Critical Praise for Taffy Cannon

"Taffy Cannon...treats Southern California as a culture, not just a region.... Throughout, the author plays up her setting well, distinguishing its identity and particular brands of looniness from those bred elsewhere in our country of regions."

—*Wilson Library Bulletin*

"Cannon deftly reveals character [in *Guns and Roses*].... The author also shows a sure touch in evoking settings."

—*Publishers Weekly*

"An author who has a wicked eye for the foibles and frailties of those who dwell in La-La Land."

—*The Purloined Letter*

"Tense, entertaining, and satisfyingly thorough."

—*Library Journal*

"Taffy Cannon creates a strong sense of place so that the reader can see, smell, hear, and feel her Southern California settings. Her gently cynical depiction of the culture is amusing, sometimes affectionate, sometimes satirical, always entertaining. Her smooth, clear prose, wry sense of humor, and keen insight make a mystery writer to watch."

—*Grounds for Murder*

Also by Taffy Cannon

Convictions: A Novel of the Sixties
Mississippi Treasure Hunt (for young adults)

.

THE NAN ROBINSON MYSTERY SERIES

A Pocketful of Karma
Tangled Roots
Class Reunions Are Murder

.

AN IRISH EYES TRAVEL MYSTERY

Guns and Roses

.

The Tumbleweed Murders
by Rebecca Rothenberg,
completed by Taffy Cannon

Taffy Cannon

OPEN SEASON ON LAWYERS

A NOVEL OF SUSPENSE

JOHN DANIEL & COMPANY
PERSEVERANCE PRESS · 2002

This is a work of fiction. Characters, places, and events are the product of the author's imagination or are used fictitiously. Any resemblance to real people, companies, institutions, organizations, or incidents is entirely coincidental.

A Perseverance Press Book
Published by John Daniel & Company
A division of Daniel & Daniel, Publishers, Inc.
Post Office Box 21922
Santa Barbara, California 93121
www.danielpublishing.com/perseverance

10 9 8 7 6 5 4 3 2 1

Book design by Eric Larson, Studio E Books, Santa Barbara
www.studio-e-books.com
Cover painting by Patricia Chidlaw

LIBRARY OF CONGRESS CATALOGING-IN-PUBLICATION DATA
Cannon, Taffy.
  Open season on lawyers : a novel of suspense / by Taffy Cannon.
    p. cm.
  ISBN 1-880284-51-0 (pbk. : alk. paper)
   1. Police—California—Los Angeles—Fiction. 2. Los Angeles (Calif.)—Fiction.
3. Serial murders—Fiction. 4. Policewomen—Fiction.   I. Title
  PS 3553.A5295 O64 2002
  813'.54—dc21   2001003725

For Chris Cannon and Bill Cannon

Acknowledgments

Special thanks to Detective Dennis Payne, Los Angeles Police Department, Robbery–Homicide Division, retired; Officer Bill Cannon, Wheaton Police Department; Carol Rogers; Janell Cannon; Sally Lynch; Linda Civitello; Suzanne Schmidt; Meredith Phillips of Perseverance Press; John and Susan Daniel and Carolyn Fleg of John Daniel & Company Publishers; Eric Larson of Studio E Books; and my agent, Jane Chelius.

As always, I am most indebted to Bill and Melissa Kamenjarin. And I am particularly grateful to the attorney who complained, after a book signing, that she was sick and tired of lawyer-bashing. She planted the "What if?" question that grew into this book.

Open Season on Lawyers

1

Somebody was killing the sleazy lawyers of Los Angeles.

In the beginning, hardly anybody even noticed.

Roger Coskins, who advertised his "Bikes & Boats Legal Services" heavily on local Los Angeles television stations, rode his Harley off a cliff along the Coast Highway north of San Luis Obispo sometime on the night of Thursday, August 29th. He had been returning to L.A. after presenting a continuing legal education seminar at the Rocky Ridge Inn just south of San Simeon.

There were no witnesses to the accident. His body and bike were noticed early the next morning in the pounding surf below the rocky cliff by a retired couple from South Dakota. Police found skid marks from Coskins's Harley-Davidson approaching the two-lane curve the attorney had failed to make. It was a treacherous curve cut into the side of a particularly steep mountain, sheer upright rock on the east, precipitous drop on the west. There was no evidence of impact with any other vehicle.

Obituaries for Coskins all noted the ironic manner of his demise. A few irreverent commentators wondered if anyone would file a lawsuit over the accident, and if so, against whom.

Warren Richardson was found dead in his garage, cherry red, on Wednesday, September 10th. His foot was jammed onto the accelerator of his late-model Lincoln Continental; the ignition was turned on, and the gas tank was empty.

Richardson was a Valencia ambulance chaser who had missed several key filing deadlines in plaintiff's personal injury cases, causing his clients to lose their opportunity for legal redress. He had allowed his legal malpractice insurance to lapse. So when the aggrieved plantiffs filed personally against Richardson, the best they could get was liens on the paltry equity in his practice. He owed more on his house than it was worth.

He left no note, but his death was officially adjudged a suicide after a hasty autopsy that failed to notice a bump behind the decedent's right ear.

Bill Burke's barely conscious body was found outside his cabin in the foothills of the Sierra mid-morning on Sunday, September 21st. Burke was slumped sideways beside a tree, wearing jeans, an unbuttoned L.L. Bean chamois shirt, and Ugg boots.

His eyes were open. He could move his head and extremities only slightly and with great difficulty. He was unable to speak. He was taken by ambulance into Fresno and placed on a respirator while doctors tried to figure out what in the hell had happened.

The medical personnel had no idea that four days earlier, Burke had won a stunning defense verdict for a San Bernardino restaurateur being sued for an outbreak of food poisoning at a wedding reception. There were two related fatalities.

The jury had come in on Wednesday morning, 10–2 for the defense. On Thursday, two op-ed pieces in the *Los Angeles Times* used the verdict as a jumping-off point for left- versus right-wing diatribes on the concept of responsibility in the personal injury legal arena. Bill Burke was quoted in both pieces.

By the time doctors at the hospital in Fresno figured out that Bill Burke was suffering from botulism poisoning, it was too late.

Forty-three minutes after the first administration of anti-toxin for *Clostridium botulinum*, Bill Burke was dead.

Three weeks later, on October 12th, civil trial attorney Lawrence Benton was found, parboiled, in the hot tub of his hillside home in Sherman Oaks.

Benton's most notorious recent trial had resulted in a multi-million-dollar award against a fast-food chain that served coffee hot enough to cause third-degree burns when spilled by a gentleman in the later stages of Parkinson's Disease. The jury had not considered the plaintiff's medical condition contributory negligence.

Benton's trophy wife was out of town when he died, so the personal injury specialist's body was discovered by his live-in housekeeper. Margarita Flores returned from a weekend with relatives in Santa Ana to discover her employer sprawled nude in the spa.

The hot tub had been bubbling so furiously for so long that it was half-empty due to evaporation.

2

Detective Joanna Davis was reading the *Los Angeles Times* and nursing a cup of exceptionally bad coffee in the cafeteria of the Santa Monica Courthouse while she waited to testify in one of her last West L.A. cases, a drive-by shooting.

Tiny, but toned and trim, Joanna was accustomed to asserting authority by sheer force of will. In another month she would turn fifty-two. She had been a detective for ten years, a cop for twenty-one, and a mother for twenty-nine. She instinctively kept her back to the wall and her radar was always on.

So she knew Detective George Watson, a former West L.A. co-worker, was in the room long before he noticed her and strode across to her table.

"Hey, Watson," Joanna said, not looking up from the newspaper's listing of recent restaurant closures by the Department of Health Services. "Says here, they closed your favorite dive last month, Pedro's on Wilshire. Vermin infestation and poor sanitation."

Watson shrugged. "Nothing a little extra hot sauce won't cure. You hear about Benton?"

Joanna looked up now, puzzled. Running the name through her personal data bank and coming up blank. "Who?"

Watson turned a chair and straddled it to sit with his arms resting on the back. "Lawrence Benton. Big-wind lawyer. Bought it out in the Valley."

"*Lawrence Benton?*" It was Joanna's impression that the

Lawrence Bentons of the world died in their sleep as octogenarians, leaving behind vast estates and anxious heirs. His most recent overreaching lawsuit sprang immediately to mind.

"What happened? Corporate counsel for Jiffy Burger shoot him at the drive-through window?"

Watson shook his head and grinned. "Better than that. Boiled in his hot tub."

"No!"

"Yes."

Joanna smiled demurely, set the newspaper aside, and folded her hands neatly on the table. "Do tell, Detective Watson."

Watson widened his grin, showing nicotine-yellowed teeth. "Don't know all that much," he admitted. "Just heard about it. Maid found him this morning. Hot tub was boiled almost empty, and old Benton was cooked like a Maine lobster."

Joanna laughed. "Fitting. I think he was from New England. Had one of those irritating accents. 'Ah hahf to pahk the cah.'"

But Watson wasn't listening. "Can somebody actually boil to death in a hot tub?"

Joanna considered. "Probably not. But people pass out and drown pretty regularly. Remember that couple in the motel in Palms?"

"As if I could forget." Watson had worked the case. A motel seeking to upgrade its image had installed hot tubs in all the rooms. Then, shortly after the grand opening, a couple grew woozy from the heat and the wine and died mid-tryst. The bodies were identified by the dead woman's husband, who had not been invited to the party.

"And we *know* Benton was a boozer," Watson went on. "Beat a couple deuces back when you still could."

Joanna chortled. "I knew the guy who wrote one of those." It seemed a million years ago. The cop who busted Larry Benton blowing a point two-three on the Santa Monica Freeway had been a friend of her first ex-husband. The tall, dour motorcycle cop was probably long retired by now, living in some heavily armed cop enclave in the remote Pacific Northwest.

"Small world," Watson told her, checking his watch. "Gotta go find my D.A. See you, Davis." He rose and swaggered away, while Joanna automatically considered scenarios in which a successful attorney might die in his hot tub.

By late afternoon, when Joanna got back to her office at Robbery–Homicide on the third floor of Parker Center in downtown Los Angeles, word had rippled through the various homicide arms of LAPD that the death of Lawrence Benton was neither natural nor accidental. The Santa Monica Courthouse, where Benton had tried and won the boiling coffee case, had swirled with rumors all day long.

At Robbery–Homicide, Joanna's partner, Al Jacobs, was discussing Benton's death with two other detectives. Joanna had known Jacobs since her second year in uniform, when she was first on the scene of a homicide that Jacobs worked as a detective in North Hollywood. The years had not been entirely kind to him. Much of his hair was gone and he was thirty pounds heavier. It had probably been a decade since he'd last shot a hole in the side of a recalcitrant beer keg to get the brew flowing again. And he seemed perennially weary. But he was still a good heart, with the demeanor of an unmade bed.

"Oh, I don't know," Jacobs was saying when Joanna walked through the door, "I've seen *lots* of suicides tidy up with one last, incredible burst of energy. No reason Benton couldn't have just fished out that boom box and put it on the counter. Hey, Davis."

She nodded and went to her desk.

"And then he wrapped the cord around the boom box real neat," Mickey Conner added. "Guy was probably a major neatnik." Conner was an old-style copper with a full head of thick white hair, a well-developed gut, and a telltale red road map on his face. *His* retirement was scheduled for next May, when he had twenty-five years in.

"Helluva suicide statement," Dave Austin added. In this crowd Austin was a mere pup, one of the youngest Robbery–Homicide Division detectives. Austin was a poster boy for the post–Nam era detectives with bachelors' degrees and great computer skills and a penchant for self-improvement. He was almost young enough to be Joanna's son, a circumstance neither of them ever alluded to. He was also a snappy dresser, not in the usual flashy cop fashion, but with a certain muted style. Detective Eddie Bauer.

"*What* suicide statement?" Joanna asked, sitting down. "And what's all this about a boom box and a cord?"

"Somebody threw a plugged-in boom box into the hot tub and zapped Benton," Austin explained, turning to face her. "Electrocution in the first degree. Actually the hundred and seventeenth degree, according to how hot the hot tub was. But that's not the good part, Davis. The good part is *what* Counselor Benton was listening to when he began his final plea bargain, trying to talk his sorry ass into heaven."

"'Good-bye, Cruel World'? 'Stairway to Heaven'?" Joanna suggested, riffling through her messages.

"No on both counts," Austin shot back. "Nope, this was a Warren Zevon tune. You know Zevon, Davis?" His tone suggested doubt.

"Of course." Joanna was a Valley Girl, born and bred. Rock and roll had been the soundtrack for her life. "Let me guess. 'Werewolves of London'?" She knew immediately that was the wrong song. As Austin shook his head she held up a hand and offered a beatific smile. "No, of course that isn't it. It's gotta be 'Lawyers, Guns and Money.'"

Austin nodded slowly. "The shit has hit the fan."

The last russet streaks of daylight were fading straight ahead of her when Joanna merged onto the Ventura Freeway heading home just after six. She felt the uneasiness that always overtook her when summer faded into fall and the light faded with it. Next week would end Daylight Savings Time, plunging the world into earlier and deeper darkness.

The romantic in Joanna loved fall, an ephemeral time when smog season segued into Santa-Ana-and-fire season and then into the brief, beautiful days of December and January. But she also knew that autumn delivered days with more darkness than light, brought nights that slithered firmly into position in late afternoon and lingered deep into each following morning. Days when it might rain and rain and rain, cloaking southern California in a wet gray shroud.

But this was supposed to be a dry winter, and so far autumn had been mild and wonderful, with an abundance of mellow, warm winds that swept the smog serenely out to sea. Quietly, too, without the atavistic howling of their more malevolent cousins, those legendary Santa Anas that bred arson and wildfires and psychosis.

Twice in uniform on night watch, Joanna had worked full moons during major Santa Anas. Both nights were wildly unforgettable. On a hot November night when flakes of ash drifted slowly out of a sky glowing crimson above Malibu, she had stood in the doorway of a Studio City bungalow where four people lay butchered, and listened to the inhuman wails of the man who killed them all.

It was fully dark when she finally arrived home, at her isolated rental house in the far western reaches of the San Fernando Valley. As always, she felt revitalized by the simple virtue of arrival at this, her nest. Single for the third time, her children grown and moved on to productive faraway lives, Joanna had created this environment to suit only herself, and she luxuriated in its idiosyncrasy.

She unlocked the cyclone fence gate, then followed the gravel drive around the two enormous California peppertrees that hid the house from the road. Programmed timers kept lights moving on and off around the small stone house while she was gone, and the place stood warmly inviting now, light seeping around the edges of the miniblinds.

She parked under the carport and went in the back door, tossed her bag on the kitchen counter, washed a handful of plump black grapes, and put them in a small glass bowl. Then she kicked off her shoes and sank into the depths of The Chair, a plush royal blue velvet marshmallow she had bought new on an uncharacteristic retail impulse. It was the only place to sit in the room. Privacy, at this stage of her life, ranked far above sociability. Only a handful of relatives and friends had even *seen* this place. Her sanctuary. Her modest monument to self-determination and a happily emptied nest and doing whatever she damn well pleased.

She lingered over the grapes, then crossed to the jukebox that stood beside the pinball machine. Her daughter Kirsten—whose own furniture was purchased in groupings featured on the HomeLife show floor—had scornfully described this room as an adult playpen.

Joanna switched on the jukebox and lifted its glass top as the fluorescent light blossomed. The Princess Rockola's visible carousel held fifty 45-rpm records, a woefully inadequate number for Joanna's eclectic music tastes. A small chest of drawers beside the jukebox was filled with six or seven hundred additional 45s, all neatly catalogued.

From the bottom drawer, she now took "Lawyers, Guns and Money," a double-sided Asylum Spun Gold disc backed with "Werewolves of London." She switched the Warren Zevon record with the Janis Joplin currently occupying A-1, one of eight readily accessible slots that she used to rotate temporary songs. She closed the machine, pressed A-1 and listened, then listened again. And a third time.

It didn't really fit, the song. Its lyrics told of jaded youth in heaps of tropical trouble, requested that lawyers, guns, and money be *sent*. The singer proclaimed himself to be "an innocent bystander." Could *that* be the message?

She listened to the song a fourth time, certain now that Dave Austin had instinctively picked up the key element here.

The shit *had* hit the fan.

Tuesday morning, the L.A. *Times*, short on hard facts about Lawrence Benton's death, ran a piece expanding on the disturbing ironies attendant not only to Benton's demise, but to the recent deaths of two other Southland attorneys, Bill Burke and Roger Coskins.

Later on Tuesday, the actual cause of Benton's death leaked, and the media gleefully reported the name of the song apparently playing at the moment when the boom box and Larry Benton's heart stopped functioning. Warren Zevon's classic *Excitable Boy* album, from which the tune came, sold out all over southern California by nightfall.

Following Wednesday's SRO Beverly Hills memorial service for Lawrence Benton, the attorney's trophy widow held an "impromptu" press conference that landed her on all the networks. Swathed in black, the stunning young Vicki Benton wiped away a tear and wondered aloud at her husband's death. "There must be some kind of madman out there," she declared breathily. "A terminator. Or maybe, since he's killing attorneys, you'd have to call him an *attorminator.*"

Which moved the story onto another plane altogether. By Thursday morning, TV newscasters and headlines alike had amended the spelling to a slightly more user-friendly *Atterminator.*

WHO IS THE ATTERMINATOR? wondered the headline in the *Los Angeles Daily News*, AND WHO'S NEXT?

<hr>

3

Ace followed the media coverage of Lawrence Benton's murder with great interest and considerable satisfaction.

Atterminator! It was more than he had ever dared hope for. And there was a certain irony that the name had come from Vicki Benton, who was obviously a total bimbo.

Atterminator. It would look mighty cool on a T-shirt, though he had no intention of making one up. Better certainly than "Legal Resolution Program," his own name for the project.

Of course, it was going to be much more difficult now to get close enough to his quarry to continue operations. The L.A. shysters would be so busy looking over their slimy shoulders that local chiropractors would need extended hours to service the cricks in their greasy necks. Ace was glad that he'd been smart enough to conduct most of his research and preliminary surveillance before the situation became publicly known. Now it would simply be a matter of confirming that established habits were being maintained. And if an intended subject proved to be absolutely unreachable, well, there were plenty of other candidates waiting in the wings. Understudies, so to speak.

As yet, he noted, nobody had connected the death of Warren Richardson to the pattern, and that was all right, too. Somewhere down the road, it might be necessary to establish his credibility. Knowing unreported details about another dead lawyer would be a compelling way to do so.

When he finished reading the newspaper coverage, he flipped through the TV channels, stopping finally on a local station rerunning Vicki Benton's press conference. It was a camera angle on the widow that he hadn't seen before, from her right. She looked exceptionally young and pretty, and when she pulled down her veil after making her little speech, he almost felt sorry for her.

But almost, as his father had always noted, didn't count.

He switched off the TV and went to change his clothes. Time to go to work.

The Atterminator, they were calling him.

My, my, my.

4

Friday morning, Robbery–Homicide took over the Benton case and it was assigned to Joanna Davis and Al Jacobs, who were on call for the week.

"Calling this a serial killing," the captain told them, straight-faced, "is probably just wishful thinking. But it's too much of a media event for North Hollywood to hang onto. And hey, who knows? Maybe somebody *is* taking out sleazy lawyers. Benton's the only one in our jurisdiction, but once you get a handle on that, check on those other two that the media keep harping about. Burke and Coskins."

"Could just be a coincidence," Jacobs said. Which was certainly true. But coincidences mattered. Any experienced detective could cite half a dozen coincidences that had tipped the scales, stilled the waters, cleared the case. Jacobs cocked his head, offered a wry smile. "Still. Three separate killers independently pick three different ways to off three high-profile lawyers? Three different ways that each just happens to send a little message? In less than two months?" He shook his head. "That ain't the kind of coincidence I like."

As they headed for the car, Joanna asked, "Just what kind of coincidence *do* you like?"

Jacobs laughed. "The kind where the guy's still standing there holding the smoking gun—the *empty* smoking gun—when I walk through the door."

They met in a conference room with the North Hollywood homicide detectives who'd caught the Benton case Monday morning. Quentin Reeves, known universally as Q, was a big man in his mid-thirties, with ebony skin, a smooth-shaven head, and a bodybuilder's strut. He wasn't going to come right out and say Robbery–Homicide was taking his case away because he was black, but he was damn sure going to think it. And though he was far too smooth to admit it, losing the case to a white *woman* really shoveled salt into his wounds.

"No need for you to be stealing this away," Reeves announced almost immediately. Very politely. Directing his remarks to Jacobs. "We can handle it."

"Not our call," Jacobs told him easily. He'd worked with Reeves before. "In your shoes I'd want to hang onto it, too. But face it, Q, once that Atterminator handle stuck, us coming in was a done deal. Nice catchy nickname like that's bound to be bringing out every weirdo west of the Rockies."

"Howling at the moon," Q Reeves admitted grudgingly. "Which isn't even full."

Jay Nestor, his partner, wasn't saying much. He was young, well-groomed, cautious, white, and junior to Reeves. Content to let somebody else do the bitching.

Q Reeves had the murder book ready. The blue loose-leaf

binder was plenty full, showing that even though nothing had broken loose yet, they'd been giving it their all. "Last time anybody saw Benton alive," Reeves began, "was last Sunday morning. There's three other lawyers he played golf with, eight A.M. every Sunday at the Riviera Country Club. Been doing it for years, same foursome. One of them was in Hawaii, but the other two both say Benton seemed just fine. Didn't say anything or do anything out of the ordinary. They played their regular eighteen holes and then drank brunch. Screwdrivers by the pitcher."

Q Reeves's tone carried a faint whiff of disapproval. Jacobs had mentioned that he was a church deacon. It was a safe bet he didn't spend *his* Sunday mornings drinking vodka and chasing a little white ball around a big green lawn.

"Benton had a rep as a drinker," Jacobs noted.

Jay Nestor spoke up. "He could hold a lot of liquor, they tell us. Nobody thought he was drunk when he left for home around one, not even the waitress who served him five drinks in an hour and a half. Just his usual self, they all say."

Q Reeves picked up now, shooting a look of minor irritation at Nestor. "When Benton left, he told the others he'd be working at home for the rest of the day. He had a big trial set to start in three weeks, first one since the coffee verdict. And that was the last anybody admits seeing him alive.

"Seems he went straight home and started working, just like he said he would," Q Reeves went on. "A young lawyer in his office gave him a bunch of papers Saturday morning and he took them home. He picked his sons up from his ex-wife's house on Saturday afternoon, took them to a Lakers game and out to dinner. Dropped them off at home in Beverly Hills around ten-thirty, saying he was tired. He probably didn't do any work that night, which means whatever work he did do was on Sunday after he got home from golf."

Q Reeves shifted his weight, leaned back slightly. "We had the woman who gave him the papers Saturday morning take a look at his office at home. She says he'd gotten a lot done. She also said he'd stopped in the middle of something, and that he didn't like to work that way. Big on closure, she put it. So if he left it, he was probably interrupted."

Jacobs smiled. "By a form of closure with precedence. As a lawyer might put it."

"A-yup," Reeves agreed.

"What about the neighbors?" Jacobs asked. "Anybody see anything, hear anything?"

Reeves and Nestor shook their heads in unison.

"Once you see the place, you'll understand," Q Reeves told them. "It's the last house on one of those twisty roads that goes snaking up the hill. Houses are all set up for privacy, fences, alarms, security gates, the whole nine yards. You could march the Bulgarian army through there and nobody'd notice. Couple of neighbors knew Benton was a lawyer, had seen him in his Jaguar. Nobody'd talked to him. One guy called him Mr. Coffee."

"I like that," Joanna put in. "Mr. Coffee. It has a ring to it."

"Mr. Coffee boiled by Atterminator," Jacobs said. "Film at eleven."

"Whatever," Reeves said evenly. This was serious business to him. Most things would be. "The long and the short is, nobody saw anything, nobody heard anything. Salvadoran maid lived in but she had the weekend off. Benton's wife was away getting starved and buffed at a health spa down by the border. She went down there Friday and wasn't due back for a week. Staff at the spa said she never left the premises."

"What's the story on the wife?" Joanna asked, ignored long enough. "She cuts quite a figure."

Reeves offered her a wide and pearly grin. "Ah yes. She does indeed. Vicki Benton, the former Vicki Vale. Thirty-three claiming to be twenty-six. A real looker. You obviously caught her on the news, dressed all in black. Goes good with the blond hair and the silicone, black does. Wore a veil like Coretta King's. High drama. Benton was sixty-two, had almost thirty years on her. He met her when he was golfing in Palm Springs. She was singing in the piano bar at his hotel. Nestor's the one mostly talked to her. Nestor?"

"Dumb as dirt," Jay Nestor announced. "And if she thought

of that Atterminator name herself, I'll eat Q's gym bag. Somebody fed that to her, maybe another nervous lawyer. The lady herself doesn't have a clue what her husband was working on, wasn't familiar with his colleagues, doesn't know of any enemies. Major talent seems to be spending money."

Jacobs perked up immediately. "Money problems?"

Nestor shook his head. "Don't seem to be. Benton's made a lot of money and he owned a lot of property. First wife died in a plane crash when he was in his early thirties. No kids from that marriage. The second wife got a big settlement and the house in Beverly Hills when they divorced. Shared custody, but only on paper. The kids live with her and didn't spend much time with him."

"He leave her for Miss Vicki?" Joanna asked. Miss Vicki and Mr. Coffee, this week's hot media couple. Cooling rapidly, in his case.

"Nope. The second wife left *him*. Miss Vicki came later." Nestor was grinning himself now. "Go figure."

"What's the story on the second wife? Bad blood there?"

"Not that you can see right off," Nestor answered carefully. "She's got her own career, some kind of interior design stuff. Married another rich man, so money doesn't appear to be a major issue. The two boys at home are eleven and fifteen, and there's a daughter, twenty, with her own apartment in West Hollywood."

"Daddy supporting her?" Jacobs wanted to know.

Nestor nodded. "She's a wannabe actress. Says she hadn't seen her father in months. Suggested we ask the child bride if we want to know what he'd been doing."

"She called her 'the child bride'?" Joanna asked with interest. "How long ago did her parents get divorced?"

"Four, five years."

"Interesting," she noted. "Not that it means anything when a teenage girl gets pissed off at a parent. Or a stepparent." The voice of experience.

"You get anything on professional grudges, unhappy clients, that sort of shit?" Jacobs asked. "Personal motives?"

"Nothing obvious," Q Reeves answered, with clear disappointment. "The coffee case seemed like the obvious place to start, but that looks to be pretty much a dead end. The guy who got burned is happy as a clam, or at least as happy as a clam can be with advanced Parkinson's. Jiffy Burger served the coffee, and the kid who served it lost his job, but he's with the Marines in Okinawa right now. Nobody else got canned."

"Who owns Jiffy Burger?" Jacobs asked.

"TLK Enterprises," Nestor answered. "With corporate headquarters in Delaware. They own all kinds of shit: seven hundred Jiffy Burgers in forty-three states, some minor league baseball teams, a chain of putt-putt golf places, lots of office buildings and apartment complexes, probably a few Congressmen and some judges. They make a lot of shit, too: cigarettes, dog food, cornflakes, lightbulbs, office supplies, money. Particularly money."

"What about the lawyers who lost the coffee case?"

Q Reeves threw back his head and laughed. "I saw those guys myself, while Nestor was off sweet-talking Miss Vicki. Let me tell you, they were some of the scaredest-looking white men I've ever seen." Given his appearance and persona, Q Reeves had probably observed plenty of frightened white men in his life. "Nerdy guys, middle-aged, with vests and glasses and skid marks in their shorts from just *thinking* about the idea that somebody was whacking lawyers. They were wondering if they ought to have police protection."

Joanna laughed. "What'd you tell 'em?"

"That we'd love to help, but there's about forty thousand other L.A. lawyers got in line ahead of them already."

5

The Benton house, perched high above the San Fernando Valley on a shelf carved into the side of the mountain, was a murderer's dream house, set up for maximum privacy at the westernmost end of a spur off a secondary residential road.

The house had been released as a crime scene, but remained

uninhabited. On her return from the health spa, Vicki Benton had checked directly into the Beverly Hills Hotel and hired round-the-clock security guards.

The detectives left the guard at the gate with his miniature TV and Playmate cooler and went to the house itself. It was about fifteen years old, custom-fit into the oddly shaped lot, set up for maximal views. From outside it was all glass and angles, landscaped in white gravel and harsh geometric topiary. Ugly as original sin and twice as expensive.

The interior was a surprise, red and black and chrome, suggestive of a high-grade, modernistic bordello. There were lots of mirrors in odd shapes and unexpected locations, and photographs of the widow Benton everywhere. Just getting from the garage to the patio, Joanna encountered two portraits that were life-sized and not half-bad, if your taste ran to airbrushed enlargements of cheesy publicity poses.

"*Ta-da!*" Jay Nestor announced as they approached the killer hot tub. He had loosened up considerably, seemed bent on making the best possible impression on the RHD detectives. Nestor was a man on his way up.

Larry Benton's spa had been constructed in the style of a stone grotto, suggestive of a natural hot spring on an isolated tropical island—except, of course, for the three million people living cheek-to-jowl in the smoggy Valley below. The hot tub was tucked into the far western corner of the property, where the shelf in the side of the mountain gave out.

There wasn't much space at all on the patio, which also held a small bar, far too many tiki gods, and a small lap pool on the opposite side.

"The maid panicked and pulled the plug out of the wall when she first saw him," Q Reeves explained. "That cut off the jets that were bubbling up the hot tub. But it also left the exact settings intact. Temperature was cranked all the way and the jets were on full blast. You saw the pictures. Benton was kind of collapsed back, floating on the far side of the tub. Almost like he was looking out over the Valley one last time."

The hot tub sat empty now, looking vaguely guilty. Shiny molded fiberglass in streaky slate gray, it featured several built-in chairs and recliners. Its walls were pockmarked with dozens of jets. Cranked up, this tub would *cook*.

Reeves continued, a bit defensively. "We drained the tub, once SID got water samples. It got crapped up, literally, when the old sphincters went. But we worked out that the water level was down over a foot from where it should've been. There's a pool boy comes by once a week on Tuesdays. It was six days since his last visit. He told us where the water level should have been."

"He figure out the electrical sequence?" Jacobs wondered, kneeling to look into the open control panel.

Reeves shook his head. "Just confirmed it. Nestor here found it first."

Nestor moved in and pointed, preening at being center stage again. "The way this spa is set up, an electrical short anywhere in the system will automatically shut everything down. The way it seems to have happened is, Benton's unconscious when he goes into the tub. The tub was kept on auto-thermostat all the time, so it would have already been hot. Our guy turns everything off, unplugs the power for the whole tub. Then he takes the cassette deck, plugs it in over here, listens to a few bars of 'Lawyers, Guns and Money' and tosses it into the tub." He pantomimed a pitch.

"*Zap!* Benton's fried. Then our guy unplugs the boom box, which has kind of melted around the plug, and winds the cord around the box. Circuit breaker's tripped on the outlet where he had the boom box, but that's a different circuit from the hot tub. Hot tub has its own breaker, untripped. Breaker box is on the wall outside the garage. Our guy sets the tape player over on the bar, goes to the garage, resets the circuit breaker the boom box blew, turns the hot tub on, turns up the thermostat to the max, sets the jets on high and splits. Leaving Counselor Benton bubbling merrily away."

Jacobs scowled. "I suppose the heat fucks up any kind of accurate time of death?"

"You got it," Q Reeves answered. "We think he was in the tub between twelve and sixteen hours. I wanted to pin that down a little closer by getting the hot tub manufacturer to see how long it takes the water to get down that far with everything cranked up high."

"They're not cooperating?" Jacobs asked. Not sounding surprised.

"Their lawyers are the ones talking to us, and you know how *that* goes. They're scared shitless the widow's gonna sue *them*, and they've got a million reasons why they could never accurately reproduce this situation. Starting with no stiff in the tub."

"Use one of the protesting lawyers," Joanna suggested. "Let's back up to where Benton was unconscious. You told us he was knocked out with a Taser?"

Q Reeves showed the pearly whites again. "Some kind of stun gun, for sure, and it's one of the ones that requires actual contact, so we know he got up pretty close. Make and model, there's a certain amount of question. Whatever it was, it hit him on the chin and he was knocked out enough so that he didn't put up a fuss when he was undressed and dragged outside. Clothes were tossed on his bed and he wasn't a clothes-tossing kind of guy. Drawers and closet look like a military supply depot."

"Any idea where he was when he got hit with the stun gun?" Jacobs asked.

"Probably at the front door," Nestor told them. "Right when he answered it. The maid vacuumed just before she left on Friday and Benton was in the habit of coming in and out through the garage. But there was a bit of debris from the front walk on the carpet. And the nap was mussed up."

They went back inside now. The carpet, which had caused Joanna to shudder on first entering the house, was thick black pile. Exuberantly tacky, and impractical as well. It would show dirt almost as readily as white. Not likely to be an issue for Vicki Vale Benton, who had live-in help.

"You send the carpet out?"

"You bet," Reeves answered, pointing. "That whole section there."

An area about ten feet square had been removed, exposing plywood. Just beyond the plywood was a silver baby grand piano with its top propped open. On the far wall of the living room, past some big puffy white couches, hung a life-sized painting of Vicki Vale seated at that very piano, wearing a scarlet satin gown and a very satisfied smile.

Walking down the hall to the master bedroom, Joanna felt a strong sense of the building's lonely impersonality. This didn't feel like a home, or even much of a house. It looked and felt like a set.

A set for some kind of dress-up game that Vicky Vale Benton had been playing. This was no male choice of decor, whorehouse overtones or no. It was an unimaginative Palm Springs lounge singer's notion of sophistication. Irregular lengths of mirror ran in parallel four-inch-wide stripes down the walls of the hallway.

In the master bedroom, Jay Nestor brought out the photos of Larry Benton's clothing on the day his body was found, casually heaped on the bed.

"The clothing give you anything?" Joanna asked.

"Not so far," Nestor answered. "No rips, stains, hairs from an Akita, fibers from a Bronco carpet, nothing like that. It's not what he wore when he went golfing. That was in the laundry hamper. He seems to have showered and changed after he got home. One of the towels in his bathroom was still a little damp when they found the body. So if there *was* anything on the clothes, it could be significant. Except there wasn't. They just seem to be real clean clothes. Now wrinkled."

The clothing didn't fit in the room, seemed totally alien to the mirrors, the black lacquer built-in headboard, the red velvet bedspread with its wide black ruffled lace edging. Very little in the way of apparel *would* fit in here, Joanna realized, though she suspected the widow's closet held an extensive collection of black lace lingerie.

Basically, this was a room to get naked in.

Benton's discarded duds were all practically new, unremarkable but expensive. His walk-in closet also held a collection of moderately garish golf apparel and an entire wall of beautiful, expensive, exquisitely tailored suits. Double tiers of custom-made dress shirts. Dozens of pairs of fine, supple Italian shoes. Everything was perfectly spaced, precisely arranged, meticulously aligned. Circumstantial evidence suggested strongly that Lawrence Benton had cut a fine figure in court.

The twin closet on the other side of the room held Vicki Benton's wardrobe, what she hadn't taken to the hotel. Here there was more of a sense of casual sloppiness. Slacks fallen off a hanger and left lying on the ground, a drawer of nylons partway open with a stocking toe peering out coyly, dresses pushed to one side and not straightened again.

Even so, there was a *lot* of clothing, including the expected surfeit of black lace. Joanna checked labels. The lady shopped at some classy stores, but she had a gift for finding the sleaziest apparel each had to offer.

Q Reeves reached up and pulled out the top drawer in a module, some six feet off the ground. "In here," he announced, with that patented ivory grin, "is an absolutely *amazing* collection of dildos." He made a production of waving it over his head before bringing it down and setting it on a small table beside a dressing chair inside the closet.

It was a showstopper.

The drawer was jammed with massive penises in a stunning variety of colors and styles. Many had discreet vibrating capabilities. An enormous pink, anatomically correct candle had been burned down an inch or so, which raised some interesting questions and gave new meaning to the term "hot in bed."

Joanna lifted a dark green, warty piece of plastic, the color and configuration of a giant kosher dill. "You ask the widow Benton about these?" Joanna knew Q Reeves had been hoping to gross her out. Now he lovingly pulled an enormous black member from a bottom corner and set it beside the pickle.

"Friend of yours?" she murmured.

Reeves glowered momentarily, then displayed his pearly whites. "None of my friends that puny."

Jacobs chuckled and Nestor hurried to get things back on track.

"Yeah," said Nestor. "I asked her about 'em. She broke into tears and said she felt so *betrayed* that we'd been going through her most private things, and how *could* we, and a woman's closet should be *sacred*, and so on and so forth. Till she pretty much got so hysterical we had to stop talking for an hour."

Joanna considered the notion of a woman's closet being sacred, decided she rather liked it. "You intervewed her here?"

"Both of us talked to her in her suite at the Beverly Hills Hotel," Nestor said. "And then the next day when she wanted to come over and get some clothes, I brought her by and stayed with her while she was in the house. She was all business. Brought in one of those rolling carts like they have in the garment district, had it out in the garage. Then she loads it up and fills a couple big suitcases with undies and stuff. I think she'd've liked to empty that drawer, but I was with her like fur on a cat and she left it alone."

"Anything else around here out of the, uh, ordinary?" Jacobs asked. "Sex-wise?"

"Depends on your definition of ordinary," Nestor replied cheerfully. "They took pictures. Basic stuff with a tripod and a timer. And some videos, which seem more spontaneous. At least on her part. He liked to spank her, but they don't seem to have been into any particularly heavy S and M. No handcuffs or leather masks, none of that kind of shit."

"The dildos make the movies?" Joanna asked.

"Nope," Nestor answered with a grin. "Benton was getting on in years. Maybe she just needed more than he could provide."

Q Reeves glowered disapprovingly. "Pictures and videos were all in cabinets back in the family room. Low enough, his kids could find them easy if they were staying here."

Shaking his head in disgust, Reeves led them into the hall, opening doors and pointing out the bedrooms used by Benton's children when they visited. The closets and drawers were nearly empty and the rooms immaculate, sterile. Mug shots from a decorating magazine.

Benton's office provided the second major decorating surprise. It was more what Joanna would have expected Larry Benton's entire residence to be like, and seemed to come not just out of a different house, but from a different corner of the country as well. It was pure New England burgher.

In this part of the house, the professional persona of Lawrence Benton shone through with exceptional brilliance. A huge oak rolltop desk filled one wall and looked easily a hundred years old, painstakingly crafted, magnificently finished, radiating Substance. It might well have been shipped west from the original Benton family homestead back east.

There were books in this room, a library in glass-fronted oak legal bookshelves, both the predictable law books and an extensive collection on the American Revolution. A large oil portrait of an eighteenth-century sourpuss—probably a Benton forebear—hung on one wall, positioned out of view of the desk. A set of much friendlier Currier & Ives prints hung over the desk. Closed heavy burgundy drapes kept out any hint of contemporary southern California.

Who had interrupted Larry Benton's work here? And why?

6

Joanna was jazzed.

This case was big, really big. And it was *hers*.

The Atterminator. A serial killer. *Her* serial killer.

In a roundabout way, a serial killer had brought her into the department in the first place. The Hillside Strangler. Back in late 1977, when Joanna was the wife of an LAPD sergeant and the mother of two small children, the nude bodies of strangled women and girls suddenly began to litter various slopes and inclines around Los Angeles. The murders increased at an appalling rate, eleven killings linked, eight in November alone.

Joanna was not exactly a helpless young fluffhead back then. She had spent endless hours on target ranges with her husband, had sufficiently mastered martial arts to be able to flip someone twice her size. But these murders utterly unnerved her, petrified her with fear. Joanna had found herself unable to function at even the simplest level, and before she realized what was happening, Don Olafson had relocated their entire family to his northern Minnesota homeland.

When Joanna returned to L.A. two years later, the hillside stranglings were over. Kenneth Bianchi and Angelo Buono were in custody. Joanna was a single parent in need of a job with good benefits, and LAPD was under court order to recruit more women and minorities.

Now things had come full circle, and she who had once fled a serial killer was charged with catching one.

LAPD had changed dramatically in the three decades since she'd first met Don Olafson, the strapping Minnesotan who had stopped off in L.A. on his way back from Vietnam and joined LAPD instead of going home. That had been the first rebellious act of Don Olafson's life; the second, not long after, was to marry Joanna.

Thirty years later it was a very different department. Joanna instinctively kept her head down, did her own job well, and stayed out of various lines of fire. She had plenty of opinions but she mostly kept them to herself. And she didn't much miss the same elements of the old paramilitary LAPD as did the old-timers, combat-toughened ex-Marines who had once ruled the streets, strong and tough and fearless. Nostalgia, she had come to realize, was always intensely *personal*.

She was not the first female to breach the masculine inner sanctum of Robbery–Homicide, an elite unit boasting centuries of collective detection experience and a group of egos unmatched outside the U.S. Senate. Still, there weren't a lot of women in RHD yet, and she knew people were watching her closely.

There was just enough exhibitionist in her not to mind too terribly much.

Best of all, she'd landed in Robbery–Homicide at the same time as Lee Walters, currently assigned to the Rape Section. Joanna and Lee had kept each other sane through the police academy. Later they'd worked patrol on different shifts in North Hollywood, while the Boys with Big Balls—the Triple-B Brigade, she and Lee had called them—left sanitary pads smeared with strawberry jam in strategic locations and muttered darkly about PMS and douche bags.

Joanna realized now that she hoped the notion of an Atterminator *wasn't* simply a case of wishful media thinking tying together three unrelated deaths. She *wanted* this to be a serial killer, and she wanted to bust his sorry ass.

Vicki Vale Benton was a little bit loaded when Joanna and Al Jacobs visited her suite at the Beverly Hills Hotel at ten-thirty on Monday morning.

Even so, she'd managed full makeup, and to cement her platinum curls into a beehive. Her black pants were skintight and her low-cut black sweater gave each curve a little squeeze. True to the evidence of her closet, the pants were pure wool and the sweater cashmere. But trash will out.

"I just *wish* there was *some* way I could help you," Vicki Benton simpered. She had an annoying little-girl voice, breathless and confused. As a lounge singer, she must have specialized in whisper tunes. "I told those other detectives *everything* I know."

Which hadn't taken long, Joanna suspected. She nodded appreciatively. "I know. But sometimes when you go over things again, you'll think of something that didn't occur to you before. Or remember a detail that you might not have mentioned earlier because it didn't seem important."

"How could my husband being *murdered* not seem *important?*" A breathless whine. Now *there* was a speech pattern.

"It's extremely important to us," Joanna assured her. She and Al had agreed on the way in that she'd take the lead, but Vicki Benton's radar screen only recognized males. Time to lob her back to Jacobs. "Detective Jacobs was just saying that he thought you probably had some important insights into your husband's lifestyle and work habits."

Detective Jacobs, who'd said nothing of the sort, obligingly moved closer. "I'm sorry that this is so upsetting for you," he began.

But the trophy widow didn't seem upset, exactly. She seemed somewhat zonked and her breath smelled faintly of wine. And she also seemed to know absolutely nothing about her husband's work. She was unfamiliar with his old friends, and described his colleagues in terms of their cars and the designer preferences of their wives. (Joanna wondered idly if those same wives referred to Vicki Benton in terms of her own apparent preferred designer, Frederick of Hollywood.) She didn't pay attention to Larry's legal work, though she *had* been familiar with the coffee case because it was "cute." She thought he had looked "real dignified" when he was briefly featured as a Court TV commentator the previous year, though she couldn't recall the case on which he had commented.

And then she broke down. "I feel so *guilty*," she whisper-sobbed. "That poor Larry died and I *survived*."

Jacobs nodded, the soul of understanding. Joanna melded into her chair, remained immobile, let Vicki Benton bond in the only way she knew how.

"Mrs. Benton, how many people knew that you were going to be away last Sunday?" Jacobs asked.

Vicki Benton frowned, thinking hard. It seemed an effort. "Not many," she admitted. "I mean, I wasn't exactly going to *advertise* that I was going to try to lose a couple of pounds. I told a couple of my girlfriends, and Margarita knew, of course, 'cause she helped me pack. I don't know who Larry told."

Probably nobody, unless his secretary made the arrangements. Joanna couldn't imagine Larry Benton chatting idly about the fact that his little cubic zirconium wife was off for her quarterly servicing at the fat farm. Joanna had worked West L.A. for years, had a well-developed eye for the telltale tightenings that showed Vicki Benton had already begun the regimen of plastic surgery that would continue till she had buried her last sugar daddy. By then, she'd be so thoroughly tightened and tucked that her mouth would fly open whenever she sat down.

"You know what I keep thinking about?" Vicki Benton asked

finally. "That my pictures were all *watching* when they killed poor Larry, that I was a helpless witness."

That her *pictures* were watching. Well, they probably had been. There weren't any portraits of the mistress of the house on the patio to see the actual killing, but there were—Joanna closed her eyes and did a brief recap—at least seven between the front door and the patio. Each would have witnessed Larry Benton being taken down by a stun gun right in the chin, then stripped and dragged by his bare heels out to the hot tub.

A helpless witness, Vicki Vale Benton said.

Or, as paraphrased by Warren Zevon, an innocent bystander.

Lucy Lanier was also dressed entirely in black. Hers was the black of stylish confidence, a dramatic floor-length shift with long, soft flowing sleeves, in rich, heavy-texture jet cotton. Larry Benton's second wife was a striking woman in her late forties, slim and calm and not terribly sorry, it would seem, that her ex-husband was dead.

Joanna and Jacobs met with her in the conservatory of her big, boxy house in the Beverly Hills flatlands. Glass walls looking into the lush backyard were thickly fogged, the atmosphere steamy and tropical. A four-foot waterfall drizzled down a stone wall above ferns and orchids. The furniture was teak, the cushions natural creamy cottons in interesting textures. Lucy Lanier seemed to be big on texture.

Lucy was an interior designer, her own home understated and welcoming, filled with warm neutral colors and perfectly selected accent pieces. The contrast to Larry and Vicki Benton's love nest was stunning.

"Larry was fifteen years older than me," she explained now. "I was twenty-five when we got married and he was forty." She smiled wryly. "Larry's brides have *all* been twenty-five, or claimed to be. Anyway, his first wife, Eleanor, had some kind of problem, so they never had kids even though he'd really wanted them. And I was obliging enough to get pregnant on our honeymoon. Larry enjoyed the kids for a while, but then, when I was pregnant with my youngest, Larry embarked on the mother of all midlife crises. Here

I was, three kids under the age of ten, and Larry decides he has to *prove* things to himself."

Joanna nodded understandingly. "And did he?"

"Did he *ever!* He tried to get in shape to do a triathlon, for God's sake, though that was pretty hopeless. He got the idea he'd take up mountain climbing, and that one never went too far either. Finally he settled on golfing on every continent of the world. By then he wasn't paying much attention to the kids he thought he'd wanted so much. Frankly, golf bores me, and as for the rest of it, I'm not exactly the outdoors type." She laughed. "Of course, neither is the third Mrs. Benton, but who'd've thought. . ." She shook her head and laughed again, an open, cheerful chuckle.

"Was she a factor in your divorce?" Joanna asked, contrasting the two Benton wives. Most men tended to stick with a type, but except for favoring blondes, Larry Benton had chosen three dramatically different women to marry, assuming that the long-dead Eleanor was the aristocratic cold fish his other wives imagined. Joanna found herself liking Lucy Lanier, a woman who related just fine to other women, who projected a sense that she'd love to get down and dish the dirt.

Except that there didn't seem much dirt to dish.

"No," Lucy answered firmly. "In fact, *I* was the one who got involved with somebody first. I did a suite of offices for Ben—my husband—and well, we just kind of hit it off. He was married, too, at the time and we were both feeling kind of neglected."

Lucy Lanier knew far more about Larry Benton's work than Vicki did. "You know, I tried to think of somebody angry enough to do that to him, and I just couldn't. Larry could be a tight-ass and he could be inflexible and he could be obsessively driven. But he always had a reservoir of charm that he could call on any time he wanted. He could sweet-talk his way out of *anything*."

She fell silent. Larry Benton had not charmed his way out of being murdered.

Through the misted conservatory glass, Joanna could see a small black sports car swiftly round the corner of the house and squeal to a halt in front of the four-car garage. Lucy turned at the sound of the car door slamming and beamed. A slim young brunette strode toward the house. She wore jeans and a tight pink T-shirt under an unstructured black blazer.

"There's Reggie," Lucy explained. "My daughter. I called her and suggested she come by. Reggie is very sensitive and I've made every effort to keep her out of the media circus end of this until she's ready to face people. I thought she might be more comfortable talking to you here."

Joanna wondered what kind of aspiring actress was so sensitive that she would shrink from media contact. A play-pretend actress, she decided a few minutes later, when Larry Benton's oldest child and only daughter was sitting in the conservatory. Up close Reggie Benton didn't seem as vivacious as she had appeared crossing the driveway. Up close, indeed, she seemed rather washed-out and vague, sincere but easily confused.

She was *studying* acting, Reggie explained, rather shyly. No, she didn't think they would have seen anything she had been in. And no, she wasn't working on anything in particular right now. "But I'm up for a really good part in an equity theater show." As she spoke, she absentmindedly rubbed her hands together. "I can't really tell you anything about my dad. I mean, the one to ask would be his wife. I hardly saw him the last few years."

Joanna led her through some personal history: Beverly Hills High, a little junior college, not waiting tables, not currently employed, taking classes in acting and yoga and dance, having some sessions with a voice coach. Reggie Benton was a bit unfocused and was, Joanna thought, one of the least likely actresses she had ever encountered. She had no spark whatsoever.

After Reggie left, Joanna and Jacobs spoke with Lucy's current husband, Ben Lanier, a likable and sincere-seeming investment counselor in his mid-fifties with a thick shock of silvered black hair and sparkling blue eyes. He assured them that his interactions with Larry Benton had been unfailingly civilized and cordial. He claimed to be devoted to Reggie and his two stepsons, Justin and Jason. He had no other children.

Ben Lanier shrugged diplomatically, lifting a bemused eyebrow, when Jacobs asked his impressions of Vicki Vale Benton, and offered only that she seemed to defer pretty totally to her husband's wishes.

When Justin and Jason Benton got home from school, their behavior corroborated Ben Lanier's claims of closeness. Neither boy was eager to talk to any more cops, and Jason, the younger, turned and asked plaintively, "Will you stay, Ben?"

So Ben stayed and Lucy left. The boys were cautious and closed-in, had been anxious to return to school today but seemed drained by the experience. They remembered details of their last dinner with Larry after the Lakers game, that Jason ordered onion rings and Justin argued strongly against Larry's picks for the year's Super Bowl.

They remembered their dad waving good-night from the curb when he brought them home. And they remembered being called out of class to be told by their mother that Larry Benton was dead.

They were tough little guys, and Joanna ached for them.

By Thursday it was clear that the Benton murder would not be rapidly cleared and that nothing else associated with this investigation was likely to be easy.

They had talked to electricians and plumbers and pool-and-spa experts. They had refilled the hot tub and run it at full blast until it reached the marked level, a process that took fifteen hours and twenty minutes. They had spoken with Larry Benton's colleagues and golf partners and employees and clients. They had reviewed his files and watched tapes of his Court TV commentaries.

They had looked into another recent colorful case of Benton's, his breach-of-promise lawsuit against a highly successful sitcom actress, Amanda León. Amanda had unceremoniously dumped her "fiancé," Emilio Montoya, after allegedly promising they'd be together through eternity. Emilio Montoya's suit against Amanda León had settled out of court for an amount sufficient to buy the pushy young gigolo a bar in Laguna Beach.

Emilio, predictably, considered the death of his former attorney a national tragedy. Amanda León met with Joanna and Al for twenty minutes in a trailer in Burbank. Chewing a big wad of bubble gum, she allowed that Emilio and his attorney were both piles of steaming horseshit, pimples on the ass of life, and various other unpleasantries.

But she, like Benton's other legal adversaries and defendants, considered it over. He'd brought suit, he'd gotten her to fork over big to avoid the public release of details of some of her more unsavory personal habits—and it was done. Finished. Caput. In any case, Amanda León was making half a million dollars a week and could buy bars in Laguna Beach for any number of additional boyfriends.

The legal picture of Larry Benton that emerged was of somebody who would cheerfully use anything and everything to gain an advantage. Who believed in winning, and winning big. Faced with a choice between stolid legal respectability in the New England towns of his forefathers or wide-open opportunity in the cutting-edge legal community of Los Angeles, Larry Benton had shipped the family desk west without a backward glance. He had moved through three wives like chapters in a book, always looking toward the future.

And eleven days after his murder, they were no closer to clearing the case than they had been on the morning when the body was first discovered.

7

Mid-morning on Monday, October 27th, Joanna Davis and Al Jacobs stood overlooking the Pacific Ocean on a windswept two-lane curve of Highway 1 between San Simeon and Morro Bay.

Frigid winds gusted viciously off the bleak gray expanse of water to the west, winds that had traveled thousands of miles from Alaska before striking land. Below them, foamy spumes of surf crashed onto the jagged rocks where the battered body of personal injury attorney Roger Coskins had been discovered two months earlier.

"I truly believe," Detective Brad Stanley repeated, leaning against his car, oblivious to the wind, looking just a smidgen bored, "I *truly* believe that this was simply an accident." Stanley had investigated the motorcycle crash back in August.

Jacobs grunted. They'd been over all this before, sitting around the conference table reviewing photographs with Stanley, who had delivered his official and pretty much unequivocal opinion that the crash was an accident. No more, no less. Stanley was forty-five, solid, unimaginative. He wanted the Roger Coskins case to remain closed and his involvement in it to remain over.

"It's a nasty curve," Stanley went on, gathering steam, "and he's not the first to go off it. Not by a long shot. Plus it was dark, almost no moon, and overcast, too. Two years ago, a family of migrant workers in an old Chevy truck went off that same curve. Six dead."

A car whizzed past them heading south. Curves and wind notwithstanding, people *moved* on this stretch. There'd be a lot of close calls, people coming into the curve just a little fast, getting through it all right, and then going, "Holy shit," and slowing down.

Stanley led them along a well-maintained six-foot-wide shoulder on the western side of the road. "Skid marks started here, for whatever it's worth. He tried to stop and left the pavement before he could control his turn. Then he bounced on the rail and flipped over. Hit the edge right about there, broke off some small rocks, and then sailed on down. I've done a lot of accident recon work and I think he stayed with the bike, rode it all the way to the bottom. Otherwise I'd expect to find the body and the bike farther apart down there."

"You were out here—when? The next morning?" Joanna asked. She was freezing, dressed in fur-lined boots, a hooded parka, woolen hat, and Polartec-lined leather gloves, a gift from her son in Minneapolis, where they knew plenty about cold-weather attire.

Stanley nodded. *He* was nonchalantly clad in a single layer of heavy, well-styled leather. No gloves. No hat. "Yeah, I know what you mean. It was at least eight or ten hours later. Plenty of other traffic had passed by here by then. But I was here when they brought up the body and the bike."

"Did anybody treat it as anything other than an accident at the time?" Jacobs wondered. He wasn't wearing a hat either, one of those guy things Joanna had long since given up trying to understand. She observed goose bumps atop Jacobs's bald head, marching in military precision across what he called, when inebriated, his "pilgarlic pate."

"Nope," Stanley answered, with only the vaguest trace of apology in his tone. "Frankly, it looked like Coskins was just one more asshole biker who wasn't smart enough to slow down for the curves. And I still think that's true."

Joanna stood near the edge, looking down, feeling the wind rip at the hood of her parka. It was scary out here, and even scarier out there. It was a long way down. In full daylight the curve offered an impressive vista and a frightening fall. At night, with no light from anything but Coskins's own cycle, it would have been a literal flight into oblivion.

The three of them hiked back up the road to where Stanley had left the cruiser, in a wide spot on the inside of the highway, tucked into a curve in the side of the mountain. The cove offered partial protection from the wind.

Joanna retrieved her coffee from the car and sipped it while her hands thawed. She turned to Jacobs. "Assume it's a homicide. How did it happen?"

Jacobs rubbed his chin. "Easy enough for somebody with a little nerve and a lot of luck. We know Coskins was on his way back to L.A. from San Simeon and our guy undoubtedly knew that, too. Coskins was featured speaker at that continuing legal education program Thursday afternoon, 'How to Get a Fortune When Your Dirtbag Client Fucks Up Big on His Chopper.' And he'd ridden up on his Harley for the occasion, being big on image."

Brad Stanley chuckled. *"Hi-yo Silver, awaaaaaay…"*

It was the tag line from the Bikes & Boats Legal Services TV ads, which had been broadcast a lot lately—as news items—while the media tried to tie together legal deaths. The ads normally ran on local stations late at night, when guys—particularly the sort of guys likely to be laid up by motorcycle injuries sustained through operator error—were channel surfing, feeling penniless and put-upon.

All the Coskins commercials ended with a gimmick: Coskins doing a wheelie and calling out, *"Hi-yo, Silver!"* In a black silk eye mask.

"Wednesday night he spent up by San Simeon," Joanna said. They'd check the hotel later, before heading over to Fresno. "But he needed to be back in L.A. on Friday morning. So he left Thursday after dinner—when? Maybe nine?"

Stanley spread his hands and shrugged. "Nobody remembered seeing him leave. But whenever he did go, it wasn't long after that that he missed the curve."

Joanna looked again around the small area where they stood, only partly protected from the wind. A wind which actually seemed to be *picking up*. Shit. She polished off the coffee and shoved her chilly fingers deep into her jacket pockets.

"So now," she continued, "you need some luck. You know Coskins is going to L.A. on that big Harley hog. There's only this one road, at least till you hit Morro Bay. You've already found a spot where there's a sharp curve high enough over rocks so you can be pretty damned sure nobody'd survive the fall."

Jacobs turned to Brad Stanley. "There other places like that along this stretch of road?"

"Sure," Stanley answered immediately. He reflected for a moment, not happily. "But if that's what you're planning, this is probably the *best* one."

"Mucho coincidento, no?" Joanna asked. "Other places might work, but this one's a sure shot. Which means you've taken the time to research this stretch of road, maybe on more than one occasion. So anyway, you know when he's leaving and you know where he's going. You scoot on ahead and park right here, walk back and hunker down in that scrub by the side of the road. There's enough brush to hide somebody, not comfortably maybe, but well enough. You wait for Coskins to come tooling along and when his chopper shows up, you jump out in front of it. He swerves, skids, bounces off the guard rail, and cartwheels into the ocean. Riding the bike like Slim Pickens on the bomb in *Dr. Strangelove.*"

"What if there's other traffic?" Jacobs asked.

"Then you abort." Joanna's tone was definite. "This guy is extremely well organized and cautious to a fault. He might be disappointed, but he'd be willing to wait for another opportunity rather than risk botching something with witnesses. And for damn sure, he doesn't want Coskins surviving to tell the tale of the mystery pedestrian. For all we know, he's been stalking Coskins for months, waiting for just the right situation."

"I like it," Jacobs said. He grinned. "I like it a lot. So, Stanley, whaddaya think?"

Brad Stanley hesitated. He appeared decidedly more glum than he had when they'd first arrived here. "I hate to say this, but you may just be right. From all I could figure, Coskins was a pretty worthless piece of scum. But he could have been forced off the road by an even *more* worthless piece."

Joanna smiled and opened the passenger door of the cruiser. Her teeth were starting to chatter. "Kind of tough figuring out who the bad guys are on this one. Adds an element of challenge."

She felt almost light-headed. It *could* be an accident. No way around that.

But still—*everything* about this location and the circumstances of Roger Coskins's death fit the notion of a serial killer, a cautious, methodical murderer.

An Atterminator.

8

Fresno was even better.

Fresno County Sheriff's Deputy Cale Cartwright had taken a special interest in the Bill Burke botulism case from the beginning, and he was delighted to have a receptive audience at last. Cartwright was a real string bean, tall and thin with a long, serious face and already-thinning light brown hair. He didn't look much past thirty. His papers were arranged neatly in piles on the table before them. He practically trembled with anticipation.

"I am so *glad* to see you guys," Cartwright told them right off, "because I've maintained from day one that this was more than a simple food poisoning case."

"Tell us about it," Joanna urged.

Cale Cartwright chose his words carefully. "On Sunday, September twenty-first, James Vlukovich was walking his two golden retrievers along a road in the foothills when the dogs ran up a driveway, started barking their heads off, and wouldn't come back. Vlukovich is a Marin County stockbroker with a weekend place half a mile down the road from Bill Burke's cabin. So he went up the drive to fetch his dogs and he found them circling Burke, who was lying on the ground outside his cabin."

"Alive," Joanna murmured.

"Alive. He couldn't talk. He couldn't walk. In fact, he couldn't much move at all. He was almost completely paralyzed. Vlukovich freaked and tried to call for help from the cabin, but the phone line was dead. Burke's cell phone was on the kitchen table, but it was out of range.

"All Vlukovich can think to do is get help. He sees Burke's car keys on the table with the cell phone and he jumps in Burke's Blazer and drives down to his own cabin. He calls for help from there and goes back to stay with Burke. It takes a while for an ambulance to get up there, and when it does, they take him all the way into town to the hospital."

Cale Cartwright shook his head regretfully. "He was in *real* sorry shape by the time he got to the hospital. I got called in to see him there. I tried to question him, but it was tough. He couldn't really respond. We worked out a system of moving one finger for yes and two for no, but that was about it. He tried to write some answers to questions, but that didn't work very well."

"Did he know what had happened to him?" Jacobs asked.

Cartwright shook his head. "I don't think so. He gave the 'no' response when I asked him that. He also responded 'no' to questions about whether anybody was with him at the cabin, had he picked any mushrooms and eaten them, was there anything un-usual that he'd eaten or drunk. Negative, one and all. I narrowed down that he came to his cabin on Friday and started to feel sick in the middle of that night. I asked if he tried to call for help, and he wrote 'dead' on the notepad. I asked if he meant the phone was dead and he gave the 'yes' response.

"By then he was having a lot of trouble breathing and they wanted to intubate him and get him on a respirator. So I didn't have a chance to ask him anything more." He paused. "You know, I've given a lot of thought to what I could have asked him, what I *should* have asked. 'Cause as you well know, there wasn't another chance. He was dead in a couple of hours."

"They figured out it was botulism before he died, though," Joanna noted.

"*Clostridium botulinum*, to be precise. They started him on antitoxin, but it was too late. I wasn't here when he went. I'd gone back up to the cabin to make sure there wasn't anything danger-ous sitting around, looking appealing."

Joanna smiled. She really liked this earnest young man. In his precision and methodic ways, he reminded her of her son, Mike. "And was there? Anything appealing?"

The young deputy grimaced. "Well, there *was* a nice-looking chocolate pie. But seeing what that guy was going through, the last thing I wanted to do was taste his food."

Jacobs interrupted. "I'm confused here. You're saying that Burke got sick on *Friday* night and he didn't do anything about it till Sunday?"

"Actually, he didn't *do* anything about it at all," Cartwright corrected. "All he did was lie down on the ground until Vluko-vich's dogs discovered him. And try to use the phone. Which is an element of this that I find particularly disturbing. Because when I got up there late that afternoon, the phone line was just fine. And the phone company didn't have any record of outages or problems with service anywhere in the area that weekend. But what was *re-ally* interesting about the phone was that it appeared somebody had been in the junction box where the phone plugs into the wall. The cabin wasn't real clean and it wasn't real dirty, somewhere sort of in the middle. But the phone box was clean as a whistle, dust-free and fingerprint-free. As if somebody had disconnected the phone and then reconnected it after Burke was taken away. Taking time to wipe anything he touched."

"There's only one phone outlet?" Joanna asked.

Cartwright nodded. "Just that one."

"Interesting," she murmured. "Very interesting." She was thinking about the wiring machinations in Lawrence Benton's hot tub execution, and she was sure Al Jacobs was thinking about them, too. She frowned. "What I don't understand is why he didn't *leave*, go get help while he was still able to."

"Botulism kind of creeps up on you," Cale Cartwright explained. "It causes paralysis, but the process is gradual. Initially it works like a really nasty stomach flu. Here's the way I think it happened. Burke was planning a long weekend at his cabin to wind down after the trial he'd just finished. I guess you know about that?"

Joanna nodded. "But I want to come back to it later."

"Sure. Anyway, the jury in that trial came in on Wednesday. Friday he headed out of town. He stopped by his office in Riverside Friday morning for about an hour, then left around eleven and drove up here. As far as we can tell, he was alone. He probably got here around five or six unless he stopped somewhere we don't know about. Maybe earlier if he really lead-footed. He brought food with him, deli stuff from a Vons in Riverside."

Cale Cartwright stopped, looked intently at both of them. "Sometime, probably Friday night, he had dinner at the cabin. Kitchen trash had remains of half a roasted chicken and empty containers of cole slaw and potato salad. He'd eaten some fruit salad out of another bigger container. The rest of that was in the fridge. There was also a big slice missing out of that chocolate cream pie I mentioned. He'd bought himself a whole pie."

Jacobs grinned. "My kind of guy."

"I confiscated all the trash, as well as any other food in the cabin. All of it, anything that had been opened. It's all still being held as evidence."

"Even the chocolate pie?" Jacobs asked, sounding concerned.

"Even the chocolate pie. Everything's in a deep freeze. And I checked the pantry for bulging cans, but there weren't any. Anyway, I figure when Burke first got to the cabin, he maybe hung around for a while, then went for a little hike. I interviewed some friends who'd been to the cabin with him—and his ex-wife, too— and they all say, whenever Burke first arrived up here, he'd take a hike and then never leave the cabin again."

"Like he'd checked off 'Enjoy out-of-doors' on his daily calendar," Jacobs noted. "Sounds very lawyerlike to me. He hunt? Fish?"

Cartwright shook his head. "No guns in the cabin and no sign that there ever were any. No fishing tackle. Anyway. He comes back, maybe has a couple Bloody Marys, eats dinner. Uses paper plates, throws the trash in his nice covered metal kitchen wastebasket. Very convenient for forensics."

And very much like a man dining alone, Joanna thought. Except for the part about throwing out the trash. "He eat any canned foods?" she asked.

"If you mean home-canned-in-a-Mason-jar," Cartwright answered, "no. And there weren't any tin cans in the trash. But he did have a lot of grocery store canned goods in a pantry cupboard, chili, that kind of stuff."

Joanna smiled. So did she. "Any of those cans bulging?"

Cartwright shook his head. "Not a one."

Jacobs leaned back. "Isn't that some kind of old wives' tale, Davis? Like, don't store your oily paint rags under an open ladder on Halloween when there's a full moon?"

"Not at all," she said. Still, Joanna had opened a lot of cans in her life and not a one of them had ever bulged, except a few badly dented ones from the grocery store mark-down bin. She'd always figured those were fresh dents, same as if she dropped the can at home, and if she could save a quarter on creamed corn, she damn well would. "It's rare, but I know it can happen. You're old enough to remember, Al. When my kids were little there was a big scare after a bunch of people died from eating Bon Vivant vichyssoise."

Jacobs's brow furrowed in exaggerated disbelief. "You fed your kids *vichyssoise?*"

Joanna laughed. "I fed my kids hot dogs. They wouldn't have eaten cold potato soup unless I starved them for a week first. Maybe not even then. But they ate Campbell's chicken noodle by the carload. So I paid attention when people died from canned soup, yeah. Mothers are like that."

"Okay, Mom," Jacobs said. He turned back to Cartwright. "You were saying?"

"Yes, sir," Cale Cartwright responded. "After dinner, he seemed to start watching a video of *Spartacus*. About two-thirds through the video, he stopped it in the machine and went to bed. Now, the docs really hedge on how long it takes for botulism to start showing symptoms. They say it can be eight hours to eight days. But they also say they found a whole lot of *Clostridium botulinum*—" he pronounced it slowly and deliberately, dragging out all eight syllables "—the bad bug, in Burke's system. Enough so that it probably gave him trouble sometime that first night. He'd wake up with a whale of a bellyache. He upchucked at least once. Had diarrhea, too. Probably took some aspirin sometime. There was an open bottle of Bayer's on the bathroom sink. Which might have helped a headache, but doesn't do much for botulism."

Botulism. Joanna shuddered. It was such a nasty, medieval kind of illness. "And you didn't find *any* source for the botulism poisoning?"

Cale Cartwright shook his head. "Not a one. We had every scrap of food in that cabin analyzed. Either he ate up every bit of whatever it was, or somebody took it away."

"Or somebody took it away," Joanna repeated slowly.

"Yeah. There's something else, too. But I'd rather wait and show it to you."

Bill Burke's hideaway cabin remained sealed, exactly as it had been on the day the lawyer died.

Burke might have been a hotshot trial lawyer, but his cabin, nestled in the woods, was basic and unpretentious. Joanna rather liked it, could imagine spending time there. It reminded her of the places she and Don Olafson had stayed when they were first married, looking for a compromise between sleeping bags under the stars and Holiday Inn.

The small cabin's exterior was rough-hewn logs, with unfinished plank walls inside. You wouldn't be able to squeeze more than one person in the kitchen, and that person had better not be overweight. It held a tiny old refrigerator with a freezer barely large enough for a single ice cube tray, and a skinny little gas stove decorated with decades worth of crud. The kitchen table was Formica, the chairs metal, the floor dirty linoleum.

The queen-sized bed in the small single bedroom was positioned dead center, its sheets and blankets twisted and disordered. The bathroom was basic—fundamental toilet and sink, cheap mirrored cabinet above the basin. A narrow metal shower stall had a mildewed once-white vinyl curtain.

"So something loaded with botulism toxin was in this cabin and Bill Burke ingested it," Joanna said thoughtfully. "And then after he was ill, somebody took it away."

"It may have been Bloody Mary mix," Cartwright said. "At least that's my favorite guess. He had a bottle of vodka and his friends and ex-wife say he drank Bloody Marys. He favored Mr. and Mrs. T's extra-spicy, which we didn't find here. No other kind of mix or tomato juice either, nothing. If you were going to add it to something, that would be a natural. You'd know he was likely to get into it early and probably also often."

Joanna shuddered involuntarily. Food poisoning had always made her nervous, tapped into something primal and maternal in her. Plus she'd seen it up close. She'd been working in North Hollywood a dozen years ago when there was a major food poisoning incident involving a maker of *queso fresco*, a soft white cheese used in Mexican cooking. Pregnant women had spontaneously aborted. Small children and the elderly had died.

"I've talked to the Centers for Disease Control in Atlanta," Cartwright told them. "The CDC tracks food poisoning episodes and they say something like this is extremely rare. In most cases, they can rely on the victims or somebody else who was there to tell them what they ate, what smelled funny, that sort of information. The ultimate irony is that if Burke had gone to town right at the beginning, they probably could've saved him."

"Did somebody check his food at home in Riverside?" Joanna asked. "Maybe it was something he ate before he left."

Cartwright nodded. "What you're suggesting is possible, but if he did, he ate up every scrap of whatever it was *and* destroyed the packaging. Riverside PD went in and cleaned out his kitchen, had everything there tested, too. *Nada.*"

"You ask Burke if he had any visitors, or saw anybody around?" Jacobs wondered.

"Yes. And he said no. Thing is, he was probably unconscious or semi-conscious a lot of the time. And he may have been suffering from double vision, too."

"Double vision?" Al Jacobs asked. "From botulism?"

"It's a fairly common symptom," Cartwright answered. "Now, who's up for a hike?"

"Me," Joanna answered immediately.

Jacobs looked as if he'd rather have his toes sucked by ferrets. "I'll hold down the fort here."

"Watch out for spiders," Joanna told him cheerfully, pleased to see him flinch.

"I got to wondering," Cartwright told Joanna as he headed purposefully into the forest behind the cabin, "just how somebody might keep tabs on Burke. I thought maybe this would be the sort of thing that a particular type of sadistic mind might want to actually observe. And guess what?"

"You were right?"

Cartwright stopped in a small clearing. "I was right."

Joanna looked around. A fallen tree rested on the ground, and through the foliage below her, she could see part of Bill Burke's cabin. "He watched from here?"

Cartwright nodded. "I think so. I didn't find any hard evidence, no trash or fabric scraps caught on thorns or anything like that. But the ground was scuffed up in this area. I think he sat right on that log, keeping track of his party down below."

"He camp here?"

Cartwright shook his head. "But further back, I found a campsite where somebody probably stayed a few days."

"You have technicians go over it?" Joanna asked.

"Uh-huh. Again, no hard evidence. C'mon, I'll take you back to see it."

The campsite was small, clean, welcoming. Joanna could imagine unrolling a sleeping bag on the pine needles, heating coffee water over a Coleman stove.

But there seemed to be an odd chill in the air, and she was sure Cartwright was correct.

9

Back in L.A. the next day, they huddled with Dave Austin and Mickey Conner, who'd been looking into the local aspects of the Coskins and Burke cases.

"The plaintiff's lawyers who lost the food poisoning case to Burke couldn't figure out what happened," Dave Austin explained. Since he'd begun hanging out in law offices, he affected more formal attire. In today's vested navy suit, he could have passed for a senior associate at Weill, Screwum & Good—except for the shoulder holster. "It never occurred to them that they could lose."

"Why don't you run through the whole lawsuit business," Jacobs suggested. They had taken refuge in a cramped interrogation room that offered a modicum of privacy from the Robbery–Homicide bullpen and its constantly ringing phones. "See what jumps at us."

"Well, as far as the disgruntled plaintiffs go," Austin told him, "they're a regular Pogo Stick Express. Here's what happened. Benny Giancana—no relation to the late Chicagoan, R.I.P.—owns a restaurant out in Montclair. Giancana's Trattoria. He's been there thirty years, nice place, family-type restaurant, 'A' health rating.

The Martinelli family had been eating at Giancana's for years, and it was a natural for the Martinelli daughter's wedding reception. Everything went fine till they hit the main course, the bride's favorite manicotti stuffed with cheese. Only that day, the cheese was bad. Ricotta, with a strain of bacteria that acted fast and dirty. By the time the newlyweds were ready to cut the cake, guests all over the restaurant were starting to get sick."

"What a nightmare," Joanna murmured. She sent mental thanks northward to Kirsten for having possessed the good sense to want a simple wedding in the park, for not even *raising* the issue of an expensive seated-dinner reception. Kirsten's wedding had been lovely, green and serene and low-key, with her father and his second wife and their three kids in town from Minnesota for nearly a week. Joanna was divorced from *her* second husband by then, and everybody had been unceasingly civil, though she had drawn her own personal line at going to Disneyland with Don Olafson's second family.

"Yeah," Austin continued. "Pretty soon things got pretty hysterical, with people fighting to get into the johns to barf. And of course, when you've got that many folks vomiting, there's a ripple effect. So probably some folks had their stomachs pumped unnecessarily. Forty-three people were treated and released at various area hospitals. Fourteen were sick enough to be admitted. One of those was a four-year-old boy who died three days later from a secondary staph infection he apparently picked up in the hospital. The other person who died was the grandmother of the bride. *She* had a fatal heart attack in the restaurant parking lot watching 'em load the bridal party into ambulances."

"How many people at the reception?" Jacobs asked.

"Around eighty. They'd paid for eighty-seven dinners and there were a few no-shows."

Conner laughed. "Bet *they* felt smug."

"Sounds like the restaurant was guilty as hell," Jacobs noted, frowning. "Why'd the insurance company ever let it go to trial?"

"Two reasons," Austin explained. "One is that there's no question but that the food poisoning was in the cheese and *only* in the cheese. The stuff was *loaded.* Giancana got his ricotta made fresh—" he chuckled "—*allegedly* fresh, by a local cheesemaker. Ralph Sortino, who closed up shop and vamoosed after the wedding. Still among the missing and very uninsured. One of the plaintiff's attorneys actually suggested that Giancana had the guy fitted for a cement wetsuit, but there's nothing to suggest anything of the sort actually happened. Our organized crime people say they'd never heard of Giancana *or* Sortino."

"And Giancana doesn't have any mobbed-up relatives back east or anything?" Jacobs asked. "Guys who like to travel?"

"Not that I can find, though that's what the plaintiff's lawyer, skinny little guy who's big on conspiracy theories, thinks. Anyway, Burke won by blaming everything on the cheesemaker. And the judge wouldn't let the plaintiff's lawyers tell the jury that Sortino was (a) judgment-proof and (b) in the wind."

"So the jury decided Giancana wasn't to blame? For *anything?*" Joanna still couldn't understand this. Society was currently so obsessed by the issue of food safety that you couldn't even take the kids out for a fast-food burger without making sure it was charred beyond recognition to avoid *E. coli.* She'd expect a conservative suburban jury to really stick it to somebody who killed a kid and poisoned a few dozen innocent merrymakers. Not to mention Granny checking out in the parking lot.

"Benny Giancana's a very charismatic guy," Conner explained. "Everybody's favorite uncle. He took the stand, testified in his own defense, broke down and sobbed while he was testifying. It also helped that he did everything right as soon as the shit started coming down at the reception, even making a few trips to the hospital himself, with people barfing in his Buick." Conner shook his head. "I liked the guy, what can I say?"

"You mentioned a second reason why Giancana got off?" Jacobs prompted.

"Greed," Austin replied succinctly. "Giancana had insurance, good insurance. The carrier would have been *thrilled* to settle, and they actually *did* settle most of the claims rising out of the incident. Most of the victims were fine once they threw up. They felt a little queasy for a day or two and then trotted their insurance checks to the bank."

"And the others?" Joanna asked.

Conner cocked his head, raised a woolly eyebrow. "They wanted *just* a little bit more. The parents of the dead boy were asking for five million and the relatives of Angela Martinelli wanted half a mill apiece for emotional distress. Seventeen family members watched Granny Angie die, including the groom who by then was technically part of the family. So that's another eight and a half million for the Martinelli family, for a grand total of thirteen-five."

Jacobs whistled. "Thirteen million is a lotta ricotta. What about all these Martinellis? And the relatives of the dead boy?"

"Spread all over the San Gabriel Valley," Conner said. "We make an official linkup of these cases, we can ask county sheriffs to check them out."

"Good," Jacobs said. "Now what about Coskins, the bike guy? Anything interesting there?"

Austin shook his head. "Not really. His customers tended to be pretty satisfied. You know, some guy's flying down the highway at a hundred—no helmet, no insurance, no brains. He piles into your station wagon, three guesses who's gonna pay. The field's not as wide open as it used to be before the helmet law and some of the uninsured motorist initiatives, but that's how Coskins made his rep. Made a lot of money, too. Didn't take things to trial, nearly always settled. He also has a lot of State Bar complaints on file, but they're jealously guarded by this ugly bitch with a bad case of 'I'm your moral superior because I'm an attorney-at-law.' Like we don't all know lawyers were put on earth so used-car salesmen would have somebody to feel superior to."

Bonita Blevins was indeed a self-righteous prig.

It took Joanna approximately three minutes to reach that conclusion after being admitted to the chief trial counsel's inner sanctum in the California State Bar's downtown Los Angeles offices. Joanna had encountered her type before, often in positions of power as school principals, welfare supervisors, dental hygienists, DMV functionaries, and Neighborhood Watch captains.

Bonita Blevins apparently believed it her sacred mission to single-handedly rid California of legal misbehavior. The agency she headed seemed to be the legal profession's equivalent of LAPD's Internal Affairs. As such, Joanna could easily extrapolate that Blevins would be universally reviled even if she'd possessed the competent cheer of Mary Poppins.

Blevins was in her late forties, her finely textured, mouse-brown hair styled in a limp pageboy and her pale brown eyes obscured by thick lenses in square metal frames. She appeared sturdy without seeming either fit or fat and was dressed conservatively in a charcoal gray chalk-striped suit with a white silk blouse and a rather jarring gold jack-o'-lantern lapel pin. Joanna had all but forgotten that Halloween was this week. Not that she needed to worry about laying in supplies of candy; there were no young neighbors in her remote corner of the Valley, where her only potential tricksters were the canyon coyotes.

"Maybe we could start," Joanna suggested congenially, "with you telling me a little bit about how the Bar's disciplinary system works. I have to admit it mystifies me."

"You're not alone," Blevins assured her. Her voice was slightly nasal, her manner defensive. "There are a hundred and twenty thousand active licensed attorneys in the state of California. Our job is to make sure they perform ethically and responsibly. California is generally considered to have the finest legal disciplinary system in the nation."

California was also home, Joanna believed, to some of the shittiest and most outrageously immoral lawyers on the planet. She nodded encouragingly.

"Our toll-free Intake and Legal Advice number handles a hundred and thirty thousand calls a year," Blevins went on automatically. This seemed to be a frequently given, well-honed little speech. "Around half the calls are simple information requests or referrals to other agencies. Of the remainder, we'll open about fifteen thousand general inquiries, and perhaps six thousand of those will advance to the investigation stage."

"That's a lot of complaints," Joanna noted.

"True enough," Blevins agreed. "But once the investigations begin, things change dramatically. Only between ten and fifteen percent of the cases we open result in major punishment: disbarment, suspension, public or private reproval. Of course some attorneys prefer simply to resign from the Bar with charges pending. Richard Nixon is probably the most famous example of that."

"Cheating the executioner." Joanna kept her tone neutral, watching for Blevins's reaction. Actually, she'd been hoping for slightly more current information.

"Anyone who resigns with charges pending will *not* be readmitted without a complete investigation," Blevins explained crisply, eyes blazing. "Frankly, if somebody shouldn't be practicing law, I don't care *how* he loses his law license, just that he loses it." Her tight, self-righteous smile suggested that she'd like to hang these wretched miscreants by their thumbs and apply acid to various tender orifices and appendages. Joanna would not want to be a lawyer caught in some kind of fuckup by this woman.

Blevins went on to explain that most State Bar investigations ended informally, and that many initial complaints simply grew out of poor communication.

Joanna frowned. "So some of your complaints are just designed to catch the lawyer's attention? Or to get even?" Move over, Internal Affairs.

Bonita Blevins pursed her lips. "And they do an extremely effective job of it. Actually, I imagine our investigative procedures are quite similar to your own."

Joanna nodded, though she doubted the State Bar got many cases where they had to chase heavily armed lawyers down garbage-strewn alleys.

Bonita Blevins leaned back in a black leather chair that was far too big for her. Her desktop and credenza held no photographs of children, no Zen sandboxes, no clever little office toys. Her diplomas were elaborately double matted in thick walnut frames.

Nothing in this office indicated that its occupant had a personality. Including the occupant.

"Are complaints to your office a matter of public record?" Joanna asked, already aware of the answer.

The chief trial counsel bristled. "Certainly not."

"Then who has access to information about pending complaints? I'm sure everybody who works here has a computer."

"Naturally our employees have computers, but that's hardly tantamount to *access.* Access is carefully compartmentalized. Only deputy trial counsels and investigators have access to all information about trials, investigations, complaints, inquiries, and so on."

"Are these records purged if the charges are dismissed?"

"No. But again, those records are only available to my staff."

"And you have—how many people in this office?"

"Fifty-five deputy trial counsels in Los Angeles," Blevins told her, "and another dozen or so in San Francisco. I head both offices. I live down here and spend a portion of my time up there."

"And what kind of investigation do you conduct before you hire somebody?"

Blevins looked startled. "Why, a standard employment investigation. We check references, of course, but it isn't like an FBI clearance or anything. Quite a few of our investigators have previously worked in law enforcement, so they're already well vetted. Why? Just what are you suggesting?"

"Nothing at all," Joanna reassured. "Some people have wondered if perhaps some of the recent attorney deaths might have occurred because somebody thought these lawyers *should* have been punished and they weren't. That perhaps somebody in your office might feel they're getting off too easily."

"That's preposterous!"

"Is it?"

Bonita Blevins was suddenly furious. Bright spots of color rose on her cheeks. "Most assuredly. We are not a vigilante force. Our entire *existence* is predicated on the assumption that the legal system works properly. I can assure you that nobody in *my* office could possibly be involved in the situations you're investigating."

They wrangled a bit over authorizations and confidentiality, but when the dance of discovery finally ended and Joanna gained access to the files of the dead lawyers, it hardly seemed worth the effort.

Bill Burke had always worked in insurance defense and had never been the subject of any State Bar complaints or investigations. Zilch.

Lawrence Benton's drunk driving conviction of a dozen years earlier was duly noted in his State Bar records, though there was no mention of earlier DUI charges he had beaten. Benton had been charged with malfeasance on two occasions and had been privately reproved for failure to communicate a settlement offer to a client. During a televised trial four years earlier, several Court TV viewers had called the Bar to suggest that Benton's conduct in court was improper, but while Benton had apparently been rude and obnoxious, those were not punishable offenses. And at the time of his death, his record was squeaky clean.

Roger Coskins, on the other hand, had received a slew of inquiries and complaints, most later withdrawn. The general thrust often was that potential clients were led to believe Mr. Coskins would personally handle their cases, when in fact Mr. Coskins was usually out on his boat or riding his Harley at warp speed through the desert, leaving the tedious legal scut work to the platoons of freshly minted, underpaid young lawyers running his mill. Coskins had also been the subject of several investigations related to the sluggish issuance of settlement checks to clients after insurance payments were received by his office. The cumulative effect of four such situations had led to a suspension a few years earlier.

But none of these people, when contacted, showed any lingering signs of bitterness. They had, after all, received hefty settlements, even if their checks *were* slightly delayed. Two had referred other clients to Coskins later, and one had retained the attorney again himself when he managed to lose a leg in a collision with a concrete bus stop.

So much for the State Bar.

• • •

On Wednesday, October 29th, the mayor of Los Angeles and the LAPD chief of police held a joint press conference at Parker Center to announce the formation of an Atterminator Task Force. Robbery–Homicide detectives Al Jacobs and Joanna Davis stood beside the mayor and chief, silent and somber.

The mayor, up for re-election in June, was a lawyer himself, a highly nervous one with a brand-new contingent of LAPD bodyguards. He explained that investigators from San Luis Obispo County, Fresno County, and Riverside County would participate in the task force's investigation.

One of the first orders of task force business, the mayor announced in an unscripted excess of zeal, would be to investigate the deaths of *all* attorneys over the past year. Toward that end, he suggested that anyone with relevant information about such deaths— or with any other information relevant to the task force investigation—call the Atterminator Hot Line. He held up a printed card with the phone number.

Joanna kept her expression solemn as he spoke, but she'd have sworn she could hear the distant rumble of crackpots by the score racing to their phones.

10

Joanna had little difficulty remaining detached from the first three legal murders. The next one, however, caught her square in the gut.

The next one might have been Kirsten.

At 8:47 A.M. on Friday, October 31st, a court reporter arriving for a scheduled deposition had just entered a Long Beach office building from the parking garage when she heard three sharp cracks. A former resident of South Central L.A., LaDonna Williams instantly recognized the sound of gunfire and dove beneath a stairwell. After several heart-pounding minutes, she cautiously opened the door to the parking area.

Richard Kinnelly, an attorney officed in the building, was just pulling into the garage when LaDonna opened that door. The two of them saw Mary Elaine McGonigle's body at the same time. While the lawyer punched 911 into his car phone, LaDonna moved warily toward the woman who had hired her for a deposition that clearly would not be going forward on schedule. She got close enough to see that there was a great deal of blood and a big empty space where the right side of the attorney's head ought to be, then about-faced with military precision and reached a trash barrel just in time to lose her breakfast.

Kinnelly, meanwhile, had power-locked the doors of his Le Baron and discovered that even after a twenty-year hiatus, he could still say Our Father pretty damned fast.

In the general confusion when the police first arrived, nobody immediately noticed the sheet of paper tucked under the driver's-side windshield wiper of the victim's car. Then one of the officers took a look at the piece of paper and everything changed.

Joanna Davis and Al Jacobs reached the parking garage about 10:15. They'd been plowing through lists of dead lawyers and fielding hot line calls when the call came through from Long Beach. By then the morning freeway traffic should have eased up a bit, but a jam-up on the Harbor forced the dilapidated unmarked to bump along the shoulder for over a mile before they passed the accident scene. A three-car pileup blocked two lanes. Cops on the scene were talking to a guy dashingly attired as Zorro, while a woman in a bumblebee outfit was loaded into an ambulance.

Happy Halloween.

News trucks from several networks were already assembled on the streets surrounding the Long Beach office building, with a vague atmosphere of carnival in the area. Many of the people who'd come out of neighboring buildings wore costumes, the usual office collection of cowboys and pirates and black cats. The RHD detectives were directed down a ramp to the garage beneath a boxy three-story office building surrounded by pyracantha bushes bearing heavy clusters of cheerful crimson berries.

Long Beach detective Ron Inouye met them at the base of the

ramp. He was a self-assured young Asian in his mid-thirties, slender with glossy, close-cropped black hair and bright, darting eyes.

"The victim is Mary Elaine McGonigle," Inouye told them. "Thirty-one years old, divorce lawyer. Looks like the shooter was waiting for her to arrive, probably back behind that Chevy in the corner. You wouldn't notice anybody back there as you drove in."

Inouye led them toward the body.

In the stark fluorescent light of the underground garage, the dead lawyer appeared appallingly young. She was crumpled beside her car, leaning up against the back fender with one leg tucked beneath her body. She'd been wearing a cream-colored wool jacket over a red silk dress randomly patterned with airy black feathers. The side of her jacket beneath the ghastly head wound was drenched with blood, blood that formed a shallow pool on the greasy concrete floor. Her sleek black hair was cut short and swept back from her face. Massive blood loss had drained any natural color from what remained of a once-pretty face. Her lipstick matched her dress, but was lighter than her blood.

"Something large-caliber, close range," Inouye said. "Not enough damage for a shotgun, but damned close. Maybe a .45. Witness heard three shots and it looks like at least one of them lodged in that wall behind the car."

"She'd closed the car door already?" Joanna asked. On the ground beside the body lay an expensive Coach handbag. "Any chance it was a robbery gone bad?"

"Purse seems untouched, and the trunk was popped open but not raised. Driver's door was closed and locked. She had her briefcase in the trunk and it also looks like that wasn't disturbed. She was probably going back to get it when he came up and fired."

The security gate to the garage was presently rolled all the way open. "That gate normally kept closed?" Jacobs asked.

Inouye shook his head. "It's locked at night, but all the building tenants have keys. Whoever gets here first in the morning unlocks it and leaves it open. Clients park under here, too, during the day. The building's all lawyers, maybe a dozen."

"You mentioned a witness?" Joanna asked.

Ron Inouye nodded. "Earwitness, anyway." He explained about LaDonna Williams. "Next on the scene was another lawyer. He says he saw somebody in a Frankenstein costume moving away from the building as he turned in. He's totally freaked."

"I guess so," Joanna said, surveying the pathetic remains of the young lawyer. Had her last vision been a Frankenstein mask? "The witness didn't see a car leaving?"

Inouye shook his head. "Frankenstein was on foot, heading west. Not running, but moving fast."

Jacobs gestured toward the front of the car, at a piece of paper angled beneath the driver's-side wiper. "That the note you mentioned when you called?"

Inouye nodded. "It is indeed. Come around this way." He led them behind the Honda to a vantage point where they could clearly see the paper. It was a plain 8½-by-11 white sheet with four words scrawled on it in uneven block letters:

OPEN SEASON ON LAWYERS.

Joanna and Jacobs stayed through mid-afternoon, avoiding the media locusts that hovered outside by the simple expedient of never leaving the building.

It was too much to hope that the OPEN SEASON ON LAWYERS note would stay secret for long, and by the time somebody brought in a bag of tacos for lunch, it was running on all the networks. Lawyers in McGonigle's office suite had a television tuned in, and updates on the shooting—most of them highly inaccurate—were being regularly inserted as news bulletins, interrupting talk show discussions of fashion tips for skydiving transvestites. Rumors crowded the airwaves, gaining credence by their simple statement: McGonigle had been raped; she'd handled a divorce for some low-level mobster; a list of potential legal targets had been appended to the OPEN SEASON ON LAWYERS announcement.

McGonigle's husband had been brought down from the Lakewood bank where he served as chief loan officer, alibied by the half dozen people with whom he'd been meeting at the time of the shooting. He moved like a sleepwalker and insisted on seeing the body. When Inouye reluctantly brought him down to the garage, he passed out cold.

The picture that emerged was baffling. Mary Elaine McGonigle was a California native and graduate of UC Santa Barbara and Western Law School. Her colleagues described her fondly as hardworking, tenacious, and dedicated to her clients. She had a four-year-old son and a two-year-old daughter.

"So what do you think?" Ron Inouye asked, carefully wiping a smear of hot sauce off his upper lip. Taco remains lay scattered on an oblong maple conference table. "Is this one of yours?" He smiled sardonically. "Do I get to be on the task force?"

Jacobs ran his fingers through what remained of his hair. "I don't know, Inouye. I wouldn't hand off your other cases just yet. This one feels different, seems off the pattern. Way off. To begin with, she's a relative nobody. Young, fairly inexperienced, low profile. The other victims we're looking at were all well known, associated with high-profile cases. Benton had the million-dollar cup of coffee, Burke got off the food poisoner, Coskins had those outrageous TV ads. Whereas this lady was doing custody agreements and restraining orders and nobody's ever heard of her."

"I'm inclined to agree," Joanna added. "But for another reason entirely. This killing lacks finesse. She was shot in a parking garage, for God's sake. How many zillion times has everybody seen *that* cliché on TV? The other three have a certain *style* to them, practically a signature. Our killer's very deliberate, into dramatic, heavy-handed symbolism."

"Nothing symbolic about this one," Inouye agreed. "It seems pretty up front, more...*personal.*"

Joanna nodded her head enthusiastically. She wished there'd been another taco; she was ravenous. "Exactly! I like a disgruntled client for this one, I think. Or, more likely, a satisfied client's disgruntled spouse, or the spouse's lover. That kind of connection. Clients in family law cases are always pissed off about something. I think what you're gonna find is that this was somebody absolutely furious and irrational because his divorce was going the wrong way, somebody who blamed McGonigle because his life was falling apart." She hesitated. "But I have to say, I *really* hate that note."

"Me, too," Jacobs grunted. "It's like a regular invitation to the deranged. Open season on lawyers. Kee-rist! I have this feeling we're going to start finding dead lawyers all over the place."

Inouye offered his sly little grin again. "There are those who might not consider that such a terrible thing."

By evening, Long Beach police still retained jurisdiction over the McGonigle murder, which was not yet officially linked to the Atterminator investigation. But if the cops were unwilling to join the case to the three previous murders, the media had no such reservations. The death of Mary Elaine McGonigle was the lead story on all the southern California TV news shows and was featured on all national news broadcasts as well.

Without exception, these reports began with an ominous intonation of the killer's latest message: OPEN SEASON ON LAWYERS.

Robbery–Homicide was an eight-to-five division and normally cleared out pretty promptly on Friday afternoons. Conner and Austin were still waiting, however, when Joanna and Jacobs returned just after five-thirty, following a bumper-to-bumper freeway marathon. Both Conner and Austin looked anxious and edgy and tired, but Austin also appeared ready to camp out for the duration.

"So?" Austin asked.

"Ours?" Conner asked.

Jacobs spread his hands wide, lifted his shoulders in an exaggerated shrug. "Who knows? It doesn't seem like it, though." He outlined what they knew about the McGonigle murder and the reasons for thinking the case unrelated to the Atterminator murders. "The most compelling part," he concluded, "is, there's a guy who looks real good for it."

"Tell all," Austin commanded, leaning back and putting his feet on his desk. He'd make a fine administrator some day.

"His name is Lenny Duran," Jacobs said, "and at the moment he's not available for comment. He's not available, period, and nobody seems to know just where he might be. But what we've got is this. He's a contractor, thirty-five, five-seven, hundred and forty. A skinny little hothead, the kind of guy who puffs up after a couple of beers and picks fights in bars. The dead woman represented his wife in a particularly nasty divorce."

Conner snorted. "There's another kind?"

"Occasionally," Joanna responded mildly. Both of her divorces had been downright amiable compared to what she had come to realize was the norm. Which maybe only meant that she wasn't normal, and she'd already figured that out. "This one was *really* ugly. Duran liked to bounce his wife down the stairwell of their apartment building. He'd already been busted twice on domestic abuse charges before the last episode, when he hung her out the window by her heels. When he made bail on that one, his wife finally wised up and took the kids to a shelter. The shelter recommended McGonigle."

"How come this eight ball isn't in jail?" Austin asked.

"Nobody seems to have a very good answer for that. Even before he started working out on the wife, he had a record for battery in some kind of construction site brawl."

"And he threatened the victim?" Austin asked.

"Happened in the courthouse, after a custody hearing." Jacobs smiled. "Those always bring out the best in everybody. Apparently Duran wasn't happy with the way the hearing went, and he started screaming at McGonigle in the hallway afterward. Bailiff remembered the incident real well. Says Duran told her, 'You're dead, you fucking cunt,' and had her backed against a wall. Bailiff and a cop nailed Duran, had him spread-eagled, but McGonigle didn't want to press charges."

"Sounds like a real winner," Conner announced. "Unless there's something you're leaving out, like he's in Washington being named to a presidential commission, I like him for this one. Like him a lot. Just where *is* the little fucker, anyway?"

"Nobody seems to know," Jacobs repeated. "He's not answering calls and there's nobody at his workshop, which is a little cubicle in the back of an auto services strip mall. Other tenants say he's been sleeping there, which is supposed to be a no-no, but nobody called him on it, not wanting to have their faces rearranged. In any case, last time anybody admits to seeing him was Wednesday."

Dave Austin grinned. "Well, he fits the FBI profile."

They all laughed. At the mayor's urging, the FBI had been consulted for a serial killer profile, and had subsequently offered up its learned opinion that LAPD should be looking for a white male between eighteen and thirty-five who lived alone, kept to himself, and had problems with authority figures. Who specifically had a grudge against attorneys. Which, Jacobs had noted when the report first came in, narrowed the field to maybe six or seven million Americans, half of them living in southern California.

"But he sure doesn't sound like the guy who's been doing the others," Austin went on. "Unless there's something you're holding out on us."

"*Nada,*" Jacobs assured him.

"Then what about the note?" Austin asked.

"Ah, the note." Joanna smiled. "Nobody hired a calligrapher, I can tell you that much. It's black marker on plain white paper. Block letters, mostly capitals. Kind of sloppy, actually, not unlike the murder itself. They've put a rush on analyzing the paper and ink, but I'll be real surprised if anything comes of it. And everybody in the western world knows the text by now."

"So what does that leave us?" Conner frowned. "A young woman probably killed by somebody who was mad at her. *Specifically* at her, not at the whole legal profession, like the others."

"But smart enough to put out a note making it look that way," Austin reminded. "You wouldn't *believe* the calls we've been fielding here all day long. Every mouthpiece who ever jerked around a client is shitting bricks. They all want personal police protection and they want it yesterday. They're all taxpayers, they lead with that one. Every one of those bastards is paying my salary."

Conner laughed. "Tell you what, if all those guys actually *were* paying me, I could afford to retire."

"Maybe the mayor could call out the national guard," Jacobs suggested, "or order up a couple divisions of marines from Camp Pendleton."

"I got a better idea," Conner said. "Let's round the bastards up and put 'em all in protective custody. See if maybe we can't scrounge around and get the plans they used on those Japanese internment centers back in World War Two."

"Detective Inouye down in Long Beach might object," Jacobs told him.

Joanna frowned. Something had been nagging at her through-out the day. "You know what's missing here?" she asked slowly. "Not one of our victims has been a criminal attorney. Whether or not we include today's killing, which is probably just opportunis-tic. Coskins, Burke, Benton—even McGonigle—all of them are *civil* attorneys. And civil attorneys just aren't the ones that the public usually gets worked up about. It's criminal lawyers who help people get away with things, get the guilty off on technicalities, *those* are the lawyers that everybody loves to hate. The ones respon-sible for the rapists who get off, the murderers who walk, the wife-beaters who get a slap on the wrist."

Her face darkened. She could feel herself heating up, sensed the anger and resentment that had simmered all day beginning to brim over. Today had shaken her badly. Her reaction to the sight of that young mother lying mutilated beside her car was purely visceral.

Kirsten. She was so very much like Kirsten.

She slapped her hands on the table in front of her. "So why isn't our guy taking out *criminal* attorneys?"

"Poor judgment?" Austin suggested.

"Lack of time?" Conner offered. "Scared of rabies?"

But Jacobs was frowning. "What's your point, Davis?"

She hesitated. "I think that whoever our guy is, his grievances with the legal profession probably came out of some kind of civil action. His lawsuit went bad and he ended up penniless. Or some-body else's lawsuit went well and he ended up penniless."

"Or he won his lawsuit and the lawyer took everything and he *still* ended up penniless," Austin suggested.

And on that note, they broke for the night.

• • •

Daylight was long gone as Joanna drove west across the San Fernando Valley, the automobile lights forming slowly undulating necklaces of diamonds and rubies that glowed in the blackness.

The image of Mary Elaine McGonigle refused to leave her. She thought about the woman's husband and her children, the little boy and girl who should be out now trick-or-treating with their parents, ringing doorbells and collecting too much candy and gorging themselves into a sugar-fueled mania. Maybe the McGonigles had planned to take the kids trick-or-treating at a mall, or to a Haunted House at some nearby park, or to a Halloween party with friends.

None of that would happen now. Halloween was permanently ruined for this young family and the people who loved them, would forever carry memories of genuine and ineradicable horror.

Joanna thought back to the Halloweens when her own children were small. Kirsten was always ultra-feminine, a fairy princess or southern belle or glamorous lady, while Mikey—back before he reached double-digit ages and dropped the diminutive *y*—invariably favored monsters, the gorier and grislier the better. Mikey's costumes featured green slime and hideous scars and dripping blood. One year, she remembered, he had been Frankenstein.

Just like the person who killed Mary Elaine McGonigle.

By the time Joanna reached her exit, traffic had thinned. She had the secondary road to her own house completely to herself, her headlights cutting arcs through the ghostly chaparral. The new moon formed a sliver above the horizon as Joanna parked outside her house and went in, trying to banish the thought that had hovered on the edges of her mind all day. She didn't yet know who within the media had made the same connection, but somebody surely had. It was such a natural. She'd thought of it on her way to work this morning, before Frankenstein ever went down into the Long Beach parking garage, while Mary Elaine McGonigle was kissing her children good-bye at their preschool.

Another season, another serial killer, another Halloween. The third victim of the Hillside Strangler had been discovered on Halloween.

Fifteen-year-old Judy Miller, the girl had been, a runaway living on the street in Hollywood, and when her body was discovered, nobody realized she was part of a horrific series. Indeed, she remained quietly unidentified for nearly two weeks. Certainly Joanna Olafson, Mar Vista housewife and mother, had been blissfully unaware that the death of this poor girl would forever alter the course of her own life.

Mary Elaine McGonigle, growing up in Orange County, would have been seven. Had Mary Elaine's mother grown fearfully overprotective of her daughter in that horrible bygone season, even as Joanna had of Kirsten? Joanna remembered sitting beside her daughter's bed on the long and frightening nights when Don worked morning watch, sleeping fitfully on a throw rug beside Kirsten's bed. Obsessed that nobody would get her child.

And nobody had.

Now she called Kirsten in Seattle, insisted on hearing every minor, trivial, joyously inconsequential detail of her daughter's day. Took comfort and delight in the minutiae.

Rejoiced that Kirsten was alive.

11

Ace was pissed.

He'd had some ideas for Halloween, just for fun, nothing serious, nothing to do with the Legal Resolution Program.

Then *this* happened.

Ace had considered a lot of eventualities, but this wasn't one of them. This was *his* show and he'd spent a long time getting it ready. He didn't want anybody else mucking around in it now.

Everybody had a script in this town. Ace had his own script always running in his head, and he could see the words of each scene as clearly as if he held the pages in his hand. Crisp black Courier typeface, with wide margins and the occasional terse dialogue block.

He anguished most of the day. Short of making a public

announcement, which would be incredibly foolish, there was no way to set the record straight. He would have to endure the linkage of the Legal Resolution Program with whatever freelance activity turned up.

Gina had called in a panic, so rattled that she actually used the cell phone. He cut her off brusquely, announced that she had the wrong number, that he wasn't interested in cellular service. He had heard her gasp, and five minutes later she rang up again from a pay phone, half-apologetic, half-hysterical.

It had taken a long time to talk her down.

He was more than a little worried about Gina.

He had never intended to undertake the Legal Resolution Program with an accomplice. It was too complicated, too risky. And you could never tell with girls. They might talk tough but they were likely to fold fast.

Gina, however, had seemed different from the first, with that sly streak he picked up on instantly. She was highly motivated. Tougher than she appeared. Deliciously amoral. Full of innovative ideas.

And she came equipped with an anti-legal agenda all her own.

Ace didn't have much use for God or religion, but he did believe that certain things were meant to be. What he was doing now was one of them. And perhaps the appearance of Gina in his life at such a pivotal point was another.

Still, she was on the verge of being a liability.

This would be particularly true if it turned out that he had actually gotten something going here, started something that could become...what? A populist movement? An armed uprising?

He reluctantly conceded to himself that he couldn't stop it. Indeed, he took some comfort and a certain degree of pride in knowing that this first freelancer wasn't half-bad. He tipped a mental hat to the author of the slogan: OPEN SEASON ON LAWYERS.

An idea whose time had come.

That's what cops all over southern California were saying about the Atterminator murders. Highly unofficial lists of possible candidates for the Atterminator's attention circulated through station houses, firing ranges, doughnut shops, and cop bars. In a newly savvy and cautious era, few were dumb enough to commit their lists to paper or make suggestions via computer or e-mail.

But there was no need, after all, to write anything down. Each cop's individual list was personalized and unforgettable.

On Monday, November 3rd, Las Vegas criminal attorney Vincent Carrigan turned the key in the ignition of his three-week-old black Porsche 911 and was blown halfway to Reno.

As technicians began picking little bits and pieces of the late Mr. Carrigan out of various cactus gardens in his upscale desert subdivision, Las Vegas detectives got on the horn to LAPD. Jacobs took the call, growing glummer by the minute, then flipped Joanna to see who'd go check it out. He lost.

By noon, Joanna was half wishing she'd offered to make the trip. Next time—and it seemed a virtual certainty there'd soon be another murdered lawyer somewhere in the U.S. of A.—she *would* go. But wait. She remembered her conversation with Mike in Minneapolis on Saturday, her son's gleeful reports of the surprise Halloween storm that had buried the Twin Cities under eleven inches of snow. She amended her resolution: next time she would go, *provided* that the incident occurred in the grapefruit belt.

The media were hot for the dramatically slain attorney, immediately prepared to add him to the list of Atterminator victims. Network film crews rushed to Vegas and everybody wanted a comment from Robbery–Homicide. Joanna referred them all to the captain, who stonewalled masterfully. The calls about Mary Elaine McGonigle, she referred to Ron Inouye in Long Beach.

Given the incessant interruptions, she was grateful she had

come in the previous Saturday afternoon to get a leg up on the Dead Lawyer List.

It was extensive.

They'd started with the lawyers that the State Bar knew to have died within the last five years. LAPD had also sent inquiries to police departments all over California, requesting info on accidental deaths, murders, suicides, and miscellaneous suspicious circumstances surrounding the demise of attorneys-at-law, both former and current. RHD's self-styled computer geek had scoured the Internet for legal obituaries.

There were a *lot* of dead lawyers.

Fortunately, most deaths could be quickly eliminated. The extremely elderly in nursing homes, their deaths balanced, in the younger ranks, by a depressing number of stress-related fatalities. There was also a good deal of cancer, including several lung cancers that could probably be cross-referenced under Stress. A surprising number were under forty-five.

Jacobs called in around one o'clock.

"So is he one of ours?" she asked without preamble.

"I don't think so," he answered immediately, "though they'd love to have it that way."

"So tell me." She sat back, pulled out the bottom desk drawer, rested her feet on it.

"Well, this is the dead criminal lawyer you asked for, Davis. A clown named Vincent Carrigan, forty-one years old, with a dozen or more folks pissed off at him for every one of those years. A guy who's gone through life irritating *everybody*, then climbing out of the hole by being charming."

He sounded a bit like Joanna's second ex-husband, though Jake Arnold hadn't been precisely *irritating*, just impulsive and immature. "So who's he irritated?"

"Well, there's two embittered ex-wives who couldn't shake the child support out of him. And a former girlfriend who *also* couldn't shake the child support out of him. He liked to gamble and lately he had this problem of blowing a lot of his cases." Jacobs laughed. "My kind of criminal defense lawyer."

"Blew cases 'cause he bungled them or 'cause he didn't fight hard enough?" Joanna wanted to know. There was a big difference.

"Bit of both, I think. But he was trying to branch out, put criminal law behind him. He'd been putting together a deal to build a strip mall, and Mr. Fuckup did it big-time here. Money was lost, which reportedly annoyed the silent partner no end. The silent partner being a guy from Chicago with a lot of vowels in his name."

"Does the silent partner have any acquaintances familiar with explosives?"

"I'd imagine so. The guys here are looking into that, and it's where I'd put my money right now. Unless Carrigan turns out to have some kind of big life insurance."

"Which would still mean it wasn't ours."

"Yeah. It's a copycat, for sure. Or maybe it would be more accurate to call it a piggyback. They haven't given this out yet, but in the dirt around the cactus, somebody'd scratched four words. Care to guess what four?"

Shit. "Would it have to do with hunting?"

Jacobs laughed. "Hey, lady, you're *good*. Yeah, it does. The copycats really seem to go for that nice little slogan. Of course it may be an elaboration, but if it isn't, our guy's gotta be wondering what's going on here."

"Maybe this is what he *wants* to have going on," Joanna pointed out. "A grassroots movement."

"Thanks. Thanks a lot. I needed that. Listen, I'm gonna stay overnight and come back first thing in the morning. That slogan in the sand is gonna leak by the end of the day, I guarantee it. And it'll look better if we still have a presence on the scene."

"Don't give me that bullshit. Partners, Al. I get a cut of anything you win. Twenty percent."

"That mean you're covering what I lose, Davis?"

"Not a chance. Now. Tell me what else I ought to know about Vincent Carrigan."

"Well, he had a way with the ladies, everybody seems to agree on that." Another similarity to Jake Arnold. "Even the ex-wives mention it first, and they mention it fondly. Plus, he was a looker. Nothing left to prove it now, of course, but I saw pictures."

Which raised an interesting point. "The ID confirmed? Carrigan didn't set somebody up so he could leave town and start over?"

"Nah. Somebody's maid was coming to work across the street and she saw it happen. Carrigan had just gotten this new Porsche, see, and he liked having the chariot in the circular drive out front of the house so everybody could admire it. Which made it totally vulnerable, of course, but undoubtedly upped the property values in the neighborhood. Anyway, this maid says she was actually checking out the car from across the street when she saw Carrigan walk out the front door, get in, and take off." He chuckled. "Just like the *Challenger*."

By the time Jacobs returned the following morning, Joanna had narrowed the lists of dead lawyers to three that seemed to bear immediate and thorough further investigation.

Alan Salter.

A thirty-four-year-old environmentalist who'd been active in several political campaigns where logging was an issue, Salter had a law office in Portland and was licensed in California, Oregon, and Washington. He was a man on the move, protecting spotted owls and gnatcatchers and kangaroo rats and anything else that might be endangered.

Salter had fallen to his death while hiking on Mount Shasta on Tuesday, August 5th.

His death could be squeezed to fit the symbolism profile. Alan Salter had taken a dive off a mountain in the midst of natural splendor, undoubtedly with *some* endangered species in attendance. He was young and healthy and fit and had hiked this particular trail in the past. It was not unreasonable to think that perhaps he had been helped over the edge.

Except that Alan Salter hadn't been hiking alone. He'd been with his wife and his brother. The local police treated the death as an accident, and their report was perfunctory.

Yes, Alan Salter was a definite maybe.

Warren Richardson.

Richardson was a suicide with ample reason to feel despondent.

He had a plaintiff's personal injury practice up in the Santa Clarita Valley, with a residence in Valencia and offices in Newhall. And—*Bingo!*—he was nearing the end of a six-month suspension by the State Bar when he died.

Warren Richardson had been forty-three and an alcoholic, the embodiment of the midlife legal crisis. According to the published disciplinary notice, Richardson had missed filing deadlines in several cases, losing his clients' chances for recovery in personal injury lawsuits. The common remedy in such cases was legal malpractice insurance.

But Richardson's malpractice premium was too far down in the pile.

Lapsed.

His clients *truly* were screwed.

He had left no note. His wife found him dead behind the wheel of his about-to-be-repo'ed Lincoln Continental at six-thirty A.M., with the engine on, the gas tank empty and the pedal to the metal. The inquest ruled death by carbon monoxide, self-inflicted.

Warren Richardson fit the profile, smooth and snug as a surgical glove. He had messed up in the legal arena, leaving behind victims with genuine grievances. His death was directly related to an automobile, adhering to the profile of condigned punishment, fitting the penance to the crime. Once again, the case was in another jurisdiction, but this one was Los Angeles County Sheriff's, which would make it relatively easy to check up on.

Richardson had died in the very early hours of September 10th, a Wednesday that fell midway between Roger Coskins's bike ride into the Pacific and Bill Burke's last bellyache. If Richardson turned out to be an Atterminator victim, that meant the guy had killed three lawyers in a single month's time.

Or possibly four, depending on what they found out about Arturo Hernandez.

Arturo Hernandez.

Hernandez had been twenty-nine, a San Diego worker's comp

applicant's lawyer. He went off Interstate 8 sometime on Saturday, September 6th, alone in his car with no witnesses. He had called home when he left Yuma, Arizona, near the California border, on Saturday morning around nine. The distance was less than two hundred miles and he said he expected to be home for lunch.

When Hernandez failed to arrive home in Chula Vista by late afternoon, his wife started making phone calls. Nobody seemed very interested in a grown man who was a few hours late, particularly one with a Spanish surname traveling just north of the Mexican border.

On Sunday morning, a westbound driver on I-8 in the mountains just west of Ocotillo noticed a bright reflection coming out of the gorge beside the highway, glanced back to spot a flash of bright red far below, and called the California Highway Patrol. Hernandez was found dead in the car with massive head trauma. He was not wearing a seat belt and had probably died instantly.

Hernandez had only been in practice a few years and his practice had nothing to do with automobiles, though it did relate strongly to accidents.

This, too, would have to be checked out.

It had been Joanna's experience, both in the work world and her personal life, that whenever things seemed to be going particularly well, something nasty and unexpected was likely to sneak up and bite you on the ass. As a cop, of course, the possibilities were limitless. The domestic call where battling spouses or lovers turn their rage suddenly upon the intervening officer. The routine traffic stop that suddenly becomes a tri-county high-speed freeway chase. The trapped burglar. The abandoned building. The dark alley.

In those situations, you had training to rely upon, and instinct, and gushing jolts of adrenaline that permitted the training and instincts to perform without thought or hesitation. With luck, a sixth sense of self-preservation would kick in soon enough to keep you whole and alive.

And if you had time to pray, luck was what you prayed for.

Joanna was fully keyed into the Atterminator investigation

now, focusing all her energy and attention on trying to find and stop this killer. And so she was totally unprepared for the call that came on Tuesday afternoon from her doctor. The Pap smear she had twice rescheduled before finally slipping away from the office on Thursday afternoon, the routine test she'd been having every year for as long as she could remember, the crushingly ordinary lab work that she never gave a second thought to—that test had blindsided her.

She listened to the doctor's calm, reasoned voice and felt icy terror coursing through her veins. The room seemed to spin, the detectives hunched over their desks tilting wildly in an uneven orbit.

"The type of test result your Pap smear gave is known as AS-CUS," Dr. Letterman explained gently, the vestiges of a Southern accent modulating the harshness of the words she spoke. "Which stands for abnormal squamous cells of undetermined significance."

ASCUS. It sounded like it ought to be a cop thing, that acronym, an in-group designation for a tactical unit or a paperwork procedure or a community outreach program.

Not a potential catastrophe lurking within her own body.

Joanna was conscious of being the only woman in the room, aware of the need to keep her voice neutral and businesslike. *Lab error*, she kept thinking. It had to be lab error. But that was not a phrase bandied about lightly at LAPD anymore, not since the Simpson trial. "We'll need to repeat the procedure then. Immediately."

"Actually, we can't," Dr. Letterman told her apologetically.

"Of course we can. This afternoon."

"The earliest we could possibly do the test again would be six weeks. It takes at least that long for the cells to regenerate sufficiently to give a true result."

A true result.

"And then what?"

"We have a couple of options. But first, let me tell you again that this type of result isn't uncommon, and there's no reason to be unduly alarmed."

"Easy for you to say," Joanna snapped.

Dr. Letterman went on as if she hadn't been interrupted. "If you want, in six weeks we can repeat the Pap and if we get the same result, then we can schedule a colposcopy a couple of months afterward. Or if you prefer, we can go straight to the colposcopy."

"Which is?"

"An examination of the cervix with a high-powered microscope. It's a simple procedure and we do it right here in the office. And at that time, if we find areas of concern, we can do biopsies."

Biopsy. Surely one of the most heavily freighted words in the English language. Right up there with the close buddy it tended to announce, *cancer.*

Joanna already had her calendar out. "Let's set it up right now."

She made the appointment for December 11th, a day that suddenly lived in personal infamy, and then she went back to work.

It wasn't until she got home that night, to the sanctity and privacy of her stone house in the foothills, that she allowed herself to think about it again. And after she had thought about it for a while, and had a couple of beers, and listened to some of the harder rock numbers on the jukebox, she went outside and lay on a chaise longue, looking up at the stars in the chilly night.

Then she cried.

13

Ace spent the early evening going over lists.

He cross-checked various maps, pulled up files on the laptop, leaned back periodically and considered. As he went about his business, he drank a glass of whole milk and ate a bologna sandwich with mayo on white bread. With Miracle Whip, actually.

Not long after he first came out here, Ace had stopped in a Fairfax District deli and ordered that very sandwich. "Bologna on white bread?" the old Jew behind the counter asked him, accent all thick and New Yorky. "Are you from *Iowa?*"

Ace was amazed that the old man knew. Only later did he

realize the insult the Jew had believed he was hurling at him. He thought about it for a long time, months maybe, before he went back. He would order the sandwich again, see what happened.

But the old man was gone. When Ace asked about him, the sad-faced lady behind the counter explained that he had passed away. A heart attack.

Justice.

Ace had felt his own heart pounding.

It was pounding again. He had lost control here and it worried him.

Ace hadn't expected things to get so big so fast. All this TV tabloid shit was weird. None of them knew anything, and yet there were all kinds of shows about everything. About serial killers. About the dead lawyers and their sorry lives. All the things they'd done and hadn't done. Information that, Ace was pleased to see, entirely validated his selections. Though he still wasn't entirely sure about Burke, who had to be picked in a hurry. Ace had attempted to screen Burke as a candidate by interviewing him over the phone, posing as a newspaper reporter. The lawyer had been smug and self-congratulatory, dismissing the deaths of two innocents at the wedding as "unfortunate." Burke had then shared his own plans for a weekend getaway on Friday and the rest…well, the rest had gone pretty well, even allowing for the regrettable intervention of those stupid dogs.

Gina would be meeting him at the apartment shortly, with something from the health food store, one of those disgusting eggplant salads or maybe gruel made out of lentils. He'd also told her to bring one of her fancy bottles of wine. Gina drank only red wine and that only from the Bordeaux region of France. California wine sucked, Gina maintained. Her father had once owned part of a vineyard in Napa.

He would find out, after she had finished the wine, just how worried he needed to be.

He needed to know, also, what else was happening out there. Were others at work? Other deserving targets being identified and taken out of the game? The notion was gratifying, but also extremely unsettling.

He had never previously considered that the Legal Resolution Program might place him at the head of some sort of movement. He was, he thought, simply an enlightened free agent.

And now this. How could he head a movement whose members he didn't even know? And, more to the point, could not control?

Maybe it would be better to move the next episode up a week or so. Take things back into his own hands.

There were seven equally ranked Potentials for the next episode. One of the women would have been the most logical choice, before that woman in Long Beach, Mary Elaine McGonigle, had died. Two women so close together, even if one wasn't really his, seemed excessive.

Of the five men remaining, any one would be perfectly suitable. Over the next couple of days, he would check out each of them again. See who was paranoid, who was cautious, who was vulnerable. Perhaps one of the alcoholics would be a good choice. They tended to be less careful.

Now all his tedious, meticulous research was really paying off. His subjects, he had realized early on, tended to be creatures of habit, habits he had mapped thoroughly months earlier. Some, he was sure, would be following exactly the same routines, certain that the Atterminator wouldn't bother with the likes of them.

One of them would soon be proven terribly, horribly wrong.

14

Joanna went to lunch with Lee Walters on Wednesday, desperate to escape the perennially ringing phones and the specter of December 11th, a date that loomed impossibly soon and yet seemed desperately far away. Since the two women had landed in RHD, they normally lunched together at least once a week. Lately nothing had been normal.

At a small restaurant in Japantown, Lee lustily ordered sashimi while Joanna—who had always found the notion of raw fish repellent—stuck to tempura. At first they recapped work, as was their habit. Lee was basking in the glory of having finally captured a serial rapist preying on elderly women in the Los Felix district.

"I tell you, nailing that worthless piece of slime reminds me of why I got into this in the first place," Lee said. She was a tall, large-boned woman with a white streak running through her short black hair, just above her right temple. Officer Skunk, the Triple-B Brigade had called her to her face when she and Joanna graduated the police academy and were assigned together to patrol in North Hollywood. Nobody called her names to her face anymore. Nowadays if anyone still used the term, it would be behind her back, and carefully. Very carefully. Lee Walters had a reputation for being a hard-ass who never got mad but always got even. And her clearance rate was awesome.

"I seem to recall," Joanna noted, "that you got into this in the first place because your mother-in-law said it was unsuitable work for a member of her exalted family."

Lee grinned. "That, too. The self-important bitch. Of course, the job's lasted longer than my membership in her exalted family."

Joanna shrugged. "Who among us hasn't married badly at least once? Hell, some of us have made it a second career."

"You may not be married anymore," Lee corrected, shaking her head, "but it's not because the marriages were bad."

True enough. Joanna had married once for love and once for fun and in both cases had reaped considerable rewards. From her union with Don Olafson she had gained two fine children, training in all manner of self-defense techniques, and a set of wonderful memories that nobody could ever take away. Their marriage had been doomed by the saddest and most improbable of causes, geography. Joanna no longer tried to explain to people that her first divorce had occurred only because neither partner could physically bear to live in the other's world, but the knowledge gave her some small comfort on nights when she lay alone and remembered the magic she had felt during her years with Don.

Her second marriage had been more problematic from the beginning, and so were the things that remained from it. From her union with Jake Arnold, she had gained a jukebox, an appreciation for restaurants and resorts she could no longer afford, and a capability to sometimes wake up in the morning with no agenda other than to have a great time.

"Well, it's just me now," Joanna told her, and heard her voice cracking. Without thinking about it—and mercifully, without actually breaking into tears—she told Lee about the failed Pap smear and the impending colposcopy.

"You'll be fine," Lee reassured her. "I know it's scary as shit, but when was the last time you heard about somebody dying from cervical cancer? And even if there *does* turn out to be something, well, you're catching it so early that you'll still be fine."

"Yeah. Right."

"Hey, what do you want me to say? That you're gonna die? Forget it, girl. It ain't gonna happen. It's probably just a fuckup at the lab anyway."

Joanna offered a snort of mirthless laughter. "Yeah. Our old buddy Lab Error. Who'da thought I'd be sitting here plugging for *that?*"

Lee reached across the table and took Joanna's hand. "You tell your mother?"

Joanna shook her head. Her mother, after bouncing back from sudden widowhood at fifty, had moved in with Joanna and her kids, making it possible for a single parent to work the impossible hours of a patrol cop. And then, with the kids grown and flown from their makeshift nest, Helen Davis had moved to southern Arizona where she lived in a trailer park and groomed poodles for the wives of retired midwestern doctors.

"Kirsten?" Lee asked.

Joanna shook her head again. "If something comes of this, then I'll tell 'em. But not now. Not when it's only a maybe."

"Your call. I'd probably be the same way. But I want you to promise that if you start getting the screaming willies, you'll at least come to me."

Joanna gave her friend's hand a squeeze. "Absolutely."

"Well, fine. So now, I want to hear all the juicy stuff you guys are holding back about the Atterminator."

Joanna's derisive snort was louder this time. "You can't hold back what you don't got."

"Oh, come on. I hear those phones ringing all day long."

"Like that means something? Actually, we're working up a telephone tree." She pitched her voice mellifluous and impersonal. "'You've reached the Atterminator Task Force. To leave a message for Al Jacobs, press one. For Joanna Davis, press two. If you're an attorney requesting police protection, press three.'" She cocked her head and grinned. "Those will automatically disconnect." She resumed, "'If you have ideas for future victims, post them on the Internet. If your lawyer screwed you, press four. If you think you know the Atterminator, press five. If you're a psychic, you already know what to do.'"

Lee chortled. "So many lawyers, so little time. I hear enrollment is way up in legal ethics seminars."

"You think that means any changes in legal ethics? Dream on. But you know, I did hear something interesting. Since this started, some folks undergoing disciplinary proceedings at the State Bar have started screaming 'cruel and unusual punishment.' I hear some of these sleazeball lawyers are looking for sympathetic judges to issue injunctions saying that to discipline them, at least publicly, is tantamount to a death sentence."

"Interesting argument," Lee agreed cheerfully. "Wish I could work up some sympathy. Wish somebody was worthy of it."

"The McGonigle family's pretty worthy."

"You're right," Lee answered, immediately contrite. "She was about Kirsten's age, wasn't she?"

Joanna nodded. "A few years older. But I don't think she was killed by our guy, and the optimists among us think her case will clear pretty soon."

Lee Walters laughed. "That leaves me out, I guess. If I were an optimist, I'd have never gone on the department."

• • •

Thursday, November 6th, Long Beach detectives charged Lenny Duran with the murder of Mary Elaine McGonigle.

The physical evidence against Duran included an off-brand black marker found in his truck that matched the note left on McGonigle's Accord. As did a ream of cheap paper in his messy "office." Duran owned a rifle, a shotgun, and three handguns, among them a .45-caliber Colt that he initially claimed had been stolen from his workshop a few months earlier, though he hadn't notified police of the incident.

Joanna and Jacobs drove down to Long Beach late Thursday morning, at the specific request of Lenny Duran's attorney. Ron Inouye was beaming when they arrived. In a well-tailored charcoal suit with a button-down blue Oxford and conservatively striped burgundy tie, he was Detective Suave, all set to meet the press.

"I guess I miss out on the task force," Inouye told them, "but I can't say I'm too terribly sorry. How you guys doing up there, anyway?"

Jacobs offered a stony countenance. "Swell. Just swell."

Joanna leaned toward Inouye. "We *have* had one recent break-through," she murmured, in a low, confidential tone. The young detective moved closer. "We have it on extremely good authority that our guy didn't kill Mary Elaine McGonigle."

Inouye moved back and laughed more heartily than the statement merited. "Duran is good for her. Got him cold. We even found the Frankenstein suit, once he told us where to look. He donated it to Goodwill. *Goodwill!* They had it sitting in a pile of Halloween costumes about to go into storage for next year when we showed up with the warrant. We've already sent it out. With luck he left some prints on the rubber head, and there might even be some fibers that match that mess we cleaned off the floor of the parking garage."

"I thought he was pleading?" Joanna's brow furrowed.

"Oh, he is," Inouye assured them. "I think of the Frankenstein suit as an insurance policy, in case Lenny tries to change his mind and go to trial. Wouldn't it make a nice exhibit in court? We could put it on a mannequin and stand it up next to the bailiff."

Joanna nodded. "I like it. I like it a lot. So—Duran told you what happened?"

"He did indeed. Lenny has given it all up and moved directly to Plea Bargain City. Go to Jail. Do not pass Go. Pay your lawyer ten thousand dollars and hand over the pink slip, too."

"Nice work," Jacobs told the detective. "I suppose it's too much to hope that he confessed to some of the others? *Any* of the others?"

Inouye shook his head. "I think you're gonna have a tough time getting him on any of the others. Tuesday, before he lawyered up, we asked about some of those other dates. August twenty-eighth for Coskins, September twenty-first for Burke, October twelfth for Benton. Lenny's been living alone and drinking a lot, so his recollections are a little vague. But he did say he was out in the desert with some buddies riding ATVs the weekend Burke was getting poisoned up near Fresno. And his buddies alibi him."

"Which desert?" Jacobs asked. A purposeful question. There were thousands of square miles of desert in southern California, some reasonably accessible to the foothills above Fresno. And devotees of all-terrain vehicles were doing their best to despoil them all.

"Out by Joshua Tree," Inouye answered. "They were camping and Lenny rode out with a buddy. The buddy says Lenny wasn't out of his sight all weekend."

"Joshua Tree's probably three hundred fifty miles from Bill Burke's cabin," Jacobs acknowledged regretfully. "The buddy reliable?"

Inouye laughed. "*I* wouldn't want to be counting on him. But he's probably okay as an alibi. There's others, too, that you'll probably want to talk to."

Jacobs pulled a face. "Yeah, we'll check it out. So where's Duran now?"

"Just down the hall," Inouye informed them, "with his counsel. *Retained* counsel. Retained by Lenny's old man, who caught on real quick that Lenny was in a shitload of trouble. The old man is afraid you're gonna try to start hanging those others on him."

"Would that we could," Joanna muttered.

• • •

They met in the hallway with Lenny Duran's lawyer before going in to see his client. Mark Steinberg had the weary air of somebody who's been practicing criminal law one-too-many-defendants long. Instructive and depressing, since he appeared to be barely thirty.

"My client," he told them after perfunctory introductions, "is happy to cooperate in any way he can, because he is absolutely adamant that he had nothing to do with any of your Atterminator murders."

Joanna smiled sweetly. Steinberg was directing most of his comments toward her, on the apparent assumption that the woman would be the soft touch. Also, she was shorter than he was and Jacobs decidedly was not.

"He have information that'll alibi him for the time frames we're interested in?" Joanna asked. Offhandedly.

Steinberg responded with an earnest nod. "During the weekend when my unfortunate colleague was poisoned up near Fresno, my client was camping with a group of friends. I'll be happy to make those people available to you."

"There are some other dates we're interested in," Jacobs reminded.

"I know." Mark Steinberg hesitated. "Listen, I'll be honest with you. I'm a lawyer and believe me, I'd like this Atterminator guy caught. Like yesterday." He offered a bit of a smile. "I might even be inclined to relax some of my opinions about capital punishment, just this once."

Lenny Duran was a wraith. The young hothead wore a jail jumpsuit, hadn't showered recently, and kept running his fingers through long, greasy hair. Once he started talking, it became clear that unless he was the finest actor in the world, he was nowhere near bright enough to have planned and executed the previous three Atterminator killings.

"I got nothing to do with them others," he insisted repeatedly. "I just thought I could put this off on him."

"On *whom?*" Joanna asked. Pleasantly. She was being everybody's favorite aunt today, the kindly teacher who pays attention to otherwise misunderstood teenagers. It was one of her more polished personas, and it generally got good results.

"The Atterminator. The killer. That *guy*." Lenny Duran shook his head. He was trembling. It looked as if Mark Steinberg, seated beside him, was also trembling. Or maybe Steinberg had just developed a tic.

"What can you tell me about him?" Joanna wondered innocently.

Lenny Duran stopped trembling and looked her right in the eye. "All's I know is this: He had a hell of a good idea."

15

The stroke that saved Joseph Tucker's life destroyed most of his remaining mental acuity. It was ironic, Ace thought, that there was no way Tucker would ever be able to appreciate—even if anybody ever found out to tell him—that he had been slated for stardom as the Atterminator's fifth episode.

Ace had been busy.

He'd checked out the five male Potentials over the last few days after reaching his decision about Gina. She kept calling, and while she claimed always to do so from pay phones, he wasn't sure he believed her. He had been foolish ever to let her get involved, and she was growing to be a real liability. She'd never really been that much of an asset anyway. Her episode could have easily been accomplished in some other fashion.

Ace owned a number of uniforms and an assortment of clipboards, all he needed to be totally anonymous around Los Angeles. To reconnoiter his previously researched subjects, he wore the "LRP Delivery Services" one—gray Bermuda shorts with a nondescript white short-sleeved shirt, an LRP plastic pocket protector, and a sewn-on name badge that identified him as Jerry. He attached the corresponding LRP plastic plates to the side doors of the white Ford van and ventured into the legal world to make some deliveries.

Last spring and summer when he was doing his research, he'd

visited many law offices, dropping off a selection of continuing legal education materials he'd liberated from various CLE programs at downtown hotels. Schedules, flyers on upcoming seminars, a few fat notebooks with detailed materials on legal ethics. The kind of stuff a guy in a delivery uniform could pick up by the boxful when the seminar staff wasn't paying attention. The kind of stuff a guy in a delivery uniform could drop off in any office without being noticed or remembered.

It had given him particular pleasure to leave ethics materials for some of the most heinous offenders.

During this same period, he'd picked up a case of specialty phone directories that somebody had dumped behind an office building. Brand-X Yellow Pages, the kind that nobody actually *uses*, but dumb businesspeople buy ads in anyway. Each was about an inch thick and fit neatly into a large padded envelope. The printed return address labels were for a company called Comtax Enterprises with a nonexistent address in mid-Wilshire.

These he delivered now. Something vaguely official in an envelope requiring signature guaranteed easy entrée to most law offices. The directories, like the man who delivered them, were even more forgettable than last summer's CLE materials. He assumed most of them went directly into the trash.

He'd favored one Potential as he began his reconnaissance, a Century City attorney who had gotten a chemical company off the hook for a "forgotten" chemical waste dump located beside an elementary school. Ace thought of him as the Toxic Lawyer.

The Toxic Lawyer was a technically challenging subject. Security had always been strong in his office building, even after hours and in the parking garage below. The high-rise condominium where he lived alone presented similar security difficulties. Should the Toxic Lawyer be selected, it would consequently be necessary to take him into custody elsewhere. The problem was that he was a workaholic who didn't really *go* anywhere else. At least he hadn't back in June when Ace spent a week researching him.

And unfortunately, the Toxic Lawyer couldn't be eliminated in place.

Like Lawrence Benton, he was intended for presentation.

His body was to be discovered inside a building tented for termites. Naked.

The poison pumped into the tented house would probably be lethal in and of itself, though Ace had no intention of leaving this important detail to chance. Another variable *truly* outside Ace's control was locating an appropriately accessible tented building when the time came. He realized now, too late, that he probably should have completed this episode earlier, before people started getting paranoid.

Because people had gotten *very* paranoid.

Ace had discovered this when he visited the Toxic Lawyer's office on Monday morning. Additional security officers were on duty in the lobby—the building was jammed full of law firms—and when he reached the reception area of the Toxic Lawyer's firm, he found two brand-new surveillance cameras mounted on the walls. With a twinge of regret, he moved the Toxic Lawyer to the bottom of the list.

His next two Potentials were both in the San Fernando Valley.

He struck out on the first one. A criminal attorney who had gotten a jury to acquit a serial rapist—who subsequently moved to San Francisco and killed his next three victims—previously had been very lax about security. But the guy was on vacation in Europe, his receptionist confided jealously. Touring the wine country of France.

Frustrated, Ace moved on to check a sleazy shyster with offices in North Hollywood. This piece of scum had gotten a half-million-dollar judgment against a gas station owner who paralyzed a gun-toting punk, by firing first during an armed robbery attempt. When his insurance company refused to pay, the gas station owner had been forced to declare bankruptcy and close a family-owned business founded in 1947.

Ace had initially avoided this situation because it hit a little too close to home. But now, when he was prepared to act on it, it turned out the damned shyster had gone into rehab. He was out at Betty Ford trying to save his miserable liver.

Ace gritted his teeth and headed for Orange County.

Where finally, in Whittier, he found exactly what he was looking for at the Law Offices of Joseph Tucker, Esquire.

Criminal negligence, general lassitude, and no discernable security at all.

Joseph Tucker was sixty-seven and *his* legal offenses had been shocking enough to get him noticed by the media, no small accomplishment in southern California. Ace had observed, in his research, that even small local newspapers rarely mentioned attorneys disciplined by the State Bar. It took a truly stunning legal lapse to catch media attention.

Joseph Tucker had caught that kind of attention.

A specialist in estate and probate work, he maintained strong connections with several retirement communities in Orange County. Tucker wrote wills. Some of them were for old people with no close relatives. In these wills, he was often named executor—at an exorbitant rate—and he occasionally rewarded himself a small bequest as well.

Spinsters were his specialty.

Tucker had already been under State Bar suspension when Ace put him under surveillance back in early July. A widower, Tucker maintained a strong, almost inviolable routine centering around his country club: eighteen holes of morning golf, lunch at the Mexican restaurant beside his nearby law office, a ceremonial visit to that office, then back to the club for dinner and an evening in the bar. Around nine-thirty each night, Tucker would pour himself into his Lexus and weave the two and a half miles home.

Ace had sometimes wondered how this routine might have differed when Tucker was still working. Maybe the afternoon office visit had lasted a little longer. Maybe he'd lunched with the elderly spinsters.

Ace revisited Tucker's office on Wednesday, November 5th. He left jubilant, planning to take the lawyer into custody when he left the country club the following evening. The episode promised to be an easy one; Tucker's body would be presented on the shuffleboard court at the club for early-morning viewing.

The plan was pre-empted. When Ace arrived at the club on Thursday evening, cutting across the darkened grounds on foot, Tucker's Lexus wasn't in the lot. A bad sign. Ace retraced his steps and drove till he found an isolated pay phone, then called the country club dining room and asked to speak to Joe Tucker.

"I'm sorry, Mr. Tucker isn't here this evening," the man who answered the phone informed Ace politely.

Ace could tell the guy was hesitating, wanting to say more but unsure if he should. Ace said nothing. Expectant pauses were usually filled.

This one was no exception. "He was taken ill earlier today," the man explained.

"Not his heart again!" Ace exclaimed, a concerned old buddy.

"No sir, I believe it was a stroke. He's over at UC Irvine in intensive care."

"Why, that's terrible!" Ace lamented, with great sincerity.

He hung up the phone, cursing.

16

Joanna was eating, sleeping, dreaming the Atterminator case. Working fourteen- and sixteen-hour days, rising before dawn and frantically working out before heading in to the office and immersing herself in the murders. She deliberately kept herself too busy to think about the Pap smear.

She called Kirsten several times a week, more often than she had in years. She was hungry for the day-to-day particulars of her daughter's life. She cherished the details of her grandson's simple adventures, his favorite toys and books. She sympathized with Kir's morning sickness, an affliction she knew firsthand to be ghastly.

And she was grateful they were twelve hundred miles away. Safe.

Of the three leads culled from the lists of dead lawyers, Warren Richardson so far seemed the most promising.

Mickey Conner and Dave Austin had gone down to Imperial County to check out Arturo Hernandez, the worker's comp lawyer killed when he went off the road in the mountains along I-8. They'd checked out the accident scene, talked with the CHP officers called to the wreck, questioned Hernandez's wife and colleagues. The totaled car was at a wrecking yard in El Centro and CHP had agreed to get somebody from the state SID to give it a thorough exam. Back at the beginning of September when the accident occurred, there'd been no reason to do more than a perfunctory check.

The cops had found skid marks where Hernandez left the road, but no evidence of any impact or of any other vehicle. Just like Roger Coskins on his motorcycle on the Pacific Coast Highway up in San Luis Obispo County. Any driver who might have accidentally forced Hernandez off the road wasn't coming forward burdened by conscience. It seemed more likely that the lawyer had swerved to avoid hitting an animal in the road—a coyote maybe, or even a deer—and lost control.

"Like the joke about what's the difference between a dead lawyer and a dead skunk lying in the road," Conner interjected into his partner's account.

"Skid marks in front of the skunk," Jacobs shot back automatically. "Anything in this guy's professional life send up red flags?"

"*Nada*," Austin went on. "Hernandez's partners seemed still really shaken up, even more when they realized why we were there. But the practice looked to be booming, and Hernandez was squeaky clean with the State Bar. Ditto the partners."

"You talk to the widow?" Jacobs asked.

"But of course," Mickey Conner replied with a grin. He was good with widows: courtly, respectful, caring. "No turn left unstoned. She *really* freaked at the idea Arturo might have been Atterminator fodder. Sweet thing, pregnant, had a toddler running around." He shook his head. "There's nothing there, guys. Hernandez was an accident, pure and simple. A nice guy, a bit on the pudgy side, no enemies, everybody misses him. Hell, one of the partners broke down just talking about him."

"You agree, Austin?" Jacobs leaned back, broke a doughnut into quarters.

"Yeah. Lake Shasta, here we come." Austin sounded chipper and enthusiastic. Today he was dressed in nicely broken-in outdoor-wear, and might have been a foreign correspondent heading off to the latest international hot spot. For his part, Conner wore his customary polyester Sansabelt slacks and a battered sport coat with out-of-style lapels. The two detectives had a plane to catch in two hours, to check out the fatal fall of Alan Salter, environmental specialist and legal provocateur.

Conner shook his head and offered a sardonic smile. "Just what I want to do in November when it's starting to get cold and rainy, go climbing up the side of some damn mountain. Some *big* damn mountain."

Joanna laughed. "Let Austin do the mountain climbing, Conner. He'll think it's fun." And indeed Austin had the air of an Eagle Scout preparing to backpack into Yosemite backcountry. "Meanwhile, you can catch the local skinny in the pub. A guy like that, there's gotta be plenty of opinions about him around town."

Conner shook his head. "'S been three months, Davis. Happened in the middle of summer. Nah, this one's not going anywhere either." He brightened momentarily. "But I'll check the local watering holes, you can count on it."

In Valencia, Joanna and Jacobs struck gold.

"I *told* them Warren wouldn't kill himself," Warren Richardson's widow insisted. "I told them over and over again, but nobody wanted to listen." Richardson had been a plaintiff's personal injury attorney specializing in auto accidents.

Lila Richardson was in her early thirties, slight and nervous. Her shiny, shoulder-length, dark brown hair was parted perfectly down the middle, a thin fringe of bangs brushing her eyebrows. She was an executive secretary for a Woodland Hills insurance company. Her makeup was precise, her jewelry simple and discreet, her beige silk dress and brown pumps as fresh as if she were starting off to work on Monday morning, not meeting a couple of cops at the end of a long week. This was not the kind of woman who ripped off her work clothes to slip on rumpled jeans at the end of the day. Any jeans she owned would be neatly pressed, on hangers.

The serenity was all superficial, however. Lila Richardson had plenty to unload, and she was ready.

Joanna and Jacobs sat in the Richardsons' immaculate, over-furnished living room drinking decaf out of porcelain cups. It was Friday evening, just after seven. They'd spent Thursday afternoon and most of today talking to Richardson's colleagues and the sheriff's detectives who'd signed off on the case. Everything pointed to Richardson having been an Atterminator victim, not a suicide. Which they hoped to confirm if Lila Richardson would agree to an exhumation.

"Warren was depressed, sure," Lila told them, becoming more animated. Her hands moved like butterflies as she talked. "He'd messed up big-time and he knew it." She grimaced. "Coke'll do that. Coke *does* do that. But he wouldn't have killed himself. Suicide *appalled* him. You see, Warren's father was a suicide when he was seven. It tore him apart, and even thirty years later, when he talked about it there was still a lot of anger."

As she shook her head, her hair floated in graceful wings. "I mean a *lot*. I tried to get him to talk to a therapist about it, but he refused. I think he was afraid of what it might open up in him. I know Warren felt horribly cheated by his father's death, thought his father should have faced up to his problems. Warren always maintained his father had taken the coward's way out."

"You told the police about this?" Joanna had slipped naturally into the lead in talking to this woman. Jacobs leaned back in a peach brocade wing chair sipping his coffee. Very slowly. He was of the why-bother school where decaf was concerned.

"Why, of course! But all they could see was that Warren was in financial trouble and depressed. They thought that it made it *more* likely that he'd kill himself when I explained about his father, because he'd had a role model. They even suggested that I hid a note."

Joanna frowned sympathetically. "Which you didn't?"

Lila Richardson shook her head indignantly. "Of *course* not! And that's another thing that makes me absolutely refuse to believe he killed himself. Warren's *father* didn't leave a note. Warren was obsessed by that, always said if he'd only explained *why* he did it, maybe it would have been easier to deal with."

"Was there any question about his father's death actually being a suicide?"

"None at all. He jumped off the Golden Gate Bridge. There were witnesses."

A horrible thought occurred to Joanna. "He didn't do it in front of your husband?"

"Oh, God no!" Lila shook her head, equally horrified. "They lived in Oakland anyway. It wasn't even their bridge. But other people saw it happen."

"You and your husband didn't have children?" There was no sign in this house that anyone under thirty had ever crossed the threshold.

Lila Richardson shook her head. "I wanted to, but Warren had a son from an early marriage, living up north. He didn't see him often, and…" Her voice trailed off.

"And he'd have been more likely to leave a note to explain to his son, even if he didn't see him often, according to what you're telling me," Joanna suggested.

She nodded vigorously. "Exactly!"

"You mentioned a cocaine problem. Was your husband in treatment?"

"He had been." Lila hesitated. "Several times, actually. But I think he was using again, to be perfectly honest."

The cops hadn't found any drugs on Richardson's person and there'd been no reason to search the house. "Where was he that night?"

"Working late. He wasn't allowed to practice law because of the suspension, but there were a lot of things he could do to service his cases, kind of like a paralegal."

"You were in a difficult position financially?"

Lila Richardson closed her eyes momentarily. When she

opened them, they were clear and sad. "Horrendous, though until Warren died, I had no idea just *how* bad. The house is in foreclosure and they took the car away as soon as the police released it. It was leased and he was behind on the payments. And the credit cards—he'd been taking a lot of cash advances. Everything's a mess."

"Did he have insurance?"

"The other cops kept harping on that. Yes, he did. But it turns out he hadn't paid that premium either, and I don't know if I'm going to get anything or not. My guess is no, just based on the way my luck's running." Her voice was heavy with resignation.

"I'm sorry," Joanna told her softly. "Mrs. Richardson, I know how painful this has been for you, and we do appreciate your help. You know that we're here because we think that your husband may have been a victim of the same person who killed several other attorneys."

"The Atterminator." She spoke flatly, then abruptly saucered her eyes. "Was he *in our garage?*"

"Quite possibly, if your husband's death was staged. Did you notice anything out of place in the garage?" The house was in such perfect order that Lila would probably notice a fork misaligned in the silverware drawer.

"I couldn't even bear to go out to the garage for weeks," she answered. "I kept my own car in the driveway and used the front door. I don't have any idea if anything was messed up out there. There were police and people here, anyway, and they wouldn't let me in there after I called for help. If something was different, I'd figure they moved it."

"It may be," Joanna went on, "that the medical examiner missed something in the examination of your husband's body. It would help us greatly if you'd be willing to sign an authorization so that we could have his body re-examined."

Lila Richardson gasped. "You mean dig him *up?*"

"We'd be very discreet," Joanna assured her.

And in the end, the widow agreed.

• • •

The following Monday, the remains of Warren Richardson were re-autopsied. This time, the coroner noticed a faint bruise on the back of Richardson's head consistent with a blow that might have rendered him unconscious. The cause of death remained inhalation of carbon monoxide.

Warren Richardson was officially named an Atterminator victim on Tuesday, November 11th.

On Wednesday morning, Joanna was at her desk early, sifting through lists of lawyers.

Confirmed victims. Possible victims. Unrelated victims.

Future victims.

There had to be some way to pinpoint people at strong risk from the Atterminator. Joanna had started with the obvious, people mentioned in newspaper reports of alleged or proven legal misconduct. There weren't really all that many in L.A. The city was too large, legal misbehavior too common.

California Lawyer and the *California Bar Journal*, however, were veritable cookie jars full of extremely naughty attorneys. Both publications offered complete listings of all the latest disciplinary actions, a veritable shopping list of potential victims. And both were readily accessible.

It was time for some preventive maintenance.

Joanna had compiled a list of men and women disciplined by the State Bar, people whose infractions had been reported in tedious detail in various legal publications. These people, if they weren't already worried, ought to be. Some had already requested protection that LAPD lacked the resources to provide. Several had engaged private security services.

All of these shoddy shysters needed to be on red alert for the duration. They needed to be interviewed, too. There was always the possibility—slim but definitely worth pursuing—that a potential victim had already *seen* the Atterminator and might remember something useful.

It seemed obvious the Atterminator had spent a lot of time selecting his victims, had stalked or at least surveilled them far in advance. The one instance where that didn't seem to be the case, Bill Burke, could be classified as the exception that proved the rule. But even with Burke, the Atterminator hadn't merely relied on luck. Had the botulism poisoning not worked as expected, the victim was still alone in a wilderness cabin, the phone conveniently dead. Vulnerable. Burke's death had, after all, been interrupted by the untimely arrival of his rescuing neighbor.

The Burke killing had demonstrated something else: this was a killer capable of spontaneity. He might normally make meticulous plans, but he could also seize the moment, improvise and leave town on short notice without being missed.

Which suggested the Atterminator wasn't punching any time clock.

They had matched the murders to weather patterns, Santa Anas, athletic events, dates and phases of the moon. Richardson's body had been found during a full moon, but the others were spread all over the calendar. All had apparently been killed or attacked at night, with the possible exception of Benton, who'd probably died late Sunday afternoon.

The timing of Burke's poisoning was even more uncertain, since there was no known source for the botulinum toxin. The poison specialists at the Centers for Disease Control weren't about to go out on a limb here, but they allowed that they wouldn't be surprised to learn that Burke had ingested the toxin on Friday evening.

Richardson and Coskins were cut-and-dried, however. Both deaths had definitely occurred at night, well after dark. And both had occurred on weeknights: Richardson a Wednesday, Coskins a Thursday.

A Thursday up the coast, again suggesting mobility.

Apart from lax ethics, the dead lawyers shared few other characteristics. They were middle-aged, ranging from the thirty-eight-year-old Richardson to the sixty-two-year-old Benton. They were white. They were male. All had been married at least twice and none had young children living in his home. Only Burke had been currently single.

There was no evidence to suggest that any of the victims had known each other. The four men had grown up in four different places and attended four different law schools. Richardson and Burke had both gone to UCLA undergrad, but there was no time overlap. Benton and Coskins had been in the military, different branches in different years. Richardson, Coskins, and Burke were native Californians, while Benton had never even visited California until after he finished law school in Boston.

No matter how they shuffled and reshuffled information about the victims, there seemed no common juncture, no instances where any might ever have even *met* the others.

They did not share the same barbers, chiropractors, doctors, dentists, health clubs, dry cleaners, temporary office services, favorite restaurants, hobbies, electricians, plumbers, computer systems, attorney services, auto dealers, insurance agents, or bookies. Benton and Coskins were Lakers fans, Burke had season tickets for the Dodgers, and Richardson hadn't followed any home teams since the Raiders moved to Oakland. Benton golfed, Coskins pumped iron, Richardson swam, and Burke ran, though not often. None were named plaintiffs or defendants in any pending lawsuits. None kept journals. None were in therapy.

Only Richardson had been treated for substance abuse, though the other three were reported to be hard drinkers on occasion, the occasion being daily in Benton's case.

Exhaustive subpoenaed searches through their case files had shown no overlap in plaintiffs, defendants, or even expert witnesses. They seemed totally unrelated.

Except, of course, that they all seemed to have been killed by the same person.

The score was Atterminator 4, LAPD zip. And nobody had any idea what inning they were in.

On Thursday, November 13th, Joanna turned fifty-two. Her mother called from Tucson. Her son, Mike, wired flowers to the office and Kirsten had quilted a cover for a book of Jamie's baby pictures.

For seventeen years now, Joanna and Lee Walters had taken each other to lunch on their respective birthdays. This time Lee picked a favorite restaurant in Chinatown, where she arranged in advance for Peking duck.

Perhaps not her best birthday, Joanna decided when she got home that night, opened a bottle of champagne, and cranked up the jukebox so loud it would have constituted disturbing the peace if there'd been any near neighbors.

But not a bad one, either. She had a year for every card in the deck, and with a bit of luck, there'd be endless jokers remaining.

17

Ace parked the van two blocks from Francesca Goldberg's house.

She lived on 9th Street, north of Montana in one of the nicest parts of Santa Monica. This area was quiet and expensive, but also folksy and as close to unpretentious as any wealthy southern California neighborhood ever got.

Around here a clean white van in good repair would not be noticed parked behind an antique shop on the south side of Montana. A clean-cut white guy in jeans and a tennis shirt could carry a gym bag down the quiet, tree-lined street without looking at all out of place.

It was now eight-thirty P.M. on Wednesday, November 19th. In the thirteen days since Joseph Tucker's unfortunate stroke, Ace had wanted more than anything to move directly to another episode.

He had been ready for Francesca Goldberg, but Francesca Goldberg was not ready for him. She was out of town. Even more frustrating, he'd been unable to find out where she was. Not that he intended to follow her, or to attempt her episode anywhere other than her own home.

Francesca Goldberg's home was the perfect setting.

And now she was back in town.

Ace strolled nonchalantly up the driveway, passing through the stucco arch that attached the house to a freestanding wall on the opposite side of the driveway. It was an older house, well maintained, despite some cracks in the wall that probably dated to the Northridge earthquake.

He stopped at the rear of the carport, pulled on surgical gloves, and deactivated the alarm system. When this house had been built, nobody really worried about security in neighborhoods like this. If she'd thought things through, Francesca Goldberg would have moved the controls to the front of the carport, where a fellow disabling electrical systems would be more obvious.

But she hadn't.

Ace moved into the backyard. He was confident that he had at least half an hour, and probably closer to twice that. He had followed Francesca Goldberg from her office on San Vicente to the restaurant on Montana where she often ate dinner. Those dinners rarely lasted less than an hour and often longer if she ran into friends.

First things first. With the alarm system deactivated, he picked the back door lock and entered her immaculate kitchen. He had noticed on previous visits that she was a tidy person, a virtue he appreciated. There was a cat, he remembered, and he was careful not to let the animal out. Starved for attention, the cat rubbed back and forth on his ankles.

Francesca Goldberg typically pulled her Mercedes into the carport through a wrought iron gate left open during the day, the same gate Ace had sauntered through just minutes ago. Then she closed and locked the gate before entering the house.

He removed a couple of items from the gym bag and returned to the yard, where he cut a dozen choice blooms from a well-maintained rose garden. Francesca Goldberg had been photographed in this rose garden when she was featured in *Los Angeles* magazine.

Now he took the flowers inside, again careful not to let out the cat. He reactivated the alarm system, readied his materials, and positioned himself in the blind spot behind the door.

• • •

When Francesca Goldberg returned to her home at 9:17, she pulled in the driveway and locked the wrought iron gate. She removed her briefcase from the trunk of the Mercedes and carried it in her left hand, holding her keys in the right. She turned the key in the lock, pushed open the heavy door with its stained-glass insert, and walked into her home.

As she turned to close the door behind her, she heard a sudden crackling and felt the sting of forty thousand volts in the back of her neck.

18

Even in death, Francesca Goldberg looked tall.

Joanna stared down at the woman who lay on the Saltillo tile floor in the kitchen of the gorgeous old Spanish-style house in Santa Monica.

It was at least fifteen years since Joanna had first encountered the criminal defense attorney, back when both of them were testing their own professional waters. Joanna had been the arresting officer for a kid caught three blocks from the scene of a robbery with the victim's watch in his pocket. Francesca Goldberg was the public defender. Any other PD would have pleaded out the case automatically, but Francesca had things to prove and places to go. The kid was convicted, but it took the jury a full six hours to do it.

Francesca Goldberg back then had cut an imposing figure. Nearly six feet tall, she wore a beautifully cut black wool suit with a very short skirt. She wore high heels and dark stockings and her legs were sensational. Her jet-black hair was pulled back into a sleek French twist and her perfectly manicured, predatory fingernails matched her plum lipstick. Even seated at the defense table beside her lanky young client, a former high school basketball player, she had appeared stately and awesome.

Now she was dead at forty-one.

Joanna had no doubt that Francesca Goldberg was an Atterminator victim. She fit the profile perfectly: someone who used the law in sometimes questionable ways to achieve sometimes outrageous results. Goldberg handled only criminal cases. Her clients never got the death penalty. She had walked several stone killers, put plenty of rapists back on the street, seen to the acquittal of entire platoons of thieves. In her spare time, she got off celebrities busted for drugs.

She was known as the mistress of reasonable doubt. Cops liked to say that meant she fucked the law.

Joanna wondered now why she had never before considered Francesca Goldberg as a possible Atterminator target. The answer, she realized, lay in Francesca's air of invulnerability. An air which had turned out to be an illusion.

The dead lawyer was carefully arranged on the tile floor, laid out on her back as if she were already installed in her coffin. Her glossy black hair was neatly combed back in the trademark French twist and provided sharp contrast to a creamy satin pillow tucked beneath her head. Her eyes were closed. Her hands were carefully arranged across her breast and her nails, Joanna noted, were still perfect, almond-shaped and painted a muted brick red that matched the suit she wore. Her designer shoes also matched the suit. What Francesca was wearing would have eaten up a month of Joanna's pay.

Two details directed specific attention to one of her more notorious cases. Four years ago, Francesca Goldberg had won acquittal for a fifty-three-year-old woman who admitted hacking apart her eighty-eight-year-old mother with a pair of pruning shears.

In her exquisitely manicured hands, Francesca Goldberg now held a bouquet of wilted roses. And a pair of pruning shears was thrust into her throat.

"Almost no blood from the throat wound," Jacobs was saying. Like Joanna, he had driven directly to Santa Monica from home on getting the call this morning that another Latina housekeeper had arrived at work to find an attorney employer murdered. "She was already dead when he stuck those clippers in. I bet he used the stun gun again. But did it kill her?"

Joanna shrugged. "I never heard anything about her being

in poor health. In fact, I'm pretty sure she ran in the last L.A. Marathon."

"The flowers are from the backyard," one of the Santa Monica detectives put in. Frank Moses was in his late twenties, with a brush cut, a well-tailored jacket, and a jaunty air. He was almost hyperventilating at the prospect of working an Atterminator case and getting on the task force.

Joanna leaned down for a closer look. Francesca's fingers were arranged to actually *hold* the flowers, as if perhaps she'd gathered them herself. *Gather ye rosebuds while you may, for time is still a-dying.* The words echoed in her mind from a long-ago high school English class. But the words weren't quite right. She was putting a cop spin on it. What were the real words? She shook her head and returned her thoughts to the bouquet.

A dozen roses, apparently home-grown, were each cut to a length of between eight and ten inches. The lower leaves had been carefully clipped off each stem, leaving only upper foliage, none of it noticeably chewed-up. The flowers themselves were of varying sizes and colors, some more open than others. Each appeared to be a different variety.

Very interesting.

The pruning shears were interesting as well. They looked brand-new and had been left in the farthest open position, blades held apart by a shiny spring mechanism. The narrower blade was stuck into the hollow of Francesca Goldberg's throat and the thicker one rested on her clavicle. There was a slight green residue on the thicker blade.

"I think the flowers were probably cut with these," Joanna said, standing up again and gesturing toward Francesca's pale throat. "Which just happen to be Felco number twos, which also just happen to be what Francesca's client, Louise Considine, used on her late mother. Nice attention to detail. And a detail not just anybody would have remembered."

Jacobs laughed. "I sure as hell didn't. What about you—" he nodded toward the Santa Monica detective "—you know the kind of garden tool Loose Louise used on Mom?"

Frank Moses shook his head and grinned. "Not me. I live in a fourth-floor apartment. With a dead Chia Pet."

Some time later, while the criminalists were still working in the house, Joanna went out into Francesca Goldberg's rose garden, enclosed by an eight-foot cedar fence. It was a beautiful place and she stopped for a couple of minutes just to appreciate it. Then she began looking for the bushes from which the funeral bouquet had been cut.

She had little difficulty finding most of them. The garden was extremely well tended, weedless and free of any obvious pest or disease problems. No powdery mildew, no rust, no unsightly foliage holes, not even any aphids. And no ladybugs, either. All of which meant that Goldberg—or more probably, her gardener—had sprayed a lot more ardently than Joanna ever would. She would readily concede, however, that the results were stunning.

All of Francesca's roses were carefully identified by oval copper markers, weathered green, the sort of decorative doodads sold by mail-order for gardeners with too much money. Joanna couldn't help contrasting this garden with her own yard, which featured only a few roses, in deference to the scarcity of water in her patch of the west Valley. The roses she continued to grow were those tough enough to make it with minimal coddling, disease- and pest-resistant enough to require almost no spraying. Like Golden Showers, whose name she never said aloud without wondering at the naïveté of the rosarian—probably some bespectacled botanist with ink stains on his shirt pocket and mud stains on his knees—who had named it. Joanna's roses were pretty much finished for the season, hanging heavy with cheerful orange hips, waiting for the week after Christmas when she traditionally pruned them all.

Here most of the hybrid teas and grandifloras were just beginning what would be their last bloom cycle of the season. Joanna worked systematically from a Polaroid close-up of the wilted bouquet arranged so neatly on Francesca Goldberg's breast. As she tracked down the source plants, she went back inside twice to check the cut ones for confirmation.

Each flower, she quickly realized, had been the prize specimen from its respective bush. All twelve roses in Francesca's bouquet came from different bushes. And each had been cut with a sharp tool, just above an outward-facing bud union with seven leaves.

Joanna thoughtfully read the identifying markers for the rose-bushes from which the Atterminator had selected his funeral bouquet: Breathless, Legend, Unforgettable, Voodoo, Buccaneer, Heaven, Taboo, Eclipse, Red Devil, Sterling Silver, King's Ransom, Secret. Each could be said to apply somehow to Francesca Goldberg and her practice of the law—or to her immediate condition. Breathless, indeed.

There were probably a hundred different varieties in the garden, and several unselected bushes featured more perfect specimens. He'd taken time and consideration in making his choices, several of which were located in out-of-the way back corners.

The selections seemed far too deliberate to have been made on the spot, and certainly not in the dark. He might have cut the flowers at night with a flashlight if he'd already made his choices, either earlier yesterday or on some other occasion. Santa Monica PD would really have to push the neighbors for memories of out-of-the-ordinary strangers in previous weeks; with luck there'd be a neighborhood busybody.

It was barely possible that he'd come by in the afternoon, selected his flowers, and waited for Francesca, but Joanna doubted it. The maid had left at noon, and she was certain that nothing but the satin pillow—taken from Francesca's ultra-feminine bed-chamber—seemed disturbed. The criminalists had found no traces of a prolonged stay by a stranger.

Trying to determine when the flowers had been cut would probably be as vague as time-of-death determinations. Joanna had already offered to attend the autopsy, with Frank Moses from Santa Monica. It felt almost like the repayment of an old debt, a belated thank-you to Francesca for treating Joanna cordially and professionally in that long-ago courtroom.

Joanna noted now that the killer had carefully avoided a really nice bush of Honor, which featured several lovely late-season blossoms. Something of a surprise for someone who normally placed such emphasis on irony. If he'd really been thinking, he'd have left a flower from Honor smashed beneath Francesca's feet.

The Atterminator had some interesting talents. He was good with wiring and alarm systems, had cut off the phone at Bill Burke's cabin, had known how to manipulate the circuitry to parboil Lawrence Benton without blowing out the hot tub, had worked around fairly sophisticated home security setups. Including this one. Overall, he was quite adept at breaking and entering, leaving virtually no trace. He appeared to be a rather skilled lock picker.

And he knew his roses.

Chief Trial Counsel Bonita Blevins arrived at the California State Bar shortly after eight on Thursday morning. Horrendous traffic on the San Bernardino had allowed her to hear almost an hour and a half of the unabridged tape of *Tess of the d'Urbervilles*. Bonita was filling in huge gaps in her literary education by commuting in L.A.

Even so, becoming more literate didn't seem to balance out the time spent on the freeways lately. She was starting to seriously consider selling the Claremont condo and making her permanent residence in San Francisco. She oversaw operations in both Los Angeles and San Francisco, with her job structured so she could make either one her primary residence. She had few strong personal ties in Los Angeles anyway.

When she reached the office, she could tell immediately that something was seriously wrong. Her mind instantly leapt to the possibility of another attorney murder, but when she learned the victim's identity, the news stunned her nearly senseless. She lost her balance for a moment, steadying herself against the doorway before stumbling into her office and collapsing into her chair.

Francesca Goldberg. Murdered.

As she struggled for composure, Bonita stared blindly out the window. Her mind swam with silly, unrelated notions, all of them forms of denial. Francesca wasn't *like* those others, she thought furiously. She didn't *deserve* this.

Bonita had gone through law school at Boalt Hall in Berkeley with Francesca twenty years earlier, and while the two women were never close friends, they were active in some of the same professional organizations. More importantly, they shared certain battle scars.

There'd been fewer women in law school back then. A lot fewer. Bonita herself had loved the study of the law, while fearing the hurly-burly of legal practice. But Francesca never seemed frightened of anything, and Bonita had modeled some of her own behavior after her classmate's awesome self-confidence.

She couldn't imagine Francesca dead.

She somehow got through the morning, but when her watch told her it was eleven-thirty, she looked blankly over her desk and saw nothing that might explain what she'd been doing for three hours. She had referred all media inquiries to Robbery–Homicide. There had been no official comment from the State Bar about any of the previous victims and there would be none about Francesca.

It happened, however, that the Women's Law Association monthly luncheon was scheduled for today. Downtown, nearby. Francesca was a past president of WLA. Bonita forced herself to go.

She arrived at the restaurant to find that nearly everyone else had come, too, most bearing slightly dazed expressions. The speaker was hastily jettisoned and the wine list freely consulted. It turned into a sort of nervous Irish wake.

Two hours later, Bonita was stopped by reporters as she left the restaurant in dark glasses, wobbling a little. The wine had loosened both her tongue and her deepest fears.

"The State Bar is *extremely* concerned about these appalling murders," Bonita told the cameras, remembering all the impromptu press conferences Francesca had held after courtroom victories. The camera had loved Francesca. She was beautiful and photogenic.

"We will cooperate in every way we possibly can to apprehend the person or persons responsible for these capital crimes," Bonita went on. The film clip would later find its way into news broadcasts around the globe. "This heinous fiend must be stopped."

• • •

It was after midnight when Joanna got home. She was tired and unfocused and angry. Mary Elaine McGonigle might almost have been a contemporary of Kirsten's, which still troubled her greatly. But Francesca Goldberg actually *was* a contemporary of Joanna's, albeit a decade younger. And however brief their interaction had been all those years ago, she still felt she somehow knew the woman.

Plus that damned snippet of poetry about rosebuds would *not* go out of her mind and it was driving her crazy.

In the second bedroom—her substitute for a storage locker, the place where Joanna kept everything she wasn't using right now but wasn't *quite* ready to get rid of—she rummaged until she found Kirsten's box of books. The books had lived on a shelf in her daughter's room years earlier, had remained behind when their owner and her life moved into new dimensions. Joanna had packed them up when she moved out of the big leased house in Encino where she'd lived with Jake Arnold. Kirsten was gone by then.

The books had been boxed ever since. Every once in a while Joanna would mention the box and Kir would promise to take care of it someday. The truth was, having the box of books felt, in some odd way, like the only remaining physical connection to her daughter's childhood. And so the books stayed and Joanna, ever ruthless in disposing of her own unwanted items, never pressed the issue.

Beneath copies of *The Secret Garden* and *Misty of Chincoteague*, she found the book of quotations.

It took ten minutes to find the book, but less than a minute after that to track down the lines she was looking for. And the quote, from someone named Robert Herrick, a name Joanna would have sworn she'd never encountered in this lifetime, was indeed an appropriate epitaph for Francesca Goldberg.

> *Gather ye rosebuds while ye may,*
> *Old Time is still a-flying:*
> *And this same flower that smiles today,*
> *To-morrow will be dying.*

19

Ace watched Bonita Blevins on the news that evening with great distaste.

There was something truly reprehensible about this woman and her sanctimony. It was, after all, *her* responsibility to maintain ethical standards for California attorneys, a task at which she had failed woefully. And she had the gall to call *him* a heinous fiend!

But he had other things to think about now. Events were moving far too quickly for his taste.

First he needed to take care of Gina.

He went to the kitchen, removed his screwdriver from its charger, and flipped the bit from Phillips to regular. In the living room, he reached behind a small corner table and unscrewed the cover on an electrical socket box. He removed the plug inserted in the top receptacle. The cord from the plug led to an ugly table lamp, but the cord was a dummy, and he'd altered the lamp to run on batteries hidden in its ceramic base.

Now he removed the fake junction box and groped inside to retrieve a small leather pouch from between the drywall supports. He pulled a neat roll of bills from the pouch, counted off twenty hundreds, considered, then counted off an additional ten. Setting those bills aside, he emptied the rest of the sack onto the carpet and looked at his savings account.

His grubstake.

His legacy from Mrs. Kowalski, bless her soul.

Mrs. Kowalski had passed away unexpectedly one night, two short days after visiting Kaiser and having her blood pressure medication changed. She had actually *told* Ace about the medication change, and he had listened intently. Mrs. Patrusak's tenants really appreciated the close attention Ace paid to their stories and complaints, their travails and concerns.

So when Mrs. Kowalski didn't pick up her morning *Times* in the lobby two days later, Ace was not surprised to find her dead, lying peacefully at rest in one of the twin beds in her ruffly little bedroom. He dutifully phoned 911, showed the responding officers to Mrs. Kowalski's apartment, and explained about her recent visit to Kaiser, helpfully locating the new prescription bottle in her bathroom for the already-bored cops. The doctor at Kaiser signed her death certificate and by then Ace had found the money.

Mrs. Kowalski had been a tenant for six years, since before he himself moved in. She always paid her rent in cash and in recent months, as her memory progressively worsened, she had sometimes not noticed when the first of the month rolled around. On three occasions, Ace had knocked politely at her door to remind her. Each time she smiled, asked him to wait just a minute, and then bolted the door in his face. Each time she was back with cash in hand—musty cash, at that—in less than five minutes.

He knew she had a stash in there somewhere.

He knew, too, that there wouldn't be any relatives showing up immediately. Mrs. Kowalski had moved to California twenty years earlier when she was widowed. Her older son was a race car driver, killed a few years back at the Indy 500, and her younger boy had some kind of business in Hartford, Connecticut. Before Ron Kowalski arrived—if he came at all, if he didn't just ask to have her furniture sold and her personal effects boxed and shipped, like the tenants' children sometimes did—Ace figured there'd be plenty of time to search out that stash.

Once Mrs. Kowalski's body was taken away, Ace went back into the apartment to remove the bedding, soiled when the old lady died. He'd been through the same drill before and hoped it wouldn't be necessary to eighty-six the mattress. Most tenants routinely slept on rubber mattress pads. But not Mrs. Kowalski. He decided he'd better pitch the mattress immediately, before it left difficult-to-remove odors in an otherwise easily let apartment.

Ace knew from previous experience that he would be able to stick the mattress out in the alley and have it disappear by morning, noxious stains and all. Welcome to glamorous Hollywood. The bedding he could wash and replace discreetly in the apartment.

He had rather been looking forward to searching the apartment, thinking of Mrs. Kowalski as something of a soul sister, but once he took the mattress off, he discovered that no search was necessary. He'd credited Mrs. Kowalski with too much creativity.

She had literally kept her money under her mattress.

Or, more precisely, in her box spring. The fabric topping of her box spring had been neatly cut along three sides of a large rectangle, which folded back to reveal the white metal tops of a dozen slender glass jars tucked into the metal coils of the box spring.

Jackpot!

Energized, he quickly slipped on a pair of the latex gloves he routinely carried in the bottom of his toolbox and lifted the jars out one by one. All contained money.

He slipped the jars back into their slots, folded the fabric topper back over the springs, and checked the box spring on the other bed. It was perfectly normal, unslit and unstuffed.

Next he walked into the kitchen and poured himself a drink from Mrs. Kowalski's Sparkletts dispenser. There was a *lot* of money in that mattress, enough that a fellow should be able to help himself to some of it with no risk whatsoever. Just imagine the freedom possible if he never had to worry about money again!

Still, Mrs. Kowalski's son from Connecticut probably also realized she was the kind of person who'd hide money in her mattress. He was bound to come out and personally go through her effects with a fine-toothed comb. Indeed, as Ace thought about it, there seemed no way Ron Kowalski *wouldn't* know. He'd probably been arguing with her about it for years. *Mom, you ought to have that money in a bank, that's what banks are for*, Sonny Boy would say. To which she'd offer a standard response: *And why? So I can lose it all like my father did in the Depression?*

A lot would depend on whether Mrs. Kowalski had left records. Ace went through the papers she kept in her little dropfront desk and found a checking account from which she paid her monthly phone and grocery bills, as well as the key to a safety deposit box. She had sterling flatware for twelve in a wooden chest in a bottom kitchen cupboard, along with a silver coffee service tarnished nearly solid black.

He replaced everything as he had found it, went back into the bedroom, and counted the money. The jars had all originally contained imported jumbo green olives stuffed with pimientos. Now each held $25,000 in green lettuce, though one jar was only partly full. It contained $12,245.

The total came to $287,245.

It made him dizzy.

If Ron Kowalski had any idea that his mother had stashed over a quarter million dollars in her mattress, he might well hop the next flight to the coast, expecting an immediate solution to any personal cash flow problems. But there was no reason why Ron—who never called unless it was her birthday, who hadn't even sent flowers the previous Mother's Day, all slights Mrs. Kowalski had shared with Ace—should get it all. Ace himself had phoned his mother weekly, wished only that he had insisted on answers before it no longer mattered.

Ace decided to leave three full jars and the partially filled one, which came to $87,245 and was more than enough for such an inattentive asshole. After replacing those jars in the box spring, he switched the mattresses, remade the other bed, scrubbed out the stains as best he could, and drenched the mattress cover with Lysol. Later he would stack the laundered, folded bed linens on the yucked-up mattress for Ron Kowalski to find. The switch seemed foolproof. Nobody but Ace and the cops knew which bed the old lady had actually died in, and the cops didn't care.

He put the eight olive jars in a brown paper grocery sack and carried it down the hall to his own apartment, where he emptied their contents into a neat pile, resisting the impulse to scream with glee. He rinsed out the jars and left them in a Koreatown recycling bin. The money he placed in two hollowed-out textbooks in a box of reference materials amid the clutter of a small storage locker he maintained in North Hollywood.

Mrs. Kowalski's son arrived the next afternoon, looking greedy. Ace let the beady-eyed, perspiring little fat man into his mother's apartment and retired down the hall to his own place, whistling softly. Three hours later, Ron Kowalski came back to Ace's apartment, knocked, and explained that he planned to ship all of his mother's effects back east and where could he get some boxes? Ever the helpful manager, Ace steered the guy to a nearby U-Haul supply store and watched with the grieving son two days later while the Mayflower folks loaded it all up. He assumed that Ron Kowalski would dismantle every item at his leisure back east.

And who knows? Maybe there *was* more, hidden someplace else.

Now the stash was significantly depleted. The Legal Resolution Program had proven expensive, and it wasn't over yet. He got out the phone book, punched in an 800 number, and negotiated his way through an irritating telephone menu. He was put on hold and while he waited he thought about Gina.

Thought with a certain measure of regret about Gina.

One of the things he had always found most appealing about her was her secretiveness. That quality was serving him well now, he realized, even as he planned her dismissal from the Legal Resolution Program. The completion of her episode had unnerved her in ways he had not anticipated. From the moment he had first involved her, of course, he had intended to later disinvolve her. Amoral though she might be, Gina was all but certain to eventually become a risk. He could barely believe he had actually once considered involving her beyond her one episode.

He had traveled this far only because he traveled alone. And because his own secretive streak left Gina's in its dust.

Still, it was almost sad.

He had already packed the van when she arrived on Friday morning, carrying her omnipresent backpack, wearing jeans and a sweatshirt. The pleasantly warm weather provided a perfect opening to suggest a spontaneous mountain weekend. They would stop and hike, he told her, then move on to a cabin borrowed from a friend.

They left early, moving against traffic up the Golden State and out through the Antelope Valley. Gina was subdued, her hands clasped tightly in her lap. She offered no specific reasons for being quiet and Ace asked no questions. Their entire relationship had been conducted pretty much in silence, watching endless black-

and-white *film noir* classics in Ace's other apartment, acting out her sexual fantasies on the rickety bed with the conventional tufted white spread.

"There's not much of you here," Gina had noted once, gesturing around the apartment.

Ace had only smiled. There was *nothing* of him there. He had established the place in a building where no one knew him and three months' advance rent in cash was sufficient reference. He kept a few items of clothing in the dresser, a few staples in the kitchen.

The name on the mailbox was M. Varner, and Gina knew him as Mike.

He left the highway and they began to climb into the Angeles National Forest. Gina remained silent beside him. She preferred the desert to the forest, she had told him once, because the life that survived in the desert was so tough; it endured by hiding and sneaking and subterfuge.

Four-wheel drive would have helped, but a dry run the week before had convinced him it was unnecessary. He left the van at the side of the road and moved off into the woods, carrying a blanket. There was a crisp sense of fall in the air. She followed him down the vague path to a partial clearing.

"First things first," he told her with a shy smile, touching the hem of her sweatshirt. She shrugged it up and over her head, revealing small, high breasts, then slipped her jeans down to her ankles. As usual, she wore no underwear. She seemed even thinner. He felt himself quicken with a new and unanticipated type of desire, pulled his own clothes off quickly, then laid his jeans on a large rock and sat on them, while she spread the blanket neatly on the ground.

"Mike, I've been very bad," she told him coyly. Gina was a champion at being coy. "I must be punished."

Then she lay across his lap, presenting her perfect little bottom. As he spanked her with the flat of his hand, she moaned and writhed, and he worried fleetingly that the sound might carry. He had never done this sort of thing before Gina, and he suspected he never would again. Still, with her it always seemed all right.

"That's not enough," she told him when he tried to stop. "I've been *really* bad."

And he dutifully walloped her some more, watching red hand-prints rise on her pale skin, deciding suddenly to fuck her one more time. He fumbled for the condom, then pushed her upward with one knee.

She lay back spread-eagled on the blanket, breathing shallowly. Ace looked at her face upturned toward his, her eyes glittering with anticipation. He quickly lowered himself and lunged into her body. They rode together for a few moments with the ease of much practice and she yelped as she came and came again.

Then, as he felt himself also begin to come, Ace clasped his hands around her throat and strangled her.

He was surprised to find, when she lay limp, that he felt a surge of genuine regret.

"It's all a game," Ace told the girl he was sending to New York. She looked enough like Gina to use her driver's license ID to get on the plane, and the round-trip ticket reassured her.

"Nobody's ever done anything like this for me," she told him seriously, and for a moment he felt like laughing out loud.

She was young and stupid, running away from an abusive step-father in Lincoln, Nebraska, finding Hollywood a large and frightening place where all her options were bad. When Ace discovered her rummaging through the Dumpster behind Mrs. Patrusak's apartment building, she was living in a burned-out building off Hollywood Boulevard with a collection of other young human flotsam.

She wanted to be an actress.

She was dumb enough to buy the story that he was taking her to New York to meet a friend who was casting an off-off Broadway play. The part was that of a young woman leaving everything behind.

She drank three little bottles of Chablis on the plane, fiddling with the good-luck scarf he had given her the night before. He watched, disguised, from four rows back, across the aisle in a window seat. He was travelling as Adam Morant.

The seat beside her was empty and she didn't talk to anybody. When the plane landed, he took the same bus he had instructed her to ride. Again she didn't recognize him.

It was already darkening when they landed in New York. The streets were still crowded when the airport bus finally reached Manhattan, crowded enough that he was able to follow her easily. She kept dutifully to the route he had instructed her to take to the apartment that didn't exist, where she thought she would be spending the night.

He sped up and passed her as they neared the corner he remembered. There he ducked down the alleyway and called her name, in the voice she knew.

She jerked around, startled. "What the—"

"C'mere," he told her. "Hurry."

She hustled down the alley toward him, looking confused. He leaned over to kiss her, then quickly twisted the ends of the good-luck scarf around her neck. It had demonstrated an impressive tensile strength earlier, crushing an empty two-liter soda bottle.

She lost consciousness almost immediately.

When he was certain she was dead, he continued to hold her upright while he checked her purse for the return plane ticket and Gina's ID. Then he zipped the purse inside his pack, lowered her to the ground by the side of the building, and merged with a steady and deliberate gait back into the stream of foot traffic.

Gina's trail had just reached a dead end.

20

On the Friday before Thanksgiving, right after Joanna returned to the office from Francesca Goldberg's autopsy, a young detective transferred a call to her. "Captain McNamara," the detective said. "He told me you'd want to speak to him."

Joanna inhaled, looked at the phone, and picked up. "Davis," she said crisply.

"I'm starting to get a little worried about you," Don Olafson's voice announced laconically. Not bothering to identify himself. He knew she'd know his voice anywhere, anytime. Even as he would know hers.

Joanna and her first ex-husband had set up the Captain Mc-Namara cover years earlier, for occasions when they might need to speak without their various office-mates being the wiser. It was an unflinchingly egalitarian system; each claimed to be Captain McNamara when calling the other. The system had been Joanna's idea and she had insisted on parity. The phone numbers they left, when messages were required, were correct, save for a phony area code in Georgia.

"No need to worry," she told him. His gentle but pragmatic concern for her safety had always touched her, dating clear back to the very first time he took her to the target range. They weren't married yet, weren't even engaged. But Joanna had known, even if Don hadn't, that they would be. And she had been both charmed and challenged by his insistence that she learn every possible method of self-defense.

"You qualified lately?" he asked.

"I could outshoot you wearing an eyepatch," she shot back, though of course it wasn't true. Don Olafson was a fantastic marksman, had turned down repeated recruiting overtures back when LAPD pioneered SWAT in the seventies. Don had grown up hunting in the Minnesota north woods and fine-tuned his sharpshooting skills in Southeast Asia, with limitless military ammunition.

"Your murders are getting a lot of attention here," he told her. "Francesca Goldberg makes a big story. People had heard about her here, you know, even before she bought it. And of course I remembered you talking about her, way back."

Way back. Joanna had testified against Francesca's young robber during a period when she and Don were speaking regularly by phone, trying to find some way to be together without actually having to live in each other's preferred—nay, essential—environments. Before they conceded defeat and moved on to other lives.

"She was a decent person," Joanna told him slowly. "She may have represented scum, but she wasn't slimy herself."

"If you say so," he replied noncommittally.

"She had a beautiful yard. Full of roses. I can't talk about why, but I spent a lot of time out there." So far they'd kept a lid on the specifics of Francesca's bouquet. "It was one of those little north-of-Montana yards, smaller than our place in Mar Vista. But it was solid rosebushes, maybe two hundred of them."

He grunted. Don had never been big on gardening, though he had uncomplainingly double-dug the vegetable beds where the kids grew radishes and zucchini. "Is this where I'm supposed to tell you we have eighteen inches of snow on the ground?"

Joanna laughed. "I guess so.... Do you really?"

"Yes, really." He hesitated. "You know, he'd never admit it to you, but your son is really worried about you."

Joanna tried to make herself angry and found she couldn't. It was primal and tribal and anachronistic and certainly unbecoming someone of her rank and experience. But she couldn't pretend she didn't like having her man and her son feeling protective. And at times like this, Don always called Mike *her* son, as if he'd had nothing to do with the matter.

"Believe me, there's no reason for worry," she assured him. "Actually, right now we're all up to our beady little eyeballs in crank calls."

His laugh resonated. "Like this one, Captain McNamara?"

"More entertaining. Though not as satisfying," she hastily amended. It was a long time since she'd spoken with Don, six months at least, since Mike had first announced his engagement to the co-worker at 3M. When they parted initially, the calls were frequent and intense, never entirely cooling even after it became apparent that neither would or could budge. Don had been desperately unhappy away from his family and roots during the years he lived in L.A. And Joanna had been frankly suicidal in Minnesota. Later, when Don remarried, the calls became briefer, less frequent, and mostly businesslike—matter-of-fact kid-related discussions. Eventually Kirsten and Mike reached full adulthood, with no further travel arrangements to make, no further support payments to negotiate.

But the Captains McNamara still chatted now and again. Just because.

"Are you trying to brush me off?" he suggested now.

Never. Don Olafson might be thousands of miles away and fruitfully married to another woman, but the sound of his voice had always quickened Joanna's pulse and probably always would. "Listen, the last call I took before yours was from a psychic who wanted us to do some fairly complicated chemical experiments involving toads and fecal matter from the decedents. Trust me, Captain, you're a breath of fresh air."

"You gonna follow up on the toad idea, Captain?"

"Maybe in June. So. How's tricks in *your* department?" Don Olafson was presently the chief of police in Duluth, Minnesota, with no retirement plans even though he'd been a cop for over thirty years. Longer if you counted military service, and they always did.

"A lot quieter than yours. But you knew that already."

Over another ten minutes of inconsequential small talk, Joanna found herself feeling oddly warm and quite pleasantly reassured.

A neat trick considering that an hour and a half earlier, she'd been staring into the bloody shell of the late Francesca Goldberg, while the medical examiner weighed miscellaneous internal organs and puzzled over what in tarnation might have killed her.

Tips were, indeed, flooding into the Atterminator Task Force hot line. By the dozens, by the hundreds, by the thousands.

There'd been a lull for a while, after the initial flurry. Word had spread throughout the legal community that no police protection would be available for individuals. "You'll have plenty of personnel available once I get killed," one angry lawyer had snarled to Joanna, a statement with which she could hardly quibble.

Shortly before Francesca Goldberg's death, a group of Los Angeles attorneys offered the task force a no-strings-attached donated computer network to link the different departments involved in the investigation. With Goldberg's body barely cold, the mayor and chief accepted the offer. Joanna personally hated the idea, certain that any system outsiders could set up, outsiders could also penetrate and monitor.

By now, the task force had contacted the offices of all attorneys publicly disciplined by the State Bar in the last three years. A preemptive strike, it was hoped, but they'd only know it worked if these guys survived. And Francesca Goldberg hadn't even been on that list.

As Joanna reviewed the case on Tuesday, November 25th, two days before Thanksgiving, she could pick out a few specific accomplishments.

Even with the addition of Goldberg, the official Atterminator casualty list was holding at five. Mary Elaine McGonigle in Long Beach and Vincent Carrigan in Las Vegas had been officially deemed unrelated copycat murders, as had similar impulse slayings in Miami, Birmingham, and Boston.

Closer to home, the death of San Diego worker's comp attorney Arturo Hernandez remained classified a single-car automobile accident. CHP had checked and rechecked both the scene of the wreck and the car in which Hernandez died, finding absolutely nothing to suggest that the lawyer's death was anything other than a tragic accident.

The upstate hiking death of environmental activist and attorney Alan Salter also seemed clean. Both Salter's wife and brother had been hiking with him and both stated unequivocally that they had watched the lawyer's horrifying plunge off Mount Shasta. Nothing learned in town had contradicted their eyewitness accounts and Mickey Conner, ever vigilant, had put in plenty of pub-time making sure there were no rumors.

Joanna continued to be fascinated by the number of buttons—including her own—pushed by the death of Francesca Goldberg. The media seemed truly aghast, even reporters who had routinely vilified the attorney when she was alive. Goldberg was the first criminal attorney killed by the Atterminator, the first Jew, the first female.

There was still no official cause of death, and the preliminary toxicology results were inconclusive. The more complex toxicology work, which normally moved at the speed of a garden slug on downers, was being rushed at the behest of the police chief himself.

Goldberg's movements throughout her final week and especially her last day had been painstakingly reconstructed, her neighborhood canvassed repeatedly and industriously in both English and Spanish. Nobody recalled anything or anybody out of the ordinary.

Ordinary.

That seemed to be the Atterminator's key: to be *truly* ordinary. To blend, to fit in, to move through different milieus and situations without attracting any attention.

How in the hell did he do it?

Joanna sighed and looked at the note left on her desk by Frank Moses, the detective from Santa Monica who'd been fielding phone calls all morning. "Melody Laughlin," it read, with a phone number in Orange County. "See me about this one."

She found Moses making faces into the phone as he stirred a cup of coffee that looked as if it had been mixed up to fill a pothole on the Hollywood Freeway. He rolled his eyes upward when he saw Joanna. Finally he hung up, shaking his head.

"You'll wanta get right on this one," Moses said. "It's a doozy. Says she buried the rind of a ruby red grapefruit in a peanut butter jar during the full of the moon and dug it up this morning. The mold on the rind is shaped like Texas and there's a hole rotted through in the general vicinity of Dallas. Our killer's a Dallasite, she says. You wanta alert the Texas Rangers or shall I?"

Joanna laughed as she sat down. "All yours, Moses. What's the story on this Melody Laughlin?"

Moses started leafing through a disorderly stack of notes. When the phone rang again he ignored it and somebody else picked up. "She's the secretary to a lawyer in Whittier." He pulled a sheet from the pack in triumph. "Joseph Tucker. He's one of the ones the task force called early on because his law license got lifted. He's some kind of scumbag preys on old ladies. You know, writes their wills, sets himself up as executor, picks the estate clean."

"A real sweetheart," Joanna murmured. Those who preyed on the elderly got no quarter from her. Her Great-aunt Edna, when Joanna was very young, had been sweet-talked out of most of her late husband's estate in exchange for a chunk of Arizona desert habitable only by scorpions.

"Yeah, well anyway, Tucker got his. He had a stroke and he's a vegetable in a nursing home. Rutabaga City. *But*—this Melody says there was a guy who came around right before Tucker had the stroke, some kind of FedEx-type messenger. There was something screwy about his visit, and she thinks he may have also come by last summer. She didn't think of it when we called before, and once we found out Tucker was out of commission, I guess he got pushed to the back burner. But I got a good feeling off her."

Joanna's eyes narrowed. "She *saw* this guy?"

On the way to Whittier, Joanna considered.

She'd been looking for ordinary, and a messenger was ordinary in spades.

A messenger would be *wonderfully* anonymous in L.A. About as anonymous as anybody could be, actually, who wasn't living in a brown cardboard box under a freeway overpass. Messengers moved everywhere, in and out of office buildings, dropping off papers, picking up packages, double-parking. Nobody paid attention to them. Folks just signed off on their deliveries and went back to work.

Melody Laughlin, bless her heart, turned out to be the exception.

"He was cute," she confided over coffee in Joseph Tucker's back office. "Things have been pretty quiet around here since Mr. Tucker's difficulties." Melody Laughlin was the one girl in a one-girl office, with an air of competence that balanced her surfer-girl blond good looks. She'd set aside a Margaret Atwood novel when Joanna arrived.

She had been with Mr. Tucker for six years, she explained. She always referred to him as Mr. Tucker. When he was suspended, he'd insisted that she stay on to reassure his clients that their interests were being safeguarded. Joanna felt confident that Melody had been well compensated to maintain the appearance of a respectable, ongoing operation, and that she was worth every penny Tucker had paid her.

The two women sat on a nice firm brocade-upholstered Victorian love seat, their bone china saucers resting on a gleaming traditional mahogany coffee table. Joseph Tucker's office, filled with tasteful antiques and fine Oriental rugs, would have inspired confidence in the wealthy elderly. She could easily picture a dowager being beguiled in this office, allowing that charming Mr. Tucker to help put her affairs in order. He'd be ever-so-slightly flirtatious while remaining utterly and impeccably proper.

Several photographs of Mr. Tucker in polished sterling frames graced a magnificent mahogany credenza. He was a distinguished-looking fellow with a great head of silver hair, a golden tan, and plenty of bright, straight teeth. One black-and-white photo, obviously taken many years earlier, showed him on the deck of a yacht with the late John Wayne, another wealthy Orange County resident. What little old lady could resist a man who had socialized with the Duke?

The State Bar records showed no ambiguity whatsoever in the charges against Joseph Tucker, a situation confirmed by the Orange County DA's office. The guy was a crook.

But from what Melody Laughlin explained gravely about Tucker's medical condition, this grifter's life of crime was over. Joseph Tucker, Esquire, had written his last will and conned his last old lady. His doctors were astonished that he hadn't died immediately, and he remained on life support only because his children were quibbling about pulling the plug.

"You've got to understand," Melody told her disarmingly, "that once Mr. Tucker was suspended, there really wasn't much of anything for me to do here. Mr. Tucker would come in after lunch, maybe make a couple of phone calls or dictate a letter or two. But he wasn't doing any more estate work. He wasn't allowed to. And there wasn't any younger associate in the office to take over. He had to refer his active clients to other counsel."

"So he was just keeping up appearances by coming in?"

Melody smiled beatifically. She, too, had kept up appearances, wore a conservative lace-trimmed burgundy silk dress with tasteful gold jewelry, even though she claimed nobody ever came by the office anymore. Tucker's children had asked her to keep the office open "for the moment," as she delicately put it.

"I suppose you could say that. He seemed lonely since his wife passed away a couple of years ago. And he was *terribly* depressed after all the trouble." As well he might have been. The file Joanna had seen was positively incendiary. There'd also been mention of alcoholism.

"Had Mr. Tucker done anything about his drinking problem?" Joanna asked. No point beating around the bush.

Melody winced. "Not really. Actually, he was a little worse lately, if you want the truth."

"Let's talk about this delivery man, then. Did he ever have any direct contact with Mr. Tucker?" It grated on Joanna to use such a respectful tone in discussing an obvious slimeball, but it elevated the conversation to the level set by the furnishings in the office.

Melody frowned, shaking her head slowly. "I don't *think* so. And I don't remember exactly what it was that he brought last summer, only that it struck me as odd at the time. We weren't getting much in the way of deliveries anymore, you see. And Mr. Tucker said he hadn't requested whatever it was."

"But the delivery man brought it into the outer office there and you signed for it?"

She nodded. "Just like this last time."

"Was he wearing a uniform?"

"Uh-huh. Shorts and a white shirt, with his name on the pocket. Jerry. He had nice legs, too," Melody reported with the casual nonchalance of one experienced in the analysis and grading of men's bodies. "You know, those courier guys all look pretty much the same, unless they're black or something. He had on sunglasses both times, not very dark. The grayish kind you don't have to take off when you go inside."

"How'd you know he was from a messenger service?"

Melody furrowed her pretty brow in concentration, closed her eyes to think. "Well, he had a clipboard, I remember that. And I had to sign for the delivery."

"Were there other signatures?"

"I guess. I really don't remember. And I probably wouldn't remember him at all if Mr. Tucker hadn't had his stroke the next day."

A safe enough way to reconstruct one's calendar. Joanna carried the subject a bit further, then paused and looked Melody Laughlin in the eye. "It's entirely possible that this delivery person is implicated in some very serious charges."

"Don't treat me like an idiot," Melody responded, a trifle indignantly. "We've both known exactly why you're here ever since you called and made this appointment. You think I saw the Atterminator, that he was stalking Mr. Tucker. And I think you may be right. Now you're going to ask me if I'd recognize him again."

"And you're going to answer—?" Joanna queried mildly, with a maternal smile.

"I think so. The hair was different last summer, but I liked the way he looked. I thought about him for a few days after he came by, actually." She shrugged. She might have blushed if she'd been the blushing sort. "It was quiet. I was bored."

Joanna nodded, waiting. Wondering if maybe this Orange County legal secretary had fucked the Atterminator even as he was stalking her boss. Nobody would ever know if she locked the outer door for half an hour and adjourned to the fine Persian rug in this inner office. Not that she would ever, in a million years, admit it.

"Do you have some kind of artist who could work with me?" Melody asked suddenly. "To try to make a picture of him?"

"I think we could probably arrange that. In fact, I know we could. There are a couple of possibilities. We have an artist down at Parker Center who could work with you, or you might want to work with one of our people using a computer program."

"Cool," replied Melody, child of the computer age.

Outwardly Joanna remained calm and gracious, but inside she

was doing cartwheels. "Why don't you come on up with me right now? How long would it take you to close up the office?"

"Five minutes." She tilted her head, trying to look bashful, playing hard-to-get. "Do I really *have* to come to L.A.?"

Joanna shook her head, offering another maternal smile. This girl was younger than Kirsten. "Of course not. You don't *have* to do *anything*, Melody. But the fact that you called us makes me think you're willing to help. It must have occurred to you that except for his illness, we might have met when I investigated Mr. Tucker's murder."

Melody cringed. She'd obviously thought of exactly that eventuality. "I *said* I'd help. But I'd like to stop at my apartment first and get some stuff. Make a phone call. I've got a girlfriend I can stay with up in Hollywood tonight." She was starting to get really into this. "That way, we can work as late as we need to."

But they didn't need to work late. Melody Laughlin was articulate and the computer artist was good. By five P.M. she'd approved a drawing and LAPD had put out a press release.

BREAKTHROUGH IN ATTERMINATOR CASE! the networks all teased throughout the evening's prime-time programs. SUSPECT SKETCH RELEASED.

21

Ace was furious.

His picture—his *picture!*—was flashing around the world. It was on his own television set, which meant it was also in newspapers and would appear in magazines. And, of course, on the Internet.

It was *everywhere*.

And with no warning. Just when he was coming down from the most extraordinary weekend of his life. A weekend he could almost convince himself had never happened at all.

He had taken the red-eye back from New York on Monday night after ditching Gina's ID and return ticket, getting back to his official residence in Mrs. Patrusak's apartment building on Orange

Grove at nine A.M. He had found it impossible to sleep on the plane.

So what was waiting for him? Crap. Literally.

On his phone machine and slipped beneath his door, he found a total of six increasingly anguished messages from old Mrs. Mc-Neill in number nine about her stopped-up toilet. Mrs. McNeill clogged her plumbing on a fairly regular basis, though she always managed to be surprised when it happened.

Ace proceeded directly upstairs to apartment 9, where Mrs. McNeill was just stepping out the front door, on her way to use Mrs. Farber's facilities across the hall in number ten. "And so where have you *been?*" she asked accusingly.

You don't really want to know, he thought as he apologized and wove his magic on the old lady. "I was called away unexpectedly," he explained in a worried tone, brow furrowed, "by a friend whose sister was *horribly* injured in an auto accident. Critical condition. The driver was drunk. He walked away without a scratch."

Mrs. McNeill bought it immediately, switched to compassion, and assured him she hadn't been inconvenienced in the slightest. Ace had known his explanation would soothe her. Mrs. McNeill had lost her husband to a drunk driver decades earlier. Now Ace made short work of unclogging the toilet and speedily changed a leaky gasket in the tank.

And all before he even got to really go *inside* his own place.

Once in, he felt suddenly and totally exhausted. He fell into a rare daytime sleep, awakening in mild confusion to find it dark again. He puttered around for a while, then turned on the late-night news.

To find *this!*

He sat riveted now, after automatically leaping to turn down the volume. Not that it mattered. Anybody else still awake in the building was probably also watching the news, though most of the elderly tenants had long since turned in. Mrs. Patrusak's heavily secured building provided sanctuary to a dozen of the aged and moderately infirm, mostly long-term residents. Younger tenants didn't tend to stay very long in such a geriatric environment.

Increasingly they didn't even move in. Usually it took only a few well-chosen comments to get them to leave without even bothering to fill out a rental application.

In any event, Ace had thoroughly soundproofed his own quarters years ago, in the course of other renovations and modifications that Mrs. Patrusak had no idea she'd paid for. "I'm so grateful to have such a handy and responsible resident manager," she always told him, a sentiment echoed less frequently now that she was bedridden and senile in Hancock Park. Ace visited her monthly to check in, but she was failing rapidly.

He watched the lead story straight through on Channel 8, then switched from one channel to another, seeing the likeness of his face fill his television screen time and again.

That it was his face seemed undeniable. He had, after all, been wearing it for thirty-one years now. He fought back an initial reaction of panic. *Stay calm. Deep breaths. Go to your center.* The last one brought an involuntary chuckle. It had been a favorite expression of a long-gone girlfriend, a total flake. Moonbeam, she'd called herself, just to drive the point home.

He stuck a blank videotape into the VCR to record the artist's sketch. Channel 5 was promising another look at it later, so he set the machine to tape that channel while he continued to thumb his way through the other networks.

His mind raced along, too.

Who was the witness who'd come up with the sketch?

He thought back anxiously through his various surveillance trips. LAPD wasn't saying, of course. The official line was simply "a witness," and there were plenty of possibilities. But it was easy enough to narrow things down, once he stopped hyperventilating and began to really think. Along with the sketch came a general warning to the public that the Atterminator was believed to have disguised himself as a messenger. That didn't limit the possibilities much, either. He'd gotten a lot of mileage out of LRP Services, had visited dozens and dozens of law offices in the past six months.

Still, it was hard to believe that anybody would make the

connection *now*, based solely on last summer's surveillance. It was too long ago and nobody'd been worried about murder back then. It was summertime and everybody was mellow.

No, it was far more likely to be some place he'd revisited recently.

Once he realized that, of course, it hit him instantly. That chick in Joseph Tucker's office, out in Whittier. Tucker may have been a widow-welshing, death-cheating creep, but his secretary was a looker and a flirt. All sweet and demure but seductive at the same time, sliding that silky skirt up her leg, looking up through those long eyelashes, offering him a soft drink. Looking hot, looking bored, looking like somebody he could have taken into the Xerox room for a quickie if he were the type to mix business and pleasure.

And now *he* was the one who'd gotten fucked.

He considered neutralizing her, but immediately abandoned the idea. They'd be watching for him to do just that, *hoping* he'd make that kind of move. He wasn't going to fall into any dumb cop traps at this point. He'd come too far. Too much work remained.

After an eternity of channel switching, the various late-night news programs ended. Now Ace played back the tape of Channel 5 and froze his image for further study.

It wasn't half-bad, he decided after a few minutes of critical examination. It also wasn't nearly as damning as he had first feared. That initial moment of panic was unlike anything he'd felt since this all began. He hoped never to repeat it. Now he peered intently at the frozen image on the screen, brought a hand mirror up beside the sketch so he could make an objective comparison.

The jaw and cheekbones on the suspect sketch were wider than his own, the eyes not quite so closely spaced. The mouth was perfect, but who ever looked at a man's mouth? The guy in the sketch wore sunglasses with clear plastic frames, as Ace himself had on his messenger surveillance trips.

Of course this ended use of the messenger ploy, but there were plenty of other arrows in his quiver. He didn't need to do much more advance reconnaissance for his Big Show anyway. He'd mapped it out early on, and subsequent revisits to the site showed that the subject remained blissfully—and erroneously—certain of his invincibility.

Ace would also need to drop any disguises that bore too close a resemblance to the suspect sketch, but that shouldn't prove terribly difficult either. He had studied makeup and wardrobe intensively, knew all sorts of tricks for aging and disguising and camouflaging. The very commonality that had plagued him through his childhood served him well now. His size, too, was a real plus here: just under six feet, in good shape without being notably buffed or gaudily muscular. Hair light brown, eyes light brown, teeth straight. Everything about him murmured "unremarkable."

He moved into his bedroom. The Orange Grove Arms was old by Hollywood standards, and its original closet space had been minimal. Ace had altered that at the same time he soundproofed the place, adding a ten-foot closet, three feet deep, along an interior wall of his bedroom. He'd built in dressers and tiered clothing rods and all of the stuff that closet organizing companies offered at four times the price. He'd also added a little feature that no other apartment in the building had, one he hoped never to have to use.

Now he folded back the French doors, looked into a full-length mirror, considered.

He'd been wearing his hair an anonymous mid-length, though the suspect sketch showed it considerably shorter. So he'd darken it several shades, streak in a little gray around the temples to give the impression of more advanced age. He'd wear only his baggy, old-man clothing when he went out in public, lose the spring in his step. And the proper hat, of course, could hide all manner of identifying characteristics.

Ace smiled, feeling better already. He had a *lot* of hats.

It was time now to see what kind of impact the release of the sketch was having in cyberspace. He removed the laptop from the hidden compartment where it lived behind the kitchen broom closet and plugged it in.

He headed straight for the Atterminator chat room.

22

Joanna woke just before seven on Thanksgiving, warm sunlight streaming brightly through the crisp white lace curtains at her bedroom window in the snug stone house built ninety years earlier by a rugged loner.

Society had crept up around the place now, not tightly enough to impinge, though close enough to provide municipal services. But the bedroom remained tiny, closetless, barely able to accommodate a double bed, armoire, and small dresser. The walls were deep forest green, the bedspread a cheerful pastel import quilt, probably constructed in a Chinese prison. In the storage bedroom she kept three other sets of bed coverings and curtains. She could change the entire character of the room in fifteen minutes.

She rose, brewed coffee, drank the first cup, and then spent forty minutes on the rowing machine and the Stairmaster. She was getting sick of the Stairmaster, she realized, should probably replace it. Joanna was a third-generation secondhand shopper with an intimate knowledge of every thrift store from West L.A. to Santa Barbara.

While she exercised, she played California tunes on the jukebox: "Hotel California" and "Car on the Hill" and "I Love L.A." and "Running on Empty" and "Surfin' U.S.A." She played "Hollywood Nights," which always reminded her of life with Don Olafson (as did "Diamonds and Rust," complete to a line about calling from a booth in the midwest). And of course there was "California Dreamin'," her personal anthem during the sixteen months she lived in the darkness of frozen northern Minnesota.

It was wonderfully soothing to lose herself in the music and the rhythms of her body on a sunny, warm late November Thursday.

It was wonderful to be alive, and to have so much to be thankful for.

She turned on the Macy's parade just long enough to note smugly how cold everyone appeared, then called her children. Twenty-five-year-old Mike in Minneapolis favored his father both physically and temperamentally. A strapping Swede with clear blue eyes and broad shoulders and a glorious grin that set his entire face aglow, Mike had passed Joanna in height before his thirteenth birthday. He had Joanna's dark hair and tanned easily, but in every other respect was a virtual clone of his father. Mike had always been fiercely protective of his mother, in a way that both captivated and irritated her; she was, after all, an expert shot who could probably still outrun him and then flip him for good measure.

When he finished high school in L.A., Mike had gone to the University of Minnesota, becoming proficient at skiing and winter sports. He was now an engineer at 3M and Joanna had come to accept that he would probably stay in Minnesota forever.

Their conversation was brief. Her son was heading off to Thanksgiving dinner with his fiancée's parents in Rochester and he was openly nervous.

"They've seen you on the news," Mike told her. His tone carried dread. It had never been easy, socially, for either of Joanna's kids to have two police parents. A cop mom had been a particular embarrassment to the teenage Mike. And now, around a Rochester urologist's Thanksgiving dinner table, her son would have to explain for the thousandth time about his mother, the cop. The currently notorious cop.

Next she called Kirsten, who had also inherited Don Olafson's height and eyes and who had gone chemically blond at fourteen to look more Swedish. Blond and tan, Kirsten was a knockout and she knew it, but she was also bright and quick and had made a great living in wholesale food marketing before she quit to stay home with Jamie. Kirsten got the morning sickness that went on for nine straight months and ran round the clock. Joanna ached at having cancelled her planned five-day Thanksgiving weekend in Seattle. Kir had been gracious, unsurprised, but the bottom line, once again, was that she was unavailable when her daughter needed her.

"Mom, I'm fine," Kirsten soothed now. *"Really.* David is taking Jamie over to his parents' for the day and once my stomach settles down, I'll drive over for some mashed potatoes. Besides, I want you to save up all your vacation and comp time to come help me when this baby finally gets here. That's when I'll *really* need you."

As Joanna dutifully promised, she offered a silent prayer that by April, when the baby was due, the Atterminator would be rotting in jail.

The third call went faster. Her mother didn't answer her phone.

Joanna wondered idly whether her mother had spent the night out with a boyfriend. Since moving to Arizona six years ago, seventy-four-year-old Helen Davis had blossomed into a new and fascinating character, equal parts desert rat, fitness champion, entrepreneur, and vivacious widow-on-the-make. She ran a small business, had had a face lift, and performed with a bunch of other "gals" in a senior dance troupe.

Joanna left a message and took her third cup of coffee outside.

She spent much of the rest of the day outdoors. It was a gorgeous day, with a warm desert wind and a cloudless azure sky. In cutoffs and an LAPD Homicide T-shirt—OUR DAY BEGINS WHEN YOURS ENDS—she worked her way through months of accumulated yard chores. Her highly informal yard was landscaped with California natives and xeriscapic imports from arid regions of Australia and South Africa and the Mediterranean.

She thought of Francesca Goldberg as she tidied the few rosebushes, wondered who would love her garden now, if it would fall into disarray with the arrival of the next owner of the Spanish-style house. The next owner. Somebody who didn't mind living in a house where murder had been committed. Something Joanna knew that she herself could *never* do. She had spent too much time at too many crime scenes.

She thought of her father, a "plant wrangler" at Warner Brothers, as she cut back perennials, remembered the backyard jungle he had cultivated from once-ailing botanical orphans pitched by the studio for being insufficiently photogenic.

From her father Joanna had learned that even the most unattractive and gangly specimens were still miraculous. That the most magnificent plant can be a noxious weed in the wrong location. That "it's not the pedigree, it's the performance," a nod to the business of illusion in which Hal Davis had labored.

They were lessons that had transferred into police work, extrapolations she could make to the human—and inhuman—worlds where she spent her working days.

Later, she roasted a Cornish hen and ate it with a baked potato and a broiled red pepper, wrapping up the meal with a dish of velvety-rich cappuccino ice cream. She had turned down four dinner invitations, but she realized that throughout the day she had not been lonely. That except for a vague and unceasing ache at her separation from Kirsten—the same concern she had always felt when her kids ran a fever, or sprained an ankle, or broke out in spots—she was quite content to be alone.

She was beginning to turn into exactly the sort of desert rat she so cheerfully accused her mother of becoming, a crusty loner unencumbered by personal ties or responsibilities.

Somewhere down the line she, too, would probably end up in an Airstream trailer on a remote concrete slab, with a propane tank and a scattering of cacti and a single Mister Lincoln rosebush.

And she would love it.

23

Joanna was in the office by seven on Friday morning, rested and refreshed and invigorated. Spending the day with her hands in the dirt had splendidly rejuvenated her.

Several other task force members also came in, which surprised her only initially. Melody Laughlin's sketch had been in circulation for sixty hours now, had been discussed around countless Butter-balls and pumpkin pies, and somebody was certain to notice something. You couldn't hide indefinitely in Los Angeles. You could hole up for a while, of course. But people eventually noticed odd things, even in L.A.

Since the Tuesday release of the Atterminator sketch, there were jillions of hot line tips. A certain number could probably be discarded without extended further investigation; it seemed unlikely, for instance, that the Atterminator was the U.S. Congressman representing Toluca Lake. Or the maître d' at the Polo Lounge. Or even Mark Fuhrman, a possibility suggested by several callers.

Jacobs had left Wednesday afternoon for his brother-in-law's condo in Palm Desert with a little shrug and a much bigger wave. "Nothing this guy does is gonna change if I leave town," he'd told Joanna. "Hell, with that picture out, he probably won't even crawl out from under his rock for another week."

Joanna had silently disagreed. And while she wouldn't dare tempt fate by saying it out loud, she half expected to learn of another murdered attorney this morning. The Atterminator might easily register thankfulness in his own nontraditional fashion.

She knew he would be furious at having his anonymity breached. Even if Melody Laughlin's approved sketch *did* vaguely resemble that odd rendition of the Unabomber that had circulated unsuccessfully for years, the one with the hood and sunglasses and chin.

The call that changed the morning came in at nine-twenty from the Beverly Hills PD. A courtesy call, Detective Ray Wylie told Joanna, with the automatic good manners that cops in an upscale community employ as a survival tactic. He got right to the point.

"Lawrence Benton's daughter didn't show up for Thanksgiving dinner at her mom's yesterday. I'm outside the mom's house. She called first thing this morning. Lucy Lanier, her name is. Says she knows you."

Lucy Lanier. Good God. "Of course I know her," Joanna answered, her mind racing to images of Larry's and Lucy's daughter, Reggie. The unlikely actress. A shadowy, pale brunette with a sad air and limpid brown eyes. Joanna had spoken with Reggie Benton twice, once at her mother's house and again at her own apartment. The girl had impressed her as being more than a little flaky, someone who actually *would* be capable of completely forgetting both Thanksgiving and her mother.

"Has Lucy checked Reggie's apartment?" Joanna asked.

"Not yet," Wylie said, "but there's no answer to the phone. We asked L.A. Sheriff's to go by and sit on it. They say her car's there."

Ah yes. That hot little black Italian sports car that Larry Benton had popped for. As he had, it seemed, paid all his daughter's expenses. Reggie Benton had been in a couple of student films, but she had finally admitted to having no TV or movie credits whatsoever.

"Have they talked to the neighbors at her apartment building?" Joanna could see this blooming as another jurisdictional nightmare, too many cops from too many places asking too many wrong questions.

Wylie's answer came as a relief. "Soon as I realized what we might have here, I pretty much put it all on hold, waiting to talk to you."

Eighteen minutes later, Joanna stood on a quiet West Hollywood street lined with tightly spaced small apartment buildings. Reggie Benton's second-floor flat was in a three-story building with a dozen units, four to a floor, each entered through a small central hallway with an elevator and staircase. Nice but not ostentatious. Anonymous. Parking beneath the building, with a keyed security gate.

Beside Joanna languished Detective Ray Wylie, who had turned out to be in his late thirties, tall and trim and handsome. Beverly Hills rarely hired ugly cops.

A man from the property management office was anxiously shifting his weight nearby, nervously fingering a key. He wore gray sweats and had arrived by bicycle.

"Let's keep this squeaky clean," Joanna told everybody as they rode the elevator. "We check to see if she's in there and if she isn't, we get a warrant before we do anything else." When they exited the elevator, the property manager used his master key to unlock the door and then stepped back into the hall.

The apartment was dark, and though the air seemed a little stale, it passed the immediate sniff test: the scent was pine potpourri, not decomposing human. So far, so good. Joanna and a just-arrived detective from L.A. Sheriff's slipped on gloves and did a fast walk-through, touching as little as possible, checking only places large enough to hold a young woman's body.

They came up empty.

Reggie Benton's apartment was neat and clean and uninhabited.

Dave Austin from Robbery–Homicide arrived next, further crowding the tiny central corridor. Joanna sent him with the guy from L.A. Sheriff's to get a search warrant and went to talk to Lucy Lanier.

On the short drive to Beverly Hills, she used her cell phone to track down Al Jacobs out in the desert. He'd just come in from an early-morning round of golf and he wasn't happy to hear from her.

"You *really* think this has anything to do with her father's murder, Davis? Sounds to me like just another thoughtless kid, not that either of us would have any experience with that." Jacobs's tone was slightly tinged with bitterness. His twenty-seven-year-old son was back living at home again, another business wiped out and another marriage gone bust. One more reason Jacobs had been so looking forward to his escape to Palm Springs.

Joanna hesitated. "I don't know, Al. It just feels weird to me. And I didn't like the vibes in that apartment. It was neat before when I was there but…I don't know. It felt almost *too* perfect. But it's not worth you coming in yet. Stay put, enjoy yourself. Anything turns up, you'll be the first to know."

"That," Al Jacobs grumbled, "is *exactly* what I'm afraid of."

Joanna had spoken to a lot of distraught mothers in the course of her career, had told far too many of them that their sons or daughters wouldn't be coming home ever again. There was a look she'd come to recognize in many of these women, the ones who were still waiting anxiously, but knew instinctively that when word came, it would not be good.

Lucy Lanier had that look today.

"I'm so scared," she told Joanna, wringing her hands helplessly. "If anything's happened to Reggie. . ."

Joanna moved to hug the trembling woman, held her for several endless moments as she felt the slender body shake.

Lucy Lanier was again dressed monochromatically, today in

beige with her customary melange of textures. Every time Joanna had seen her, the woman wore neutral shades, with an occasional accent in some bold, vibrant hue: turquoise, hot pink, tangerine. It seemed to be a kind of upscale interior decorator's uniform. Neutrally dressed, Lucy Lanier could blend effortlessly into any environment. Today there was no color accent.

"I just know something's happened to Reggie," Lucy told Joanna again. She had barely acknowledged Detective Ray Wylie, who had been waiting outside in his car when Joanna arrived. Wylie's goal seemed to be to extricate himself from this mess ASAP.

Lucy's affable husband, Ben, came out of the kitchen, carrying a mug of coffee. He seemed deeply disturbed as he offered a concerned nod to Joanna and a distracted handshake to Ray Wylie. Wylie took Ben Lanier off to the kitchen while Joanna and Lucy adjourned to the conservatory. Different orchids bloomed today, including a pink cymbidium with a breathtaking flower spike over two feet long.

"Something terrible has happened," Lucy repeated. "I just know it. I can *feel* it."

"Has she seemed worried lately? Different? Not herself?" Joanna made the questions sound casual, offhand. She wanted Lucy to tell the story her own way. Leading questions closed too many doors.

"How could I tell? It's been such a nightmarish month. The boys can't sleep and we're still *hounded* by those media people—" she shook her head, suddenly wide-eyed "—and they'll all be *back* again, now, won't they? Shit!" She shook her head, picked up one of the natural, undyed cotton pillows from the teak settee, began turning it. Over and over and over. "Was she different? We're *all* different than we were before Larry was killed."

Lucy Lanier wore her silver-blond hair in an expensive tangle. Now she set aside the pillow and began nervously stretching out and releasing the long, thin curls that dripped over her forehead. Strands of hair bounced like coiled metallic springs in the diffuse light.

"Have you spent much time at her apartment?"

Lucy shook her head. "Not since I decorated it. I wanted to encourage her independence." Suddenly she crumpled into tears. "I should never have let her leave home, no matter what she wanted."

"It's hard letting them go," Joanna commiserated. This she knew from her heart. "Does Reggie still keep things here?"

Lucy shook her head. "I haven't redone her room yet, but she pretty much stripped it clean. She's been living on her own two years now. Would it help to see her room?"

"I don't know," Joanna admitted. "But it might. If you don't mind."

But Lucy Lanier was right. Any signs of individuality that might have once been displayed in Reggie Benton's room were long gone. Joanna spent ten minutes checking under and behind drawers, beneath the mattress, places a teenage girl might hide pictures or dope or a diary. She found nothing, and no signs that anything had ever been hidden.

Another half hour's questioning only made it obvious how little Lucy knew about the details of her daughter's current life. "I promised her I'd continue her allowance at the same level for at least another year. Larry was *so* adamant that she shouldn't have to take some menial job." Lucy mimicked her late ex-husband, as she had a month earlier. "'No daughter of mine will *ever* wait tables.'"

Lucy had no clues about Reggie's current friends, boyfriends, leisure activities or hobbies, though she did report that the girl was a staunch long-term vegetarian. Her daughter enjoyed nature hikes, music, movies, and the beach.

Which sounded, Joanna decided as she took her leave, more like an ad in the personals than a description of a twenty-year-old individual.

Things got more interesting once they had the search warrant and brought a criminalist into Reggie Benton's apartment.

In this impersonal neighborhood, people kept to themselves. None of the neighbors had seen Reggie for at least a week, and none remembered ever seeing visitors.

The only messages on her answering machine were from her mother. Her refrigerator held a selection of now-slimy sprouts, carrots sprouting thick white hairs, yellowed broccoli, and spoiled acidophilus milk. There was no sign of the backpack she carried in lieu of a purse, or of any of the items she might have carried in it: checkbook, address book, cell phone, wallet, car keys. Her toothbrush, makeup, and contact lens accessories were gone. There were condoms in a bathroom drawer.

The windows were all closed and locked, the curtains all fully drawn. A spindly plant had keeled over limply in a ceramic pot of bone-dry dirt. The VCR was empty. In a drawer of her dresser they found a thick stack of identical black-and-white 8x10 glossy photos, the kind actors take to auditions. The composite had four separate poses in two changes of clothing, but the images all carried the same air of haunted melancholy.

Joanna smashed a fist on the perfect beechwood kitchen table. Dammit, why hadn't she paid more attention to the girl? Pushed harder during the two earlier interviews? The task force now was investigating five possible murders, but it was Larry Benton's death that had brought Joanna to this table. Had Reggie seen something? Known something? Suspected something?

All day Joanna had been flogging herself, castigation for sins of omission. Had she screwed up by not recognizing the importance of Reggie Benton? *An error only becomes a mistake if you don't correct it*, Joanna's father had always maintained.

Paying insufficient attention to Reggie Benton seemed to have become a mistake.

A calendar hanging in the kitchen had only a few notations. On Thanksgiving, it read: "Mom." Back on the 12th, it noted: "Dentist, 11." And on Monday, November 24th, was a cryptic note: "AA 9A."

All of which would have been interesting but inconclusive except for one detail. One detail that made everything look very different indeed.

There were no fingerprints in the apartment.

None.

Anywhere.

24

Ace had managed, through judicious examination of various obscure databases, to gain two key addresses he wished to investigate further.

Unfortunately, they were at opposite ends of the sprawling Los Angeles basin. Getting to either one would take the better part of an hour, even without traffic tie-ups. He decided to wait until Saturday morning to choose which to explore first.

Saturday dawned cool and slightly foggy, the kind of day that could lead to rain but probably wouldn't. He dressed in jeans, sweatshirt, and baseball cap, then flipped a coin. Heads he'd go west, tails he'd go east. The nickel landed with Monticello facing up.

He took Mrs. Lancaster's car, as she had requested on Thanksgiving Day when he joined half a dozen tenants for their customary turkey potluck. Mrs. Lancaster couldn't bear to give up her sturdy old blue Chrysler, a car she firmly believed would freeze up into a solid block of rust if not exercised on a regular basis. Since her eyesight was failing rapidly, information she avoided sharing with the DMV, she increasingly relied on Ace to drive the car for her.

He reached his destination in just over forty-five minutes. The complex was an older one, close enough to the freeway so that even thick shrubbery around the buildings couldn't entirely muffle the continuous roar of tens of thousands of vehicles passing by daily. The residents would be oblivious to the white noise, he knew, likening it to surf if they mentioned it at all. But it wasn't surf. Even in winter, the thick, corporeal air seemed to twine through trees and bushes like so much noxious Spanish moss. And on a day like today, when the air was already heavy and moist, it was almost unbearable.

He parked near a small cluster of buildings with a pool and tennis courts and a community center. Inside he visited the men's room, then read notices on the bulletin board, and struck up a casual conversation with a guy trying unsuccessfully to start a fire of pressed-wood logs in a big fieldstone fireplace. Once Ace located the flue and opened it, things went much more smoothly. From the incompetent fire-starter he learned that several units in the complex were currently on the market, though the fellow seemed uncertain whether Ace's aging aunt would find the place to her liking, the residents being mostly younger. On the plus side, the fire-starter added, children were discouraged.

Ace took his leave and meandered around the grounds, stopped briefly to watch a spirited tennis match, then strolled in the general direction of the unit he was seeking. But before he could reach it, a Ford Taurus came squealing around a corner. He leapt out of the way and realized, with a sudden frisson of delight and terror, that he had almost been mowed down by State Bar Chief Trial Counsel Bonita Blevins. Well, *what* a coinkydink.

Impulsively, he abandoned his plans to case Blevins's unit and hurried back to Mrs. Lancaster's car, jumped in, and raced after the Taurus, which was merging onto the San Bernardino Freeway by the time he caught up with it.

She was easy to follow. She moved over into the number-one lane and stayed there at a steady sixty-three miles an hour, ignoring faster vehicles that came up behind her, hovered on her bumper, and then irritably passed to the right. He gave her plenty of room and stayed two lanes to the right. She negotiated the downtown interchanges smoothly, then cut back on the Pasadena, which surprised him. He'd been expecting her to go to her office.

Instead, she drove into Pasadena, where crowds were congregating in the streets. And then Ace realized, with genuine shock, just where she was heading, what was happening today. When Blevins parked, so did he. He changed baseball caps, slipped into a navy UCLA nylon windbreaker, and went to find his quarry.

Bonita Blevins had come to the Doo-Dah Parade.

The Doo-Dah Parade had begun as a counter-event, a gentle mockery of the Rose Bowl Parade that passed on this very route every New Year's Day. Over time, however, Doo-Dah had become its own proud entity, nobody's counter-anything, a conglomerate of the loopy and bizarre. It was, in a sense, the quintessential L.A.

event. Ace had attended once long ago, finding it rather silly, not considering it really worth his time.

He followed now as Bonita Blevins, dressed in a black, straight-skirted suit with a severe white blouse and low black heels, joined a group of similarly clad professionals. She apologized profusely for her tardiness. Milling about like a colony of penguins, several dozen of them waited, each carrying an attaché case.

He watched them move into formation and run through a few fast warm-up maneuvers. Bonita Blevins—that humorless, self-righteous priss who so irritated him every time she opened her whiny yap on TV—Bonita Blevins was a member of the Precision Briefcase Drill Team. Who *ever* woulda thunk it?

He retreated into the crowd, finding anonymity easily in this collection of slumming yuppies. The Briefcase Drill Team stopped directly in front of him: presenting cases, right-facing, left-facing, lifting cases, about-facing. Making regular jackasses of themselves, though the crowd seemed to love it. They flung tortillas through the air with abandon, a pastime he couldn't begin to understand.

Several other goofball groups passed, and then Ace felt his heart skip a beat as a cluster of approaching marchers caught his eye. He froze, scarcely able to breathe.

Carrying various instruments of mayhem—giant water pistols, phony swords, plastic cudgels, even a couple of chain saws—they wore dark shorts and white shirts and carried clipboards.

The banner under which they marched was labeled:

ATTERMINATOR TRAINING SCHOOL.

25

The "AA 9A" notation on Reggie Benton's calendar glowed like roadhouse neon, a veritable taunt. The letters were written in tidy black ballpoint, probably by the designer pen hanging on a golden cord beside the calendar, which featured black-and-white stills from classic films. The designer pen had been wiped clean.

Wiped clean.

What was going on here? And what, if anything, did it have to do with the hot tub electrocution of the girl's father seven weeks earlier?

AA. The best-known AA in Los Angeles was, of course, Alcoholics Anonymous, and there seemed no reason not to check the obvious first. Nobody had characterized Reggie as an alcoholic or even much of a drinker, despite several unopened bottles of French Bordeaux in her pantry. But her father had been a juicer of some renown, and if she saw herself heading down the same path, she might have caught herself early. A lot of *very* young people were in twelve-step programs these days.

So Joanna called downtown and set Frank Moses to locating all the AA meetings held around L.A. on Monday mornings at nine. She was willing to bet there were a gazillion. And penetrating the curtain of anonymity would present a definite initial challenge.

Joanna maintained a healthy respect for twelve-step programs, which had turned around the lives of several people she cared about deeply, but she'd gotten a little sick of them over her past few years in West L.A. They were *so* ubiquitous, so terribly *chic*, often seeming to feature a defiant reverse snobbery—not whose recovery was most exemplary, but who had been the baddest of the bad *before*. Furthermore, L.A. offered twelve-step programs for a bewildering array of interrelated addictions and dependencies. Two years ago, Joanna had investigated a killing that arose out of a relationship initiated at a group for alcoholic lesbian incest survivors.

And yet, nobody had founded Cigars Anonymous, a program she considered desperately overdue.

Lucy Lanier seemed as certain as a mother ever can be that her daughter was not a substance abuser. Reggie liked a little wine now and then, Lucy conceded, and in her early teen years she had flirted briefly with bulimia, a problem that pretty much cured itself once her parents divorced. But that was it.

So if it wasn't Alcoholics Anonymous, what then was AA?

Abigail Adams? Ace Auto? Absolute Asshole?

American Airlines was the next obvious answer, and a fast call to the airline's 800 number determined that American flight #2 left LAX daily at nine A.M., headed nonstop for JFK in New York.

Bingo.

Joanna hung up, got more coffee, and considered. Had Reggie Benton gone to New York without telling anyone, or at least without telling her mother? If so, why? And did it really matter? A twenty-year-old with ample personal funds could easily make such a trip, and it wouldn't be anybody's business but her own. Given the media circus attached to her father's death, a desire to get away was even more understandable.

Except, of course, that a twenty-year-old anxious to get away for a while wasn't likely to bother wiping every single fingerprint out of her apartment before she got on the Super Shuttle. Somebody had been in Reggie Benton's apartment after she left it, somebody anxious to obliterate any traces of outside identities. Why? Because he or she had spent a lot of time there and couldn't remember just exactly what had been touched? Or was it to remove traces of somebody else, somebody who might be publicly compromised by association with the aspiring actress? This was, after all, Hollywood.

She had Dave Austin follow up on American Airlines flight #2 and took another stab at reaching a live human in the medical examiner's office. The L.A. Coroner's office had found time to put together a mail-order catalogue—a *mail-order catalogue*, for Chrissakes, like Brookstone or Land's End—of beach towels and T-shirts and toe tags. Unfortunately, they still hadn't quite gotten the knack of swiftly determining unusual causes of death. Nine days after the discovery of Francesca Goldberg's body, all they really knew was that she'd been jolted in the back of the neck by a stun gun. That pruning shears had been thrust into her throat after she was already dead.

And, of course, that she *was* dead.

By sunset Saturday, Dave Austin had traced Reggie Benton to New York.

A round-trip ticket in the name of Gina Benton had been

reserved by telephone on November 19th and paid for in cash at the airport the following day. On Monday, November 24th, a woman had shown acceptable identification, boarded American flight #2, and been seated in seat 17A. She had checked no luggage. The flight made no stops, so she presumably disembarked with the other passengers upon arrival in New York at 5:28 P.M. The flight was seventeen minutes late.

Gina Benton was scheduled to return on flight #1 from JFK on Monday, December 1st, also departing at nine A.M. and arriving nonstop in Los Angeles at 12:08 P.M.

Joanna drove to Beverly Hills and told Lucy Lanier what they'd found out.

Lucy didn't buy it. "Reggie doesn't know anybody in New York," she protested. She looked drained by the events of the past two days. "And she wouldn't take a trip like that without telling me. I don't think she's ever gone *anywhere* by herself. Furthermore, that girl doesn't pay cash for anything. I've seen her charge a tube of toothpaste."

All legitimate, even compelling arguments. Joanna didn't point out that Reggie's Visa and MasterCard accounts had shown no activity since Thursday, November 20th, when she charged $37.21 at Trader Joe's on Santa Monica Boulevard.

"Well, *somebody* took that flight," Joanna pointed out, "and used Reggie's name to do it. And if it *wasn't* Reggie, we need even more to know who it was. We need to find her friends, Lucy."

But they'd been through all this before, and Lucy continued to be chagrined that she was so little help in the friends department. She hadn't really known who her daughter's friends were since Reggie had moved out two years earlier. At Joanna's direction, she'd already checked with a couple of the girls Reggie used to hang with in high school, but they all claimed not to have heard from her in ages.

"Maybe somebody from Reggie's acting class?" Lucy suggested hopefully.

Which would have been nice, except they had no idea who was in that class. Lucy knew only the name of the teacher, a one-time semi-celebrity with a vaguely familiar name, and *her* phone message coyly announced that she was away for an amorous weekend. The storefront studio to which Lucy Lanier's large monthly checks were mailed was dark.

"Look," Joanna suggested, when they had reached what seemed to be a total impasse, "let's just keep our fingers crossed that Reggie's planning to be on that return flight on Monday. Somebody from NYPD will meet her at the airport when she shows up, and they'll call us before she gets on the plane." It sounded like a cheerful enough scenario, Joanna thought. Except that she didn't believe a word of it, and she was pretty sure Lucy didn't either. "Meanwhile, unless you want to take this public, there isn't much else we can do."

"We've managed to keep it quiet so far," Lucy answered with a sigh. "But if I have to go public, I will. What do *you* think? Would it help to make a public appeal? I know that's what Larry would have done. And *he* would have done it this morning."

Joanna felt torn. As a mother, her instincts told her to go public. Way public. Slap up the billboards, hire the skywriters. HAVE YOU SEEN REGGIE BENTON? As a cop, her experience told her that publicity right now would probably only muddy the waters, though there was always the possibility that it would flush a scarlet-cheeked Reggie from some Manhattan love nest. Having been one herself, Joanna had no illusions about the innocence of twenty-year-old southern California girls.

As for what Larry would have done, Lucy's other consideration, that struck Joanna as totally irrelevant. The kinds of things that Larry did seemed to have gotten him killed.

The real answer was probably a lot simpler, way too simple. And it was nothing that a mother would want to hear.

"If Reggie doesn't turn up at the airport Monday morning," Joanna said gently, "then we'll announce her as a missing person. And we'll launch a full, very public investigation. Can you wait another thirty-six hours?"

"I suppose," Lucy Lanier answered, her voice flat and deadened, her eyes lifeless.

• • •

Monday morning came and Reggie Benton didn't board American flight #1 at JFK. Nor did anybody else use her ticket.

With Lucy's guidance, Joanna had selected a picture from Reggie's acting composite, the one that looked most like her, with a poignant expression suggesting somebody'd just run over her pet schnauzer. That photo was released when the police chief and mayor—who were getting pretty good at their tandem announcement act—told the world at a hastily called mid-morning press conference that recently murdered attorney Lawrence Benton's daughter was missing.

Dave Austin was pegged to head the Reggie investigation, and more cops were assigned to the case. Detectives checked with her former teachers at Beverly Hills High School, and with classmates from yoga and acting and dance classes.

Nobody knew anything.

Joanna watched Lee Walters chomp into an enormous burrito with entirely unladylike gusto. Lee pumped iron and ate like a stevedore.

The café at the entrance to Olvera Street was remarkably quiet at one-fifteen on Tuesday. Normally this area near downtown that featured the oldest buildings in Los Angeles—the original pueblo from the era of Spanish colonization—was clogged with tourists. But today Joanna saw only one Japanese tour group, and a mere smattering of the snowbirds who normally flocked south and west for mild L.A. winters. Was the Atterminator discouraging tourism? Probably not, though she'd be willing to bet lawyers weren't making many impulse trips to southern California this season. Oh, darn.

"God, I was hungry," Lee announced with a satisfied smile and a little burp. She had practically inhaled the burrito. "The colposcopy this week or next?"

"A week from Thursday." Joanna shook her head. "You know, I've really tried not to dwell on it, and God knows we're busy, which helps. And I try to be positive when I *do* think of it." She hesitated. "But optimism doesn't come easily to me."

"Of course not. You're a cop. When you're geared for the worst, it can't take you by surprise...."

"And anything better seems like a bonus," Joanna finished.

"Exactly. So, if you don't want to talk about that, how about giving me the hot skinny from the hallowed halls of the task force."

"Hallowed indeed. Actually, our only real news is the toxi report on Francesca Goldberg. And you already know about that."

"Only through multiple hearsay. Tell me again. I always like a good poison story."

"I know. You don't get that many of them anymore. Hell, there were only half a dozen poisonings in the entire *country* last year that qualified as homicides."

Lee shook her head. "Hard to believe it. You watch TV, you'd think it happened eight, ten times a week."

"Not practical. Why bother with complicated chemistry when you've probably already got an AK-47? So what we have is poisoning, an extremely rare method of murder, and *two* victims killed by two *different* esoteric poisons. Botulism for Counselor Burke and now nicotine sulfate for Francesca Goldberg."

"Nicotine sulfate," Lee said thoughtfully. "That sounds like something out of a British murder mystery. Like hemlock in the crumpets at the parsonage." She pushed aside the wreckage of her burrito and grinned as she lit a cigarette. "Well, they always did say tobacco was a killer."

"Actually, I've learned in the last few hours that if you soak enough cigarettes, you *can* end up with a kind of tea that will probably kill you."

"But it would sure taste like shit."

Joanna turned her palms upward. "I guess. I ain't trying it. But that's not what this was anyway. This was an insecticide. Just like the nicotine for spraying roses they always have in the gardener's shed in those Miss Marple stories. And I'm sure I don't have to remind you that Francesca was noted for her roses."

"Did it come from Goldberg's house? Can they tell?"

Joanna shook her head. "Nothing on the premises contains nicotine and her gardener says there never has been. He uses a lot of poisons, but not that one. As far as I can tell, nobody much uses nicotine-based garden poisons anymore."

"How would—"

"Probably skin absorption. It's fast. They still have the body, so now they're checking it again."

Lee frowned. "I hope they put her away somewhere." The county morgue was legendarily overcrowded, bodies stacked like seasoning cordwood.

"Yeah. I insisted."

Lee rubbed her chin. "So you've got botulism from badly canned food—"

"Or from something."

"What else is there? Isn't bad canning pretty much a given?"

"Not according to my new buddies at the Centers for Disease Control," Joanna answered. "Turns out there are all kinds of ways you can get botulism. Food-borne is the most common, though there aren't nearly the number of incidents of botulism from home-canned foods that there used to be."

"Well, of course not. Nobody cans their own food anymore. That's why God made Del Monte."

"Maybe not here, people don't can, but they sure do it in the country. When I lived in Minnesota, people had fruit cellars just loaded with home-canned stuff. Don's mother had a whole wall of blue ribbons from the county fair. Piccalilli was her specialty."

Lee wasn't interested in Olga Olafson's famous piccalilli. "So if not canning, what?"

"Well, there's something called wound botulism, as in a wound getting infected, and that's probably pretty unpleasant because botulism has some really nasty close relatives. Gas gangrene, for one, and tetanus. Infant botulism is usually caused by babies eating *honey*, if you can believe it. Talk about having natural goodness turn on you. And then they have a whole vague category of botulism that they just can't explain. Cases that seem utterly spontaneous. Somehow or another the spores move into your guts and colonize."

"Colonize?" Lee's hand crept to her abdomen.

Joanna nodded. "All these diseases are caused by anaerobic spores that can exist for long periods of time, waiting for just the right warm, dark place to set up shop. It's a nasty, nasty family."

"So what does that tell you about your killer? That he's inept at canning and out of date on rose poisons?"

Joanna laughed. "That sounds like a description of Norman Bates's mother. Or somebody who works at a midwestern garden center and comes to southern California when the place closes for the winter." She nodded toward a septuagenarian couple in matching kelly green windbreakers, double-knit brown pants, sturdy white sneakers, and baseball caps that read CORNHUSKERS. "Like those Nebraskans over there."

Lee furrowed her brow. "Why do you say a *midwestern* garden center? What about one right here?"

"Actually, I guess it's 'cause I was just thinking about northern Minnesota. There was a place like that in the town where we lived, Pine River Falls. Pesticides and rosebushes and lawn rollers and canning kettles all under one roof, with a farm stand that sold fresh corn in season." She grimaced. "The season was about two weeks long."

"You checking places like Home Depot?"

Joanna nodded. "Yeah. There's a bunch of guys from Metro going out with the suspect sketch. We always knew there was a chance our guy worked someplace like that, just 'cause of the odd range of skills he's got. But without a picture, there wasn't any real way to check it. There's too much turnover in those places."

"You could get lucky."

"He could walk into Parker Center and confess, too. But I'm not holding my breath." She finished her Coke. "Actually, something else interesting has turned up. You know how they've been using botulism therapy in cosmetic surgery?"

Lee narrowed her eyes. "Yeah, right. Is that part of the strychnine diet?"

"No, it's for real. You remember that stalking case last year in Brentwood? The washed-up actress stalking the washed-up actor?" It had been a study in pathos, all around, with a lot of media play.

"Oh, yeah. That was yours?"

"No, but it was West L.A.'s and I paid pretty close attention. I had a big crush on him when I was a teenager. Anyway, the washed-up actor had been having botulism injections to cure his wrinkles. That's where he was coming from the day she turned up naked in the front seat of his car. The dermatologist's office. He'd just had botulism injected into his frown lines."

Lee shivered. *"Men* do this?"

"They do. Mostly it's women, but more guys than you'd think. Anyway. The point is, these doctors have the stuff in their offices. On hand, readily available whenever Mrs. Too-Much-Money struts in to get her forehead done. It's called Botox. We looked back into burglaries of medical facilities that keep Botox on hand— doctors' offices, hospitals, and the like. And guess what?"

"I'm on the edge of my chair," Lee said, leaning back deliberately.

"Last March there was a burglary in a dermatology office in Beverly Hills. The security system was dismantled very professionally to make the entrance. A bunch of stuff was taken, including various sedatives and all the Botox in the office."

"How come these guys didn't come forward when the Burke death was first broken?"

Joanna frowned. "They *say* that it never occurred to them. But Beverly Hills thinks the original police report was fudged, that a lot of drugs were stolen that the doctors didn't want to admit they had in the first place. And that consequently they didn't want to remind anybody that anything had happened at all."

"Makes sense to me. You think your guy stole this stuff from the doctor's office? How would he know it's there?"

"Once you know it's used for cosmetic medical work, you can let your fingers do the walking. Call dermatologists and plastic surgeons in Beverly Hills and West L.A. Read the ads in the back of *Los Angeles* magazine. But I'll tell you, Lee, what *really* interests me is that this happened way back in March. Our boy has spent a long time getting ready."

"What's he doing with the rest of the stuff he stole?"

Joanna shrugged. "No way of knowing. He doesn't seem to have used any of it on anybody. At least not that we know. Maybe he's got some habits of his own. Jacobs is gonna go lean on the docs, see if they'll give up what actually got taken."

"They won't."

"I agree."

"So. You still haven't told me what they *do* with this botulism toxin that people are paying for. I assume they're paying?"

"Big-time. It's all based on the way that botulism functions as a poison. It's a paralytic that freezes up muscles. And it also has some other, more respectable medical applications."

Lee frowned. "Such as?"

"Such as, in some voice disorders where the larynx is all twitchy, it freezes that twitching so the person can talk properly again. They use it sometimes for cerebral palsy and to stop muscle tics, like if your eyebrow won't quit twitching. But if you just want it to make you *look* good, it's injected directly into the area that's wrinkled, and it smooths those little wrinkles right out."

Lee winced, bringing her fingers to cover her mouth—an area which, if she were a West Side matron, she would definitely be considering for botulism therapy.

"But the kicker," Joanna continued, "is that it's only a temporary fix. No wonder the docs love it. If you like the results, you have to keep doing it, over and over and over. A single treatment lasts maybe three to six months."

"Yeah," Lee added, "although think what you'd save on facials."

26

Ace entered the mid-Wilshire office building through the parking garage in the late afternoon of Tuesday, December 2nd, slipping inside when the guard ran back to check on a valet-parked car. He carried a compact, efficiently packed toolbox.

Outfitted as a telephone repairman, he went directly to the tiny room that housed the building's phone cables in the basement, off the parking garage. It took only a moment to glove up and pick the lock. Then he slipped inside, relocked the door, and wedged a towel beneath it to block any light or shadows he might inadvertently create. The odds of a bona fide telephone service person showing up in the remaining two hours of the business day were too slight to worry about.

Except, of course, that worrying about *everything* had made it possible for the Legal Resolution Program to move so smoothly toward its conclusion.

He settled in a corner, made himself as comfortable as possible, and waited. He was good at waiting, at playing mental games to keep himself alert. But today he had an additional task: to plan a relatively spontaneous—but, he believed, potentially satisfying— addition to his plans for the week.

Yesterday morning he had watched the mayor and police chief announce the mysterious disappearance of Reggie Benton, with Detective Joanna Davis at their side.

He had taken the opportunity, an opportunity that seemed to have been personally delivered to him by winged messenger, to drive into the western reaches of the San Fernando Valley to check out the address he had ferreted out for Detective Davis.

The odd stone structure was wacky by almost any standard. Joanna Davis apparently lived alone, and she had very little furniture, very little food—very little, indeed, to suggest much serious habitation at all. In a dark and cozy little bedroom, he checked out a blond art deco armoire filled with expensive clothing. He couldn't imagine how she afforded such a wardrobe on a police salary; was she somehow on the take? He glanced only briefly at a junk-filled storage room, and spent most of his time on the premises in her intriguing living area.

It seemed to be all toys. A pinball machine, a large-screen television, a stair-stepping machine, a rowing machine.

And a jukebox.

A jukebox with "Lawyers, Guns and Money" in the A-1 slot.

Even as he had first gazed upon the jukebox, Ace had felt a plan begin furiously percolating in the back of his brain. The only remaining question was when to do it.

Shortly after two A.M., Ace disconnected the phone lines to the entire building and crept up the stairway from the basement to the fourth floor, where the Law Offices of Lorenzo J. Taft were located. He hugged the wall, stopped frequently to listen for unexpected noises, touched nothing even though his hands were safely encased in gloves.

He had watched the building for a week of nights back in September, had even spent part of a night inside once, accustoming himself to the building's circadian rhythms. Lorenzo J. Taft owned the building and his law offices took up the entire fourth floor. The lower floors were occupied by various small businesses, mostly minority-owned: accountants, a temporary secretarial service, a court reporting service, a travel agency. All but Taft's law offices emptied promptly at the end of the standard working day and the night staff was skeletal: a parking attendant until seven, a security service that swung by and checked the entrances and exits several times a night, no on-site security guards. Two cleaning people did the entire building, and they arrived promptly at nine, staying till around three-thirty or four A.M.

Ace couldn't have designed the situation better himself.

He was pleased to see that he wasn't even the tiniest bit out of breath when he reached the fourth floor. Cautiously he peeked out of the door from the stairwell and located the cleaning service cart at the far end of the hall, outside the ladies' room.

Perfect.

Up at the front of the building, at the opposite end of the hall, the door to Taft's private office was closed. According to Ace's calculations, Taft was the only occupant remaining at work in the entire building. His Cadillac Seville was the only car still in the downstairs garage. Taft employed two younger attorneys, several secretaries, and a raft of paralegals, but they all generally cleared out by nine.

Taft himself often remained much later. As media profiles always noted, he functioned on five hours of sleep a night, which had advanced his career but cost him two marriages. He was currently between wives, and had recently been photographed at the NAACP Image Awards escorting last year's February Playmate, an ebony stunner.

Ace slipped soundlessly up the hall, his rubber soles silent on the flashy white marble floors. Taft had a thing about marble; the building was full of it. Ace paused outside the open door to the ladies' room and heard the cleaning lady softly humming some tune he didn't recognize.

Action.

He pulled the length of nylon stocking down over his face and entered the rest room. She had her back to him, a stout black lady in a shapeless blue uniform dress bent over inside a stall, emptying a little trash bin. She wore Walkman headphones and continued humming, oblivious to his presence.

He gave her a fast zap in the ass with the stun gun and watched her begin to crumple into the stall. He reached down and broke the fall before she could actually crash, then pulled her out into the center of the floor. Here in the Ladies', the marble was pink. He gagged her tightly with a pair of pantyhose and carefully secured a fabric bag over her head. Next he bound her hands and feet with duct tape, anchoring her feet around one of the stall supports.

When he was finished, he issued a guttural warning that if she moved he would kill her. Then he gave her another quick jolt and slithered cautiously into the hallway.

On his way up from the basement, he had opened the lobby door just far enough to determine that the other cleaner was running a waxing machine on the first floor. No telling when he might come looking for his partner, and if he showed up too soon, things could become messy.

Speed was critical.

Ace approached Taft's inner sanctum through the office of his secretary, a woman who had been with him since he first relocated to L.A. from Chicago. There was no window here, but the cubicle was spacious, full of neatly arranged piles of paper and elaborate silk plants, many in hanging baskets.

He stopped and took a deep breath. This next part would be the trickiest.

A door to Taft's office opened into the secretary's office. Ace stopped for a moment to place a few drops of lubricant on each of the hinges. Then, standing to the side, he slowly and carefully turned the knob, anxiously listening for creaks or noises.

The knob turned silently. So far, so good. He inched the door open enough to get a foothold, then abruptly kicked it all the way back and leaped through the doorway, landing like a commando with the gun in both hands.

Taft was a good twenty feet across the room in a big leather chair by the window, working at a wooden table strewn with papers. His shaved head gleamed as it reflected rays from a track light aimed at one of a dozen vivid pieces of contemporary African-American art hanging on the interior walls. It was a very *shiny* room.

Astonishingly, Taft was fully dressed, hadn't even loosened his tie or removed the natty, broad-shouldered jacket from his olive-green suit. When Ace exploded into the room, Taft dropped the papers he was holding and half rose from the chair. His right hand shot toward a phone on the table beside him.

"Freeze, asshole!" Ace commanded, in the same Germanic tone he had used on the cleaning lady.

Taft froze.

"Back in the chair," Ace commanded. "Hands way up high." *Vay* up high, he pronounced it.

Taft dutifully eased back into the chair, but he sat tensed, ready to spring.

Ace approached cautiously, moving lightly on the balls of his feet, glancing swiftly around the room to assure himself it was empty. He was fully prepared to shoot the lawyer, but he hoped to avoid the noise, the mess, and the inconvenience.

He hugged the wall until he reached the window, then swiftly twisted the vertical blinds closed. The chance of anybody watching at this hour was remote, but Taft's office overlooked Wilshire Boulevard and anything was possible.

"Hey, man," Taft began, his voice soft, crooning. "You want money, I got ten grand in the safe. Small bills, unmarked. Emergency money. It's all yours, man." He sounded friendly, confident that something could be worked out. A real hustler.

Ace was six feet away from the lawyer now, standing behind him. He switched the gun to his left hand and pulled the stun gun from his pocket.

He saw Lorenzo J. Taft's body stiffen, realized in a heartbeat that the lawyer could see him in the reflection off the black marble wall.

Taft's eyes widened in recognition and fear. This guy was a criminal lawyer, down in the trenches, defending his people against police brutality. He knew what a stun gun looked like, even in a dim reflection. Earlier subjects, practitioners in more rarefied fields of the law, hadn't a clue. The Goldberg bitch might have, but she never saw what hit her.

"Aw, *shit!*" the lawyer muttered. Then he suddenly lunged from the chair.

But Ace was right behind him. He got him in the shoulder with the stun gun even as the lawyer feinted to the left. Lorenzo J. Taft fell to the marble floor with a resounding thud, landing with his head on a thick area rug. He lay on his right side, twitching from the electric shock, curled in a semi-fetal position. His eyes bulged as he watched Ace slip both weapons into the deep pockets of his jacket and remove a small vial.

Ace carefully poured five drops from the vial into Taft's left ear and began undressing the lawyer.

Then he crossed the room and retrieved the toolbox he had left in the secretarial office. He swiftly removed various items and began dressing and positioning Lorenzo J. Taft. Set decoration time. Midway through the task, the lawyer stopped breathing with a loud gagging noise.

Literally croaked.

Five minutes later Ace contentedly surveyed his handiwork, gathered his materials, and slipped back down the stairs.

27

Joanna looked down at the dead attorney with a feeling of satisfaction that appalled her.

She was a cop, a homicide detective, sworn to uphold the law, to protect and serve. To get the bad guys and all that bullshit. Bullshit she *believed* in. Her job required—no, demanded—that she feel outrage any time a human life was taken.

Yet here she stood, feeling an almost uncontrollable urge to holler, "Right on!" and go out to breakfast.

Lorenzo J. Taft was in a class all his own. He wasn't merely an extraordinarily successful criminal defense attorney. He was a criminal defense attorney who could send a cop's blood pressure soaring, just at the mention of his name.

He was a first-class, gold-plated son of a bitch.

For years he'd been at loggerheads with LAPD, successfully bringing actions for police brutality, pleading out assholes who should have fried, walking scum, always right up front gloating at the press conference when LAPD fucked up.

But that was okay, sort of. He was just doing his job.

Until fourteen months ago, when he won acquittal for a young black man charged with the murder of an LAPD patrol officer.

Lorenzo J. Taft had walked a cop killer.

The case had outraged cops nationwide, and for a while there was a black market (so to speak) in photographic blowups of the attorney's face and upper body, concentric rings neatly superimposed for easy target practice. Nowhere had the anti-Taft anger been felt more acutely than here in L.A. Now Lorenzo J. Taft himself was dead, and Joanna had to remind herself that she was supposed to be upset about it.

The Atterminator had really done a number on him, too.

He sat in a three-thousand-dollar leather chair wearing nothing but racy red ladies' lingerie from Frederick's of Hollywood. A generic police hat perched at a jaunty angle on his smoothly shaven head.

And a thick coating of bright red lipstick graced his full lips, from which protruded a police nightstick.

Joanna shook herself out of her reflections and went to work. But as she talked to the cops who were first on the scene, assessed the general situation, began making investigative decisions, a naughty thought kept flickering in the back of her mind.

If Lorenzo J. Taft's murderer should ever come to trial, it was inevitable that photographs of the victim would have to be introduced into evidence.

The uproar over the death of Lorenzo J. Taft was immediate and extraordinary.

It was fueled in part by the swift and deadly undercurrents of racial ugliness which had flowed through Los Angeles since the night Rodney King tried to outrun the cops. And it was given a considerable goose by the inevitable speculation and innuendo regarding the state of the corpse. Phrases like "compromising position" didn't begin to cover the scene in that leather chair. News that a police baton was involved leaked early on.

Word on the street was that it had been found sticking out of the lawyer's ass.

Two messages from Kirsten were waiting when Joanna returned to the office that afternoon. Instinctively assuming the worst, Joanna punched in her daughter's number before she even sat down. True, they'd been speaking frequently in recent months, but Joanna always placed the calls. Kirsten had been trained from childhood to call work only in a genuine emergency.

No emergency, Kirsten told her, in a small, worried voice with a definite catch in it, nothing really *wrong*. "Mom, is this going to turn into some big, ugly racial thing?"

"I hope not," Joanna answered fervently. After six hours at the crime scene, she had a bad feeling about how the community would react to this latest killing. A very bad feeling. "But it certainly isn't anything that *you* need to be worried about, honey."

Kirsten sighed. "I've always been worried, Mom. You know that. Every single time you went out the door to work, I just knew it was the last time I'd ever see you alive, that something horrible was going to happen, that you'd be shot and I'd be orphaned and you were never going to come home again."

Oh, man. Her daughter was teetering on the edge of overwrought, which probably had a lot to do with pregnancy and hormones. Normally Kirsten was stoic and uncomplaining, like her dad. Still, there was no pretending that her fears weren't valid, or justified.

"But I always did come home again," Joanna reminded her gently. "And I do understand what you're saying, honest. I always worried the same way whenever your father went to work when he was on the department here. But *he* was always just fine, too."

"Well, how do you think I felt when *both* of you were going off each day, risking your lives?"

Joanna chose her words carefully. "Honey, when both of us were cops, it was after your father went to work in northern Minnesota. And once *that* happened, his likelihood of being injured or killed in the line of duty went *way* down, practically off the charts. He's much more likely to be accidentally shot by a hunter than a criminal, if you absolutely *have* to worry about something. And once I got off patrol and became a detective, the same thing applied to me. Even in L.A."

"What? You're likely to be shot by a hunter?"

Joanna laughed, relieved to see Kirsten regaining her sense of humor. "Actually, Kir, you'd have more reason to worry right now if I were a *lawyer*, not a cop."

"I suppose." Kirsten still sounded dubious. "But who *is* this Taft guy, anyway? Am I supposed to know who he is?"

Joanna made a snap decision. "Honey, I really don't have time to talk now. Let me call you when I get home tonight."

"And when will that be? Midnight?"

Ouch. "Not a minute past eleven-thirty, I promise."

It was actually only eight when Joanna curled up in her blue velvet marshmallow chair and called Seattle.

"Saw you on the news again," her son-in-law, David, told her when he picked up. Joanna had been caught by reporters leaving

Taft's office, had spoken a few noncommittal words. She hadn't seen it herself and didn't really want to.

"Hope they got my good side," Joanna told him lightly. "How's Kir feeling?"

David was a math professor at the university, a very solid and controlled and linear man. Joanna liked him well enough, though she could never imagine feeling truly comfortable with him. At Kirsten's side during twenty-three hours of agonizing, drug-free labor, he had never lost his composure.

Now he answered methodically. "Miserable and pregnant. Also tired. Once she got Jamie down, she nodded off, but she made me promise to wake her when you called."

"I *am* awake," Kirsten put in. "I've got it in the bedroom, David. So tell me all about this Lorenzo Taft guy, Mom."

"Certainly. Lesson number one: the name is Lorenzo *J.* Taft. He *always* used his middle initial. And probably the most relevant thing about him now that he's dead is that a lot of cops are very discreetly rejoicing."

"Really?"

"Uh-huh."

"Interesting." Kirsten sounded as if she meant it, which was unusual. Normally her daughter steered clear of the sordid details of her mother's workplace. "Why?"

"Well, there was a young gentleman named Desmond Johnson," Joanna explained. "A nineteen-year-old African-American gangbanger with a criminal record dating back to the second grade. Somebody fingered Desmond as the shooter in the death of a Korean grocer who got shot during a robbery near Normandie and Florence."

"Normandie and Florence," Kirsten said slowly. "Why does that sound familiar?"

"It was a key location in the L.A. riots. Anyway, Jack Tangier and Frank Sheldon were partners, on routine patrol one night when they recognized Desmond Johnson slipping into an alley. They knew he was wanted for the Korean grocer, and Tangier had busted Desmond before. Apparently he thought he could pop him again without backup. *Big* mistake. Johnson opened fire with an assault rifle. Tangier was killed outright and Sheldon went down." She hesitated. "Are you sure you want to hear this?"

"Yes."

"Okay," Joanna went on doubtfully. This was exactly the kind of situation Kirsten had described as her personal nightmare, just this afternoon. Cops shot in the line of duty. "Sheldon got off four shots before he collapsed, and one of them nicked Desmond's spinal cord. Turned him into an instant paraplegic. There's a lot of gangbangers in wheelchairs these days, you know. They've just about got chapters at some of the rehab facilities. Sometimes the gangs deliberately shoot to cripple, not to kill."

"Hmph," Kirsten muttered. "That's pretty shitty."

"Yeah. Anyway, Desmond Johnson's assault rifle vanished before the paramedics and LAPD backup arrived. Which wouldn't have mattered, except that Lorenzo J. Taft took on the defense and put the cops on trial."

"How could he get away with that?"

"The usual way." Joanna sighed. "The pisser was that he had good material to work with. Jack Tangier and Frank Sheldon turned out to be bad cops, exactly the sort of guys the Christopher Commission said LAPD should get rid of. Tangier was even on the list of forty-four." The commission had publicly identified forty-four officers with significantly disturbing records of violence; most by now had left LAPD, though Tangier was the only one actually killed in the line of duty.

"So what were they? Bigots?"

"And more. Tangier had been up more than once for unnecessary use of force, and he couldn't exactly explain the situation at Desmond's trial, since he was too dead to take the stand. As for Frank Sheldon—well, Taft struck *gold* with Sheldon. Sheldon came to LAPD after ten years on the job in Montgomery, Alabama. Where he collected Nazi memorabilia and belonged to a 'study group' called the Caucasian Ascendancy League. CAL for short."

"You're making this up," Kirsten said. "Nobody's *that* stupid."

"Unfortunately, it's all true. Taft brought in a whole parade of witnesses who put Frank Sheldon right at the heart of CAL, starting with Sheldon's sister and his first wife. Pickets outside the courthouse carried posters with photo enlargements of Sheldon wearing Klan robes on horseback."

"Genuine pictures?"

"Sheldon claimed that the photographs were faked, and they probably were. He also said the Caucasian Ascendancy League was just a youthful indiscretion, blah, blah, blah. But it didn't much matter *what* Sheldon said. He was fucked and so was the case against Desmond Johnson. Desmond put on a coat and tie and testified from his wheelchair that he was unarmed and minding his own business when officers opened fire on him with no provocation at all. That he did hear shots come from somewhere behind him, but only *after* he fell, wounded and crippled."

"And Lorenzo J. Taft walked this Desmond?"

Joanna offered a half laugh. "So to speak. The case was tried in Compton with a jury of seven men and five women, all but one of them African Americans. They acquitted Desmond Johnson in fifteen minutes."

"Well, wait a minute. What about killing the Korean grocer?"

"That case fell apart. A key witness disappeared and half a dozen people turned up saying that Desmond Johnson was at a Bible study class when the shooting went down."

"You're right," Kirsten announced suddenly. "I don't like this story. What happened to the cop who survived? The racist?"

"He went back to Alabama, opened a firing range, and set about making himself the finest sharpshooter in the world. They say he blames himself for not being a better shot in that alley, for leaving Desmond Johnson alive."

"Where was *he* last night?"

"In Mobile, teaching a self-defense class to nervous white women."

Kirsten exhaled deeply. "How can you *do* this work, Mom?"

"Is that a serious question?"

"No. But I still do wonder sometimes."

"So do I, honey. So do I."

28

Ace watched the videotaped segment of Joanna Davis on the evening news for the seventh time.

The more he saw the Davis woman, the more she reminded him of Meredith Finch, his high school drama coach. Mrs. Finch had been so supportive, assuring him he had real talent when his father, usually taciturn, got chatty enough to suggest that actors were sissy fags and to proclaim unequivocally that going to Hollywood was out of the question. And to remind him there was a family business to run.

Mrs. Finch had encouraged him on the sly, even after he confided his father's disapproval. She had led him on, in a way, though he couldn't fault her for it; she had no way of knowing how things would work out. Mrs. Finch had been delighted when he went off to the state university and majored in drama. He'd returned to tell her good-bye before he moved to Hollywood after his father died, when it was pretty clear that going into the family business was no longer an option.

But she was gone. Had moved away, and the people at the high school wouldn't tell him where or when or anything.

Detective Davis was a *lot* older than Meredith Finch, was old enough to be her mother. But she had the same kind of short, sleek hairstyle, with neat little wings tucked behind her ears, and she moved her hands in the same smooth, authoritative way.

It surprised him the first time he saw her on TV and noted the resemblance. Small world and all that. Everything moved around in circles. The more things change, the more they stay the same, like the old man used to say. In the old man's world nothing had ever changed, which was ultimately part of the problem.

Ace wondered now just where Mrs. Finch had gone, what she was doing, if she had kids of her own. He knew that no matter how this all ended, he'd never see her again. Just as well. She'd be disappointed to learn that he hadn't made it. He hadn't come to the same ignominious end as Peggy Salk, the last hometown girl who went to Hollywood, the one his father had thrown up to him.

Peggy Salk, who made porn flicks and then OD'd. But he hadn't ended up with his name on marquees, either.

Any name.

Though he had, after his own fashion, become very famous indeed.

Detective Davis was being very earnest right now, as she was interviewed outside Lorenzo J. Taft's office. "Obviously this person harbors a deep-seated resentment toward the legal community."

Ace laughed at this part, as he had each time. *Deep-seated resentment.* Yeah, you could say that. The camera was right in front of Detective Davis and she seemed to speak directly to him. She wore a burgundy wool suit he had admired in her armoire. He'd been surprised how small her clothes were, how tiny *she* was, by extension. She seemed larger on TV, had a lot of on-camera presence.

A clot of microphones was thrust beneath her chin. "We have no evidence," she went on, "that he had any professional dealings with Mr. Taft or any other victim."

"Is this somebody trying to set straight a grievance?" a reporter's voice asked.

She shrugged, another gesture she shared with Meredith Finch. It was really quite uncanny. "That would certainly appear possible. But I don't see how anybody can hope to set a grievance straight if we don't know what it is."

Did she think he was going to pick up the phone and call her with a detailed explanation? How dumb did they think he was?

"In the meantime, we're suggesting that all attorneys take additional safety precautions until we catch this killer."

Which would be never, Ace told himself with satisfaction. He was done now. He knew when to quit. It only remained to sit things out for a little bit and then take the remainder of old Mrs. Kowalski's grubstake and leave.

Oregon would be lovely in the spring.

He'd been in Hollywood far too long, even though the last couple of years he had remained only to implement the Legal Resolution Program. Hollywood sucked, was evil at its very core.

But it was never dull. He worried a little that he'd find the wilderness cabin in Oregon too isolated. He wondered if he'd miss the human contact. Not that you could call most of the contact in this sewer human. But even so.

Maybe, he thought, what he *really* needed to do was find some small town where there was a hardware store for sale and no Wal-Mart within a hundred miles.

And start over. At the very beginning.

Ace opened a slim compartment concealed between two kitchen cabinets, retrieved the family photo album, and brought it into his living room. There he sat on the sofa and carefully opened the dark blue book on his lap. The gummed pages under the clear plastic overlays, he noticed, were browning at the edges.

He worked his way slowly through the book. Black-and-white pictures of his parents when they were young and carefree, honeymooning in Florida, standing in front of the house they bought on Mulberry Lane, holding the baby boy who had died in infancy and then, abruptly, holding the baby Ace.

The replacement.

The replacement went through boyhood in the pages that followed. These pictures were in color, but the hues were aging badly. Yellowing, mostly, like the pages they were displayed on. It seemed to have a kind of morbid symbolism, that the book and the pictures were decaying practically in front of his eyes.

He looked at his school pictures, one from each year, and at his birthday parties and at fishing trips with the old man up in Wisconsin. The old man considered photography an extravagance, and as time passed, there were fewer and fewer pictures. Lots of shots when Ace was a baby, a fair number in boyhood, and then things started tapering off drastically. Some high school shots from *Brigadoon* and *Our Town*. The graduation portrait. Production stills from college performances in *Othello* and *Death of a Salesman* and from his dinner-theater role in *The Mousetrap*.

And that was that.

There were no pictures from his life after he came to California.

And there were no pictures of the store.

Not from the good times, when it probably had never occurred to either of his parents to waste film on such an obvious and central part of their lives. And certainly not from the end, when times were very bad indeed.

The store had been his father's life, and his grandfather's before that. A place where a man could find just about any tool or gadget or gizmo, and if it wasn't on the shelves, the old man knew where to get it or could figure out a way to jury-rig a substitute.

But wait—there *was* one picture of the store, when he was in second grade and his mother had surprised the old man by bringing a birthday cake to the store on the day the old man turned forty. After school Ace and his mother had lit the candles just outside the front door and marched in singing.

The old man had not been pleased and she never did anything like that again.

Ace himself had shot four rolls of film at the very end, pictures of the house and store and a few pictures around town. That was on the second-to-last time he went back there. But once the pictures were developed, back in California, he knew he couldn't keep them. It was just too damned painful. So one night he went down to the beach and built a bonfire and burned them.

He regretted now only that he hadn't burned down the store itself the last time he was there, when he inaugurated the Legal Resolution Program. At the time, it had been tempting but seemed foolhardy; no reason to call attention to the store while the other, more important, business was going on. In retrospect he knew he'd made the correct decision.

Of course, back then he hadn't been as confident of his own abilities.

He smiled now with a decided measure of self-satisfaction. At this point in his life, burning down a hardware store would be a piece of cake.

He closed the book, put it back in its hiding place, and went back to listen to Joanna Davis's news clip one more time.

Tomorrow morning he would leave his message to her. He had

the materials all ready. Because this situation had arisen unexpectedly, it was more crude than he would have liked. Not a message so much as a statement designed to unnerve her.

Maybe he ought to send a real message, too. Explain a few things, as she'd suggested. But that would be stupid. To assure his success, he needed to fade away quietly now, to drift out of the picture as he had always intended.

On the other hand, right now he had *everybody's* attention.

Maybe this was *exactly* the time to issue a manifesto.

29

The murder of Lorenzo J. Taft provided a vast array of physical evidence, at least compared to the previous killings.

For starters, there was an actual witness, the cleaning lady found trussed in the ladies' room. Fifty-four, semiliterate and deeply religious, Elmira Stokes had been badly shaken by her experience.

Elmira Stokes was no fool. Joanna interviewed her in a guarded private hospital room on Thursday, hearing the edge of hysteria in the woman's protestations that she had seen nothing. *Nothing!* Elmira had no idea whether the assailant was black, white, or green. She couldn't identify him from Melody Laughlin's sketch, since she hadn't seen him. Period. End of report. Elmira was certain the Atterminator would be back to tidy up later, to remove the witness he had inadvertently left behind.

Joanna didn't think there was anything inadvertent about it. Sparing Elmira Stokes seemed to make a clear differentiation between those the killer considered culpable and those who merely served. It also made a racial statement of sorts: that Taft might be a worthless, death-deserving, African-American shyster, but his race was not the primary issue.

And there were other clues.

Elmira had been found with a calico flour sack tied over her face, from a brand found in groceries serving Latino neighborhoods throughout L.A. The sack was tied in place by pantyhose,

Ralphs' house brand. There were fresh drops of 3-in-1 household oil on the hinges of the door connecting Taft's office to his secretary's. And the duct tape was...duct tape. The Atterminator was very good at acquiring anonymous materials.

But the highly polished marble floors of Taft's office building offered more promising information, starting with imprints of size-ten Nikes leading up the stairway into the ladies' room and finally into Taft's office, where there was a throw rug askew and other evidence of a minor struggle. A lot of blurred but similar shoe prints were found in the tiny telephone service area down where the phone lines had been disconnected, suggesting that the killer had waited out his quarry rather than attempting to breach the building's fairly good electronic system at night. Not that this guy probably couldn't circumvent the alarm system with a bobby pin and a stick of chewing gum.

Mid-morning, word came from the medical examiner's office that, like Francesca Goldberg, Taft had died of nicotine sulfate poisoning, probably within ten minutes of exposure. Taft had also been zapped first, on the shoulder from behind, with the same type of stun gun used on Goldberg.

As she pondered this latest death, a nagging question kept pushing itself toward the front of Joanna's brain: How many people had the Atterminator actually killed? Was Roger Coskins really his first victim? The Coskins killing was such a complex and *showy* crime to lead with. Too good, really, to be just beginner's luck. The initial certainty with which it was accepted as an accident only confirmed Joanna's suspicion that their guy might have officiated at some other accidents, prior to last August.

But what? Where? They'd scoured years' worth of accidental attorney deaths, most of which had turned out to be exactly as represented. And they couldn't very well check out every accidental death in California going back indefinitely.

If, indeed, California was where this guy had started out.

If, indeed, he was one guy and not two guys or two gals or a guy and a gal.

She was haunted as well by previously repressed memories of

that garden/feed/hardware store in Pine River Falls. The year and a half she lived in northern Minnesota had been the most difficult period of Joanna's entire life, and as much as possible, she had buried memories of that time. This one, however, was increasingly insistent.

Cops had taken the suspect sketch to every home improvement center, nursery, and hardware store in Los Angeles County, and had come up empty. They'd been back to the security services and the companies that manufactured and installed burglar alarms. Zippo.

Still. The Atterminator hadn't simply awakened one morning and decided to start killing lawyers. He'd been working up to it for a long time. His plans were comprehensive and he was patient. They knew he'd been researching possible victims since at least early summer, when he first visited Joseph Tucker's office. The Botox had been stolen in March.

Joanna ran a fast mental tally.

Roger Coskins. Flew off the cliff into the Pacific Ocean on Thursday, August 28th. San Luis Obispo.

Warren Richardson. Asphyxiated by carbon monoxide in his own garage on Wednesday, September 10th. Valencia.

Bill Burke. Poisoned by botulism in his Sierra cabin sometime on the weekend of September 20th. Fresno County.

Lawrence Benton. Electrocuted in his hot tub on Sunday, October 12th. Sherman Oaks.

Joseph Tucker's office. Visited on Wednesday, November 5th. Whittier.

Francesca Goldberg. Poisoned by nicotine in her home on Wednesday, November 19th. Santa Monica.

Lorenzo J. Taft. Poisoned by nicotine in his office early Wednesday, December 3rd. Mid-Wilshire.

Six murders, six very different locations, five different agents of death. *Five* different police departments, six if you included Tucker's office in Whittier. Each killing was separated from the others by at least ten days, and over a month had elapsed between Benton and Goldberg. That delay coincided with the explosion of publicity: public linkage of the murders, copycat killings in Long

Beach and Las Vegas and points east, the addition of Warren Richardson to the death list.

Joanna and most other task force members remained convinced that Joseph Tucker had been the intended fifth victim. His office was visited midway between Benton and Goldberg, which fit the ten-day-interval schedule. And the maître d' at Tucker's country club had—when prodded by detectives—remembered an unusual call on the night after the lawyer's stroke. The maître d', a supercilious ass with a bad toupee, couldn't recall any elements of that brief conversation. But he acknowledged that it was highly unusual for *anyone* to call Joseph Tucker, who drank his dinner nightly at a window table overlooking the golf course, flirting with the waitresses as he quietly pickled himself.

Everything related to the lives and deaths of the murdered attorneys had been analyzed six ways from Sunday. They had backtracked to childhoods, cross-referenced client lists, interviewed State Bar complainants, leaned hard on the people involved with the incidents that had led to disciplinary charges against Coskins and Richardson and Tucker.

All for naught.

Joanna remained deeply troubled by the disappearance of Reggie Benton. While airline personnel and people in neighboring seats had tentatively identified Reggie as being on the pre-Thanksgiving flight to New York, her trail went stone-cold once she got to JFK Airport. She seemed to have vanished into thin air at thirty thousand feet.

Everything about Reggie's trip was wrong: having no obvious (or even plausible) destination, paying cash for the ticket, picking the ticket up at the airport, leaving without telling anybody, and of course, the absolute lack of fingerprints in her apartment.

Dave Austin and his cohorts had spent a lot of time running down the people who knew Reggie Benton. Problem was, nobody really did seem to know her. Her acting instructor was a melodramatic ditz and her fellow students claimed no interaction outside class. Her high school teachers remembered her dimly as a girl who sat in the back of the room and got Cs when she bothered to do the work. Her West Hollywood neighbors didn't know her. Her former therapist cited confidentiality, and they could find no current therapist. There was no indication that she participated in a twelve-step program or any other group therapy. Reggie no longer saw her high school friends, who all agreed that several years ago she had hated her father and deeply resented her parents' divorce.

There was, in this father-daughter relationship, a whiff of something seriously amiss. Molestation? Reggie's mother hotly denied the possibility, unwilling even to consider it, but mothers in these situations could be incredibly dense. Vicki Benton, the trophy widow, said that in the four years she had been involved with her late husband, Reggie had remained uniformly cold and distant. All of which fit the incest profile tidily, but none of which helped much now.

Increasingly, Joanna believed that both father and daughter were dead.

It was nearly ten when Joanna arrived home on Thursday night, passing houses festooned with Christmas lights as she moved away from the freeway toward her own place, where Christmas decoration was on hold.

The lights-on-timers in the house were burning as always, but the moment Joanna walked through her back door, she knew something was very, very wrong.

The jukebox was lit.

No music played, but the interior fluorescent lights shone brightly from the Princess Rockola across the room. The box was turned on and ready for action. Joanna knew she had not left the machine on herself. She always turned it off when she stopped listening to music, and she hadn't played it for several days.

She could see from across the room that some of the record labels on the program menu were different. Joanna used standard red-on-white blank jukebox labels bought in mass quantities from a used record store. Most of those jukebox labels were still in position.

But the first four records in the upper left-hand corner of the selection panel and the last four in the lower right-hand corner had been changed. She couldn't read them from across the room, but the slips of paper in those slots were now neon-pink.

Somebody had been in her home.

Had tampered with the jukebox.

Might well still be here.

All of this awareness took barely a second to compute. Her heart pounded as adrenaline pumped into her system by the quart. She had her gun out before she even realized it, sweeping her eyes around the room as she pulled the cell phone from her purse with her left hand and flipped it open. She punched in 911.

In a loud, clear voice she identified herself and explained the situation. The operator was calm and competent, telling her to stay on the line and to leave the building.

Joanna passed on relevant information: precise directions, that the gate was locked, her location inside the building, Al Jacobs's cell phone number. Jacobs had left work half an hour before she did and was probably home by now.

The back door still stood wide open and she left it that way as an escape route. She waited just inside the doorway with her back to a solid wall, facing unobstructed views of the kitchen and living area. Outside lights on sensors had turned on when she arrived and she now flipped switches inside the door to keep the area outdoors illuminated.

What to do? Where to go?

The 911 operator notwithstanding, Joanna knew she was more vulnerable to ambush outside, where darkness and isolation offered superb cover to any waiting assailant. She decided to stay put and wait for backup. She could tell there was nobody in the living area; the paucity of conventional furnishings precluded hiding anything larger than a squirrel.

What's more, anybody hiding in her bedroom, storage room, or bathroom would have to enter the living area through the single central hallway, and anybody who exited through windows in those rooms could only re-enter the house through the back door.

The chain and deadbolt on her never-used front door appeared across the room to remain locked and intact.

Wait. Keep waiting.

Her muscles were tense and locked. She flexed first her right leg and then her left, to the rhythm of her pounding heart. She knew the precise location of her Kevlar vest, in the bottom drawer of the armoire. She hadn't worn it for years.

She felt naked without it.

She knew that time *had* to be passing, but it crawled past in the slowest of increments. Every second seemed an eternity.

Finally she heard the first siren, distant and then growing louder with a familiarity that offered immediate reassurance. That siren was joined by a second one, and Joanna felt waves of relief course through her body, passing clear down to her toes. More sirens followed, and more, a delicious cacophony of noise.

And then there were uniformed officers running into the yard and swarming into the house.

With a composure that enormously pleased her, Joanna took charge. First she had officers check the other rooms in the house. They came up empty. As additional cops arrived, she had them fan out through the fenced area surrounding the house. If anybody was still here, she wanted him badly.

But there was nobody. That much was clear by the time that Al Jacobs arrived from his house in nearby Simi Valley. A West Valley sergeant was on his heels, while the West Valley watch commander and Robbery–Homicide captain remained on separate open phone lines.

Which allowed Joanna the luxury of finally looking at the jukebox.

Eight records had been changed, those that could be reached and removed without manually operating the carousel. Some titles were songs she knew she owned, ones she kept in the chest of drawers beside the machine. Others couldn't possibly be hers. Without opening the jukebox, she could see that A-1, at least, was what the new neon-pink label proclaimed. The pink labels had been typed and only one side of each record was identified. But that was enough.

A-1 was the Rolling Stones. "Dancin' with Mr. D."

The others followed a similar theme, one that made Joanna's blood run icy as a glacial waterfall.

C-1 was the Bobby Fuller Four, "I Fought the Law." E-1 and H-1 were "Eve of Destruction" and "The Man Who Shot Liberty Valance."

C-O was Roberta Flack's "Killing Me Softly." E-O and G-O were "Teen Angel" and "Last Kiss."

And down in the lower right-hand corner of the jukebox selection menu, the pink label for H-O offered a tune by Eric Clapton:

"I Shot the Sheriff."

30

Violated.

It was the only word to describe the way Joanna felt, but it seemed hopelessly inadequate.

By the time she reached task force headquarters the following morning, she felt as if she had spent a weekend in a cement mixer. She wore the same clothes she'd had on the previous day. She'd spent last night with Al and Marie Jacobs in Simi Valley, had stopped at an all-night drugstore for a toothbrush because she could take nothing from her house until SID had examined every square inch of the place. She knew they would be extraordinarily thorough.

But there would be no fingerprints, no trace evidence. She was sure of it. This guy was too careful and this attack too specifically focused.

Everyone believed that the records in her jukebox had been changed by the Atterminator. Which made it obvious that this was not his first visit to Joanna's home. He had been there before, seen the jukebox, chosen his calling cards carefully.

Their message terrified her.

Killing me softly.

The eve of destruction.

I shot the sheriff.

Was she in personal danger? This question—currently being hotly argued throughout Robbery–Homicide and at the highest levels of LAPD—was one that she didn't really want to think about at all. It made no *sense* to target her personally. There seemed no *reason*, apart from her visibility on the task force. She didn't fit the victim profile in any respect. She was not a lawyer, did not coddle criminals, had no previous notoriety.

And yet, for whatever reason, this message had been delivered to *her*. To her *home*.

How had he found her home?

Like most cops, Joanna zealously guarded her privacy. Her phone was unlisted, her address known only to personal friends and family members. She was not a joiner.

But she sometimes shopped by catalog. She got junk mail. She voted.

Nobody in today's society had absolute privacy. She knew that, had always known it. But it hadn't seemed to matter before. She had always believed that with minimal effort, she could achieve and maintain a level of personal privacy that would protect her.

She had been wrong.

And in a way, what angered her even more was that because this criminal had invaded her personal space, her home and life-style were now fair game for cops, technicians, administrators. The goddamned mayor would even make it his business to find out just what had happened and where. For all she knew, he and his good buddy, the police chief, were out there right now, pawing through her lingerie.

Strangers would now know about her jukebox and her pinball machine and the dearth of love seats and coffee tables. People she had never met would examine her bedding, her medicine chest, her accordion file of personal papers.

Her home was, now and forever, a crime scene.

As she worked through Friday morning, methodically reviewing the same lists and materials on which she'd been working before

Wednesday morning's discovery of Lorenzo J. Taft's chiffon-clad body, she wondered how long they could keep this development from the media. Because her home was so remote, no media had monitored her cell phone call to 911, at least not that she knew of. LAPD had clamped on a tight lid and the word from above was to protect her quietly, to call it a burglary attempt.

She knew that wouldn't last. There'd been too many cops at the scene, each with a spouse or significant other or buddy or all of the above. Somebody would slip something. It was just a matter of time.

When she realized that she had reviewed the same list four times without processing one scrap of information on it, she found a private office and called a familiar number in northern Minnesota. She told the young woman who answered the phone that Captain McNamara was calling Chief Olafson.

"The Atterminator was in my house last night," she told Don without preliminaries when he picked up. "He was gone when I got there, but he'd been there yesterday."

She could hear him inhale, very slowly.

"Are you all right?" he asked quietly, deliberately. Don Olafson never got ruffled. When Mikey fell from the fig tree and had an inch of shiny white femur sticking out of his bloodied leg, Don had picked up his screaming son and said calmly, "Guess we oughta get this looked at."

"I don't know. He was gone when I got there. But he'd been there before, Don."

"Can you tell me about it?"

She knew he didn't mean are-you-capable-of-discussing-it, but rather is-it-okay-with-your-brass. And realizing that it was probably anything but okay with them, she told him the whole story anyway.

"The kids' addresses in the house somewhere?" His question was casual and pointed at the same time, vintage Olafson.

"I called them both this morning," she said. "And the captain's talked to brass in Minneapolis and Seattle. They'll be watching both of them until further notice."

"That's not good enough," he said, with a career cop's awareness of how inadequate police protection could be. "Kirsten in particular can't stay where she is." He considered for a moment. "She can come here and stay through the holidays. There's plenty of room."

Joanna felt an eerie echo of twenty years past, when Don had bundled them all off to his hometown, not revealing till it was a done deal that he'd accepted a job with the Minnesota state police and that the vacation was actually a permanent relocation. But she let it go. The fact of the matter was, Don's idea was just dandy and she only wished she'd thought of it first.

"Will it be all right with Carol?" Carol was Don's second wife, a kind and solid and likable Norwegian who had produced three little Olafsons of her own.

"Of course," he answered shortly. "And I'll talk to Mike, too, but I don't think he'll be willing to come. I don't like this, Joanna."

She felt anger pushing its way up and forced the rage back. "I don't either. But I really think this visit to my house was meant to be a distraction. Maybe we're closer to him than we realize. This guy is focused, Don. He stays on task. If he'd wanted to take me out, I'd be dead. He doesn't give warnings."

"Even so, this might be a good time for you to take a little vacation," he suggested. "And don't forget to get your mother covered out there in Arizona."

"Taken care of." She smiled at the memory of the conversation with her mother earlier that morning. "*She's* going to take a trip, with a gentleman friend. But I can't leave. I won't do that. I can't let him think he won."

"Your safety's the issue, Joanna, not who's winning what. Sometimes getting away really is the best answer."

There was a moment of silence and she knew they were both thinking of the same thing. When the Hillside Strangler had so traumatized and paralyzed Joanna that she allowed herself to be moved to Minnesota without even really noticing, the move had ultimately torn them asunder and ended their marriage.

"Oh, I'm safe enough," she answered with a certain bravado.

"I've got bodyguards from Metro who look like combat-trained redwood trees. And SID is ripping apart the house even as we speak. There'll be surveillance on it in case he comes back."

"Do you think he will?"

"No. And I don't think I can either. Which *really* pisses me off. It was my *home*, dammit. My sanctuary. And now it's ruined for me."

"Where will you go?"

"To live? No idea. But in the meantime, I've got all sorts of offers. I stayed at Al's last night and I'm moving out to Lee Walters's place tonight."

"Is it secure?"

Joanna laughed for the first time since she'd walked through the back door last night and seen the beacon of the lighted jukebox. "Her husband's an ex-cop who raises pit bulls, Don. You met him at Kirsten's wedding. Yeah, I'd say it's safe. And anyway, I've got the bodyguards, remember?"

He was quiet for a minute. "Do you think this guy means to hurt you?"

She answered slowly. "No. But I'm not sure I understand what he was trying to prove. I mean, we already *know* he can get in almost anywhere. Why focus on *me*?"

"I guess that's up to you to figure out, Joanna. You're the detective. I'm just an administrator. But do me a personal favor, okay? Take those bodyguards over to the academy this afternoon and give yourself a nice workout on the target range."

Feeling oddly reassured in the way that only Don Olafson could reassure her, Joanna went back to work, trying to find comfort in routine.

By now the morning mail had arrived, and she began sifting through the stuff addressed to the investigation, a nice uninvolving task that occasionally got interesting. Today there was a three-page letter from a true-crime writer in Virginia, suggesting what the Atterminator might be up to next: judges. The next piece of mail, unlike most Atterminator letters, was addressed specifically to her.

She pulled the sheet of paper from the envelope and froze.

It was a single sheet of plain white 8½-by-11 paper with a few lines printed in the center:

Rockola makes a fine jukebox, don't you think? You asked for an explanation. No explanation is necessary. The acts speak for themselves and for all those who have been wronged by the legal profession. Warren Richardson had a Hobie surfboard and Lorenzo Taft wore Scarlet Passion by Revlon and Francesca Goldberg was Breathless with Voodoo.
P.S. Why so much Bob Seger?

"Holy shit," she said out loud. The other detectives in the room—all of whom were treading a knife edge, trying to be solicitous without *appearing* to be soliticitous—looked up expectantly. Anxiously. She let the paper fall gently onto the desk. "It's from *him.*"

They surrounded her in seconds. Mickey Conner, who got there first, read the letter aloud over her shoulder. "Sonuvabitch," Conner muttered. "You're right, Davis. Addressed to you?"

She nodded. The envelope lay upside down on the desk where she'd dropped it as she pulled the sheet from inside. She remembered, though, that it was block-printed in ballpoint, addressed to Joanna Davis, no title or honorific, at Robbery–Homicide, LAPD, with the correct zip code for Parker Center. Everything spelled right, and no return address. The stamp was a standard American flag off a roll.

This letter was for real. She would have been certain of that even without the jukebox references. The withheld details of the three killings were too specific and too well-chosen. Indeed, the note seemed designed to point out some of the killer's most ironic touches, just in case the cops were so dumb that they'd missed them.

The public knew Francesca Goldberg was found holding roses, but not which ones, or even the colors. There'd been no reason to publicly mention the surfboard in Warren Richardson's garage, but Joanna could close her eyes and picture it hanging on the wall behind the spot where the lawyer's car and body had been found.

As for the lipstick on Taft, that was a specific they didn't even *have* yet, something the lab was supposed to be tracking down. It ought to be a snap to confirm with this info.

Around her, the room carried the electrically charged buzz of a freshly disturbed beehive. By the time the captain arrived, Jacobs had already bagged the envelope and letter.

"I'll hand-carry this to the lab myself," Jacobs announced. "Unless you want to?" He nodded at the captain.

"Be my guest," the captain told him. He looked concerned, which was significant, since he prided himself on a stony-visaged Dick Tracy demeanor. "You okay, Davis?"

"Yes, sir." She shook her head. "I'm just not used to being… *involved* like this."

"It sucks," the captain said unexpectedly. He also prided himself on detachment, and on purity of language. He had come to her house late last night, grim and controlled. And very, very angry. He was taking this almost as personally as Joanna herself.

Now he gazed around the group, stony-faced once again. "For whatever reason, this guy's got a fix on Davis. He may try to get through to her by phone, e-mail, something else. I want everybody paying close attention here. All the time. Davis, I think we should find you a safe house."

She shook her head. "I'd really rather not. Like I told you, I'm planning to stay with Lee Walters, sir. I'd rather do that."

He frowned. "Your call. But keep alert. I'll assign Walters to work with the task force for now. You can carpool. And go on over to the range this afternoon."

She nodded, wondering how he'd react if she told him he was the second police administrator to give her the same instruction within the hour. As if conventional shooting expertise could help against a sly killer who prided himself on breaking all the rules.

But when she went to the academy that afternoon, she shredded every target and outshot both her bodyguards.

31

Joanna and Lee Walters took her bodyguards back to the west Valley Friday afternoon to retrieve some clothing and personal items from what she already regarded as her former home. The bodyguards were okay guys, she realized, comfortable enough companions if you had to hang with people trained to thwart assassins.

But Joanna wondered again, as she often had when working West L.A., at the lack of privacy endured by the famous. She tried to put herself into a mind-set that might *enjoy* having every movement monitored, but it was impossible.

There were guards on her house when they arrived and somewhere up on the hill others watched the entire surrounding area for unusual or suspicious activity. Never mind that everybody agreed the Atterminator wouldn't be back. This was one cop's house that was *not* going to be broken into again. This task was handled with zealous enthusiasm by all involved; the notion of a serial killer creepy-crawling the home of *any* LAPD officer was very scary and hit everybody hard.

"Oh, dear God," Lee said softly when they walked in. "Oh, Joanna, I'm so *sorry!*"

Joanna herself said nothing at first, simply regarded the mess that she'd considered home until eighteen hours ago.

The house was a wreck.

SID had finished and departed, and Joanna could tell that they *had* taken some care, but not enough. Things were askew everywhere and fingerprint powder filmed the place like fallout from a volcanic eruption.

The wall where the jukebox had stood since the day Joanna moved in seemed starkly naked. Princess Rockola had left the building. The entire jukebox had been removed for close examination in the lab—where, she reflected glumly, they were probably jiving to Bob Seger right now. *Why so much Bob Seger?* the fuckhead had asked in his letter. Why? Because it gets me moving and reminds me of my ex-husband, asshole.

The word so far was that there was absolutely no physical evidence from inside the house. Or from inside the jukebox.

There was nothing on the letter that had come in yesterday, either.

No fingerprints on the paper, none clear on the envelope but Joanna's. No saliva on the stamp. The ballpoint ink on the envelope was bottom-of-the-line Bic and the letter itself had been produced on standard photocopy paper by a brand and model of electronic typewriter displayed beside stacks of try-out paper in office supply warehouse stores from coast to coast. Dave Austin had just been returning from an Office Depot as Joanna and Lee left the office. He reported with a scowl that he'd meandered into the office machines display area and produced a similar note without ever once attracting the attention of a salesclerk.

There was, however, one bit of physical evidence outside the house.

Footprints. Chilling footprints at that, the same kind of anonymous size-ten Nikes found on Lorenzo J. Taft's marble floors. The footprints were in a particularly secluded back area where someone had jumped the fence. Joanna had no desire to examine the site. If this guy had been skulking around her yard, then the grounds were every bit as emotionally destroyed for her as the house.

"You know," Joanna said, leaning on the kitchen counter, popping open a Diet Coke from the fridge, "Kirsten once told me this place looked like it was furnished by a teenage boy. But now it looks like it's lived in by one, too. Shit!"

"We'll come back and clean it another time," Lee said matter-of-factly, forestalling any notions Joanna might have harbored about setting things straight just now. "You need to get some time and space between last night and cleanup, trust me."

It was an enormous comfort having Lee around, and Joanna was secretly relieved that the captain had reassigned her. If the idea was to baby-sit Detective Davis, well, then Detective Davis didn't mind a bit. Lee was a large and physically formidable woman, a decided plus under the circumstances. More important, though, her years as a detective in Sex Crimes had helped burnish a natural gift for warmth and empathy. Right now Joanna sorely needed just that kind of TLC.

Joanna put on her Kevlar vest before leaving the bedroom, replacing one she'd borrowed at Parker Center. The borrowed vest was so large she'd also had to borrow an extra-large sweatshirt to cover it, giving her the contours of a fleecy gray trash barrel.

As she gathered clothing and personal effects, she realized that she could leave here easily enough. She'd lived in lots of places, moved with few regrets, transported less and less to each new address. It would not be difficult to move.

But she had *wanted* to stay here. Damn that bastard anyway!

Out in Diamond Bar, she was given her own room with a window overlooking the dog run.

On his retirement from LAPD three years earlier, Alex Walters had decided to breed dogs and had—with a cop's unerring instinct for security—swiftly narrowed the possibilities to Rottweilers, Dobermans, German shepherds, and pit bulls. A childhood fondness for the *Our Gang* series tipped the scales and he now had four adults and a litter of puppies.

The neighbors were not troublesome; nobody was especially inclined to argue with a family consisting of two cops and a dozen pit bulls.

Joanna didn't much like dogs, though she and Don had owned a mutt for a while in Mar Vista when the kids were little. The problem with dogs was that they required constant attention. In many ways, she believed, a dog was more of a responsibility than a child. A child would eventually be able to fix her own breakfast, but a dog would never be able to pour his own kibble, or independently use the toilet.

Nor did she like pit bulls, a prejudice she had harbored for many years. These dogs frightened her and they were damned ugly to boot.

But it was nice to think that they were between her and anybody who might want to make trouble.

Blanche Dodsworth was enjoying one of her favorite indulgences, reading the Sunday newspaper. On this gray and blustery day, the light was already fading through the barren treetops. The dull pewter sky outside promised snow before morning, and wind howled across the frozen cornfields.

Inside, the house was chilly and something was wrong with the radiator in her parlor, a problem she feared would be expensive to resolve. And on top of all that, her arthritis was acting up. Even turning the newspaper pages was a painful and laborious process.

Still, reading the newspaper on a Sunday afternoon was a pursuit she had always enjoyed, and one she was not prepared to abandon at this late date. On Sundays, Blanche read the *Des Moines Register*, as well as the local *Kingsfield Clarion*. The *Register* had a long article about those terrible murders out in California. Admittedly, some of the dead lawyers sounded fairly disreputable, but that was no excuse for taking another human life.

What *was* it about California, anyway? Why would *anybody* want to live there? Earthquakes, fires, floods, eye-burning smog, it just never stopped. And the *crime!* She could only assume some sort of statewide dementia. Blanche herself had never been out of Iowa, had never felt the slightest stirrings of any desire to leave.

KILLER HARBORS GRUDGE AGAINST LEGAL PROFESSION read the headline, which certainly belabored the obvious. Nobody seemed to respect lawyers anymore. Things had been very different when she was a child, daughter of the town's most respected attorney. People had always been grateful for the services her father provided, had showered the family with gifts at Christmas, and filled the church to overflowing when he passed away.

Blanche looked again at the sketch that accompanied the story, a picture that was supposed to be the killer. The Atterminator, that silly, trivializing name. There was something oddly familiar about the face in the sketch and she moved the page back and forth in front of her eyes to focus it more sharply.

The Pearse boy, she thought suddenly. That was who it looked like. The Pearse boy, Ethel's grandson. What *was* his name, anyway? His father had been Edward, called Ted, and his mother, Ethel's daughter, was Sarah. A mousy little thing, she'd been, totally lacking Ethel's sparkle and zest for life. But *what* had they called the boy? It annoyed her that she no longer had the recall for names she had once prided herself upon.

Kevin.

That was it! Kevin Pearse. She peered again at the smudged newsprint. The resemblance was there, all right, and it was strong. Kevin had been off at college when the troubles began, Blanche remembered. She seemed to recall something about him moving to California after his parents were gone. Off to make it in Hollywood, some had said.

After a light supper, Blanche put the refolded newspapers in the bin on the back porch. She washed her dishes, took a bath, and settled into her comfortable reading chair with an historical novel set in Restoration England.

But later, just before she drifted off to sleep, she found her thoughts returning to the Pearse boy. What ever had happened to him, anyway? It was ridiculous to think that he might be that killer, of course, but the resemblance was startlingly strong. Don't be silly, she chided herself. You're an old lady living alone, letting your imagination run wild.

But that night she dreamed of Pearse Hardware, and of her friend Ethel, and of little Kevin who had been so helpful when a confused older lady came into the store needing help.

In the morning, she retrieved the newspaper section with the sketch of the California killer and looked at it again. She thought she could see something of Ethel through the forehead of the young man in the sketch. Poor Ethel had died young, had keeled over without warning while they were setting up the church Christmas bazaar on a snowy December afternoon a quarter century ago. Little Kevin had been very young then, perhaps not even in school yet. Once Ethel was gone, of course, she didn't hear much about her friend's grandson anymore. And the occasions when she required hardware were mercifully limited.

Still, she decided as the teakettle began to whistle, perhaps she might mention seeing the story and picture to some of the girls this afternoon at Bingo.

It couldn't hurt to see if anybody knew just what *had* happened to Ethel's grandson Kevin.

33

State Bar Chief Trial Counsel Bonita Blevins called a press conference shortly after returning from a long liquid lunch on Tuesday, December 9th. By the time reporters arrived, she had freshened her mascara and begun to wonder if this was actually such a good idea. But what the hell. They were here, she was angry, and she might as well go for it.

And so Bonita Blevins faced the cameras defiantly and decried the lack of progress in solving the Atterminator killings.

"There is a despicable fiend running loose," she announced, "and so far the Los Angeles police have been absolutely stymied. Surely we can do better than this! This sort of greasy little terrorist cannot be permitted to intimidate and destroy our legal system."

By the time the reporters realized that Bonita had nothing new to contribute, she'd been talking nonstop for nearly ten minutes. The best part had been right at the beginning.

The sound bite about the "greasy little terrorist" was broadcast around the globe.

Ace watched Bonita's extended remarks on one of the local L.A. television stations and pointed his finger at the set, fanning an imaginary hammer on an imaginary six-shooter like the toy guns of his youth.

Shooting the chief trial counsel repeatedly.

Yearning to see her fall.

But that was silly and self-indulgent, and he could little afford to be either just now. Things were much hotter than he'd ever expected them to be. Indeed, he was seriously considering leaving right now. Cutting his losses and bailing out before something *really* bad happened. He remained only because his departure might draw too much attention, attention which simply would not do. To end the Legal Resolution Program effectively, he needed to slip away later, when things were quieter, when nobody would notice.

That would constitute success.

In the meantime, though, he was increasingly tempted to teach that self-righteous Blevins bitch a lesson. A *real* lesson, an unforgettable one. The lesson of a lifetime. He felt an almost uncontrollable urge to make an example of this woman who had so publicly maligned him. He couldn't, after all, sue her for libel. And for the life of him, he couldn't understand why the media hadn't been harder on her and her office, those alleged watchdogs of legal propriety who seemed to specialize in wrist slaps and second chances.

He'd also toyed with the notion of doing something about LAPD's Joanna Davis, who had similarly defamed him, but he'd abandoned the idea at least partly because of her resemblance to Mrs. Finch, his high school drama teacher. Also, he knew it would be too hard to get to Detective Davis, particularly after the stunt he'd pulled at her house.

She'd be watching now, on full alert all the time.

And a cop on full alert was nobody to be messed with.

34

Blanche Dodsworth walked deliberately up the salted stone steps of the Kingsfield County Courthouse, taking extra care not to slip, clenching the handrail tightly, feeling the cold, smooth metal through the palm of her thin leather glove. Her appointment with Sheriff Colwell was at nine-thirty and Reverend Moyer had promised to drive over from Ames to meet her at the sheriff's office. It was still a little difficult to realize that this odd and dreadful thing was actually happening.

Blanche had felt slightly uncomfortable bringing her concern to Reverend Linscott, the very young new minister at Trinity Methodist Church. She didn't really know him very well, and he had ideas about certain social issues that she and some of the other older parishioners were not entirely comfortable with.

But Reverend Linscott was smart and he knew how to listen. He had taken her seriously when she presented herself at the church yesterday afternoon, had listened intently, and then asked several very focused questions. It was only when he excused himself to call his retired colleague, Reverend Moyer—who had been pastor of the First Lutheran Church when the Pearse family were members—that Blanche realized he believed her.

And she was consumed with an almost overwhelming sadness.

Reverend Moyer lived over in Ames now, where he'd retired near his daughter, a physics professor at Iowa State. Rather to Blanche's surprise, he had insisted on driving over immediately after Reverend Linscott's call. In the forty-five minutes it took him to get to Kingsfield, Blanche chatted cautiously with the new minister, an earnest if misguided young man. Imagine sanctioning homosexual marriage! She wasn't ready and neither was Kingsfield.

She knew she would feel more comfortable with Reverend Moyer. Blanche had known the Lutheran minister for many years, had attended numerous weddings and funerals for members of his congregation. It was several years now since she'd last seen him and he looked suddenly old.

He was, however, as sharp as ever. From the very beginning, he made it clear he considered Blanche's fears both reasonable and well-founded, which in some ways made matters even worse. The notion that she, Blanche Dodsworth, might know the identity of such a horrible killer was really quite unnerving.

That a man of God shared her concerns caused her to literally tremble.

"Good morning, Mrs. Dodsworth," Reverend Moyer told her now, rising to greet her in the waiting area outside the sheriff's office. He helped her off with her coat and hung it beside the door. "How are you feeling this morning?"

"Perfectly dreadful," she admitted. "On the one hand, I really feel really quite foolish being here. On the other hand, I'm very frightened. Reverend Moyer, what if we're *right?*"

He helped her into a chair and sat beside her, leaning in and resting a hand on her quivering arm. "Nothing would make me happier than for both of us to be totally wrong. I spent a long time last night thinking about the Pearse family. I didn't sleep at all well, and as I tossed and turned, I remembered some other things which make me even more convinced that we belong here this morning."

The door to Sheriff Colwell's office opened and the sheriff filled the space, resplendent in his blue wool winter uniform. The sheriff was a very militaristic sort, a Vietnam veteran. Even as a Cub Scout, his uniforms had always been crisp and spiffy. It was a fond community joke that not even Clarence Colwell's wife had ever seen him out of uniform. He owned and alternated among a dozen different styles.

Reverend Moyer did the talking once they were seated in the sheriff's office. Blanche tried to watch the sheriff's face, but his desk was set up so that the window—and therefore the morning sun—was directly behind him. It was difficult to gauge his expressions.

They had not told him why they were coming, only that they considered it urgent.

"Mrs. Dodsworth and I, for separate and compelling reasons, are concerned that a former Kingsfield boy may be involved with or responsible for the murders of a number of attorneys in California," Reverend Moyer began.

Sheriff Colwell frowned. "You mean those Atterminator killings?" he asked, sounding surprised.

Reverend Moyer nodded. "We do. And we're hopeful that you might be aware of information that would tend to either corroborate or disprove our theory."

"It's possible," the sheriff conceded carefully, still frowning. This was obviously not what he'd expected. "Just which Kingsfield boy is it you think might be responsible?"

Reverend Moyer took a deep breath, looked at Blanche, and then spoke clearly. "Kevin Pearse. Whose family owned Pearse Hardware."

Blanche watched the sheriff process the information. Up until that moment he had, she was certain, simply been tolerating the whims of a couple of respectable senior citizens. But now the sheriff sat straighter, with a definite glint in his eye. Clarence Colwell had lived in Kingsfield most of his life. If he was even an occasional Mr. Fixit, he'd have been a regular customer at Pearse Hardware for many, many years.

Blanche felt simultaneously exhilarated and numb.

"Why don't you tell me just what makes you think that might be the case?" Sheriff Colwell suggested cordially, sitting back as if he had all the time in the world.

35

The first call from Iowa came into task force headquarters at 9:47 A.M. on Tuesday, December 9th. It was taken by a young detective from the county sheriff's office, a woman who'd been assigned to the task force after Warren Richardson was added to the list of victims. She'd been fielding silly phone calls for weeks now, and her initial youthful enthusiasm was beginning to falter seriously.

She placed the Iowa message atop a pile of other messages she delivered when Joanna returned from visiting her jukebox in SID. Joanna had wanted to see the box again to consider whether she might one day wish to reclaim it, and had quickly realized that the answer was no. The creep had been in the machine. Had been all over it, replacing records and labels. He'd probably even played it. She would never be able to look at the jukebox again without seeing neon-pink labels glowing in the corners of the program menu.

She might get another box. In fact, she almost certainly would. She loved having a jukebox, loved being able to select and program her own soundtrack at will. But she'd have to restock it from scratch, replacing all the records that were in the machine when it had been violated. Including, dammit, all the Bob Seger.

Detectives had found the used record store in Santa Monica where the substitute 45s had been purchased, though the clerk on duty at the time was unable even to remember if he'd sold them to a man or a woman. That they'd managed to keep the nature of her "burglary" from the media was tantamount to a miracle. The guards on the house itself were gone now, and patrol officers drove by regularly. But Joanna saw no reason to add an expensive security system to this particular horseless barn. It wasn't as if she'd be back.

"This caller sounded really worried," the young detective told Joanna now, tapping the message on top of the stack. "Thinks the Atterminator's a home boy who went to Hollywood and never came back." Her tone was flip and her smile ironic. "Like that never happened before, somebody liking it better out here than back in the boonies."

Joanna looked at the message slip, at the unfamiliar area code. Sheriff Clarence Colwell, of Kingsfield, Iowa. "Thanks," she told the young woman. She got a fresh cup of coffee and punched in the number. She was put through immediately.

As she listened, she felt her spine straighten. She'd heard out plenty of crackpots in the past weeks, talked to a lot of cops with dead lawyers they hoped to foist off on her.

This cop sounded different. This call *felt* different. She took a lot of notes, asked questions, requested further information, and closed by exchanging pager numbers. She promised to get back to the sheriff soon and hung up. Wondering.

She took it to Jacobs. "About thirteen years ago in Kingsfield, Iowa—which is apparently an hour and a half away from nowhere—a kid named Kevin Pearse went off to state college. His family owned a hardware store, and Kevin had worked there since he was little, helping out his old man."

Jacobs nodded encouragingly. "A hardware store. Sounds good so far."

"Yes, it does. A midwestern hardware store is the kind of place where a boy could learn all *sorts* of useful things. Like wiring basics, and plumbing, and how to set up and dismantle security systems. Garden poisons."

"Locksmithing?" Jacobs asked.

Joanna nodded. "I'd assume so. In any case, Kevin Pearse was an only child and he wanted to be an actor. He wanted to go to Hollywood. And he *did*, Al. But what's even *more* interesting is what was happening back home in Kingsfield while young Kevin Pearse was away at school, before he ever left Iowa."

"Yes?" Jacobs leaned forward encouragingly.

"Wal-Mart came to town."

He got it immediately. "Which put the family hardware store out of business."

Joanna nodded. "Exactly. It didn't happen right away, of course. The Wal-Mart wasn't even *in* Kingsfield, it was fifteen miles away. But Pearse Hardware couldn't compete. They closed within a year."

Jacobs frowned. "So? Seems like, if this kid wanted to kill somebody, he'd've taken out Sam Walton. Or his minions."

"Well, yeah. The guy I talked to didn't know anything specific about him hating lawyers. But he *did* know that Kevin Pearse's father died shortly before the store closed and six months after that, his mother killed herself. Kevin had already moved to Hollywood. After he buried his mother, nobody in Kingsfield ever heard from him again."

"So?"

"So he looked like the Laughlin sketch—there's two preachers and a nosy old lady sure of it. He was a little weird, they say."

Jacobs shook his head. "Davis, the kind of kids who leave those podunk towns and come to L.A. *always* seem weird to the locals. That's *why* they leave."

"True enough," she conceded. "Anyway, the local guy's going to try to get a photo and send it out here. Maybe nose around a little."

"This sheriff been running his yap to CNN?" Jacobs asked, rubbing his chin. He didn't seem nearly as excited about this as Joanna.

"He says not. He promised not to talk to anybody right now. I laid it on him pretty heavy about how this could be really big, but if it gets out, the whole thing is blown."

"Assuming this guy isn't just another failed actor selling insurance in the Valley."

"Or dead. I already thought about that. But I ran Kevin Pearse and came up empty. No license, no California ID, no arrests. He took a stage name, the sheriff said. He was going to call me back when he found out what that was." Her pager went off. "If this were a movie, he'd be on the line with the name right now."

But it wasn't, and he wasn't.

The captain came by Joanna's desk an hour later. "See you, Davis?"

She followed him to his office. He'd been solicitous but distant since the previous week, the night he'd driven to her house at midnight and stood in front of the jukebox, slowly and deliberately reading through the selections. Joanna truly *hated* it that he had been in her house. Had been in every single room of her house.

"Jacobs told me about your Iowa lead," the captain said now. "He suggested sending you out there to follow up. He says you've had experience in the midwest."

Hmmm. Joanna didn't really think that narrowly avoiding a nervous breakdown as a transplanted housewife constituted experience the captain would find meaningful. But she was not about to tell *him* that. And she hoped Jacobs hadn't either.

"I lived in Minnesota for a while. It's not exactly a foreign country, the midwest. They speak English and all that." She smiled, then reached a snap decision. "But I do think we should follow this up, and I *would* like to go."

The captain offered a rare smile in return. "Take the red-eye. You'll probably have to go through Chicago. I've been told there's no sign of anybody trying to get near you since the incident at your house, but I want you to take a bodyguard. Who do you want?"

"Nobody." Her answer was firm and immediate. The prospect of being alone again, even if it meant braving an Iowa blizzard, was deliciously seductive. "Keep your manpower here where it can do some good."

He argued briefly, then acquiesced.

She would be, once again, deliciously *alone*.

36

As the feeder flight out of O'Hare descended into a frigid central Iowa Wednesday morning, Joanna felt acutely aware of just how fast the clock was running.

There was, of course, the very real possibility that this lead would come to no better end than any of the thousands they'd already pursued and abandoned. But it felt real and Joanna was quite comfortable trusting her instincts, though she was savvy enough to find external justifications wherever possible. No point taking crap about women's intuition.

She was also acutely aware that it was probably only a matter of hours before word would fly electronically around the world that the Atterminator Task Force was nosing around Kingsfield, Iowa, seeking information about potential suspect Kevin Pearse. Back in L.A., detectives continued their frantic attempts to trace Pearse without releasing his connection to the Atterminator case.

The stakes were high.

If Kevin Pearse *was* the Atterminator and they spooked him now, nobody doubted he would disappear again. He might be able to elude them indefinitely. Maybe forever.

She looked again at the high school graduation picture Sheriff Colwell had wired the previous day.

Kevin Pearse had a certain Nobody look. His photo was almost deliberately bland, showing an attractive-enough fellow with light brown hair and regular, unremarkable features. There was nothing about the picture to suggest that a dozen years later, its subject would be suspected of terrorizing an entire profession, and one not easily terrorized, at that.

Kevin Pearse, for now, remained a cipher.

Sheriff Colwell had come across as sharp and perceptive on the phone. In the flesh he appeared a bit of a buffoon, albeit a well-organized one. For the past twenty-four hours, he'd been gathering information, obtaining the necessary search warrants from a discreet and friendly judge, and generally greasing the skids for Joanna's visit. He knew the appropriate players and had made appointments on the q.t. with several of them. He was, in short, a fine advance man.

With a little luck and a tailwind, Joanna might just learn what she needed to know before some clown from a network showed up to shove a microphone in her face. The luck might be problematic, but she had the tailwind already. Biting blasts of icy air howled relentlessly across the frozen prairie.

They began at the First Bank of Kingsfield, where the lobby was festive with silver tinsel and shiny red garlands and strings of tiny white lights. Immersed in both the investigation and her own trauma and anger, Joanna kept forgetting that Christmas was only two weeks away. She'd done no shopping, not even for her grandson.

Bank vice-president Mark Andersson was sixtyish, pale, soft, and extremely Scandinavian, a type she had known well during her Minnesota sojourn. He wore a boxy gray suit, white polyester shirt, and blue knit tie, and he began by noting officiously that he could speak only of matters in the public record. How like a banker to reflexively start covering his ass. Then he explained that he was also an attorney, and the clouds suddenly parted.

"Ted Pearse was always an extremely responsible man, fiscally," Andersson stated carefully. "But if we had realized that he was terminally ill, I doubt very much that we would have issued the loans that we did." First Bank of Kingsfield had given Pearse a second mortgage on his nearly paid-for house and a business loan on his store, both in the final year of his life. "We were already experiencing some economic decline here in town, even before the Wal-Mart came in over in Payneville, and businesses like Pearse Hardware were hit hard. The hardware store wasn't the only business that went under."

But it was the only one that Kevin Pearse cared about, Joanna thought grimly. They were on the right track here, she just knew it.

"Ted Pearse insisted on paying all his medical bills as he incurred them," Sheriff Colwell put in. "Mark here didn't know it, but Ted was already a sick man when he took out those loans, and he didn't have any health insurance at all. Cancer bills mount up fast, too. Ted spent a couple weeks in intensive care after an operation that took a wrong turn. By the time he died, those loans and just about every other penny he had were gone."

"So you foreclosed?" Joanna asked, her tone cordial and understanding. Trying to forget the time another light-haired banker—a California surfer, not a pallid Scandihoovian—had turned down her car loan because of bills her second ex left behind.

But *of course* they would foreclose. It was their *job*. They were a *bank*.

She was beginning to feel a certain empathy for the Pearse family, whose luck seemed to have taken a spectacularly bad turn a decade earlier.

"We didn't foreclose initially, of course." Round pink spots rose high on the banker's cheeks. "Sarah Pearse didn't know anything about the loans, as it turned out. Ted had kept her totally in the dark. She came in to see me the week after the funeral and it was obvious right away that she had no idea whatsoever what a tight spot she was in. We tried to help, but payments on the store loan were already several months behind. We hoped that perhaps giving her more time would help, but business just kept getting worse. Within six months, she agreed that the best solution was to close the store."

He spoke as if Sarah Pearse had had a choice. Freshly widowed and a financial neophyte, how could she possibly have known what to do?

"Her husband didn't have any life insurance?"

Banker Andersson looked uncomfortable. "A small policy, from his military service. Enough to bury him, but no more."

"You said Mrs. Pearse was unaware of the loans. Had she been involved in running the store?" Joanna asked.

"Oh, no," Sheriff Colwell said, clearly stunned by the idea. "Never. I don't believe anybody ever saw her in there until after Ted died. It was very much Ted's store. Sarah was a housewife, a homemaker, whatever you want to call it. And she wasn't the sort to go out flitting around, or even do much with the PTA or Scouts. She *really* stayed home."

"She didn't even have a checkbook," Mark Andersson added. "She didn't know how to write a check. Her husband always gave her cash to run the household."

Great life, Joanna thought. "When the store went out of business, did she take it hard?" The answer seemed self-evident, but she wanted the hometown male take on the subject.

It was even less sensitive than she expected.

Mark Andersson shrugged. "I really don't know. I never saw her again after the store closed. I tried to reach her by telephone when it became obvious that something had to be done about the home loan. Not only had she stopped paying on the second, the mortgage itself wasn't being paid, either. She didn't answer her phone and she didn't respond to letters. We sent those registered, of course," he noted, "and she did sign for them."

"So she lost the store. How long after that was it before she lost the house?"

"She didn't actually lose it," Andersson said hurriedly. "We were in the process of foreclosure, but she was still living there."

Under seige, it sounded like. "But what was the time sequence? I'm sure you've looked through your records."

"I have," he admitted. "Ted Pearse died in August. The store officially went out of business the following February, and Mrs. Pearse passed away in May."

Passed away indeed.

"I understood that she hanged herself," Joanna said nonchalantly, as if it were the sort of detail anybody might forget.

"On what would have been her forty-fifth birthday, according to the note she left," Sheriff Colwell said. "Unfortunately, she wasn't found for almost two weeks afterward. She'd become a bit of a recluse, so nobody missed her right off. Then some kids playing softball over Memorial Day weekend hit a wild ball that broke the window in the side garage door. When they went to retrieve their ball, they saw her right away. She was hanging between the car and the snowblower and by then she wasn't pretty."

"Did Kevin come back then?" Joanna asked.

Both men nodded.

"He came in here and met with me," Mark Andersson said. "Sat right in that chair where you're sitting, Detective Davis. I explained the situation vis-à-vis the property. By then, of course, we'd already taken possession of the store building."

"Did Kevin sell the house?"

"The bank held legal title to the house by the time that Sarah Pearse died," Mark Andersson said carefully, "even though we hadn't taken any steps to formally evict her. Kevin understood the ownership situation, and that he was not entitled to any proceeds from the sale of the property. We gave him the opportunity to remove the contents, of course."

"How did he seem when you talked to him?"

"I didn't really know him before," Mark Andersson said, "so I can't tell you how his behavior might have been different from normal. He was, however, quite cold and formal when he spoke to me."

What a shockeroo!

"I understand you haven't been able to sell the store," Joanna noted. They had driven past it on Main Street, standing forlornly empty.

"True enough," Andersson admitted. "And it isn't the only piece of property we acquired in the same sad fashion, I'm afraid. Expansion in Kingsfield has been limited in recent years."

"But you *did* sell the house, didn't you?" Joanna asked.

"Yes, eventually, to a young couple named Donnelly. They're both teachers at the junior high school."

Candy Donnelly was on maternity leave, totally immersed in the wonder of her first child, a chubby baby learning to roll over on a quilt on the living room floor. He was a cheerful child, very gurgly. Candy was evidently a crafter; the house was jammed with tole-painted wood and dried herbal sprays and ducks and bows and cows and gingham and cutesy pastel knickknacks. Plus a *lot* of pastel country-style Christmas decorations.

Clarence Colwell introduced Joanna as Mrs. Davis from the state, in a previously planned attempt to confer anonymity. A woman home alone with a napping baby might be inclined to pick up the phone and call CNN.

The sheriff explained that they were trying to locate Kevin Pearse, whose family had once lived in this house.

"Actually, I never met Kevin Pearse," Candy Donnelly told them. "He had gone back to Florida or wherever it was by the time we moved here. The house had been on the market for a while, because of...well, because of what happened. We were initially hesitant, but we couldn't have afforded such a large place otherwise."

"It seems like a lovely house," Joanna agreed. What was going on here, anyway? Was something wrong with her? She—a hardened police officer with nearly twenty years' experience on the mean streets of Los Angeles—had fled a house which had merely been trespassed in. There wasn't any really appropriate charge in the California Penal Code for felony record-changing. You couldn't even call it burglary, because he hadn't taken away the records he removed. He'd actually *donated* a few discs to her collection, if you wanted to get technical about it.

While this pleasant young mother felt no compunctions about raising a family in a place where a putrefying corpse had dangled in the garage for several weeks.

The house seemed stunningly ordinary, a forty-year-old wood frame two-story box on the outskirts of a small, dying town. Joanna wondered what the interior had been like when the Pearse family lived there. It was a safe enough bet that it hadn't been this cheerful when Sarah Pearse climbed up on the snowblower and knotted that noose.

"Was there anything unusual you noticed when you moved in?" Joanna asked now.

"Well, some of the furniture was still here, though we got rid of most of it. Of course if you mean *unusual*-unusual, there's a secret cupboard under the front stairs. And a false back on the closet in the boy's room. They were both totally empty, but *still*. They were *there*."

False closet backs. Secret hidey-holes. The boy's room would be where Kevin Pearse grew up.

Joanna's pulse raced. "Do you suppose I might see those places?"

Candy Donnelly was happy to oblige. Both hiding places were quite capacious, large enough to hold an adult temporarily without causing acute distress, but not so large as to be obvious. Like priest's holes in old English houses, or Underground Railroad hiding places. The compartments were very cleverly set up, with no outward signs to reveal their existence. Hinges were hidden and the carpentry was superior.

Joanna closed herself into each of them, screwed her eyes tightly shut, and tried to put herself into the mind of Kevin Pearse, who had almost certainly inhabited this very space himself at some point, years ago. What had he been thinking?

Where was he now?

"Did you look around for other secret places?" Sheriff Colwell asked. He was also fascinated by the compartments, but could barely squeeze into the one in Kevin's closet and couldn't fit at all under the stairs.

Candy Donnelly smiled. "Well, sure. And there might be more, but we haven't found 'em yet."

"You said the place was still furnished when you bought it," Joanna noted. "Does that mean things like pots and pans and dishes were here, too?"

"Some. It looked like somebody had taken a few things. There were some empty places on the shelves. But not much was gone."

"Was there any canning equipment?"

"Yeah, there was. Cartons and cartons of Mason jars, too."

"Any home-canned food?" Joanna held her breath.

"A bunch. But I've gotta tell you, none of it had dates on it and some of it looked kind of funky. So I just brought a big trash can down to the cold cellar and pitched it all."

"You were asking about the canned goods 'cause of the guy who got it with the botulism, weren't you?" Sheriff Colwell asked as they picked their way carefully down the slippery front walk past a group of plastic carolers on the lawn. The walk had been salted, but not quite enough.

The big, barrel-chested sheriff wore no overcoat and his improbable uniform featured a lot of silly cords and complicated braids and shiny hardware. He looked like an organ grinder's monkey on steroids.

"That's right," Joanna answered, her teeth chattering. She was dressed appropriately, too, still owned a comprehensive cold-weather wardrobe and was proud that she could fit into every scrap of it after two decades. "Was there ever an incident that you recall around here involving botulism and home-canned foods?" They had speculated, at the task force, that perhaps the killer had chosen that unusual method of poisoning because of an early or vivid exposure to a botulism outbreak.

"Not since before I was born," Colwell answered. "But back during World War Two, there was an outbreak at a church supper. Some people died."

And people would have talked about it, now and again. Would make self-conscious comments as they set out the hot dish at church potlucks. One more puzzle piece clunked into place. "People talked about it while you were growing up?"

Colwell chuckled as he opened the driver's door of the squad car. "That they did. Now, we can go by the high school, but that'll set the rumor mill grinding."

Joanna nodded as she got in the squad. "I agree. But as soon as the story breaks, I want to find any teachers who remember Kevin. Will you be able to help me with that?"

Colwell adjusted himself behind the wheel, slammed the driver's door, and peeled off, skidding on a little patch of ice. "You bet. But you know, once this story breaks, *everybody's* gonna remember Kevin. Your biggest problem is gonna be sorting out the bullshitters from the folks who might actually know something."

Which was, Joanna reflected, a succinct enough definition of all detective work.

The building that had once been Pearse Hardware sat on Main Street between a barbershop and a storefront insurance office. Too bad, Joanna thought, that Ted Pearse hadn't walked next door one day and gotten himself a health policy. Everybody might have been saved a *whole* lot of trouble.

Signs painted on the front window and on the brick above the door still read PEARSE HARDWARE. The display windows had five-foot backboards, behind which the store yawned dark and vacant. Sheriff Colwell had the key and a search warrant. As he unlocked the front door, Joanna shivered.

Inside, save for a few abandoned shelves arranged in lonely aisles, the place was empty, dusty and desolate. The floor plan differed, but this abandoned shell of a business carried the same general feel as L & L Hardware, Feed & Garden in Pine River Falls. The inside of the building was nearly as cold as the street outside, where the wind kept caterwauling. More snow was expected by nightfall.

"There's been nobody in here for about ten years now," Sheriff Colwell told her, closing the door. "I never heard about anybody even *considering* buying the place. It's too big and too basic. You'd need to completely renovate the building."

Hands jammed in her pockets, Joanna walked slowly to the end of an aisle and looked up at the wall where snow shovels had once been displayed. The price sign hung slightly crooked now, the dollar figure slashed through and reduced by half. The going-out-of-business sale for a multigenerational store like this would have been a heartbreaker. How much of it had Kevin Pearse been around for? What had it done to him?

Colwell sighed as he looked around. "This was a mighty fine store. For some of us, this town hasn't been the same since it's gone. It's hard to second-guess somebody like Ted Pearse, but I honestly think that deep down he must have believed Kevin would do the right thing and come back to run the place. Pay off the debts."

Do the right thing. Funny how that could mean so many different things to so many different people. "But he didn't."

"Nope."

Joanna passed through the depressing store interior until she reached a small office in the back where a beat-up desk and a couple of wooden chairs remained. She took off her lined leather gloves, flexed her icy fingers, and then put on latex replacements. She systematically opened desk and file drawers. All empty.

"Is there some way we can secure this building for a few days?" Joanna asked.

"Depends on what you want to secure it from," Colwell told her with a shrug. "Been sitting here empty ten years and nobody's bothered it yet. I can put a police seal on it, but then people will start wondering why. I can get some people out from the state crime lab if you want, good folks, FBI-trained and all them apples. But if you're figuring on bringing your own techs out here, best you do it fast."

"I'll get right on it," she promised.

"Let's go talk to Jerry Williams," Colwell suggested, "before he needs to go in to work. He probably knew Ted better than anybody. After Ted took sick, Jerry ran this place by himself and I thought it was gonna kill him to close it down."

"Were he and Kevin close?"

"Can't rightly say. Even pumping my brain like I've been doing these last couple days, I can barely remember Kevin myself. I know he was here a lot of times when I came in on the weekends and such. A nice kid, polite and all that. But that was fifteen years ago. And I never did have any kind of sense of who he was. No scrapes with the law or anything, no J.D. stuff. Never struck me as being any kind of a wrong'un. Of course through the mirror of hindsight, I can see that maybe he was a bit squirrelly."

Joanna thought of what Jacobs had said about hometown perceptions of the "misfits" who left small towns for the big city. Being different wasn't the same as being squirrelly, not by a long shot. "Anything specific?"

"'Fraid not, and believe me, I've tried to come up with something. Maybe there was stuff I didn't know about."

Clarence Colwell's tone suggested that very little transpired in Kingsfield of which he was unaware. He must have been out of town when Sarah Pearse's body was swaying silently in her garage that bygone May.

"The guy who worked here, he still lives in town?"

"Oh yeah, Jerry's still in town." Colwell's smile was ironic. "Same line of work, too. Manager of the hardware section at Wal-Mart in Payneville."

"Ted purely *hated* that Kevin wanted to be an actor," Jerry Williams stated emphatically.

On Wednesdays, Williams didn't go in to work until five. They'd found him in his immaculate, extensively stocked home workshop, joining bands of fine hardwood into a beautiful burgundy-and-gold kitchen cutting board. Everything glistened and gleamed in the virtually dust-free space. Joanna had spent time in emergency rooms that weren't this clean.

"When did that become an issue?" Joanna asked. They had moved into the adjacent pine-paneled rec room and sat on sturdy, angular homemade furniture that Jerry Williams self-deprecatingly referred to as "a bunch of old two-by-fours."

"When Kev was in high school." Williams shook his head. He was in his late thirties, slight, wearing wire-rimmed glasses and a red plaid flannel shirt neatly belted into jeans. "Why are you asking about him, anyway?"

"Can't tell you yet, Jerry, but you'll know soon enough," Clarence Colwell answered, in an official-sounding tone.

"He's not in some kind of trouble, is he?"

Well, there's an excellent chance that he murdered half a dozen people, Joanna thought. But other than that, not really. She smiled noncommittally.

The sheriff went on. "You know I'd tell you if I could, Jerry. How long'd you work at Pearse Hardware, anyway? Twelve, thirteen years?"

"Ten exactly. Almost to the day."

"Kevin worked in the store part of that time, didn't he?"

"Oh yeah. He came in after school and Saturdays all through junior high and high school. When he went away to college, he'd come in a bit on vacations, but it wasn't the same. Like as not, he'd get into an argument with Ted and bug out early."

"That happen a lot?"

"Three, four times when I was there. I'd make myself scarce in the back. Ted was a quiet fellow mostly, but something about Kevin and acting just set him off."

"What was Ted's objection?" Joanna asked.

Jerry Williams smiled a little nervously. "That acting wasn't a very, um, manly way to make a living."

"Did he think Kevin was gay?" Nobody had mentioned this possibility, but nobody had said anything so far today that would contradict it, either.

Williams shook his head vigorously. "Oh no, I really don't think so. Ted would never have said such a thing anyway. I think it was more a general feeling about immorality in show business than anything specific about Kevin. You see, there was a girl from Kingsfield who went to Hollywood a few years before Kev did, and things worked out pretty bad for her. She made some porno movies and became a heroin addict. It was quite a scandal around these parts when she overdosed. Her parents moved to Des Moines, where nobody knew them. I think what happened to that poor girl was on Ted's mind, too. But you'd really have to ask Kevin about that."

"We will," Joanna promised.

"Sarah Pearse was absolutely distraught when she learned what Ted had done, taking out those loans." Reverend Henry Moyer spoke slowly, with a reluctance that seemed to emanate from deep within. "I feel uncomfortable, somehow, discussing this. As if I'm betraying her confidence."

Which, of course, he was. But the lady was dead. And so were a lot of other people.

"I appreciate your concern, Reverend. But I can't help wondering why you agreed so readily with Mrs. Dodsworth's suspicion that Kevin might be responsible for these murders?" Joanna sipped strong Earl Grey tea from a saucered cup. On the tray that Blanche Dodsworth had set out upon their arrival, a quilted sleeping-cat cozy covered the porcelain teapot.

"It was such a tragedy," Reverend Moyer went on, ignoring the question. "And on so many levels, too. Ted Pearse was a terrifically proud man. He didn't want anyone to know he was sick, and I suspect that he probably ignored his health problems far longer than he should have. By the time he began treatment, he was a very sick man. He wanted to protect Sarah, but there again his good intentions led him astray. Instead of protecting her, he made her more vulnerable." He smiled sadly. "I haven't forgotten your question, what made me so ready to accept that Kevin might be responsible. I suppose I've been wishing that I didn't have to answer it."

"We all feel that way," Blanche Dodsworth interjected softly.

"I know." And Joanna *did* know. Nobody ever wanted to believe that those they cared about could do the sorts of dreadful things that would bring around a homicide detective.

Reverend Moyer set down his teacup, still nearly full. "Sarah consulted several attorneys after Ted died. His affairs were really quite a mess; he didn't even have a will. Sarah came to me in tears on more than one occasion after she met with the lawyers. There was an expression she used that I keep hearing in my mind.

"She would sit in my study, tears streaming down her face. I can hear her as if it were yesterday, saying, 'Oh, Reverend, I've been *so* abused by lawyers.'"

Sheriff Colwell phoned his office before they left the Dodsworth house. He'd been checking in routinely throughout the day. This time his expression clouded. "When?" he asked, sounding angry. "What'd you tell 'em?"

He listened a minute or two longer, then hung up. He made no reference to the call as they put their coats back on and prepared to leave Mrs. Dodsworth's house.

Outside Joanna looked up at him expectantly.

He glared straight ahead, not meeting her eyes. "The NBC station in Des Moines heard LAPD is in town and they're sending over a camera crew. Looks like we're busted."

"Shit!"

"Couldn't have put it better myself. But there's something else I wanted to tell you ever since the Reverend started talking about Mrs. Pearse. Something that hadn't occurred to me before."

"Yeah?"

"The lawyer Sarah Pearse finally hired to handle her end of the foreclosure and bankruptcy. Sven Lundquist." He stopped.

Joanna waited a moment, till it became clear that he really didn't want to tell her the rest. How bad could it be? "What about him?" she prompted.

Sheriff Colwell looked grim. "Sven Lundquist was killed in a single-car automobile accident a year or so after Sarah Pearse's suicide."

37

How had they gotten onto him?

Ace desperately wanted to know.

He'd accepted for a long time that sooner or later somebody might recognize him and make the connection. He'd actually been lucky it hadn't happened sooner, given that he'd spent several years in a profession where it was important to distribute your photograph constantly, to anyone who'd take it.

But it wasn't Hollywood that had caught him.

Lane Spencer hadn't been identified, not yet.

Kevin Pearse had.

It was Kevin Pearse's high school graduation picture from thirteen years earlier on the front page of the *Los Angeles Times*, in all its wide-eyed teenage glory.

But if they knew about Kevin Pearse and were prowling around Kingsfield, they'd get Lane Spencer soon enough. Linda Moraine had written him that letter after he was in the TV movie and he'd answered it. "We're all very proud," she wrote, which he took to mean she'd blabbed it up around town. At the time, that had made him feel good and he had read the letter so many times he still knew it by heart. Back then, he still believed he was going to be an actor.

Suddenly it seemed very important to know who had remembered him, who in Kingsfield had made the connection.

After he had heard the first news bulletins last night, Ace had gone into various Atterminator chat rooms on the Internet and found lots of Iowans online, speculating. Everybody claimed to have a Kingsfield connection. A guy's brother knew somebody who had a cousin whose buddy from the Marines lived in Kingsfield, that sort of shit. Somebody who was actually *from* Kingsfield came on for a while, but the guy didn't seem to know anything. He'd called himself Roy, which probably wasn't his real name. Certainly Ace never used *his* real name—not any of them—while on the Internet.

Now he needed to mobilize. Assess contingencies. Formulate his battle plan.

He didn't want to leave town now unless it became absolutely essential. More than ever it seemed crucial to hunker down and wait it out. His absence would be noted. That was the one real drawback to the geriatric tenants at the Orange Grove Arms. They read the papers and listened to TV all day long and had far too much time on their hands. If they hadn't suffered from such universally poor eyesight, one of them would probably already have recognized him from Tucker's secretary's sketch. Some were pretty far gone mentally, not unlike his employer, Mrs. Patrusak, and his late benefactress, Mrs. Kowalski.

But they weren't all dumb and forgetful, not by a long shot. If he skedaddled, one of them would catch on for sure.

A group of attorneys had offered a $100,000 reward after the death of Lorenzo J. Taft. That made him nervous, too.

He had spent a long time analyzing the graduation picture that had been released. He'd never liked it, not even at the time, and it certainly didn't look like he did now. But there were other pictures in that yearbook that more accurately represented his appearance. And once the Lane Spencer connection was made, there'd be much more recent photos, shot by professionals.

So—he would lie low.

He had all the food he could possibly need for several weeks. He would leave the building only through the back exit and he would never go outside looking less than sixty-five years old. The geezer disguise was a great one. Nobody looked very hard at old people except other old people, and their eyesight was generally shot.

Now he made a mental checklist:

The other apartment. The apartment where he'd tarried with Gina was thoroughly cleaned and the rent paid through February. Nobody was likely to enter the place before then, unless a water main burst or something. And unless they went in because they'd made him, the message he'd left behind would be meaningless to anyone who found it.

The place in Oregon. It was ready. Certainly ready enough for immediate occupancy, anyway. He'd moved some favorite tools up there in the fall, stocked the place with canned goods, and used a chain saw to cut up enough wood for several months' fuel.

His other tools would have to be left behind, and that rather hurt. But he could replace them. And he liked the idea of working on the place in Oregon with only hand tools. It felt right, in keeping with the rustic simplicity of the place. The American West had not been conquered by people operating Sears band saws. Like those who homesteaded before him, he would forge a simple pioneer existence.

The money. It was time to start wearing the rest of old Mrs. Kowalski's grubstake in a money belt. At all times. Ace doubted he'd have to bolt with no warning, but fuckups happened. He also would need to be frugal for a while to stay on the safe side, though that shouldn't be a problem. His expenses would be pretty much zilch.

The laptop. Funny how attached he'd gotten to the damn thing in recent months. He wouldn't be able to use it in Oregon anyway, not out where he was with no phone lines and no electricity. Meanwhile, it was probably time to replace the hard drive, melt down the old one, and start over. The replacement drive had been waiting in the hidden broom closet compartment since June.

The loose ends. Joanna Davis. Bonita Blevins.

Davis, he'd pretty much given up on, for purely practical reasons. Only a fool would intentionally kill a cop. He was no kamikaze.

Blevins, however, was a different matter. She continued to piss him off, over and over again, like she was *working* at it. She'd been on the news again last night, saying that she hoped the identification of the Atterminator would lead to the fiend's immediate apprehension. She routinely made public pronouncements in which she referred to him as a fiend, an animal, a dastardly coward, a barbarian.

There was no indication that she was under any particular police protection. He'd gone out to her condo again the other night, watched her shadow cross the curtains, seen no evidence of increased security other than the pathetic system she had always had.

He would try to resist temptation, but he wasn't sure he could. Blevins was such an *appealing* target, and she could be used to make an extremely cogent closing statement for the Legal Resolution Program.

If he dared.

38

Joanna lay in the predawn darkness of Barbara Colwell's sewing room and relived the chilly sense of despair she had known as a young mother in Pine River Falls. Frost painted spiky angular designs on the inside of the window beside her. Snow fell steadily outside.

She had intended to stay in a motel while in Iowa, but once the media arrived in town, Clarence Colwell insisted that she move in with his family. She had readily agreed, never dreaming that the experience would give her the sort of flashbacks that raised gooseflesh now beneath three blankets and a down comforter.

Flashbacks to the long and gloomy Pine River Falls winters after Don Olafson quit LAPD and signed on with the Minnesota State Police, buying a snowmobile and a four-wheel-drive Jeep and a house twice the size of the one they left behind in Mar Vista. It had a basement and an attic, two new concepts for Joanna, who had never before lived in a house with either. A massive boiler in that basement extended huge tentacles upward to heat the rooms above. To *try* to heat the rooms above. From Joanna's point of view, it had never quite succeeded. She never felt entirely warm.

She had tried to fit in, even as she found herself sliding into a deep and overwhelming depression. Seasonal Affective Disorder was being tentatively discussed in medical journals of the period, but everybody in Joanna's limited Minnesota circle seemed to go about life's business with robust vigor.

While Joanna had trouble getting out of bed. Found herself sobbing uncontrollably. Grew to dread the threatening skies that signaled yet more snow and even greater darkness. Only sleep could banish the depression. She dreamed of warm, sandy beaches and gently swaying palm trees and tanned surfers striding onshore carrying custom-made long-boards.

Then she would waken.

And find herself lying beneath layers of blankets, in a second-story bedroom where she could frequently see her own breath. Once she realized where she was, tears would begin to seep out the corners of her eyes. Time to get up, to get the kids dressed, to fix breakfast, to begin another day. A day whose sunrise was still two hours away.

Lying here now, watching the snowflakes pass, she knew she had been right to leave when she did, even though it ultimately meant abandoning a man she adored, a man she still loved so much it sometimes hurt to think about. She had saved her sanity by returning to southern California, at a price she no longer even tried to calculate.

And now, she realized suddenly, she was about to miss the appointment for her colposcopy. Damn! She had deliberately blocked out awareness that she was supposed to be in her doctor's office this morning at nine A.M. In Los Angeles. An appointment she couldn't possibly make.

But the colposcopy could wait. Would have to wait. She would call in later this morning and reschedule. If the procedure resulted in good news, that good news would be just as welcome later. And if it didn't, and the next step was taking a chain saw to her innards, well, what was the rush?

The public revelation that Kevin Pearse was a prime Atterminator suspect swept through Kingsfield, Iowa, like a howling summer tornado.

Nobody could believe it.

Everybody could believe it.

At first nobody remembered him and then everybody remembered him. The town was aswarm with reporters extending open mikes to all comers.

Jerry Williams was taking the day off—with the blessing of the horrified Wal-Mart store manager—to help search the former Pearse home for additional secret compartments that might yield evidence. Personally, Joanna didn't believe they'd find anything useful. Kevin Pearse had left town without looking back and he'd have cleaned out all his hidey-holes before he left.

And they might not be Kevin's hidey-holes at all. Maybe they'd been his father's. Nobody had a clue what they might have been intended for, or how they'd been used.

By midday Friday, various witnesses who knew a little bit more about the elusive Kevin Pearse had worked their way to the front of the line. Former neighbors. Hardware store customers. Teachers. The pattern that emerged was surprisingly vague.

Kevin was quiet, everybody agreed on that. Well mannered. Polite to the elderly. Hardworking. Quick with his hands. Skilled with tools. Knowledgeable about hardware. Conscientious.

University of Iowa records showed Kevin Pearse enrolled for two years as a drama major. The third year he signed up for a reduced class load and then withdrew abruptly in October. The month after Ted Pearse died.

Back in Kingsfield, Kevin's high school records showed an average student with no particular strengths or weaknesses. Except for drama, a senior elective. He aced that one clear through the year. The teacher was an M. Finch, finally recalled by some veteran teachers as an energetic young woman who'd stayed at Kingsfield High only one year. Meredith Finch had been married to a graduate student in Ames.

Nobody had any idea what had happened to her.

Until she called in from Kansas.

• • •

Joanna pushed open the side door of the courthouse housing the Kingsfield cop shop on Friday afternoon and found herself plastered against the wall by a truly shocking wind.

She was sneaking out to take Clarence Colwell's Jeep back to pack her bag, shower, and await the arrival of the deputy who would drive her to Lawrence, Kansas. But first she'd have to *reach* the Jeep, parked half a block away.

The streets and sidewalks looked slippery, too, and she wasn't sure she could drive the Jeep back out to the Colwells' without running off the road, which would be decidedly embarrassing. She had been a terrible winter driver, fearful of skids and getting stuck and running into things, all of which had happened when she was behind the wheel in the endless winter of Pine River Falls. But it hadn't been windy like this in Pine River Falls. Just cold and dark.

As Joanna well knew, there were some extremely tall trees between here and the North Pole. Kirsten was in the midst of some of those trees right now at Don's house outside Duluth, with little Jamie. In fact, Kirsten actually sounded as if she were enjoying her unanticipated winter vacation. Maybe she was. Seattle was pretty dreary in winter, and snow was prettier than rain.

But apart from those trees, the earth was perfectly flat between central Iowa and the Arctic, with no natural obstacles to slow a determined wind. Right now, it was beginning to snow again. Little warning snowflakes whisked past, going sideways through the bitter chill, reminding everybody that they had a lot of relatives headed for town.

Somebody stood across the street, leaning on a streetlight pole, a hulking figure in a heavy, hooded dark parka. No obvious video camera.

Joanna's hand moved automatically for her gun. The gun that was deep inside her purse, a purse she could barely open in the wind, wearing heavy gloves. The figure started toward her, crossing the deserted street.

Shit!

She held her ground a moment, huddled against the wall,

watching from under the thick knitted cap she had borrowed out of the Colwell odds-and-ends bin. There was, she reminded herself, no reason to be worried about her safety in Kingsfield, Iowa. This was the last place on earth where Kevin Pearse was likely to show up just now.

Then the figure spoke. "Welcome to the midwest, Jodi. Ordered up this weather just for you." She hadn't heard that voice in years.

She peered more closely at the shadowed face beneath the hood. There was a moustache there, a moustache coated with frost. Yes, it was definitely Stampley. John Stampley of the *Los Angeles Times*, and years earlier, of Poly High in North Hollywood, Joanna's alma mater.

"John!" she exclaimed, feeling genuine delight at seeing a friendly, familiar face. "What on earth are *you* doing out here?"

Stampley grinned. He was a couple years younger than Joanna, which would put him in his late forties. Too old for a Valley boy to be hanging out in frozen Iowa cornfields. Stampley was, and always had been, a likable, easygoing guy. Their paths had crossed regularly when he was in the *Times* Westside bureau and she a freshly minted detective in West L.A. Both were married at the time, but she'd enjoyed having a drink with Stampley now and again. He was bright and honest and he kept his word. Then he went off to the Miami bureau and she hadn't seen or heard from him in years.

"Hoping to waylay you, Jodi," he admitted cheerfully. His heavy jacket, she could see now, was dark brown. His arm looked like an enormous sausage as he waved one gloved hand toward the front of the courthouse, where several TV news vans had taken up permanent residence. A shivering reporter with big hair and an even bigger parka was doing her stand-up. "I knew you were in there somewhere and that sooner or later you'd have to come out. I also figured you probably weren't any fonder of the press than you used to be, so you'd try to *sneak* out."

It was too cold to stand outside and talk. She nodded at the door she'd just left and dug out the key Colwell had given her after

CNN arrived and the courthouse went into lockdown. "C'mon inside for a minute." She turned the key in the lock.

Stampley pulled open the heavy door, followed her inside, and stomped his feet on the big black rubber mat. He slid back the hood of his jacket, peeled off his gloves, and grinned. "Much better. Mighty cold out there. So how's Kingsfield treating you, Jodi?"

Joanna smiled. Stampley was one of a *very* few people who even knew she had once been called Jodi, and one of even fewer she permitted still to use the name. Jodi was what she was called as a child and teenager, for her first two decades, until Don Olafson walked into the stereo store where she worked, seeking four-foot-tall KLH electrostat speakers and changing her life forever. Joanna was a beautiful name, Don had told her on their first date, and Jodi Davis had ceased to exist.

"Swell, thanks. They send you out from L.A. on this?"

He shook his head. "Naw. I'm with the *Times* Chicago bureau right now. Actually, I *am* the *Times* Chicago bureau. You here by yourself, Jodi?"

"Yep, I guess I'm LAPD's Iowa bureau. You know, I truly am glad to see you, but I can't tell you a damn thing."

Stampley shrugged. "That's perfectly all right. When I got the call to come out here, I was slogging my way through the regional angle on new approaches in solid waste management. The absolute pits. But Jesus, Jodi, the Atterminator! Is he really Kevin Pearse?"

"Nice try, John." An idea had been circling in the back of her head ever since she first recognized the hulking figure outside the door. "You in town by yourself?"

He wiggled his eyebrows, nodding. "And very available."

"I'm not looking for cheap thrills," Joanna told him, laughing. "But you may be able to help me with something, and if you can, then I can help you, too."

Stampley humbly bowed his head. "You know any time that I can be of assistance to any officer of the law, it makes me a happier and more fulfilled person."

"Can it, Stampley. You got a car?"

He nodded.

"One that can make a road trip even if the weather gets worse?"

"Within reason. It's a Jeep Ranchero."

The same car Clarence Colwell drove. Maybe this was a portent.

"Here's the deal," she told Stampley impulsively, speaking softly, mindful that others roamed the halls of the Kingsfield County Courthouse on this blustery Friday afternoon. That even with security technically airtight, somebody inside could easily be feeding info for dollars to a reporter. The miracle would be if there were only one such somebody.

Of course, she herself was about to compromise security by actually *co-opting* a reporter, but that was different. This was the enemy she *knew*. Her homey. "I need to go and talk to somebody in another town. If you take me there and bring me back without telling *anybody*, particularly not anybody at the *Times*, I'll give you first crack at this particular information. And by extension, at the person, too. It may not last long, but it'll be a great exclusive while it's yours."

"I need to check with my editor."

"You check with your editor and there's no deal. I already had a plan for doing this and I can still use it, no problem. Somebody from the Kingsfield PD will take me and you'll be left in the dust." She grinned. "And don't bother trying to follow, either. I'll be tossing roofing nails and broken glass out the window behind us as we squeal out of town. You haven't got a chance."

"Roofing nails from Pearse Hardware?"

She laughed.

"And where would we be going?" he inquired, after a moment.

She shook her head. "Uh-uh. You agree to my terms and give me your word of honor—*and* your cell phone, not that I don't trust you—and then we can leave. From now on you're my shadow. And if you fuck me on this, Stampley, you'd better hope you never get transferred back to L.A. I've got a long memory and a lot of friends."

"And it's my sincere desire to remain a pleasant part of that memory and one of those friends," he assured her. "I can live with your conditions, and I'm willing to skip the editor if you insist. But I need to call my wife. I always call and tell her where she can reach me, even when I'm *not* in possible danger from a homicidal maniac."

"He doesn't kill reporters, Stampley."

"Not yet," he noted. And it wasn't a bad point. If you were seeking the ethically challenged, a lot of the media qualified handily.

"Of course you can call your wife. Same wife?"

Stampley nodded. "Same wife."

"Good for you," she told him approvingly. "And the kids?"

"Same kids, too," he answered with a grin. "We thought about trading in the little guy, but his blue-book value was too low. Now he's got a kid of his own."

For the first time, Joanna considered the possibility that she might actually *enjoy* the drive to Kansas.

The two hundred and eighty miles from Kingsfield to Lawrence, Kansas, was nearly all due south and mostly on Interstate 35. Some four hundred miles in the other direction on I-35 was Duluth, where Kirsten and Jamie were holed up, celebrating Santa Lucia and baking butter cookies. Joanna's son, Mike, in Minneapolis, was actually *closer* than her destination. Joanna briefly considered these ironies, then resumed packing.

Around four-thirty, just as it was getting really dark, Joanna and John Stampley slipped away from the Colwell home. "Aim for Kansas City," Joanna told Stampley, and he tipped his hat and headed toward the highway.

Once they got to the Interstate, an insistent tailwind whooshed them along. The night sky remained rich and black and star-strewn, with no hint of snow. The roads were clear and dry. By six-thirty, Des Moines was behind them and the car interior was perfumed by the drive-through fast-food dinner they'd just picked up. Stampley was sailing at about eighty-five, playing Van Morrison, stuffing a supersized order of fries in his face.

"I hope you realize," Joanna told him mildly, "that if you get stopped for speeding, I can't help you. We need a low profile here, and I don't plan to bring out my badge unless it looks like they're hauling you off to the hoosegow. In which case you're in deeper shit from me than the state troopers."

"Duly noted, Officer Jodi."

She smiled. "I'm not officially telling you to slow down, John, being as how I'm a bit outside my jurisdiction. But when you see that light-bar go off in your rearview mirror and it looks like the Fourth of July, you're on your own."

Stampley looked over, grinned, and lifted his foot from the accelerator. "I was just trying to speed the course of truth, justice, and the American way. But listen, Jodi, I could *really* use a little break here. I left Chicago at four this morning and I'd already driven over three hundred miles before I took up my vigil outside the courthouse. My *lengthy* vigil. This is very un-macho of me, and I know you cops set a lot of store by manliness, but I need some rest. You think you could maybe drive for a while?"

Joanna had just settled into a comfortable position and was contemplating closing her own eyes. But she wasn't really tired and she'd filled a coffee thermos when they stopped. "Sure thing, Stampley. Pull off at the next truck stop and while we change places, the citizens of Los Angeles will buy you a tank of gas."

They were registered in connecting rooms at the Lawrence Holiday Inn in time for the ten o'clock news. Before retiring, Joanna locked Stampley's cell phone, laptop, and modem in her suitcase and extracted his Scout's honor promise that he wouldn't use his room phone.

That accomplished, she was asleep in two minutes.

39

The warm southern California rain began late Friday and continued steadily, the sort of quietly methodical storm that might end in twenty-four hours or could go on for a week.

Bonita Blevins heard raindrops insistently pummeling the shake shingles of her townhouse roof when she woke at six, the hour she normally rose to go to work. The room was very dark and she moaned reflexively; the freeway would be a nightmare.

But wait a minute.

The alarm hadn't gone off. She realized after a moment that today was Saturday. That she planned to work at home this weekend and could lie in bed all morning if she wanted. Not that she would, of course. But maybe she'd just rest a little longer. She rolled over and tucked herself snugly into the goose-down duvet.

As the rain let up slightly, became steady and soothing and monotonous, Bonita drifted back to sleep.

At four-thirty that afternoon, it was still raining steadily and Bonita's dining table was covered with files and papers. She was inordinately proud of the progress she had made in this controlled environment, free of unwanted and irrelevant interruptions. Lately it was impossible to get anything done at work.

The doorbell rang.

Bonita jumped, then froze. She wasn't expecting anybody, wasn't friendly with the neighbors. And it was too late to be the mailman or UPS. It was nearly dark again.

She decided to ignore the doorbell.

A minute passed and it rang again. Twice this time.

Curiosity and annoyance got the better of her. In her Isotoner slippers, she tiptoed across her living room to the doorway. There she peered out through the fish-eye peephole.

An elderly man stood just inside the overhang of her tiny front porch. Behind him, rain cascaded off the edge of the roof in a solid sheet. The building had no gutters. The old man gave a rheumy cough, then reached forward and tapped tentatively on the door.

Bonita had two deadbolts and a chain lock securing the door, plus the security wiring she'd installed after what happened to Francesca. And this guy looked truly pathetic. What possible danger could there be in talking to him through the door?

"Yes?" she queried, speaking loudly and firmly.

He jumped back, startled, almost losing his balance. As he stumbled unsteadily, he got thoroughly drenched by the sheet of water pouring off the roof. He wore a shabby brown suit under one of those cheap clear plastic raincoats sold by the checkout at Sav-on for when you get caught out in an unexpected deluge. The raincoat's hood was pulled up over a battered brown felt hat, the kind Bonita's grandfather had worn to church.

"I am sorry to bother you," he began. His accent was vaguely eastern European. "I am looking to find the apartment of my niece and it is not making sense. She is in number 1107-A and you are number 1107-B. But why are you here and she is not?"

Because the street numbers in this place were assigned by an idiot, Bonita thought. She relaxed slightly. "Each complex has a letter," she explained, "and within that complex the numerical sequences mirror each other."

The confusion on his wrinkled face was evident. "Mirror? I am not ..."

She started over. "Each section of the development has the same set of numbers as all the others. You can tell them apart by which one has which *letter*."

Comprehension did not seem to be dawning. "So then she is not by here?"

"No. She's over on the opposite side. Where you turned right and drove in here, if you'd turned left, you'd find her complex. Just drive straight across when you go out. Her place will be in the same position as mine, only backwards." Even to Bonita this sounded needlessly muddled. Had so many years in the law rendered her incapable of simple communication?

The expression on the old man's face grew more dumbfounded. "I am sorry," he said, starting to turn. "I am bothering. I go."

Bonita felt suddenly sorry for him, and that she'd been unnecessarily mean. "Why don't you give me your niece's phone number and I'll call her and tell her to go outside and watch for you."

He shook his head. "Oh, I could not do...I will go. I will find her."

"Don't be silly," Bonita insisted. "Do you have her phone number?"

He fumbled in a pocket, pulled out a battered little brown

address book, and opened it, moving it back and forth to focus. "Her name is Elizabeth Jacoby," he said, "and she is at 555–2359. But you really do not need…"

"Just wait on the porch out of the rain," Bonita told him. She crossed quickly to the telephone and punched in the number. It rang. And rang and rang and rang. After a dozen rings she hung up and tried again. Same thing.

She went back to the door where the old man stood, patient and stoop-shouldered in his dripping raincoat.

"I'm sorry," she told him. "I'm afraid she didn't answer. You *did* say 555–2359, didn't you?"

He pulled out the address book again, examined it. "Yes."

Bonita frowned. "Is she expecting you?"

"Five o'clock, she told me come," he answered. "I am early. Perhaps she is at store." He turned. "I will go over, try to find. I am sorry to trouble you."

"No trouble," Bonita told him, stepping back and moving away. She noticed, since she'd been moving around, that she was hungry, realized she hadn't eaten since the bagel and half grape-fruit she'd called breakfast at ten.

A sudden sharp cry came from the other side of the door, followed by a distinct and heavy thud.

Bonita whirled, put her eye back to the peephole and winced. The old man had fallen and his head rested on the planter beside the door. Rain off the roof was pouring onto his splayed legs.

She punched the numbers into the security keypad to disarm her system and hastily undid the locks, clumsy with anxiety. What seemed an eternity later, she swung open the door. The old man lay utterly still, awash in rain. Good Lord, was he *dead?*

As she leaned down, panicked, to see if he was breathing, she saw his right hand dart suddenly from beneath his body. It was holding something small and black and gunlike.

You bastard! she thought. *How could I be so stu—*

But then there was an incredible, searing zap in the side of her neck.

And that was that.

Meredith Demetrius lived in a huge old two-story house that looked, on a December Saturday morning, like a Christmas card. Drifts of pristine snow frosted the gabled roof and icicles dangled from the porch roof.

From the sidewalk out front, Joanna could see an eight-foot tree covered with blinking lights through the lace-curtained living room window. Beyond that, a young woman walked into the living room carrying a baby. This lady was about to have her life changed, and not for the better. Why was it, Joanna wondered, that being a good citizen so often entailed paying such horrendous dues?

She had left John Stampley in the car reading science fiction and—even though she sort of trusted him—she was still carrying his various techno-toys in her oversized shoulder bag. At breakfast this morning she'd given him the ground rules. After Joanna talked to Meredith Demetrius, she would apprise the woman of the inevitable arrival of a horde of media jackals. Then she would suggest a single interview with Stampley as an alternative, an interview that would conceal her current name and hometown, running only after she had a chance to decamp for some other location.

Her identity would be leaked sometime, by someone. This Joanna knew. So it seemed a logical compromise for someone who had announced at the very beginning of her call to the Kingsfield Police that she *absolutely* did not want to be publicly identified.

Joanna had awakened feeling antsy, had called in to let the captain know the arrangement she had in mind with Stampley. He didn't like it, but he hadn't forbidden her to do it.

Now she rang the doorbell and heard chimes inside. The foresty pungence of a large wreath on the door made Joanna wonder fleetingly just where *she'd* be living at Christmas. She watched through the lace curtains in the beveled glass door panels as the woman carrying the baby hurried toward her. Joanna held up her badge at the window and the door swung open.

The woman was slim and petite in evergreen sweats decorated with red and white poinsettia blossoms. She had to be at least thirty-six or thirty-seven, but she looked younger, and the cheerful baby appeared to be about nine months old. A single long braid hung down her back and she wore no makeup on her fresh young face. It was a face that looked oddly familiar and it took Joanna a moment to realize why. The hair was very different, but Meredith Demetrius looked a lot like Joanna herself had, many years ago. Back when she was still Jodi, and during her first few years as Joanna.

"Good morning, Mrs. Demetrius, I'm Detective Davis." The ghost of Christmas future.

"Please, come in." She pulled the heavy old door open wider and Joanna stepped inside. "I'm Meredith. This is my son, Nicholas, Jr. Would you like some coffee? I just made a fresh pot and there's some baklava that my mother-in-law made yesterday."

"That sounds lovely," Joanna lied. She loathed baklava, baked paper drenched in supersweet honey.

Joanna followed the young woman back to a large, cheerful kitchen, with lavender gingham curtains at the windows and matching cushions on the captain's chairs at the round oak kitchen table. Meredith set the baby down in front of a busy board in a playpen and poured two cups of coffee. In front of Joanna she set a plate of gooey, dripping baklava.

"I really appreciate your calling us," Joanna told her. "It can't have been easy to do. But we really are grateful. So often people don't want to get involved."

Meredith Demetrius looked down into her coffee cup. "I didn't even know about the killings," she said softly. "I don't read the newspaper and we don't have a TV."

Come again? *No TV?* Joanna had heard about people like this. Sometimes they wrote letters to the editor of the *Times*. But she couldn't remember a single residence she'd been in as a cop—from the raunchiest crack house to the most luxurious mansion—that didn't have at least one television somewhere. More often there were half a dozen, including a large-screen for sports and a little guy in the car.

"It was my ex-husband who called me," Meredith went on, "and asked if I'd heard about Kevin Pearse. He remembered me talking about Kevin years ago. When he told me what was happening, and that they thought Kevin was *responsible* for it, I was just horrified. I knew I didn't have any choice. I had to tell you."

Joanna sipped her coffee, nodding and murmuring as the young woman talked. The ex-husband was troubling; they'd need to put a gag on him right away. In her initial call, Meredith had explained that she had divorced shortly after leaving Kingsfield and then quickly remarried.

"I taught school for six years in three different states before we finally settled down here," she said now. "The first job I ever had, right out of college, was in Kingsfield, teaching high school English. Kevin Pearse was in my drama class and then he joined the Drama Club. He had some problems with that, and with rehearsals, too, 'cause he was supposed to work a lot in his dad's store after school. But of all the kids in that first class, he was the only one who'd even *thought* of the possibility of acting as a career. Which was odd, 'cause he was so self-conscious at first that he almost couldn't perform at all.

"One time I had the kids break into little groups and then act out some scene of family strife." She looked a little embarrassed. "I didn't realize yet just how much of an intrusion that kind of assignment could be. Anyway, Kevin did his scene with another boy and a girl but it was Kevin's show. It upset me no end. Kevin played the father, berating his 'son' for wanting to be an actor. I was shocked. Kevin was so *into* the role, and so verbally *abusive* that I couldn't quite believe it. I mean, up until then Kevin was pretty vanilla pudding. Average looks, average behavior, average grades, average *everything*."

Meredith Demetrius took a deep breath. "That skit was the first I realized that there was this other…this *dark* side to him. I got to know him better because he sought me out. I asked him about the skit and the father's anti-acting diatribe and he swore the whole thing was taken straight from life. Down to and including that the mother never said a word. That was one of the comments I made when I was grading the scene, that the mother just kind of hovered around but never spoke. 'That's what she does,' Kevin said."

"Did you ever meet his parents?" Joanna asked.

Meredith shook her head, just as the baby started to kick up a fuss. "Gimme a sec." She scooped the baby out of the playpen, pulled a bottle from the refrigerator, and microwaved it. Soon Nicholas, Jr. was back in his playpen, lustily guzzling the nasty beige concoction.

She sat back down. "Both Kevin's parents came to Open House in the spring, and I know they were at the plays when Kevin performed. But I never did get to talk to them. At Open House, they looked in while I was talking to some other parents and left almost immediately. Kevin's dad was built like him and he had the same kind of ordinariness. I honestly can't remember having any impression at all of his mother. Except I *think* she was there. Isn't that a horrible way to remember somebody?"

Joanna nodded, pushing around her baklava, pretending to take a bite. "You told me on the phone about a play that Kevin wrote."

The young woman looked pained. "Yeah, I did. The assignment was to write dialogue for a scene in a familiar setting, to hear the way people talk. But Kevin wrote an entire little play, with quite a few scenes. Called it something like *Blue Ribbon Veggies*. It was set on a farm run by a widow. She kept hiring different men to help work in her vegetable garden and we never saw any of them again. Real fast little scenes. Then it had this kind of Alfred Hitchcock ending where she hires another man and takes him out to the vegetable garden. She has him dig up a section of the garden and then she kills him and plants him. Then she picks a bunch of vegetables and goes to the county fair and wins a bunch of blue ribbons."

Joanna shuddered. "Holy moley. That is *really* creepy."

The message was clear and terrifying. Kevin Pearse had been giving serious thought to serial murder since he was in high school, thirteen years ago. Had been, at seventeen, organized enough to plot out what would have made a creditable "Twilight Zone."

"Of course, the writing wasn't really very good," Meredith went on. "The exercise was about dialogue and the dialogue was all stilted. But what a story line!" She shook her head in wonder. "But you know, you really ought to talk to the girl who played the farm wife. Linda something. Morelli? Moroney? I had the impression that she was Kevin's girlfriend."

"I was never Kevin's *girlfriend*," Linda Moraine Gilhooly explained carefully. She was probably eighty pounds heavier than the plump senior Meredith had identified from pictures in the Kingsfield High yearbook. Linda's husband managed a toy store in the local mall, which explained both the knee-deep litter of plastic trucks in the house and his Saturday absence two weeks before Christmas. Through the family room window, Joanna watched rambunctious five-year-old twin boys conduct a snowball war around a pair of Little Tykes log cabins.

It had only taken an hour to locate Linda Gilhooly in St. Joseph, Missouri, once Joanna called the name in to Clarence Colwell. By then the Kingsfield grapevine was humming so loudly you could almost hear it in Lawrence by sticking your head out the window. And St. Joseph was barely an hour and a half away from Lawrence.

Once again Joanna had a deal with Stampley to interview Linda when she finished, and this time he waited more genially in the car, laboring diligently on his laptop on the Meredith Demetrius interview. The timing had been close to perfect; by the time Colwell found Linda's mother and got her address, Stampley was just about finished talking to Meredith. Real teamwork.

"I *knew* Kevin," Linda explained cautiously, "but I don't really know what Mrs. Finch means about this girlfriend business. I don't think he *ever* had a real girlfriend in high school. I maybe knew him a little better than some from being in drama together and sometimes going into the hardware store with my brother. Kevin never really struck me as having close friends, boys *or* girls, but he was always nice enough to me. Anyway, he went away to school and the next thing I knew there was all that horrible stuff about his family."

Joanna nodded. It didn't seem worth pushing the girlfriend issue. Linda had been heavy in high school and might not have dated much herself. If she'd nursed an unrequited crush on Kevin, it hardly mattered at this point, except to the extent that it might have made her more observant. "Did you see Kevin when he came back for his parents' funerals?"

"When his dad died, yeah. There was a great big funeral for his dad and I went with my folks. But I didn't *talk* to Kevin then, other than to say I was sorry. He was with his mom and everything, and we weren't close enough to go back to the house after. And then when his mom died the next spring, there wasn't any service or anything. On account of the way it happened and all. I heard he'd been in town, but I didn't see him before he left. And he never came back again." She sighed. "Would you like more coffee?"

"Sure," Joanna agreed, following Linda into the kitchen. It was excellent brew, designer coffee having insinuated itself even into remote corners of the heartland.

"I *did* talk to Kevin around when the store closed, though," Linda continued as she poured Joanna another cup and set some Christmas cookies on a plate. "I'd heard he was back that December after his dad died. I went in to get a Christmas present for my brother, a set of socket wrenches I knew he wanted. Kevin let me have them for half price. He said not to tell anybody he gave me that price, cause the going-out-of-business sale wasn't till after the first of the year. That was the first I knew for sure that the store was gonna close."

"Did Kevin say anything about where he was living or what he was doing?"

Linda Gilhooly's eyes glittered with the memory. "Oh yeah! He told me he was living in Hollywood, that he was going to be an actor, just like Mrs. Finch had suggested. I thought that was just about the most amazing thing I'd ever heard. Kevin Pearse, somebody I *knew*, was in *Hollywood!*"

It did boggle the mind.

"He like it out there?" Joanna wondered neutrally, leaning on the kitchen counter and biting the head off a gingerbread girl.

"You know, it was funny. One minute he was going on about what a great place it was and how much he loved being an actor and then in the next breath he called it a cesspool." She shook her head.

"A cesspool. I was shocked. Anyway, after that he went back and like I said, I didn't see him when his mom died. But I do kind of watch a lot of TV and I kept looking for him. And then one night I saw him. He was in a TV movie about a teenage girl who had some rare disease and died. Kevin played her brother. He wasn't on all that much, it was mostly about the girl and her mother, but I knew right away it was him. And then I looked for his name at the end but it said the brother was played by Lane Spencer."

Lane Spencer.

Lane Spencer.

The stage name. The L.A. name. The connection they'd been waiting for, searching for, yearning for. Joanna could barely contain herself. She wanted to scream and do cartwheels.

Instead she smiled graciously. "Really," she murmured.

"I wrote him a letter," Linda went on, appearing mildly discomfited by the admission. "To Lane Spencer in care of *A Harvest of Tears*—that was the name of the movie—at NBC. And about a month later, I got a note back from him. Saying thanks for writing."

Joanna held her breath. "You wouldn't still have that note by any chance?"

This time Linda Gilhooly definitely blushed. "Yeah, I do. After you called, I dug around and found it."

From there, matters began to move with stunning speed.

Stampley came in to interview Linda—a far more willing subject than Meredith Demetrius—while Joanna closed herself into the Gilhooly guest bedroom and called the task force office. It was Saturday afternoon, but the whole gang was in. As she passed along the new information to Jacobs, he let out an uncharacteristic whoop of glee.

"Attagirl, Davis!" he shouted. He took down the pertinent information. "Now we can *move!* Listen, Walters wanted to talk to you when you called in. Hang on."

And as her co-workers moved into an Atterminator blitzkrieg in L.A., Lee Walters came on the line. "So good things sometimes *do* happen in the midwest."

"Now and again." Joanna felt an instantaneous sense of connection, as well as unabashed jealousy. Back in L.A., they might well move in on the Atterminator within the hour. And here she was, stuck in a town she'd never heard of before this morning, waiting to go back to Kingsfield, Iowa. She told Lee what she'd already told Jacobs.

"Even if he's not working now, once they get into SAG records, there'll be an address for residuals," Joanna told Lee confidently. "And if he was in an NBC movie, he had to join SAG." Not that joining the Screen Actors Guild would be any kind of burden for an aspiring actor. Acting wannabes would do almost anything to gain the coveted SAG card. It was validation of the highest order.

"What would you know about residuals?" Lee wondered. "You moonlighting or something?"

"No, but I grew up in the Valley. And trust me, any actor who isn't working regularly—which is to say just about *any* actor—will stay in touch with SAG. Residuals come in from odd stuff, foreign markets, God knows what. And even if the money isn't much, it's a reminder that they're *actors*. That they've been paid to act, and God willing, it'll happen again."

"But you can't count on actors to be *reliable*," Lee noted. "Actors are the ultimate flakes."

"Tell me about it."

Lee laughed. "Doesn't sound like I need to. Wait a minute, it's coming back. Wasn't Kirsten hooked up with an actor for a while?"

"Yep. When she was in college. A real charmer he was. Eric Landon. You've never heard of him because he's deservedly a nobody. But Christ, was he a looker! And sexy, too. Very sexy. *Shit!*" She smashed her palm on the desk. Even now it infuriated her to think about that smarmy bastard. Who had possessed the unmitigated gall and incredible poor taste to hurt and reject Joanna's firstborn.

"So what happened?"

"Kir moved in with him, and I bit my tongue bloody. Don had a fit, but he was halfway across the country and besides, she was just as stubborn as he was. The relationship lasted maybe a year altogether. And wouldn't you know, when they split up, Eric owed Kirsten a lot of money. He was into her big-time, at least by her standards. She's a tightwad Swede like her old man."

"Oh yeah, and you're a real wild and crazy spendthrift. Queen of the Valley thrift shops. Lady Goodwill."

Joanna laughed. "Your point. Anyway, she didn't want to tell me right away."

"I can see her position," Lee noted. "You tell your mom the cop a story like that, she might just go over and shoot the asshole's balls clean off."

"She might indeed. Kirsten knew how pissed I'd be, but she wasn't going to let him get away owing. She got his current address through somebody she knew at SAG."

"Very resourceful girl."

Joanna grinned. "It's in her genes. And whaddaya know? It turned out Eric was living on a boat in Marina del Rey with an attractive young restaurant manager. When she found that out, Kirsten stopped being so proud. She called her old lady and asked for some muscle." She shook her head. "But I don't imagine you want to hear about senseless police brutality."

"You know I *love* hearing about senseless police brutality. It's one of my very favorite subjects."

Having the name Lane Spencer didn't yield an instant arrest after all.

Joanna and Stampley drove back to Kingsfield, where it was dark again and three inches of fresh snow glittered on the news trucks outside the courthouse. When she called in to the task force, holding her breath, she found out that Lane Spencer hadn't picked up his acting residuals for ages. He'd long ago gone inactive, and SAG claimed not to have had a current address on him for five years.

She learned that Kevin Pearse had changed his name in Hollywood because a Kevin Pearce with a *c* was already a member of the Screen Actors Guild. SAG rules were inflexible on this point: one customer per name, no exceptions, no matter what you were called at birth. If somebody else had registered it—even if that person was already dead—you were shit out of luck. Kevin Pearse couldn't have joined SAG under his own name any more than he could have called himself Humphrey Bogart or Clark Gable.

In other bad news, the nine-year-old return address on the letter to Linda Moraine in Kingsfield turned out to be an apartment complex in North Hollywood that had been razed years ago as part of a road-widening project.

On the plus side, they finally had something to release besides Kevin Pearse's high school graduation photos. Composite photographs of Lane Spencer began surfacing from dormant files all over town and became the top media story of the day.

In the nation.

And from them came the first genuine connection to the Atterminator case.

Late Saturday afternoon, Patricia Marquette, a young woman who had taken acting classes with Reggie Benton, marched into the Beverly Hills Police Department and announced that she had once seen Reggie with somebody who looked just like Lane Spencer, going into a small apartment building off Santa Monica Boulevard. Patricia had never mentioned to Reggie that she'd seen her and she'd never seen the guy again.

But she *did* remember the building. It was right next to a house where she had attended a wrap party for a UCLA student film in which she had starred.

The seedy little fourplex was still there, Jacobs told Joanna when she called in after Stampley dropped her off at the Colwells'. All four apartments were rented, but only three were occupied. None of the other residents knew M. Varner, the purported tenant in apartment B. None of them recalled ever even *seeing* M. Varner. And M. Varner didn't respond to knocks.

Jacobs called again after they went into the apartment with a search warrant. It was empty, wiped clean. No food, no clothing, no personal effects. A few pieces of battered yard-sale furniture.

And a message scrawled on the bathroom mirror in lipstick: *Sorry I missed you.*

"The lipstick was sitting right there on the sink," Jacobs announced. His tone was an odd combination of triumph and defeat. "Wiped clean like everything else. Scarlet Passion by Revlon."

The very shade and brand smeared on the lips of the late Lorenzo J. Taft, as mentioned in the Atterminator's note to Joanna Davis.

41

Apart from that one little trip out to Claremont, Ace stayed in over the weekend, roaming restlessly around his apartment, two televisions running constantly.

He felt a bit silly having two TVs in the same room, actually, or having two sets at all. Still, he'd seen no reason to leave behind that nice little Trinitron when he abandoned the Mike Varner apartment. Turned out to be a lucky thing he had both sets going, too, when a local station he wouldn't normally watch came on with a breathless bulletin: a police raid in West Hollywood believed to be a major breakthrough in the Atterminator case.

Nobody had any details yet, but it sounded as if they'd found the Varner apartment, much sooner than he would have liked. Not particularly good. Still, he had made it as dead an end as one could hope for. It would have been even deader if he'd resisted the impulse for set decoration, but hey, this was show biz.

The TV stations were really scouring Hollywood, he had to give them that, talking to every lowlife and wannabe that Ace had ever known in his brief tenure as Lane Spencer. People he didn't even remember were claiming they'd been best buddies. And the ones he *did* remember were something else.

Jeremy Randolph, the faggy Brit agent with the bad teeth and the worse breath—a man who had briefly represented Lane Spencer nine years ago simply because he was the *only* person willing to—had been interviewed in London, where he had apparently retreated to bugger schoolboys. "He was a very determined young man," Randolph told reporters, "but he had difficulty infusing that determination into his characterizations."

Nobody followed up the Randolph interviews with what struck Ace as obvious: that he had managed to infuse *quite* a lot of determination into recent characterizations.

But all told, Ace's favorite Atterminator Moment so far was when a girl he had fucked in a bathroom at a party—her sitting on the sink with her ass on somebody's toothbrush—described him as "brooding."

Brooding? As if that girl could possibly have noticed. She was yelping like a litter of puppies.

Lane Spencer, overall, didn't seem to have made a very enduring impression on Hollywood, which was certainly no surprise to Ace. There was a clip they kept playing from *Harvest of Tears* that he rather liked, both from a technical acting standpoint and also because it didn't look at all like his current appearance. He had streaked his hair blond for the role of a self-centered skateboarding rebel.

It was a sad commentary on his so-called acting career that there was so little to show for it. And it *really* graveled him to hear that stage of his life dismissed by blow-dried asshole TV anchorettes busily trying to fuck their way to the middle.

Nor were things much more satisfying online.

The various Atterminator bulletin boards and websites were jumping, and he periodically downloaded and devoured their information. Sometimes he couldn't get through at all. Meanwhile, in his favorite Atterminator chat room, he found the conversation to be pretty much horseshit. Everything was theoretical, and discussions kept moving into half-assed psychobabble—subjects like Acting versus Reality—carried on by people ignorant of both.

The one thing that did interest him was a suggestion—from a lawyer in South Carolina—that perhaps the Atterminator was planning a grand finale. Specifically, infiltrating an American Bar Association banquet and then letting loose with an Uzi.

Not a bad idea, if you were into cheap theatrics with no possibility of escape or survival.

Ace, however, intended both.

Keeping pace with new developments in the story required a

certain amount of concentration. While out yesterday, he'd stopped and bought all the papers. He'd also listened to talk radio in the van. Thus he learned, as he negotiated the merge onto the Hollywood Freeway, that Kingsfield police were opening an investigation into the death of Sven Lundquist.

It surprised him how quickly they caught on to Lundquist.

Not that he hadn't expected them to. After all, Joanna Davis was in Kingsfield; he'd seen her on TV walking into the court-house, just down the road from Pearse Hardware. It was the first time he'd seen new pictures of her since he'd been in her house.

Somehow he hadn't expected all this to happen so quickly. It made him a little angry how fast everything was moving, how far out of control this entire situation had gone.

He remained, however, quite proud of Lundquist. In certain respects, the killing of that self-righteous Swede lawyer had been the most satisfying of all the episodes.

His hatred for Sven Lundquist had smoldered and raged from week to week and month to month after he returned, orphaned, to Hollywood. The insensitivity of the man stunned him. It wasn't bad enough that Lundquist had orchestrated the legal maneuverings that ended with Ace's mother dangling from a noose in her own garage, and this after promising her he could somehow make everything better. No, he had to make it even worse. In a meeting the day after Sarah Pearse's burial, the lawyer had actually told Ace that his mother had killed herself because her son had moved to California and was not man enough to accept family responsibilities.

Ace had always been patient. Fishing with his father, he could sit for hours without stirring. Assembling models, wiring lamps, helping construct the hidey-holes the old man believed would buy him time in case of Communist invasion—through all of these he had infinite patience and a willingness to give each project the time it deserved.

So he waited, almost two years. And then, on a secret sojourn to the midwest, he carried out the plan he had been developing and fine-tuning all that time. He stole a wallet from a fellow student in his acting class and went to Iowa as James Barton. He took a room in a modest motel on the Kingsfield side of Des Moines and rented a big sturdy van, careful to take out full collision insurance.

Sven Lundquist had made a point of his community involvement, had lectured Ace on how he toiled for Rotary, led Boy Scouts, served as a trustee at the Lutheran church. At the church after burying his mother, Ace had picked up a chatty newsletter that noted the trustees met on the third Tuesday evening of the month.

On the third Tuesday of January, Ace sat in his rented van down the street from the Lutheran church as a light snow fell. Around eight-fifteen, half a dozen men left the church and got into half a dozen late-model American sedans. He recognized most of them. Sven Lundquist was hatless, his pale hair glowing in reflected light from a street lamp.

He drove slowly and cautiously to the outskirts of town, seemingly unaware of the van that followed him. Lundquist lived out in the country, on a road Ace had driven hundreds of times, a road that followed a bluff above the river for almost half a mile.

There was no other traffic. Ace held back, driving without lights when he left town. Once the attorney reached the stretch of road beside the river, it was all wonderfully easy. Ace roared up behind him and slightly to his left, high beams flooding the rearview mirror with blinding light, giving the back bumper of the lawyer's Buick a little nudge. The lawyer tried first to pull over to give passing room, then fought briefly for control as he fishtailed on the slippery road. Finally he crashed through the flimsy guardrail and flew into space.

Ace stopped just long enough to see that the car had broken through the frozen river down below, watched the headlights abruptly go out beneath the ice and water. Then he drove back to Des Moines, turned the car in the next morning, and flew home.

Au revoir, Counselor Lundquist. See you in hell.

When he returned to California, he felt somehow purified.

Within a month he gave up the Lane Spencer identity and became George Lange, another identity he had been developing for some time. And he began to plan the Legal Resolution

Program, realizing that this was his mission in life, the reason he and his family had endured such outrage and pain. Vengeance for the loss of his beloved mother. He would be a force of retribution for all the powerless who had suffered unfairly.

When the time was right, he metamorphosed into the identity he'd been building as Henry Mason. And when the time was *really* right, he began to implement the Legal Resolution Program. It had taken a long time, but it had been well worth the wait.

42

Joanna wasted no time going home.

She retraced her path through Chicago to Los Angeles, so eager to get back that she almost didn't mind flying, which normally terrified her. She compulsively read stories about plane crashes, knew all about the failure potential of de-icing agents, not to mention human error and sloth. Every time she tightened her seat belt and sphincters for a takeoff or landing, she remembered the apologetic voice of a pilot who had somehow survived a horrific crash: "We ran out of runway."

But the plane landed uneventfully at LAX Sunday afternoon— to radiant sunshine, a vibrantly blue sky, and the fresh-washed splendor that invariably followed a southern California winter rain.

It was glorious to be home, even though "home" remained a problematic concept at the moment. To be back in L.A., she'd settle for that.

Just to be warm was almost enough.

Lee Walters picked her up at the airport. Joanna had declined the offer of bodyguards for the moment; she felt certain that Kevin/Lane had other things on his mind just now besides harassing her. He'd be worrying about survival and escape, much more fundamental issues.

As meticulous as he had been in every previous detail, she felt rather certain, actually, that he had probably *already* escaped. Unless he had some kind of suicide mission planned, a grand finale.

They'd already checked to be sure there were no legal conventions planned in the area for the next couple of months, and found the calendar for large legal gatherings in the Southland miraculously cleared. No lawyer with any sense wanted to *come* to L.A. from elsewhere, and the ones already there were lying low. Praying.

"For three months this guy has been a phantom," Lee said, as they sped along the freeway toward task force headquarters, "and now his face is everywhere. If he'd gotten this kind of attention when he was trying to act, he probably wouldn't have killed anybody."

Lee waved at the *Los Angeles Times* Joanna was perusing. The paper's coverage was awesome, page after page crammed with minutiae about the Iowan's failed acting career. Under the heading FACES OF KEVIN PEARSE, pictures marched across a page, many of them by now familiar. The Melody Laughlin sketch was the final shot in the series.

"Where were all these pictures when we were beating the bushes before?" Joanna groused.

"In truckloads full of other ones just like them, all the thousands and thousands of wannabes who never are."

Task force headquarters was buzzing. After weeks of spinning wheels and listening to crackpot hot-line callers, people finally had something to do besides engage in fruitless evidence searches around freshly discovered corpses. Jacobs was there, and Mickey Conner and Dave Austin, completing the foursome that had started down this road back in October. It was a regular old home week, including various detectives from Santa Monica and L.A. Sheriff's. Joanna wouldn't have been surprised to see that macho nonbeliever from San Luis Obispo show up.

The mood was upbeat and determined. Surely, in the face of such widespread and endless publicity, Kevin Pearse would be flushed out of whatever den he had created for himself. Whatever hidey-hole. The folks in Kingsfield had found three other hiding places in the old Pearse homestead, none of them large enough to conceal a human being, but all intricately constructed and designed to secrete *something*. Their origin and function remained a mystery and all were empty.

After a few hours at the office, Lee and Joanna returned to Pit Bull Acres, where Alex Walters and the dogs had been busy smoking beef briskets in a pit in the backyard. Through the evening, the three of them ate barbecue and worked their way through countless bottles of Alex's home-brewed beer. Even as every hamlet in America had been nurturing its own microbrewery, Alex Walters had taken his retirement as occasion to perfect his own brewing operation, something he had dabbled in sporadically for years. Alex had bottle-washers and crates of wire-bailed Grolsch bottles and two refrigerators full of different brews in varying stages of readiness.

That night, sharing the giddy sense of finally being on to something, they seemed to try them all.

Nobody discussed the subagenda. Alex might not even be aware of it, Joanna realized, though she assumed Lee had told him. Theirs was a marriage of solidity and sharing. But if Alex knew, he disguised his awareness masterfully.

And so there was not a single reference to the fact that in the morning, Joanna would proceed directly to her doctor's office for the long-delayed colposcopy. It was a swift and simple procedure, Dr. Letterman had assured her. And Joanna felt fairly certain nobody would be checking her blood-alcohol level to see if she'd gotten shitfaced the night before.

So she did.

In the morning she was hung over with an intensity she couldn't recall ever feeling before. Beer wasn't supposed to *do* this to you, she thought miserably, as she sipped from a huge car mug of black coffee and nibbled halfheartedly on a bran muffin. Beer was the *friendly* alcohol. But even your friends could turn on you, she knew, and besides, she was old and out of practice.

She was also terrified.

Not of Kevin Pearse, high school drama student turned internationally acclaimed serial killer, though the thought of Kevin certainly continued to rankle her.

This fear was far simpler and exceptionally personal.

She was afraid she had cancer and was going to die.

She was ashamed, too, that a perverse corner of her mind kept whispering, *At least it's not your breast*, as if it really mattered, once they started hacking at your female organs, whether they began inside or outside.

Traffic was light in the cool gray morning as Lee expertly maneuvered through the cars and trucks that crowded the L.A. freeways night and day. An hour from now, Joanna realized, it would all be over and they'd be sending her biopsies off to the lab.

Biopsy.

Now *there* was a word to put you right off your feed. And yet doctors always tossed it around so easily. *Oh, we'll just take a little biopsy and check that.* Casual as can be. *Check that.* When what they were usually checking was whether there was something truly horrible wrong with you, something that would forever alter the course of your life.

And in her own case, after they took the biopsies, they wouldn't even be able to *tell* her anything. She wouldn't know anything for three days.

Three days.

Joanna was accustomed to waiting for lab results, sure, but for patients that were already dead. *That* was annoying. *This* was something else altogether.

They arrived early, as was Joanna's habit even when her life wasn't on the line. She skimmed John Stampley's pieces on Meredith Demetrius and Linda Moraine Gilhooly in the *Times*, relieved to see that he had kept his word in every respect. Linda had not minded the idea of being publicly identified—had, actually, seemed to savor the prospect. By now, Joanna knew, there'd be TV trucks parked outside her house, reporters eating sugar-speckled Christmas cookies.

Meredith Demetrius, however, had been given a pseudonym, and alternately was referred to as "the drama coach." The drama coach who by now had fled with husband and child to a lodge in the Ozarks, yet another Atterminator displacement. But she ought to be able to go home soon. This situation was moving so quickly that in a few more days, Meredith Demetrius would be old news, very ho-hum. For all their failings, the media locusts did have one unintentional positive attribute: an extremely limited attention span.

Article finished, she leaned back. "If you hear anything or if anything happens, come get me," she instructed Lee. "Just break right in." Lee had confiscated Joanna's beeper and cell phone, an odd flashback to the Kansas motel room where Joanna had done the same to John Stampley, two nights before last. Stampley had taken it with good grace, she realized now. Her own reaction was close to fury.

Lee raised an eyebrow. She had drunk even more than Joanna the previous night and showed not a sign of hangover. "Girl, *relax*. This is no big deal, as we've already discussed. And discussed. You're gonna be *fine*. And the task force will get along somehow, I promise. What could possibly happen in the next hour?"

What happened in the next hour was that Bonita Blevins did not arrive at the State Bar offices in downtown Los Angeles.

Normally Bonita was entrenched at her desk by seven-thirty, a self-proclaimed early bird with no empathy whatsoever for night owls. Circadian rhythms was not a subject that had ever interested Bonita. Her way, she truly believed, was best.

Speculation ricocheted about the office. Bonita had not intended to go to San Francisco until Wednesday. Everyone was quite certain of that, and her calendar confirmed it. Nobody had seen or heard from her since she left the office late on Friday, wheeling a banker's box of files that she intended to work on over the weekend.

When repeated calls to her home phone and the cellular in her car went unanswered, one of the investigators took a deep breath and called LAPD, which immediately transferred the call to the Atterminator Task Force. It was one of those this-is-probably-nothing-but calls that people hate to make because they almost never *are* nothing.

Everybody hovered and waited, in a flurry of inactivity that would have displeased Bonita Blevins mightily.

They didn't have to wait long.

• • •

Claremont police broke into Bonita Blevins's townhouse at 1107-B Calle Caminito at nine-ten A.M. on Monday, December 15th and found the chief trial counsel facing the doorway.

Waiting for them.

She sat in a simple wooden armchair, wearing only a white blindfold and a white sheet, arranged toga-style on her body. Her left arm had been propped on the chair arm to hold an old-fashioned scale.

Lady Justice was dead.

43

Beatrice McNeill's kitchen drain was clogged with bacon grease.

She truly dreaded calling Henry. He had been so *short* with her the last time she had difficulty with her plumbing, as if a seventy-eight-year-old woman would deliberately humiliate herself by stopping up a *toilet*, for pity's sake. As far as Beatrice was concerned the plumbing in this entire building was deplorable. The other tenants were always having difficulties, too, and when Henry replaced the old fixtures a few years back with those water-miser commodes, matters had further deteriorated.

Last night when she realized her terrible blunder, she had decided to wait till morning and see if perhaps the problem wouldn't correct itself. In any event, she needed to wait until the bacon smell dissipated, or Henry would know immediately what had happened and she wouldn't be able to get away with being a helpless old lady.

Henry had lectured her on previous occasions, could somehow tell after he used his little rooter machine just what had caused the stoppage. You should know better, he had scolded. Nicely—Henry never raised his voice—but scolding nonetheless. And she *did* know better, of course, at least now. The problem was, she'd been pouring bacon grease down the drain her entire life and until she lived in this building she had never had a bit of trouble from it.

It seemed so unfair, like a public punishment for her secret indulgence. Beatrice loved bacon. Always had and undoubtedly always would. And every once in a while, in defiance of the dictates of her doctors and her children, she would cook herself up half a pound, and eat it. All by itself: no eggs, no tomato and lettuce sandwich, no chicken livers and water chestnuts, no embellishment whatsoever. Just meaty strips of thick-sliced Farmer John's, beautifully browned, slowly and lovingly cooked to flat, golden perfection.

Last night, without even thinking about it, as she was cleaning up after one of these occasional binges, she poured the grease right down the drain. Then the phone rang, her daughter's weekly call from Dayton, before she had a chance to run enough hot water to get rid of it. And sure enough, by the time she hung up, she'd forgotten all about the fool drain.

She surveyed her kitchen now for evidence. She'd foil-wrapped the bacon packaging last night, then carried it out to the trash can in the back hallway and buried it beneath her coffee grounds. She had washed her dishes and the skillet in the bathroom, and all were dried and put away. Her tracks were covered.

On the TV, she noticed, they were showing how to stuff a Christmas goose, as if anybody could afford one at four dollars a pound for something that was half fat and would all cook away anyway. There it was again. *Grease*. She couldn't seem to escape it.

She sighed and sprayed more cinnamon air freshener. Then she braced herself and called Henry.

44

Lee Walters was still clucking maternally when they arrived at task force headquarters, and between that and the hangover and the experience of having little chunks of tissue excised from her body, Joanna was not in the best of moods.

And would not have been even if they *hadn't* been making their hasty return because of a death they all should have anticipated.

How could they have let Bonita Blevins get killed? Why hadn't they realized that—failing a legal convention bombing—this highly symbolic attorney was *precisely* the next victim this killer would want to select?

The mood inside the office was glum. Joanna knew she probably ought to go out to the crime scene, but she was feeling a little woozy and wanted to just sit for a few minutes. So far as she was aware, nobody in this office knew where she'd been, or why.

"Is the story out yet?" she asked Jacobs.

He shook his head. "But I figure we've got maybe half an hour more. If we're lucky. I don't think we can get away with cutting the phone lines at the State Bar. Of course they all swore they wouldn't let out a peep." He grinned. "Goes back to that old chicken-and-the-egg question: do lying sacks of shit just naturally gravitate toward being lawyers, or is being a facile liar something they teach in law school?"

Lee remained nearby, not precisely hovering but close enough to take part in the conversation. "Law school," she said definitively. "Without a doubt. You're right, Jacobs, those fuckers are probably burning up the lines already, trying to get through before the prime-time sleazefests are all booked."

"Did she do anything while I was out of town that would have particularly pissed him off?" Joanna asked.

"Not that I know of," Jacobs answered. "She did call a kind of impromptu press conference on Tuesday, but that was before you left. Once the story's out, we can subpoena somebody's uncut footage. I don't know exactly what she said, but I do remember seeing part of it and thinking she'd been in the sauce."

Joanna shook her head, feeling anguished. "So he saw it and got mad. Damn, damn, *damn!*" She rubbed her hand across her forehead. What ever had possessed her to get so drunk last night? She was too old for this sort of shit. She probably ought to eat something, but the mere thought of food was nauseating. "Tell me what happened."

Jacobs shrugged. "Don't know much yet. Conner lives out that way so we headed him off on his way in and he's at the scene. He says she's been dead a while, maybe a day or two. There's marks from the Taser, no other obvious cause of death. They've already swabbed the ear canals to start checking for nicotine sulfate." He sighed unhappily. "And that's not all."

What else could there be? Even as her mind considered and dismissed the possibility of rape, Joanna knew what else there could be. Theatrics.

"He posed her?" she asked flatly.

"Yeah. He posed her. Dressed her up like the blindfolded justice lady and sat her in a chair holding scales. And he left a business card on one of the scales."

Joanna stared blankly. "A business card? Surely not his own."

"Unfortunately, no. And it wasn't the victim's, either." Jacobs sighed. "*This* card was from the late Lorenzo J. Taft."

45

Ace felt panicky.

He was reading Mrs. Finch's interview with the *Times* when he got the call from Mrs. McNeill in number nine about her clogged sink. More damn bacon grease, he figured, though he was certain she'd deny it. At least it wasn't her toilet this time.

He made her wait while he finished the story, though. It left him sadder than he would have expected. Mrs. Finch really *did* remember him, much better than he would have thought. They called her Caroline Wintergreen in the article, but he realized instantly who it was when he saw the headline: TEACHER RECALLS SUSPECT AS DRAMA STUDENT. Sometimes they referred to her as "the drama coach," which he didn't particularly like. It made her sound like somebody brandishing a bullwhip, thundering orders to a locker room of sweaty thespians.

Next he read the story about Linda Moraine, which was far less interesting, and then he quickly reread the one about Mrs. Finch before gathering his tools and going upstairs. Any minute now he expected them to find the Blevins bitch, and he really didn't want to be with any of the old folks when the TV bulletin broke.

Mrs. McNeill chattered nervously when he arrived. She'd sprayed a lot of cloying air freshener but the underlying scent of bacon was unmistakable. He pretty much ignored her, went to work, cleared the clog, and then turned to her.

"Mrs. McNeill, do us both a favor and next time pour the grease into a can. If you don't have a can available, call me and I will *get* you one. All right?"

"I'm sure I don't know what you're talking about," she sniffed.

As the door closed behind him, he heard the heavy intonation beginning on the TV running inside her apartment: "We interrupt our regularly scheduled programming for this special news bulletin."

He zipped downstairs and was back in his own place by the time the bulletin itself came on. They'd found her, all right.

And through the rest of the morning, as he monitored the breaking story on his television and online, he wondered.

Had she looked at him funny, Mrs. McNeill? Somehow it had felt as if she had. Was looking at him like maybe she *knew*.

Beatrice McNeill hadn't known, though. Hadn't ever once thought of the possibility until after Henry left, his rebuke still ringing in her ears.

Then the bulletin came on about that poor lady lawyer being killed. Another woman. Victim number seven.

There was no evidence of forced entry, the reporter said. And for some reason, that made her think of Henry's pass key.

Then they came on with pictures of the boy they were looking for, that Kevin something from Iowa.

She stopped, riveted, as the picture flashed on her screen.

It couldn't be.

Could it?

She sat down, trembling. After a while, she realized that as absurd as the notion might be, she had to discuss it with somebody else in the building, somebody she could trust. Anna Farber, that's who she'd ask. Anna, like Beatrice herself, suffered certain hearing deficits, but she had excellent eyesight and a definite open-mindedness.

Anna would be willing to consider the possibility without laughing in her face. But Anna also wouldn't hesitate to say if she thought Beatrice was being a silly, overly imaginative busybody.

Because it couldn't possibly be. Could it?

Detective Manny Rodriguez listened to the two old ladies who had arrived unannounced at the Hollywood Division of LAPD, insisting that they needed to talk to a detective immediately, about the Atterminator case.

Plenty of nutcases had been dropping in over the past few days, brimming with hot flashes on the Atterminator, and at first Rodriguez figured to give the old gals the hot-line number and send them home. Let Robbery–Homicide deal with them; that was why they got the glory. But these two ladies were nice enough, so even though they were probably just goofy old flakes, he figured he'd humor them.

Then, to his utter amazement, he started believing them. And by the time they had finished their tale, he could barely contain his excitement.

He got sodas for the old ladies, excused himself, and started trying to get through to Dave Austin. Austin had been his former partner in Hollywood detectives before moving up to RHD.

Maybe breaking the Atterminator case could be Manny's ticket up and out as well.

Beatrice McNeill and Anna Farber returned separately to their apartments late on Monday afternoon. Each carried colorful holiday shopping bags and was accompanied by a blue-jeaned female police officer, acting with the fond familiarity of a favorite granddaughter.

Inasmuch as both of the older ladies were hard of hearing, it was agreed that all communication inside the building—with their police escorts and each other—would be conducted by written notes or electronically over phone lines, on the laptop computers the policewomen carried.

Around four-thirty on Monday afternoon, just as it was getting dark, Manny Rodriguez left a Pac Bell truck parked outside and walked into the Hollywood apartment building managed by Henry Mason. Dave Austin waited across the street in an unmarked van with the technicians, listening in.

Rodriguez was wired, both psychically and electronically.

The Orange Grove Arms was an older, two-story stucco building, with an unlocked outer door leading into a vestibule holding a dozen mailboxes and a sturdy, bolted-down bench. In this once-nice neighborhood, unsecured furniture had a tendency to travel. The outer lobby was clean, however, and in immaculate repair. Some throwaway newspapers and a pile of circulars from a local Chinese takeout were strewn on the bench.

In one corner overhead, Rodriguez registered a discreetly positioned video camera.

Through thick, narrow safety-glass panels on either side of the locked interior door, he could see a central carpeted corridor, with stairs and an elevator on the left. He pressed the button above the mailbox belonging to E. FENSTER, reported by the old ladies to be visiting her sister in Boise. He waited when he got no answer, then pushed it again.

After a few moments, he shrugged and pushed the button over the last mailbox on the right, labeled H. MASON, MANAGER.

In a moment, a voice came through the intercom. "Yeah?" Male, youngish, wary.

"Pac Bell," Manny said. "Got an installation order for Emily Fenster in apartment twelve and there's no answer. Can you let me in?"

"Mrs. Fenster?" the voice answered. "She's already got a phone." The sound came through the speaker with remarkable clarity, much clearer than the customary static-ridden transmission of an apartment intercom.

"This is for a second line," Rodriguez went on, reading from the hastily forged work order, "with three extensions."

A clear laugh came through the speaker. "That *has* to be a mistake. I can't let you in to do that, not without Mrs. Fenster being here."

"Could be we screwed up somehow," Rodriguez acknowledged cheerfully. "I'll check it out. But hey, if I can't do the work, I need somebody to sign that I came by. Then when she calls and starts squawking, I'm covered."

There was no answer. Rodriguez was starting to wonder if he'd pushed too hard, if he maybe ought to ring the bell again. Then he saw a guy coming down the hallway toward him. He could feel adrenaline coursing through his body.

Jesus H. Christ, it was *him*.

Five-ten, one-eighty, hair darker than the sketches, some gray at the temples. He wore jeans and a flannel shirt in a dark blue plaid. Sneakers. He moved lightly, with the nervous tension of a cat.

He reached the vestibule, propped the door open with his foot, and leaned against the doorjamb. Poised, ready to spring either forward or back. Again Rodriguez had the sense of feline energy.

Rodriguez lazily turned his clipboard to him and held out a pen. "Could you just initial here, sir, to show that we attempted installation?"

But the guy had his own pen. He leaned forward and initialed the indicated place on Emily Fenster's bogus order. And he did it without touching the clipboard or anything else.

Manny Rodriguez looked at his watch and grinned. "Hey, guess I got lucky here! This is my last job of the day." He turned, nodded, and opened the door back out to the street. Outside it was almost totally dark, Hollywood moving into the shadowy rhythms of its night. "Have a good one."

Ace didn't like it.

He'd gone into too many places himself armed with fake papers on a clipboard. Old Mrs. Fenster had lived in this building for seventeen years, more than three times as long as Ace had been here, and every December she went to Idaho for the entire month. The idea that she would have ordered a second telephone line— and one with three extensions!—was absurd. She lived in a one-bedroom apartment on a fixed income. She didn't have a computer and probably didn't even know what a fax was. And she wasn't the kind of person who'd set up some kind of boiler-room scam in her living room. She was the kind of person who embroidered pillowcases.

Were they on to him?

Was the repairman with the phony order a phony repairman?

Should he leave now?

Yes, he told himself. Yes to all three.

His instincts all told him to walk right out the back door and never look back. Get into the van and drive to Oregon. He was already wearing the money belt. He could pick up the laptop and the family photo album on one last swing through his apartment.

There wouldn't be time to wipe his fingerprints out of the apartment. Realistically, though, he knew that his fingerprints were everywhere in this building and it would be absolutely impossible to get rid of them, short of blowing up the building.

Which maybe wasn't such a bad idea either, a bit of improvisation he hadn't previously considered. He thought about the logistics for a moment. Explosives weren't exactly a specialty, but he knew enough to rig something in a hurry if he had to.

He could leave behind a bomb threat and give them enough time to clear out the old folks.

And he could hide a dozen bombs in this building that nobody would find in time.

46

Joanna was floating in a deep and dreamless abyss at seven-thirty on Monday night when Lee shook her shoulder.

"Joanna! Jacobs is on the phone. They think they've got him."

The events of the past few days had dropped Joanna in her tracks by late afternoon, when Lee insisted on bringing her home, a decision she didn't even try to argue. Eleven days ago, she'd come home unsuspecting to find her jukebox aglow and her personal space violated. Now she'd worked eight days nonstop and topped it off with a drunken debauch and a terrifying medical procedure.

Enough was enough. She stripped, slipped into sweats, and was asleep before she was entirely horizontal.

Now she picked up the phone and felt herself springing awake as she listened to the note of jubilation in her partner's voice.

"He looks awfully good, Joanna," Jacobs told her. "*Awfully* good. Austin's buddy says yes, for sure, and he actually saw and talked to the guy. What we know about him all fits. DMV has a Henry Mason at that address and the picture looks right. Claims to be twenty-nine, one-seventy, five-ten. Henry Mason surrendered a current Illinois license when he took the test in California five years ago."

"And these women just came in off the street?" She tried to sit up in the unfamiliar bed. But though her mind was already racing, her body was slow to follow. She lay back, wishing for the array of pillows she kept on her own bed. *Had* kept on her own bed, in what was starting to feel like a previous lifetime.

"Walked into Hollywood and asked for a detective. Pretty sharp old gals, according to Austin and his pal both. We had to let them go back into the building so our guy wouldn't get suspicious of them disappearing. So we sent them back with undercover officers ready to spend the night."

"Come again?" Joanna had a flash of Kingsfield's Blanche Dodsworth entering an apartment building on the arm of one of her own recent beefy bodyguards. Not exactly a coupling that would blend into the woodwork.

"Couple of young gals took them in," he said patiently. "I woke you up, didn't I? I *told* Walters not to wake you up."

"She knew I'd want her to. Keep going, Al. The old ladies went back in. So what is this place, anyway? Some kind of nursing home? And *where* is it?"

He gave her the address. "It's just an apartment building, way I understand it, but it's only seniors living there. The one younger person on the premises is the resident manager. Our guy, Henry Mason."

"Tell me about him." She was now totally awake. Getting revved again. Almost ready to take another shot at sitting up.

"Well, he does all the maintenance and wiring and plumbing for the building," Jacobs began. "He lives in an apartment in the rear on the first floor. Very handy, according to the two residents who made him, the kind of guy who can fix anything. About half an hour ago we pulled out one of the old ladies again. Had her call and tell Mason she was going to visit her grandniece in Northridge and then she and her bodyguard split. They're bringing her in to help work up floor plans. Captain wants to give it to the D-team."

"That's what they're there for," Joanna said, thinking of Don Olafson and how he had refused overtures to join SWAT, known as the D-team, because he said he hadn't become a cop to spend his life in armor, preparing for urban Armageddon. "Are we sure Mason's in there?"

"So I'm told. They've had the building covered front and back since before Austin's buddy made him. Lights are on in his unit. And remember, we just had one of our old ladies call him to say she was spending the night out. She says she's sure it was him."

"Don't forget call forwarding," Joanna said, not really believing her own words. He was in there. He was *in there*. They *had* the miserable SOB. "So how soon are we going in?" She felt almost panicked. She had come too far with this to miss the end. "Don't you *dare* go in before I can get there. I can be there in twenty minutes. Fifteen if Lee's driving."

Jacobs laughed. "Nah, do yourself a favor and go back to sleep. Nothing's happening tonight. Word right now is we wait till morning. SWAT says it's easier logistically to get in when it's daylight."

Joanna knew that SWAT, once brought into a case, did not have the autonomy that Jacobs was suggesting. That when SWAT went in for Henry Mason, it would be because she and Jacobs *sent* them. And that they could also call them off, any time, without backtalk. Joanna herself had never actually called in SWAT, but she'd been around twice when it happened. It was pretty awesome.

And it was scheduled for tomorrow morning.

When they'd be arresting the Atterminator.

Joanna slept restlessly and awoke at three forty-five. The house was pitch-black and there wasn't even a yip from the kennels. As soon as she realized she wouldn't be able to go back to sleep, she got up and went to the back room where Lee and Alex kept their athletic equipment. She started warming up on the Universal.

She was rusty, out of shape, could feel her usually toned muscles protest. The midwest, in only a few days, had robbed her of her edge. The NordicTrack in the Colwells' basement in Kingsfield had been buried by boxes, and it hadn't seemed worth further inconveniencing her hosts by trying to dig it out. Besides, she'd been busy.

Now, however, she could feel her sluggish muscles slowly revive as she put herself through a routine taught her long ago by a fitness trainer at one of the dozens of health clubs she'd belonged to over the years.

By the time Lee appeared, fully dressed, at quarter to five, Joanna was starting to feel a little more like herself again. She showered and dressed in warm layers, starting with a few wisps of lace-trimmed mauve satin and the Kevlar vest.

They were in Hollywood at five twenty-three.

Electricity charged the misty darkness of predawn Hollywood.

It was, in fact, damned chilly, but by now Joanna felt oddly warm. Her blood was a lava flow of adrenaline and anticipation.

The Hollywood streetlights glowed through the darkness as they drove down nearly deserted streets to their destination. An intense young African-American uniformed cop stopped them at a roadblock near the address, then pulled aside the sawhorse once Lee flashed her badge. Surrounding streets were blocked on all sides of the target building, leaving the neighborhood in spooky silence. Lee cut her lights, drove into the restricted area, and parked behind a huge white trailer.

This would not be a neighborhood of early risers, but there were bound to be a few sleep-over lovers heading home to shower and change before work. Joanna was pleased to see, as they approached the trailer, that LAPD was prepared for just this exigency. Up the street, a slightly disheveled young man in a sport coat emerged from a building, giving a casual and mildly furtive glance in each direction. Like an apparition conjured from the morning mists, a woman in a black sweatsuit and running shoes met him at the sidewalk, showed him something nestled in the palm of her hand, then escorted him up the block to his car. She'd be back a few minutes later, Joanna knew, waiting for more early risers, getting them out of the way. There was a big, nicely oiled machine at work here.

The large, anonymous white trailer, command post for this operation, was the sort used by film crews on location. GDS PRODUCTIONS was painted on its side. GDS stood for either God Damned Sneaky or Get Da Scum, depending on who you asked; LAPD had used this ploy before. The target building, where Kevin Pearse/Lane Spencer/Henry Mason remained holed up in his resident manager's unit, was across the street and a few doors down.

The building didn't look like much. It sat in the middle of a long block, the sort of nice-enough, two-story apartment building found in older L.A. neighborhoods. Similar buildings stood on either side of it. At one time, this would have been a very good address. Now it had wrought-iron bars on all the ground floor windows.

Inside the command trailer, Jacobs and the captain and a tough-looking fellow in stylish SWAT black sat at a small table at one end, looking over floor plans. At the opposite end of the trailer, amidst a collection of industrial-strength weaponry, half a dozen more lean and lithe D-team guys in black body armor waited, sipping from Styrofoam cups. Others were already in position around the neighborhood. The inside of the trailer fairly reeked of testosterone.

"Ready to rock and roll?" Jacobs asked, with more enthusiasm than he'd shown for months. He probably hadn't made it home last night, but he still looked ten years younger than usual. He also seemed a bit wistful, as if he secretly yearned to be wearing some of that body armor himself, carrying an antiaircraft gun. Boys will be boys.

"Boogie down," Joanna answered, offering a small wave of greeting to the guys in black. "Morning, everybody."

She herself felt not the slightest desire to be first into any dangerous or unstable situation. Never had, when you came right down to it, even though she'd done what she had to over the years, always kept up her end, and never shirked. By the time she left patrol, however, she did feel she'd pretty much used up her lifetime allocation of street luck. She'd taken a headstart on that as a teenager in the Valley, after all.

She was introduced to Carver, the SWAT lieutenant, who projected the image of somebody who'd just breakfasted on a hearty platter of glass shards and cactus, with a few rashers of razor wire on the side. He explained how the detectives would be able to monitor events via closed-circuit TV from cameras mounted around the trailer. And then they reviewed the plan, which had been continually revised throughout the night.

"We'll bring out the old lady we have in there before anything starts," Carver said. "But we can't get anybody else out without making too much noise and risking tipping him."

"Beatrice McNeill," Jacobs explained to Lee and Joanna. "She's with our undercover gal, Penny Delaney, in an upstairs apartment, same side as Mason. We've got Penny on an open computer hookup through the phone line. They're ready to leave now. Soon as we give the signal, they're down the front inside stairs and out the door."

"And we can't get out *anybody* else?"

"Well, we already *do* have Anna Farber out," Jacobs reminded her. "The woman who helped with the floor plans and the tenant information. Thing is, a lot of the residents have hearing problems. And mobility problems. No way to evacuate them quietly."

"Where's the building owner?" Lee Walters asked. They'd speculated about that on the way in.

"In Hancock Park with Alzheimer's," the captain responded. He offered the ghost of a smile. "She's the one person not in a position to complain if this goes sour."

"It won't," Carver grunted, personally affronted.

"So let me see if I've got this straight," Joanna said. "You're going to storm a building full of little old ladies, and those guys—" she gestured toward the ninja cops at the other end of the trailer "—will be the first thing these little old ladies see when their doors get broken down? I hope we've got somebody standing by to handle assembly-line coronaries."

The captain nodded, stony-faced again. "One block over. Two ambulances that I sincerely trust we won't need."

Joanna considered the elderly residents, all but one female and all on the sunset side of seventy. Her initial inclination was to view them as uniformly frail and helpless. On the other hand, her own mother was seventy-four and *she* was off on a romantic tryst somewhere in southern Arizona. Age was highly relative, particularly in southern California, where Ponce de León was probably still ensconced in a two-bedroom at Leisure World.

Those old ladies would probably be just fine.

Jacobs was worried, though. "The other part of the problem is that these old gals all really *like* Henry Mason. Austin pretty well pumped Anna Farber dry, and what he got makes Mason sound like a cross between Forrest Gump and the Eagle Scout of the Year. He didn't just fix their dripping faucets. He gave them cupcakes and helium balloons on their birthdays, for Chrissakes."

"Shit," Lee Walters muttered, shaking her head.

"Once we go in for Mason, my men are poised to immediately evacuate the other residents," Carver told them. He seemed uninterested in negativism of any sort. "It's not perfect, but we're still better off doing it this way in a dense residential neighborhood. These buildings are all crammed with geezers. We let them wake up, they're bound to get in the way. And then we'll *really* have problems."

The captain scowled. "Tough call and we're screwed either way."

As streaks of light began to filter out of the east in the eerily quiet dawn, the captain gave Carver the go-ahead. Carver immediately began issuing orders to the D-team men, both those already invisibly positioned around the neighborhood and the ones now slipping like combat-armed wraiths out the back door of the trailer.

Meanwhile, the Robbery–Homicide detectives hunched around their TV monitors. Inasmuch as this operation was taking place in LAPD territory, other members of the Atterminator Task

Force had expressly been disinvited. And were, Joanna was certain, royally pissed about it.

The truth of the matter was, from the point of view of the investigating officers, this wasn't going to be too terribly dramatic. They were sitting in a trailer watching the collar of a lifetime on TV. They wouldn't even have the satisfaction of reading Henry Mason his rights. Whoever got into the apartment first would take care of that.

Now things started to happen visibly.

Two women exited the building, stepping gingerly down the front stairs. The older one wore a pink knit beret and a long, fully buttoned gray wool coat. Her chin jutted forward determinedly and she clutched a sturdy square handbag. This was Beatrice McNeill, suddenly positioned to collect enough serious reward money from various attorneys and legal organizations to move her into a *far* nicer neighborhood. Her cop companion, Penny Delaney, was a buff young brunette in a leather bomber jacket and jeans. Delaney steered Granny's elbow with one hand and kept the other deep in her jacket pocket. At the sidewalk, they turned right, walked ten steps, then slid into the back seat of an idling unmarked Chevy and sped away.

SWAT now closed in on Henry Mason's apartment. Some entered the building through the back service entrance beside the apartment, while others positioned themselves outside Mason's barred windows, all completely obscured by opaque brown draperies.

Carver, listening intently through earphones, never changed his expression or his tone as he asked, "Say what?" Not "oops," but not a good sign, either. A minute later, he turned to the detectives. "We've got a situation with the apartment," he told them, now permitting himself a feral scowl.

"Where's Mason?" Jacobs snapped.

"That's the situation. We don't know yet."

Meanwhile, SWAT officers began bringing out old ladies, a surprising number of whom were already dressed. They hadn't fully considered the hours maintained in Geezerville, it seemed. Miraculously, not a single resident went into cardiac arrest, either, the combination of long-term Hollywood residence and media savvy making them all too aware what SWAT team members look like.

As they came out, SWAT handed them off to detectives. Lee Walters went out to join in the interviewing process, meeting other detectives already waiting at a commandeered coffee shop a few blocks away.

And almost as soon as the first old lady hit the pavement, the sky seemed to explode with noisy news helicopters. Other geriatrics in adjacent buildings, it seemed, were also up. They had watched the SWAT team ninjas creeping past their windows and had promptly speed-dialed 1–800–HOT–NEWS.

"The tenants are all out," Carver reported. "I'm going to check on the apartment."

"And we're going with you," Joanna told him, already halfway to the door.

The captain had resumed his customary dour expression. "Just you and Jacobs," he said. "Till we know what's happening. And be careful."

They went in the front door, passing through a vestibule leading to an inner hallway. Joanna noticed, with some surprise, that the interior of the building was truly immaculate. The creamy walls were freshly painted and the hall carpets were both clean and recently vacuumed. This place didn't have the slightly dispirited feel of most older apartment buildings. It didn't even smell of cabbage or chorizo.

At the end of the hall stood the splintered remains of Henry Mason's apartment door. SWAT had bypassed half a dozen various locks and deadbolts by simply smashing out the door itself.

Immediately inside the door, resting on a wooden kitchen chair, stood a nasty-looking little green bottle labelled SureKill-43, an obvious pesticide. A neatly lettered note was propped on the bottle.

"Don't touch anything," the SWAT man waiting beside the door warned them. He was extremely tall and very wide, a grain elevator in combat boots. "We think this space may be rigged somehow."

"You got it," she answered. Henry Mason had the know-how to blow them all to Maui. She moved cautiously toward the door and read aloud:

> *By entering this room you triggered a device that will render the entire building uninhabitable in 45 minutes. Get the residents out fast. As for me, my actions speak for themselves. There's nothing to discuss and I won't go to jail. I'd rather end things on my own terms, like my mother did. Say hello and good-bye to Mrs. Finch.*
>
> *P.S. Watch out for booby traps!*

"He's daring us," Carver said. He was a man not easily dared.

"Is this supposed to mean he's dead in there?" Joanna asked incredulously. She felt suddenly cheated. She had things to *say* to Henry Mason. To Kevin Pearse and to Lane Spencer. To the Atterminator.

"My men stopped right here," Carver told them. "They're putting on Hazmat suits to go further. We take comments about booby traps real seriously. And your boy is good at that sort of thing. Bomb squad's coming and I'd suggest that right now we get our asses out of here."

Joanna examined as much of the apartment as she could without actually sticking her head through the hole in the door. Like the hallway, it was clean and neat, a plain place with the sort of inexpensive tweedy furniture young bachelors buy so they'll have something to sit on while they watch football games. You could see almost the entire interior, except for part of the bedroom and the bathroom. The bathroom door was completely closed.

Interestingly enough, the television was running, tuned to the local NBC affiliate and aimed at the doorway. As they watched, the *Today* show was interrupted for helicopter footage of the street just outside.

• • •

They went back out to the trailer.

"How soon can we find out if he's in there?" Jacobs asked. "This is his building, has been for years. He could have all sorts of hiding places in there. How many'd they find in his house in Iowa?" He turned to Joanna.

"Five," she answered shortly.

Carver frowned. "You want my guys to start ripping out walls?"

"Not yet," Jacobs told him. "Where are we on the time line, the forty-five minutes he gives in the note?"

Carver checked his watch. "The door came down eleven minutes ago. Thirty-four to go if he's telling the truth."

Joanna looked at Jacobs. "A big *if*, Al. I don't believe him. Where the *hell* is the bomb squad?"

"On their way," Carver said.

"Look," Jacobs reminded, "we *know* he's in the building. There's only two entrances, front and back, and we've had them both covered continuously since three o'clock yesterday afternoon. And his van is still here. We staked it out last night, too, half a block away. So where is he?"

"We'll know in a minute," Carver told them, stopping for a moment to bark a few orders into a radio. "If he whacked himself, he'd've done it in the bathroom. So I got Mastropierri getting ready to take a crack at busting out the bathroom window. It's painted over. We'll take it real slow and easy, on account of him mentioning booby traps. Same reason we're not opening that bathroom door just now."

They watched on closed-circuit TV as a black-clad cop in a gas mask cautiously climbed a ladder outside Henry Mason's bathroom window and broke the glass. The window was high and tiny, maybe one foot square, and the cop had a set of shoulders on him like a sumo wrestler.

As they watched, he backed down the ladder and radioed to Carver. "There's some kind of gas in there," Mastropierri reported. "And there's a body in the bathtub."

Joanna felt her heart go into free fall.

"Can you see him? Is it our guy?" Jacobs asked.

"His head's behind the shower curtain. The body's crumpled. Blue jeans; running shoes, Nikes. It looks like he was standing up when he ate the gun. Classic blood splatter on the shower walls."

Dead.

So Kevin Pearse had actually *done* it, had killed himself like his mum.

The sneaky little bastard.

The cheat.

After brief discussion it was agreed that the Hazmat people would first clear whatever gas was in the bathroom before attempting to bring out the body. As they spoke, the bomb squad arrived and went in the back door with bomb-sniffing dogs. The Orange Grove Arms was a busy little building this morning.

Carver checked his watch again. "If he was telling the truth, we've got twenty-one minutes before the building blows."

"He didn't say it was going to blow," Joanna corrected him. "He said 'render uninhabitable.' That sounds like some kind of gas or poison to me. If there's anything at all."

There wasn't.

But to be on the safe side, everybody left the building five minutes before the forty-five-minute deadline and stayed out for another half hour afterward. Upon their cautious return, there were no obvious changes. Nothing had blown up, nothing was hissing or ticking, and orange gas didn't spew from the heating ducts.

After much discussion—and some irritating instructions from the chief, who had just arrived, and from the mayor, who was phoning in *his* suggestions—it was agreed to bust down the door of Henry Mason's bathroom. Just in case, all but the two SWAT cops involved in the venture left the building.

High-quality microphones were set up around the apartment now, so the cops in the command post heard quite clearly the loud and furious cry of "*Shit!*"

Joanna stared down at the body in the bathtub beneath the classic blood spatter pattern on the tiled wall. It wasn't a body at all. It was a very lifelike department store dummy, artfully arranged behind the shower curtain. The blood spatter pattern, while indeed classic, wasn't blood. It was paint. And the gas in the bathroom was a simple little stink bomb.

Working from photos and diagrams of secret compartments in the Pearse family home in Kingsfield, Iowa, it didn't take long for searching cops to find an empty cupboard hidden in the back of Henry Mason's broom closet.

A few minutes later, somebody else came upon the trick opening in Mason's bedroom closet, behind a section of elaborate shelving. The shelving swung forward far enough to admit a full-sized human body, though there didn't seem to be one in it now. But there was something else. The closet compartment opening was in the end of the closet by the outside wall of the building and it dropped into a narrow tunnel that ran beneath the vegetated walkway separating the apartment building from the one beside it.

On its other end, the tunnel came up behind a plywood wall in the back of a storage area for tenants of the neighboring building. This wall, too, had a trick opening built almost imperceptibly into it. Outside the opening they found broken glass from a discarded bottle of cheap wine and blood—real blood, this time, and quite a bit of it—where somebody had apparently stepped into the glass. A brand new men's undershirt had been hacked apart and the section left behind was drenched in blood, tossed in a corner. Drops and smears of blood led to the stairway up to the ground floor and from there out the apartment building door and onto the street, where they disappeared a hundred yards to the north.

There was no further trace of Henry Mason, aka Lane Spencer, aka Kevin Pearse, aka the Atterminator.

He had vanished.

47

There was no way to pretend they'd arrested Henry Mason, not with the air full of news choppers, the streets full of nosy neighbors, and the evacuated building residents—many of them still in their pajamas—clamoring to go home.

Task force detectives interviewed the residents of both Mason's own building and the one next door through which he had apparently fled after he was identified the previous afternoon. Given the extensive array of clothing, wigs, and makeup found in his apartment, he might have exited the building next door dressed as anything from Scarlett O'Hara to Godzilla. It being Hollywood, nobody'd noticed.

SID moved into Mason's apartment with a vengeance, looking for anything and everything, starting with additional hidey-holes. The goal was to find evidence that might match up with any of the seven murders. Eight if you counted Reggie Benton, as Joanna was inclined to do. Nine if you wished to include Sven Lundquist, the Iowa attorney who had handled the financial ruin of Sarah Pearse and the demise of Pearse Hardware.

And God knows who else.

The man had a gift for murder, and now that they had a trail on which to backtrack, Joanna believed they might well find more suspicious deaths. For all they knew, he'd been bumping off elderly tenants for years, though the tenants themselves regarded him with great fondness. Most were shocked and appalled by the aborted arrest. They did not want to believe that Henry—that dear young man who fetched their prescriptions when they were ill and took such *pride* in the care of their building—was actually a calculating serial killer with a cupboard full of poisons and some unspeakably vile habits.

At nine-thirty A.M. on Tuesday, December 16th, the mayor and police chief held a press conference, carried live around the world. They conceded that a predawn raid on a Hollywood apartment building had failed to result in the arrest of one Henry Mason, the alleged Atterminator.

They admitted that Henry Mason was still at large and that they didn't have the foggiest notion where he might be.

This last was discussed with vigor in the task force office as the day wore on. "He's in Rio," Dave Austin insisted. "Or someplace like that, outside of the country. He's *gone*. He's good with fake IDs, we know that. He'll have a choice of phony passports and he wouldn't hang around LAX waiting for the perfect flight. He'd get on the first plane for Mexico City and then move on from there."

Some thought he'd return to the midwest, where he could blend in, though Joanna figured Kevin Pearse's days of midwestern blending were over for good. Others believed he had another apartment in L.A.—or maybe several apartments—that they hadn't found.

The issue of money was another great big question mark. How would he finance a getaway? How had he paid for the Mike Varner apartment? For that matter, what had he been living on?

Henry Mason's bank accounts were skimpy and unremarkable and his apartment suggested no expensive habits. He seemed to have no income apart from free rent and a small stipend for managerial services. He hadn't picked up a royalty check in years. And while someone had come forward who recalled working with him years ago at Builders Emporium, a now-defunct home-and-garden chain, nobody knew of any recent employment. The tenants reported that he was usually available when they needed him.

They also recalled, when pressed, occasions when Henry Mason had been unavailable for several days at a time. Detectives were trying to pin down those occasions more precisely to match them with the Atterminator's busy schedule.

Henry Mason liked to hide things. They also knew that. In addition to the getaway tunnel, they'd discovered a phony electrical outlet in his living room, with evidence suggesting that something had once hung from a nail inside the wall. There were other hidey-holes as well, including one that contained a poignant photo album of the Pearse family, late of Kingsfield, Iowa.

But Henry himself was gone.

Joanna's sense of disappointment was so profound that she could barely acknowledge it to herself.

Nothing was resolved.

Nothing.

And there was no reason now to believe that anything *ever* would be resolved.

Kevin Pearse had planned everything else so carefully that she could only assume his own escape was equally well orchestrated. Austin was right; he was gone and he wouldn't be back. Mission accomplished.

Which meant they couldn't close any of these cases. They couldn't hold out the prospect of death-penalty revenge to relatives of the deceased, a group now large enough to fill a good-sized hall. They couldn't offer assurances of safety to any attorneys, anywhere.

They were fucked coming and going.

Around eleven A.M., Jacobs took a good long look at Joanna. "You had any sleep in the last two weeks?" he wondered idly.

She shrugged. "Three or four hours on the plane to Iowa. And last night."

"Go home," he instructed. "We've got manpower out the wazoo right now and nothing to do but pretend we hope to learn something significant from the apartment."

"I can't leave *now*. This is the biggest day of the investigation."

He shook his head. "The biggest day of the investigation was when we made Pearse in the first place. Get some rest, Davis. Give yourself time to recover. Go home."

She frowned. "I don't have a home, Al."

"I didn't mean you had to go out to your own place yet," he backpedaled hastily. "Go to Walters's house. Shit, go to *my* house. Just go someplace where you can get some rest."

Nearby Lee Walters was flipping through notes on her interviews with the tenants from the Orange Grove Arms. "Actually," she told Joanna softly after Jacobs went to the john, "you *could* go to your place. Alex and I went out Saturday morning and cleaned it up."

Joanna was shocked. "You shouldn't have done that."

"I'm too much of a Tidy Tillie not to," Lee admitted with a shrug. "The thought of how nice you had the place and how we messed it up kept bugging me. It wasn't Mason who trashed it, after all. It was LAPD. Anyway, it may not be exactly how you had it, but I think it's pretty much okay."

Joanna felt overwhelmed at Lee's generosity. She felt, indeed, moved almost to tears, that in itself suggestive that she needed more rest quickly. Atterminator Task Force headquarters was not the sort of place where a prudent female professional burst into tears.

"Thanks," she said. "I dreaded having to deal with it." She frowned. "When were you planning to mention this, anyway?"

Lee waved an easy hand. "When the moment felt right." She grinned. "It feels right. Go home."

Joanna could feel her conflicting emotions engage in spirited hand-to-hand combat. From the battle rose a strong sense of anger and irritation. Kevin Pearse was long gone. He'd briefly visited her house and had primarily concerned himself with only the jukebox, an item no longer even on the premises.

She had been prepared to give up all the happiness she had gotten from that house, simply because a criminal chose to play mind games with her.

Which would be an admission that Kevin Pearse, the Iowa nebbish with the part-time job at the hardware store, had *succeeded* in playing mind games with her. Had *won* those games.

Well, screw that.

"I'll give it a shot," she told Lee, watching the caution behind her friend's eyes. Lee knew how freaked she had been. "If I don't want to stay, I'll just head up to the Holiday Inn." She smiled. "Al's right. I'm wiped. Soon as I can rustle up a car, I'm out of here." Joanna's own car was out at Pit Bull Acres and had been for almost two weeks.

Lee tossed her keys across the table. "You don't need to fuck with one of the regular junkers. Take mine. Wheaton lives out my way. I'll catch a ride with him."

And so Joanna got on the familiar freeway and drove home, savoring the feeling of being by herself, looking forward to being in her own space again.

There'd be time later to be disappointed and angry about losing Henry Mason. Who might not be in Rio, but was probably at least in Guadalajara.

48

Ace had intended to be long gone by now, halfway to Oregon.

Once Mrs. Farber called to tell him she was spending Monday night with her grandniece, he knew they had him. Anna Farber *had* no grandniece. She'd told him her entire family history on more than one occasion.

He realized then that time had run out, that he had to leave immediately. He swung into his pre-evacuation activities with calm precision. The dummy was waiting, fully dressed, hanging in the tunnel on a heavy hook. It took only a few minutes to apply red paint to the shower walls with the template he had created after consulting a criminology textbook. He rather enjoyed arranging the dummy, thinking of what he was doing as an allegory, or a metaphor, one of those English-lit things.

He was creating the death of Henry Mason, who had never really existed in the first place.

He quickly decided that there was no time to sabotage the building, and there seemed no point to it anyway. He could achieve pretty much the same result by merely *saying* he had sabotaged it. That way he'd also avoid endangering the tenants, most of whom he was genuinely fond. Throughout the entire Legal Resolution Program, he had endeavored to harm no innocents, even to the extent of choosing no victims with small children. With the possible exception of the girl who'd taken Gina's ticket to New York— a girl whose innocence had already been sucked dry by the streets of Hollywood—he had succeeded in maintaining that goal.

He wrote his note and set up his stink bomb and gathered the few essentials he would need for the thousand-mile journey to his new life in Oregon, where the few folks he had dealings with knew him as Jim Hansen.

Then he made himself up as an old man, stripped to his underwear and socks, and pushed his duffel bag ahead of himself through the tunnel. Everything went smoothly until he emerged in the darkness of the below-ground garage next door and stepped on a broken bottle.

In a thrill of pain and panic, he felt glass slice deeply into his right foot, followed immediately by the warmth of his own gushing blood.

He fought the terror of this unexpected event as he sank to the concrete floor and used his flashlight to examine the wound. It was almost two inches long and went deep, deep enough to pour blood out onto the gray concrete. He peeled off his undershirt and wrapped it around the wounded foot, pressing hard against the cut, elevating it as high as it would go.

He frantically considered options.

He couldn't call for help. He couldn't go back into the apartment. And he certainly couldn't seek medical attention.

Under other circumstances he might have brazened out an emergency room visit, or found one of those nasty storefront urgent care places that catered to indigents and illegals. But right now that felt too much like a trap. Logically he knew that nobody realized he was in this garage, that they were waiting for him to come out of his apartment next door. His entire escape plan was predicated on this assumption. But still...

After a while, he cautiously released the pressure on his makeshift bandage and found the bleeding had slowed to a trickle. He then tied the sodden undershirt tightly around his foot and struggled to dress without standing up. A giant hassle, but not unmanageable. The baggy brown suit slipped on easily, but once he was fully clothed, he still had to deal with the foot.

He examined the pair of brown wingtips he'd found at the Salvation Army, then loosened the laces on the right one. He used his pocketknife to cut off the only remaining dry section of the undershirt, twisted the fabric tightly around the injured foot, then pulled the cut and bloody sock over the whole business, cringing with pain. Finally he attempted to slip his bound foot into the shoe.

No go.

He gingerly extricated his foot and went to work with the pocketknife on the battered shoe. The shoe seemed constructed to last through eternity, but finally he succeeded in separating the upper from the sole along the outside edge. This time when he worked his foot into the shoe there was sufficient room, though the sole was inclined to flap. He considered a moment, then undid the laces down to the first holes, brought the loose ends around under the shoe and then back up top again, where he slipped them through two empty holes and tied a neat little bow.

He had no idea how long all this had taken until he consulted his watch and discovered, to his horror, that it was nearly ten P.M.— a bit late for a senior, even a Hollywood senior, to be heading out on the town.

He took a series of deep breaths, then cautiously stood and tested the foot. The pain was blinding and he was sure he could feel the blood starting to flow again.

Don't think about it. Just get out.

Grateful for the impulse that had led him to include a cane in his getaway costume, he cleaned up the most obvious blood with the remains of the undershirt, then cautiously made his way to the stairway. He supported himself on the handrail to keep his weight off the foot as he climbed to the lobby. Then he walked out the front door and hobbled down the street, looking neither left nor right. Half a block away, he got into an unlocked Nissan Sentra, hot-wired it and split.

He headed automatically for the freeway, trying to think.

He'd lost a lot of blood, he knew, and felt light-headed, woozy, nearly as frail as the image he was trying to project. His right foot on the accelerator felt sticky, and when he slipped his hand down to investigate it came back up red and wet.

This was not good.

He again considered a hospital or an urgent care and rejected both. He had no insurance and would only call attention to himself by pulling out a wad of cash. Furthermore, in the harsh fluorescent light of an emergency room, it would be immediately apparent that he was fifty years younger than the age he was trying to appear.

He realized, too, as he mechanically moved down the freeway, that even before he lost all that blood, he had been utterly exhausted. Too much had happened too quickly. The Bonita Blevins episode on Saturday had drained him. Then there was Mrs. Finch's interview with the L.A. *Times*, which he now wished he'd brought with him. That fat cow Linda Moraine, who knew *nothing* about him, was all *over* the television, which greatly annoyed him. He'd had to deal with Mrs. McNeill and her damned bacon grease, followed by the phony telephone installer.

No wonder he was so wiped.

With a start, he realized that he'd screwed up his freeway merge. Good God, couldn't he do *anything* right tonight? Instead of heading north to connect with the Golden State, he was now moving straight west on the Ventura. Was this what it meant to go into shock?

He couldn't possibly drive to Oregon tonight. At this rate, he wouldn't be able to get out of Los Angeles County. He'd have to find a motel somewhere and rest, stop for bandages at an all-night drugstore, look into stealing a different car. This one had 120,000 miles on it and really crummy brakes.

And then, in a sudden jolt he realized exactly where he had headed, without even thinking about it.

Joanna Davis's house in the west Valley was sitting empty in an isolated area that was practically country, while its owner chased Kevin Pearse's ghosts across the midwest. Ace had liked her house quite a lot, appreciated the simplicity of its design and the fact that she kept it so spare. Now he decided that it would make a fitting coda to the Legal Resolution Program to spend his final night in Los Angeles in the bed of the Robbery–Homicide detective who had failed to catch him.

As far as he knew, she was still in Iowa. And before she left town, she'd abandoned the house to stay someplace else. Ace had always played the odds, and they were clearly in his favor here.

And even if she happened to turn up, well, those were the breaks. He was traveling light, but he still had the gun he'd used to threaten Lorenzo J. Taft. He had the Taser and some pesticide. He could cope.

He arrived just in time for the eleven o'clock news, after leaving the stolen Sentra a bit down the road. Scaling the fence out back was difficult with his injured foot, but the realization that he was almost safe gave him new strength.

The lights were still on timers, as she'd had them before, but as he approached the house, the property felt abandoned. He checked around the premises carefully for indications of hidden cameras or other security devices and found nothing.

Once inside, he made sure the blinds were all tightly closed, then went into the bathroom and stripped, carefully folding his old-man clothing before sitting on the closed toilet and removing the shoe from his wounded foot. As he painstakingly peeled back the sock, he realized that he was somehow expecting a geyser of blood.

It didn't come.

His foot was a mess, but not nearly as bad as he had feared. He'd started a little fresh bleeding in his climb over the cyclone fence when his foot slipped once, but for the most part, the wound had clotted nicely. He decided against trying to clean it up too vigorously, not wanting to start the blood flowing again. With a wet washcloth, he began carefully wiping away dried blood from areas he knew to be uninjured. There were a couple of little cuts that didn't worry him, but even the big wound didn't look so bad in the comfort and relative safety of Joanna Davis's pale blue bathroom.

In her medicine chest he found Band-Aids and a little tube of antiseptic, both woefully inadequate for this job. But there were also minipads, and he hopped into the bedroom to retrieve some pantyhose he remembered seeing in a dresser drawer. He carefully dressed the wound, smearing antiseptic on a series of Band-Aids that he marched along the cut. Then he secured a minipad over the whole works with strips of pantyhose. Maybe not the state of the art in emergency medicine, but not half-bad.

In the medicine chest he also found Tylenol and an outdated bottle of amoxicillin with four pills left in it. He took a couple Tylenols and two of the antibiotics, setting the rest aside for later. He rinsed out blood from his trouser leg and hung the pants to dry over the shower curtain rod. He was cold, he realized, so he put his shirt and suit coat back on, then hobbled into the bedroom and pulled the quilt off her bed, wrapping it around his waist. He looked, he imagined, quite ridiculous. But somehow he didn't care.

He still felt woozy, and decided it couldn't hurt to eat something. The refrigerator contained no perishables, had been emptied since his last visit when—now that he thought about it—it hadn't held much food either. All that remained was some mustard and pickles and a half gallon jar of enormous stuffed olives. He ate a few olives while he nuked some canned chili and mixed up a packet of hardened hot chocolate mix he found in a cupboard.

As he ate, he catalogued his successes and accomplishments with growing pride. He'd caused people to think about lawyers and their perfidy, had inspired others to follow his lead, had brought extremely public attention to the shameful abuses of the legal profession.

What he had done had muted the echo of his mother's sobs on the telephone in the months before her death, softened her repeated, anguished cry: "The lawyers are killing me."

He looked back on that time with an overwhelming sense of guilt, shamed that he hadn't returned to help, that he had allowed her to be ruined by legal machinations that stripped her of what little she had left after her husband's death. It was too late to help Sarah Pearse, and that he truly regretted. He'd been blinded by dreams of his own acting success, a success he believed would sweep his mother out of the wreckage of her life in Kingsfield and give her the comfort and luxury she deserved.

But now, even though it was too late to help her directly, he had avenged her honor, and there was a satisfaction in that, almost strong enough to balance the guilt. Others had been warned. Attention had been paid.

After eating, he felt much better and no longer the least bit sleepy. He would have liked to play the jukebox, but it was gone. The pinball machine remained, however, and he brought a bar stool from the kitchen counter to rest his foot while he gave it a try. He hadn't wanted to risk taking time to play it when he was here before, but this visit was different. Joanna Davis was in Iowa and he had all the time in the world.

It was a simple game, actually, not much fun at all. But after he played a few rounds—stopping to open the machine and figure out how to reset it for additional free play—it occurred to him that he had the opportunity to *really* get the last word here. The service manual was tucked inside the machine. He read it carefully, went to the kitchen to find her tools, set to work making one last statement before he disappeared into the ozone.

It took longer than he'd expected, and he didn't finish till nearly five A.M. Tuesday. When he was done, the pinball machine was rigged to send a shower of rice down onto the playing surface when a certain combination was triggered. He played enough test games to figure that she'd probably hit that combination within ten or fifteen games.

At the same time the rice cascaded down onto the playing field, a Scarlet Passion lipstick by Revlon would roll to the front of the machine.

And when she opened up the machine in shock and outrage, she'd find his final message, written in lipstick: SVEN LUNDQUIST.

Satisfied, he repacked his duffel bag, rebandaged his foot, and laid out his clothes neatly in preparation for the journey north. He packed the gun in the duffel bag, put the Taser in his right pants pocket, and the small vial of nicotine sulfate in the breast pocket of his shirt. He brushed his teeth, turned down the blankets on Joanna Davis's bed, and slipped between the sheets. It was a double bed, an odd size one didn't often encounter anymore, the same size bed he'd kept in the Mike Varner apartment where he'd tarried with Gina.

Ah, Gina. Regina Benton. He could see her clearly, sitting naked on the bed watching *Double Indemnity*, announcing matter-of-factly, "I'm going to kill my father."

The fact that Gina's father turned out to be an attorney—and a scummy one at that—seemed too serendipitous not to act upon, and after much soul-searching, Ace had decided to make Lawrence Benton a part of the Legal Resolution Program. Gina had not known about the LRP, of course, or about any of the other subjects and episodes. Ace had orchestrated matters so she thought every detail was her own idea, and she had insisted on being the one to zap her father with the Taser when he answered her unexpected ring at his door. She had also tossed the boom box into the hot tub, laughing with girlish glee.

It had been a rather spooky episode, actually. Not as business-like as the others. Less controlled. But undeniably dramatic. And it had put the Legal Resolution Program onto the map.

Poor Gina. He realized, as he finally drifted off to sleep, that he really did miss her.

He was startled awake, some time later, by the sound of a car door slamming.

49

Joanna unlocked the padlock on the gate and gazed fondly at the little stone building nestled behind the huge pair of California peppertrees. In the week since she had come here to collect her cold-weather wardrobe for the trip to Iowa, her revulsion for the place had significantly mellowed.

It was not the house's fault that Henry Mason had invaded it, and Mason himself had done no real physical harm to the place. She no longer felt absolute disgust at the notion of being here, though she wasn't quite sure that she could actually live there again.

She wandered briefly around the yard. Less than three weeks

since Thanksgiving when she'd done so much yard work, and already there were other obvious chores. Roses to prune, buddleia to cut back, spent asters to hack to the ground. The garden's next cycle was already beginning, narcissus and homeria poking their spiky leaves through the ground. And the peppertrees out front were absolutely loaded with delicate pink pepperberries, the best crop ever. Maybe *this* would be the year that she finally got around to figuring out how to make a holiday wreath from them. She could take it with her to Seattle.

She was stalling, she realized suddenly. Better just to go inside and not worry that things might not be exactly as she kept them. Better just to check and see if the *feel* of the place was all right. Whatever Lee and Alex Walters had done to clean things up was important, but superficial. What mattered ultimately was whether or not it still felt like her home.

She took a deep breath and unlocked the back door, then swung it open and started to walk inside.

And froze.

Something was wrong.

She knew it immediately.

The atmosphere inside the house felt electrically charged. A faint scent of chili lingered in the air. And something—*someone*—was behind the door.

It was him. It had to be.

And if she wasn't fast enough, he'd zap her and she'd be dead. Stone cold dead, like all the others.

All of this registered in a microsecond as she sensed the person behind the door coming toward her and twisted around, focusing on the black object in his right hand.

The Taser.

It was the last thing they had seen, those others. Bonita Blevins. Lorenzo J. Taft. Francesca Goldberg. Lawrence Benton. Every one of them had felt the sting of the voltage and then gone on to ignominious death.

It was not going to happen to her.

She could feel her body move automatically, in fluid motions and lightning reflexes she had mastered over three decades of self-defense and physical training. She used her body as a tool, aware through ample experience that she had two advantages a larger opponent would not immediately expect. She was supple enough to slip like a greased eel out of most conventional holds, and she was strong enough to exploit the laws of physics and throw an unsuspecting adversary.

But first she had to avoid being jolted into eternity.

She concentrated on keeping the weapon away from her, the way she'd been trained to disarm an opponent bearing a firearm, a type of weapon that at this point seemed downright benign. All four of their hands were joined together, locked around the weapon and each other as he tried to bring the muzzle around to connect with her flesh.

"You zap me," she shouted, "you'll get yourself, too. So *drop it now!*" There was so much adrenaline coursing through her system, she thought surely she would explode.

She could sense him testing what she'd said, realizing its truth. Their bodies were twisted together, their flesh joined in several places. Any voltage that hit her would pass right through to him, and now he realized it. Which made it even more crucial that she not let go of him before the Taser was out of the equation.

They were braced in position like a bizarre statue, too-modern art.

"Just let it go," she ordered again. "Drop the fucking Taser. You need to tell us your story, Kevin. People want to hear it. Every word. You're a star now, you know that, don't you?" Was it a mistake to call him Kevin? He had so many identities, so many versions of his own reality. "It's all wasted if you can't tell us why." Her voice was calmer now, almost soothing, and she could sense him hesitating. "We need to know. There's so much we want you to expla—"

Before he could think, in mid-sentence, she twisted, brought her knee behind him, shifted her weight and felt him fly above her, coming round on his back with a crash on the floor, still clutching the blasted Taser in his right hand.

This was it, her only chance. She kicked it out of his hand as he struggled to regain his breath, saw the black nightmare skitter across the floor and land beneath her pinball machine. As he grunted in dismay, she smashed her left foot down hard on his right wrist, wishing she wore heavy, metal-toed boots instead of rubber-soled athletic shoes.

But then he screamed in pain and she felt a shameful satisfaction. There was no time for niceties here, and even better, there were no witnesses. Whatever happened in this room, it would be her word against his.

Assuming that they both survived.

He was kicking upward from the floor now, even as he concentrated on his ruined wrist, and she jumped out of range of his flailing legs. How to hold him while she called for backup? How to even reach the goddamned phone? It was years since she'd physically grappled with someone she was trying to arrest, and never in her career had she been in such a situation without a partner somewhere nearby. She was too damned old for this kind of shit, she thought, but the awareness of the twenty-year gap in their ages only invigorated her.

Moving behind him, she decided that a sharp kick to the head was probably a very prudent move. She deliberately took aim.

With all her strength she kicked first the side of his head and then his jaw, not sure whether or not she wanted to break his neck. It would be so much simpler all around if she could just kill him right here. He would not, she knew, shrink from killing her. Would probably have already done so if she hadn't moved so fast.

It was tempting. Nobody could ever argue that she'd used unreasonable force. He had seventy pounds and nine inches on her and he'd already killed at least eight people. Folks would marvel that she'd been able to do it at all.

But she realized, with sudden and absolute clarity, that she *didn't* want to kill him.

She wanted him alive.

She wanted to be able to sit across a table from him and ask questions until her jaw muscles ached and her voice grew weak from overuse. She wanted the hows and the whens and the what-ifs and the wheres and most of all the whys.

And she knew he'd *want* to talk. To explain, to justify, to validate what he had done by expressing it aloud, by telling the anxiously waiting world every disgusting detail.

He reached out for her ankle, his hand moving like the tongue of a lizard, and as she jumped back out of range, she saw that there was something wrong with his *own* foot. He wore a baggy brown suit but no shoes, and there was blood flowing from his right foot. She remembered the broken wine bottle at the end of the tunnel out of the Orange Grove Arms, the bloody undershirt they'd found nearby.

Here, then, was his vulnerability. She grabbed his injured right foot, squeezed hard, and used it to twist his entire body. She listened in satisfaction as he screamed again. Then she smashed him facedown onto the floor—and heard an odd small sound, the tinkling of broken glass. Almost immediately, the air was killed with a foul, fishy, chemical odor. But there was no time to stop and think about it.

She landed on the small of his back, grabbing his left arm, twisting it high between his shoulder blades, hearing him give a little whimper of dismay.

He was dead.

Ace knew it as surely as if he'd been reading the Judgment Book out loud. The glass vial of nicotine sulfate in his shirt pocket had been crushed when he hit the ground and it was a matter of minutes, maybe only seconds, before he'd be gone.

"You killed me," he told the detective, his voice stunned and accusatory. How could this have *happened?* She was straddling his back, had his wrist pulled excruciatingly high. The *good* wrist, not the one she'd jumped on like some kind of playground bully.

"Shut the fuck up," she snapped at him, pulling his hair back and banging his face into the ground.

He tried to laugh. Already he could feel his muscles freezing up on him. He'd watched this process too many times not to know exactly how this poison would work. Not to know that he was doomed.

"I only have a couple of minutes," he tried to tell her. Maybe he could play on her sympathies. Maybe, it struck him suddenly, *he could take her with him.* "You've got to get the poison away from my skin. It's in my shirt pocket." He could feel his heart racing, his head pounding, waves of dizziness sweeping down his body.

She released his hair, but still clenched his arm, still sat on his back, grinding the crushed vial of poison into his chest.

"Please," he tried again, his tone wheedling. He didn't want her to think he was begging. Balance was important here. If he could just get her to touch it, to pull the wet fabric away from his body, to get it on her own hands. That would do it. At this concentration, that's all it would take to kill her, too.

And then, when they found him, they'd find her as well. Both of them dead. The Atterminator's final statement.

"Too late for favors," she answered brusquely. "What we're gonna do now is move over toward the door. You're gonna crawl on your belly like you're going through boot camp and I'm gonna sit right here on your back every inch of the way, like I'm riding a rocking horse."

"Just take off my shirt first," he told her. It was harder to talk now, more labored. Saliva dripped from his mouth and his tongue seemed to be afire. He felt bile rising in his throat, fought the nausea.

"I don't think so," she answered tartly. "I'm not feeling very helpful just now."

He started to speak again and found he couldn't. That he had lost the power of speech. That he could never tell them why.

Joanna felt herself growing woozy from the fumes. She was not about to go fiddling with whatever this shit was in his pocket, but she didn't want to pass out, either. If it was nicotine that had gotten him—and she was pretty sure it was, based on everything she'd learned about it—then she, too, was in danger, from inhalation. She would have to get up, leave him, go outside.

But what if it was simply a trick?

As she pondered this, he twitched, and twitched again, and went suddenly slack.

The hand she was holding high on his back was limp now, and when she searched for a pulse, she couldn't find one.

Fifteen minutes later there were ten cops at the house.

Forty minutes later, they'd been joined by a dozen detectives from the task force, the Robbery–Homicide captain, a flock of criminalists, a coroner's van, the police chief, and the SWAT team lieutenant, who was almost petulant with disappointment. How could Kevin Pearse have died before he had a chance to blow him off the face of the earth?

Still later, Joanna wandered outside in her garden while the hordes swarmed in and around her former home. The windows were all open, the double-bagged body gone. Above her in the bright December midday sun, the air was thick with *thupp*ing news helicopters, being held at bay by a police chopper that hovered directly overhead.

Kevin Pearse had slept in her bed, had left rumpled sheets and the indentation of his head in her pillow. His duffel bag sat on her bedroom floor and his blood had dripped upon her bathroom tiles. Ten minutes ago, a criminalist had gleefully discovered his sabotage of her pinball machine. The only way the violation of her space and her home and her life could have been more absolute, she realized, would be if Kevin Pearse had killed her.

But he hadn't.

She heard the chirp of her cell phone coming from her bag, which she'd brought out of the house and stashed in the garden shed. She needed to call people, she realized suddenly. Kirsten. Mike. Don Olafson.

"Davis," she announced into the phone, in a voice so crisp it startled her.

"Joanna, it's Susan Letterman."

Dr. Letterman. For the last few hours, Joanna realized suddenly, she'd managed to completely forget about the doctor. About the

colposcopy, the biopsies, all of that. She stopped breathing, bac]
into the shed. This was not a call she wanted witnessed.

"My staff's been listening to the radio," the doctor went o]
"and they tell me you're probably real busy just now, but I kne\
you'd want to know right away. I got your lab results back. You're
fine, Joanna. Everything is negative."

Joanna felt waves of relief wash over her, tempered with suspicion. "But how—you said three *days*."

Dr. Letterman laughed. "I put a rush on it. Seemed to me you
had enough on your mind already. Anyway, everything is fine.
Benign. You're all right."

You're all right.

Was she?

She interrogated the doctor for a few minutes before finally
believing her, then put the phone away. Beside her on the wall of
the shed hung her gardening apron, and sticking out of the pocket of the apron were her pruning shears. The criminalists hadn't
yet checked over the shed, but that was too damned bad. Very
deliberately she pulled out the shears.

Then she walked around to the front of the house and started
cutting sprigs of pink pepperberries to make a wreath.

Christmas was coming.

• • •

MORE MYSTERIES
🙂 FROM PERSEVERANCE PRESS 🙂
For the New Golden Age

Available now—

Too Dead To Swing, A Katy Green Mystery
by **Hal Glatzer**
ISBN 1-880284-53-7
It's 1940, and musician Katy Green joins an all-female swing band touring California by train—but she soon discovers that somebody's out for blood. First book publication of the award-winning audio-play. Cast of characters, illustrations, and map included.

The Tumbleweed Murders, A Claire Sharples Botanical Mystery
by **Rebecca Rothenberg, completed by Taffy Cannon**
ISBN 1-880284-43-X
Microbiologist Sharples explores the musical, geological, and agricultural history of California's Central Valley, as she links a mysterious disappearance a generation earlier to a newly discovered skeleton and a recent death.

Keepers, A Port Silva Mystery
by **Janet LaPierre**
ISBN 1-880284-44-8
Patience and Verity Mackellar, a Port Silva mother-and-daughter private investigative team, unravel a baffling missing-persons case and find a reclusive religious community hidden on northern California's Lost Coast.

Blind Side, A Connor Westphal Mystery
by **Penny Warner**
ISBN 1-880284-42-1
The deaf journalist's new Gold Country case involves the celebrated Calaveras County Jumping Frog Jubilee. Connor and a blind friend must make their disabilities work for them to figure out why frogs—and people—are dying.

The Kidnapping of Rosie Dawn, A Joe Barley Mystery
by **Eric Wright**
Barry Award, *Best Paperback Original 2000*
Edgar, Ellis, and Anthony Award nominee
ISBN 1-880284-40-5
A Toronto academic sleuth is on an odd odyssey, to rescue student/exotic dancer Rosie Dawn—and find out who wants her out of the way, and why. One part crime caper, one part academic satire, and one part love story compose this new series entry.

Guns and Roses, An Irish Eyes Travel Mystery
by Taffy Cannon
Agatha and Macavity Award nominee, *Best Novel 2000*
ISBN 1-880284-34-0
Ex-cop Roxanne Prescott turns to a more genteel occupation in this new series, leading a History and Gardens of Virginia tour. But by the time the group reaches Colonial Williamsburg, strange misadventures and annoying pranks have escalated into murder.

Royal Flush, A Jake Samson & Rosie Vicente Mystery
by Shelley Singer
ISBN 1-880284-33-2
Jake and Rosie infiltrate a dangerous far-right group, to save a good kid who's in over his head. The laid-back California private eyes will need a scorecard to tell the ringers in the gang from the real racist megalomaniacs.

Baby Mine, A Port Silva Mystery
by Janet LaPierre
ISBN 1-880284-32-4
The web of small-town relationships in the coastal California village is fraying, stressed by current economic and political forces. Police chief Vince Gutierrez and his schoolteacher wife, Meg Halloran, must help their town recover.

Forthcoming—

Another Fine Mess, A Bridget Montrose Mystery
by Lora Roberts
Bridget Montrose wrote a surprise bestseller, but now her publisher wants another one. A writers' retreat seems the perfect opportunity to work in the rarefied company of other authors...except that one of them has a different ending in mind.

Flashover, A Novel of Suspense
by Nancy Baker Jacobs
A serial arsonist is killing young mothers in the Bay Area. Now Susan Kim Delancey, California's newly appointed chief arson investigator, is in a race against time to catch the murderer and find the dead women's missing babies—before more lives end in flames.